# Heaven's Hell

E.A.Gray

# DEDICATION

~ Kat for endless nights of discussion, (ordering an entire overhaul of Michelle after (I thought) the book was done)
~ CK for her repeated editing prowess in shaping the first few drafts of this monster.

To my Yaywhore kittens for chasing endless shiny things, "Look, Ma, it sparkles!"
Finally to Max who caught cherry blossoms, marvelled at snow and did not like being ignored in favour of a manuscript.

# 1 Cupid's Introduction

*Psyche was a captivatingly attractive Princess. Jealous, Goddess Venus ordered her son Cupid to make Psyche fall in love with an outcast of a man to reduce her popularity. But once Cupid looked at the Princess, he instantly fell in love and whisked her away to Paradise.*

*Venus was furious. She plotted to kill Psyche under the guise of motherly tests of loyalty to her son - she arranged seemingly impossible tasks but Psyche passed them all, securing Cupid's love.*

Excuse me, I have to jump in here. What a weird interpretation of a story. Firstly, I'm a she. Secondly, when I met Psyche I didn't fall for her, I fell over her. I was carrying some temple gifts for Ma when Psyche walked right out in front of me, and let's just say I didn't expect to see a feast like that outside of a banquet hall. With her ultra kissable lips and legs that inspired too many urges, Psyche simply had to get my attention. It's why I fell for her - after I fell over her.

Ma wasn't a happy camper.

"Don't play with mortals, Cupid. They carry all sorts of diseases."

She banished Psyche and locked me in the Heavens. And for that I gave her three solid weeks of intense whining. Ma caved in the end, gave Psyche an easy task to save face. Anyone can complete a hundred piece jigsaw in under a week.

You're thinking we lived happily ever after, right?

You see, I was being very Presley about my singledom - after six months of infidelity my sorry ass got dumped. Of course Ma was beyond angry I'd screwed up again. Day after day of the cracked record classics ensued.

"When are you going to grow up and realise your responsibilities, Cupid? I let you have her and you throw it all away, Cupid. Blah blah blah blah, blah blah blah blah, Cupid."

It's not like I was wearing gang colours and participating in drive-by shootings. I'd just had some fun, not realising it'd suddenly become illegal.

Ma threw her usual curveball then, wiping Psyche's memory and letting her go back to being a plain lickable mortal.

So my point, and yes I have one - what you read and what really happen can be two distant cousins. Take Medusa, she went to the islands and got

1

badly done cornrows. Combine that with legendary PMT and suddenly she's a bitch with snake hair? Give the girl a break. As for the Sirens. The family love Karaoke, what, it's a crime? Okay, the way they sing clearly is for that story to have lasted this long, but they are cool girls.

Now we've cleared all that up I'll carry on with my original job. I am going to be your hostess with the mostess. I'm here to set some records straight, and let you know what's really going on.

The most misunderstood story is of Elle. We call her 'The Caretaker' you know her as God. To me that makes no sense. There are hundreds of us Gods, I don't know why you've picked her to go all Hollywood starlet about. Either way, you think she's a man too. Have to say, I'm not happy with all this innate sexism.

Back to my point: Elle. She's five foot four of pure sex appeal. Her petite body is covered in designer clothes not white flowing sackcloth. She isn't an ethereal mist-like voice from above or omnipotently sitting on a golden throne, either. We're not living Cecil B. DeMille.

Listen, why don't you cut those expectations loose and look for yourself.

# Chapter One: Elle
## 1st April, Year 2, 15:00
## Mice-Capades

"Sam, can you come in? Bring your pad, there are notes I need you to take about Discord's graduation."

My finger slides off of the intercom button. I wait, staring at the silent, black plastic box, tapping fingertips on my desk. I push the button again, moving closer, saying my one word very slowly.

"Samantha?"

You'd think being a God meant dedication, unswerving loyalty and attention...or at least getting an answer from your assistant. I tap the box and it crackles loudly. Like a bullet I sit back in my seat as it starts to smoke.

I have terrible luck with electrics. I killed my toaster at the beginning of the month, my garage door spent last week opening and closing whenever it felt like it and yesterday my hairdryer tried to electrocute me. I expected today to hit an all time low, and it has.

After another minute that feels like an hour I realise: Samantha is not coming, my intercom is not working, and, as I peer into my glass, I'm out of fruit juice.

My reception area is curiously empty. The vending machine fills my glass with fruit juice, and, as I take a sip, I'm not impressed. I peer into murky depths then up at another uncooperative piece of electrical machinery. The lights flicker, it throws a cup out, and another and another. Clicking and crunching noises echo through reception. I bend, fighting the tidal wave of cups, batting them away. My finger hovers over the power switch. What are the odds of being electrocuted by an automated machine, and would my epitaph read, 'Killed by the fruit juice she loved'?

There are some things that should be risked and some that shouldn't. I remove a Manolo and tap the switch with the four-inch heel. It crackles an answer, throws another handful out then grinds to a successful halt. After slipping my shoe back on, depositing the odd tasting fruit juice in the bin and kicking all of the escaped cups into a little pile, my work here is done. Yet throughout all of this I'm *still* alone.

"Hello? Sam?"

When I employed Samantha as my assistant I may have been a little optimistic. Her typing was terrible, her phone manner appalling, organisational skills clearly absent and the theory regarding spell-checking documents simply did not exist in her universe. However, she was well intentioned and got on with everyone. I assumed even a village idiot could learn office etiquette: the layout of a keyboard, how to put a call through without losing it. Years later Sam has proved my assumptions wrong.

Suddenly her blonde head pops up from under her desk like a submarine periscope, turning around quickly, trying to ascertain who called. Her glasses sit comically askew on top of her head. I sigh. Where did I go wrong?

"Your Eminence. We have mice. Isn't it fantastic?"

Whiter than white teeth accentuate an even tan and golden blonde hair. She'd make a beautiful Angel of Mercy if she had the I.Q. to carry it off.

"They're so cute. Here mousy, mousy."

Lucy. Thousands of years of the same old, same old stunts, yet she never tires. Astounding. I deal with my problems at hand, first.

"Vermin? As in ones that carry, let's say, the Black Death - a plague that destroyed a big chunk of Earth's civilisation with bleeding sores and a horrifyingly painful death? That kind of vermin?"

A second later and Sam's screaming and clambering on top of the desk. Office doors open and everyone's looking to see what the noise is. A chorus of, "Your Eminence," echoes along the hallway.

I hold a hand up before some bright spark calls security. My one word explains the incident clearly.

"Samantha."

Eyes roll, heads shake, doors close, and our emergency is oddly over. I wonder what it's like in Sam's world, never having anything to worry about.

"The mice are in my office, too, Your Eminence."

It's a recognisably friendly drawl. I turn, coming face to face with a pair of broad shoulders and a tight shirt that hugs every curve, especially two. When significant amounts of your staff are over six foot you have to invest in a collection of very high heels.

Michelle bows elegantly, her blonde hair pulled back in a plat that sits on a shoulder.

"Can we get Lucy up here to take control of her little subjects, Michelle?"

"I've been on at them since yesterday. I've tried calling her but she's, 'Out of Hell today'. I spoke to Bee and persuaded her to recall them."

I raise an eyebrow. Bee is not easily persuaded.

"Don't ask how I did it."

"Probably wise I don't know." My eyes rake reception for movement.

3

"I'm not sure what's sparked Lucy to life but she's being a pain lately."

"She needs to find a hobby that isn't destructive."

Michelle stares at Sam who's sitting cross-legged on the desk with her eyes squeezed shut.

"Is she meditating?"

"No, she's testing my ability to stay calm under stress." I squeeze my eyes shut for a moment. "She does it every day we're together."

I open them. Sam's on all fours, glancing over the edge of the desk, holding a pencil like it's a spear. Michelle's mouth twitches into a diplomatic smile.

"At least no two days are ever the same."

Some uniformity would be helpful. Yesterday she almost sent a letter out referring to me as Her Remnants.

Michelle's head tilts one way then the other as she watches.

"I have some papers that need signing off for the graduation." Eyebrows rise as she shakes her head then finally peels her gaze away from our comedy moment. "Last minute things so everything runs smoothly. Should I...?" Her thumb hooks over at Sam. "Or...?"

"Straight to me will be fine."

Michelle nods, her eyes darting back to Sam.

"I'll go chase Bee up, make sure she's not dragging her heels on Operation Mice Hoover. Your Eminence."

The commotion has brought some life to my reception area. Several heads turn as Michelle walks back to her office. Tall and athletic, her movements are fluid and seamless. No need to wonder why her combat training courses fill up so quickly.

I turn back to Sam. Michelle's right, no two days are the same.

"Sam? Page someone from facilities management to fix the machine. Also, come into my office when you get a chance. We only have two days and I have some notes I need you to take about the graduation."

...and some extra patience just waiting to be exhausted.

Her hand shoots out, thumb pointing high, quickly followed by a wide-eyed look of embarrassment. That same hand covers her mouth, fingers splaying as she speaks.

"Sorry. I meant, yes, I'll be there in one minute." A pause and I wait for her to finish. "Your Eminence."

I just watch her then sigh.

"Thank you, Sam."

In my safe office I recline in my chair and kick my shoes off, taking a moment before she comes in. Something skims my foot. I pull both feet up and drag my shoes to safety, too. I hug my knees. My heart pounds. I glance under the desk. A scurrying mouse pauses, glares back then runs away. Even her vermin have attitude! I take a long breath, trying to calm down but fail miserably. I seethe one word under my breath.

"Lucy!"

## 2 CUPID'S INTRODUCTION

That was Elle and her Head Office in Hell. You also heard about the flip side of Elle's coin, her nemesis, Lucy. Lucy's short for Lucifer. Well, if God's kitted out in four-inch heels and designer clothes you don't still think the Devil's half-man/half-goat, do you? You Earth people are too melodramatic with your views. Lucy doesn't eat children or kill kittens. As for horns and fangs, what do you think we look like? I don't have stupid feathery wings and Elle isn't all glowy - normally. I mean she *can* glow but it's a cheap trick and she can do so much better.

Still, you're half right because they both have some cool tricks. They can transport to and from places. Picture it, you're having dinner and suddenly Lucy appears perched on the edge of your table trying to stick a finger in your dinner. It's off-putting. They can also heal wounds which is a redundant skill since Elle versus Lucy - that was a fight that didn't want to go away, but I'll come to that later on. Healing is a bit theatrical and draining on energy levels. Imagine, you flash in, fix a broken leg then have to sleep for a day. Not great on the social life.

Back to Lucy. She is by every race and religion, angelically beautiful. Remember, she was one not too long ago. A few thousand years since her and Elle's fight might seem a long time to you, but to us it's nothing. When Lucy turns it on she can charm the most brutal warrior up to the most holy of men. She can make people do things they wouldn't normally consider. Not because she bewitches them but because she knows how people tick. If you link that mind with a body that could cause pile-ups, you see why Elle has her hands full.

Anyway, back to Lucy. There are so many things I want to tell you about her but there's a whole story in front of us so I'll let her do the talking.

# Chapter Two: Lucy
## 1st April, Year 2 - 15:00
## Hell is a Paperwork Jungle

I flick through the mountain of files sent by Elle. Letters of complaint,

5

evidence of misbehaviour by my staff, and general accounts of interference. I roll my eyes at the latest addition: a file full of reports on vermin infestations allegedly sent by me. Can I help it if Elle attracts rodents?

Note to self: send mice up more regularly.

I slowly push the entire pile off of my desk. I rest my chin on the edge and watch them fall, hitting the bottom of my bin with a satisfying thump. This is the most efficient way of creating a paperless office. It's also the only way to deal with Elle's tyrannical need to castrate my fun by drowning me in bureaucracy. For example, I want to spread a disease? Six forms filled out in triplicate and that's before I get a disease order number. After that another three procedures before I can submit a time and place for my incident, and that's only agreeable if there's an over population issue or an increase in violence. Natural disasters? Five separate forms. An assassination? I only bother if I have three weeks spare for the paperwork. By that time the fun has gone and I no longer want to be bad. Naughty is such a spur of the moment feeling, which is something I assume Her Perfectness has realised.

As for stealing souls, that joy was curtailed with the addition of the statistics man. Stats Man is my ball and chain. He is the manacle that keeps Her Godliness unfairly in charge and poor little me under her thumb. I have to justify the souls I take. I have to show him they deserve it. I have to prove to that little spy that I'm behaving myself. At the time I tried to tell Elle, "I'm the Devil. The day I start to behave myself is the day the known universe is about to implode." Her Godly smile was my only answer. It was like talking to a pristinely whitewashed brick wall. Now I'm ruled by figures. In my sleep and waking hours all I think about are percentages. It's all about them and winning. And winning wouldn't be as hard if the all souls assigned to me could be taken by my people. But, oh no, I'm not trusted - which is a recurring theme Elle has.

My door opens. Arms loaded with paper, my assistant comes in. I pout.

"I'm bored, Bee. Let's kill someone."

Her paperwork drops on my desk. Eyes narrow as she taps her bottom lip with the end of her pen.

"Do you have someone specific in mind?"

"Any high-ranking religious figures been disavowing me lately?"

"All of them as usual. Elle's got Mother Theresa. There's always the Vatican but we'd have a real struggle to get anyone. It's not worth the effort."

She shrugs unhelpfully. It doesn't take me long to come up with an alternative

"I know what we can do, Bee." One of her eyebrows barely quirks. "Why don't we both take an early day? I've just had my Jacuzzi refitted..."

"Thanks but I have lots of work to do."

In the time Bee's been my assistant she's developed an ability to ignore my suggestions. For me it's encouragement to try harder, like a game. I lean over my desk, knowing my cleavage is on full view.

"Come on, Bee. I know a great way for us to relax. You won't even need a swimsuit if we..."

"Charity's auditors are coming for the inspection in an hour. There's paperwork to shred."

My voice takes on the tone dedicated to the woman who has my investments over a barrel. There's less room to be naughty with Charity. Her bank holds my entire portfolio.

"Charity Nature. Almost as bad as Elle."

I fall back in my seat with one word echoing in my head: auditors. We used to have annual visits. Elle said, "It's to make sure your paperwork and monetary contributions are up to date and in order." I told her she could kiss my contributions. She made the visits monthly.

"The audit takes priority. Go on, scoot. Don't want to be caught with our panties down."

Bee leaves to get on with other things. I glance at my clock. Two hours until my most important meeting of the day, my masseur. Therefore I'm making an executive decision to fill my time with something of serious importance: beauty sleep.

I close my eyes and relax.

## 3 CUPID'S INTRODUCTION

Okay, now onto the new addition in the ranks. You need to understand that no one, especially a God, is infallible. Everyone has something that inspires crazy stuff. With me it's lap dancers. It's something to do with their pliability. But with Elle it was this woman, Discord Knight - not a blood Angel but a mortal.

Quick run through. All new souls are screened to see what section of the Heavens they'll go to. Almost all end up in the party-zone for mortals, where everything's provided and they can bask in a fun-filled eternity. But pre-screening tagged Discord's soul and temperament as an ideal Angel of Vengeance - that division cleans up the messes Earth's society can't cope with: serial rapists, child killers, large-scale drug dealers. And to pre-empt any comments about their effectiveness, Elle's guys and girls try their best but their ranks are almost static and you people are multiplying like rabbits.

To make it short but sweet, souls are judged according to their deeds. If you're good you go to the Heavens, if you're bad, to Hell, but if you're really bad, Vengeance will remove you from Earth to prevent your influence.

Discord Knight died and was snatched out of the party-line and shoved straight in the training deep end. She did well and sucked up everything thrown at her. Either way, back to the sex and loving 'cause that's why you're here.

Listen, we're going to have to go back in time for this one because I don't want you missing the good stuff. Think of it as a sixties style cartoon flashback. Let's go back to last year, a couple of months after Discord's arrival in the Heavens. After settling in and training, training, training, Elle met Discord.

Hold on to your hats for the roller coaster ride.

# Chapter Three: Elle
## 30th May, Year 1 - 13:00
## Rush Of Blood

"**T**hat was Sam." I wiggle my mobile in the air, trying not to crush the plastic. "Bee called to say Lucy will be late. Again."

The elevator doors close. Charity expels a frustrated sigh as I shift my pile of heavy files to my other arm; I like to keep the stretching of limbs even.

"Why the deep-seated need to keep us all waiting? This meeting is designed to help with her sneaky little soul stealing..."

I rub her arm, making her bite that rant back as she leans against the elevator wall.

"Count figures, Charity." Floor numbers go whizzing by until, with a ding, we arrive at the sixth. "We help her count figures because she can't seem to do it herself."

The doors slide open and we make our way along the pristinely white corridor towards the meeting room.

Charity sighs.

"I'm glad she doesn't drive. Imagine the speed limit confusion if she thinks ten is a hundred."

A loud noise makes me start, sending the contents of a folder fanning to the floor. I stare at the mess. This skirt was not designed for bending. It was barely designed for walking. I carefully make it to the floor without incident and grab the papers, jamming them back into the folder. I glare up at the inconsiderate source of the interruption. At the other end of the corridor Michelle holds the door open with a trailing arm and through it looms a shadowy figure.

My papers float back to the floor. Inky black hair slinks across broad shoulders as charcoal eyes focus on an indefinable point ahead. My fingertips connect with the cold marble. She stalks closer, top clinging to sculptured sinews stretching up forearms to distinct biceps that look powerful but still clearly feminine. My lips part as a breath forces out. I close my eyes, the negative image branding into my brain. I open them and she's still there. My body rises as she slices a swath through the sudden atmosphere in the hallway.

Charity's words drift towards me.

"Who's that?"

My mouth opens but all that exits is a sigh.

"Elle?"

There's only one fresh soul I've had to sign off forms for.

"Sorry. It would have to be Discord Knight. Mortal. New."

I glance at my best friend, trying to ground myself. Her head tilts, eyes watching what I just did. She mutters simply.

"Wow."

My gaze resumes its magnetic attraction as I flounder in the visual shock. Twenty feet away shadowy eyes float over me like a shameless caress.

Charity's amusement is obvious.

"An admirer, Your Eminence?"

I watch as each methodical footstep is carefully taken. I bet the Amazons would've loved to have her because she looks every inch a fighter: lean, muscled, and broad, broad like a swimmer.

"Why it would seem that way, yes."

"She doesn't know who you are, does she?"

My voice slips to a monotone as all higher brain functions begin to shut down.

"Why it would seem that way, yes."

Michelle bows quickly as she passes, whereas our new soul decides to take a different approach. Dark eyes glitter as they slide the length of me. She cocks her head in a hello. I blow a breath out, shaking my head and watch her walk away.

"Did I just see that? Good grief, Elle, she mentally undressed you."

"Why it would seem that..."

With a poke to my side my autopilot disengages.

"Charity to Elle, come in Elle."

I try to shake the heat from my cheeks, engaging enough of my brain to make words tumble out.

"Michelle, a moment, please?"

Both stop. Michelle is the first to turn. Next, but by no means least, Discord slowly pivots on her heels, shoulders squaring off beautifully. She carefully brushes a dark strand of hair from her shoulder. Michelle bows and probably does something else but my attention has been kidnapped.

"Your Eminence. Ms. Nature." She motions to her guest. "Your Eminence, this is Discord Knight. Discord, this is Her Eminence, or the Caretaker." She leans in, whispering to Discord. "You know her as God."

Discord's eyebrows plummet sharply as Michelle takes a step backward leaving the new arrival to my scrutiny. The rest of her reactions to my introduction are just as transparent. Her jaw sets and eyes widen. I can't help my smile as I hold out my hand.

"It's a pleasure to meet you. Welcome to the Heavens, Discord."

Her gaze slides down to my hand, then hesitatingly meets mine again. Tanned skin does well to hide most of her blush. Her arm extends suddenly, muscles flexing under her smooth skin.

"You're God?"

My blink isn't just at the warm fingers that slip against my palm, grasping it gently. Charity snorts, trying to cover the sound with a cough. Me, I stare up into eyes that hold my own without reservation.

"Last time I checked the name plate on the door that's what it said. Well, a God, anyway. Were you expecting something a little different?"

A fingertip glides over the sensitive skin of my wrist and my entire arm jerks. Another cough from Charity and I pull my hand away, aware that Michelle is by no means blind. I glance down, fingertips rubbing together, missing what they just held.

The low timbre of her voice pulls my attention back.

"I didn't mean to be rude. I thought you were supposed to be a man. You know, that's what they teach."

Michelle's cheeks flush as she squeezes her eyes shut. I wouldn't like to be the one trying to teach this woman some diplomacy, but then in her new position I doubt she needs it. Vengeance doesn't require politeness or astute comments. It needs tactical brilliance and controlled brutality. I have a feeling she has those.

My eyes float across strong shoulders that rise and fall with each breath. I lean closer, dipping my voice to a whisper. My skin prickles from the heat she radiates.

"They? The good book, you mean?"

I get a bare nod so I give a barely thought through reply.

"It's been re-written too many times. There was a lot more fun in the original."

For a moment everything nearby fades and all that's left is this arresting woman and me. I watch as her tongue flicks out to moisten her lips before she speaks.

"You're the good guys, though? That bit was right?"

I catch Charity clutching her case to her chest and looking away, the corners of her mouth twitching.

"Yes. We're the good guys."

Discord maintains her stoic composure.

"That's all that matters then, Your Eminence."

As her sombre aura attempts another assault I remember who else is here. I turn to the serious face of my Head of Combat Training.

"Michelle, you're doing a good job. Are all of my Angels of Vengeance so confident and sure of themselves?"

She bows deeply.

"Thank you, Your Eminence." She looks quickly at Discord. "The Vengeance legion is unique in its physiological and psychological make up."

"Mmmm." I glance across to Charity. Her eyebrows slowly rise. I try to add

something a little more sensible. "They certainly are."

My best friend interjects, dragging me back to safer ground.

"We'll have to say goodbye. The meeting with Lucy started five minutes ago. Not that I expect her to be there but if we're too late we can't throw disapproving looks at her tardiness when she strolls in."

Discord glances at Charity then me, eyelashes fluttering in a heavy blink. Her hand stretches out once more, daring me to teeter from the precipice I precariously cling to.

"It was good to meet you, Your Eminence."

I take that taunting hand. Like coming out of the shadows into bright midday sunlight, the effect is instantaneous. My skin burns.

"You too, Discord."

As with all teases it leaves too soon. Her hand slips away. Michelle bows, saying goodbyes I barely register. My Angels turn and carry on their journey. Heavy footsteps echo in our confined space.

I stare at Charity, unable to form a single sentence that could convey what that woman just did to me. Suddenly the rhythmic noise of boots on marble stalls and I glance over at that tall shadowy figure once more. She spins, walking backward, keeping up with Michelle. The acoustics carry her sentence.

"Your Eminence?" No smile on her serious face. "My first religious experience was a pleasure."

She bows courteously, holding it for three steps then spins back around. Michelle mouths an apology. They turn a corner and disappear.

I stare at the space Discord occupied a few moments earlier and blow a long breath out. A cool hand touches my hot cheek.

"Oh dear. Two words, Elle. Ethical. Violation."

"Not if it stays in my imagination."

I take hold of her shoulders, trying to steady the flood of intense emotions exploding through me. Charity grins widely.

"You can manage that? All you didn't do was have sex in front of me."

I close my eyes and lean my cheek onto that shoulder, the material of her top softly comforting.

"I didn't mean to be obvious but she's..." Words stutter as I try to regain my composure. "...compelling. Did it show too badly?"

A hand rubs up and down my arm, dissipating a sudden chill.

"I was watching Michelle because you obviously had eyes for only one person. She thought Discord was being obliviously rude. She was too focused on that. You don't have much to worry about - if you keep it in your head. Remember, ethical..."

My voice exits in a sultry whisper I can't stop.

"Violation. Hmm, I know."

"Anyway, she's not your type."

I straighten up and readjust my suit.

"I know but it doesn't change what happened to me here." I point to my heart. "And here."

She grabs my hand, stopping it from pointing somewhere else.

"I can imagine. But she's too strapping. She'd damage you."

I turn and stare at the corner that stole Discord.

"It'd be fun seeing how she'd go about that damage." I sigh heavily. "I know she's too broad. I know she's too muscular, too intense. It's just..." My revelation is sudden. "...she's tall dark and handsome, and I want her."

# 4 CUPID'S INTRODUCTION

See what I mean? Discord was the irresistible cowgirl who rode into town and made Elle swoon. Now, Elle's always been the steady hand up in the Heavens but with Discord she made up for lost time. Elle lit the fuse, forgot to take ten steps back to safety and the blast radius shot all of the Heavens to Hell.

See the problem is simple: a God falling for a mortal and living happily ever after? Like that could ever happen without mayhem erupting. Life doesn't cut us any more slack than it does you people, remember that.

Back to the story. After the initial meeting, days of tension turned to weeks of, well, tension. Elle did whatever she could to be near the new arrival. Not that Elle knew but Discord was doing the same. At its most simplistic it was a boiling attraction Elle couldn't control. At its most complicated it was a God finding her soul mate.

Remember, we're still in our sixties style flashback last year. Discord had shown exemplary skill in combat, but she'd also annoyed a couple of Amazons by kicking their asses in training. An unofficial cat-fight was barely avoided and turned into, well, an official cat-fight: an Arena battle.

Just over two weeks after Elle and Discord met, the tension exploded.

# Chapter Four: **Discord**
## 15th June, Year 1 - 14:00
## A Fight on our Hands

I take a sip of water, trying to rinse the taste of blood out of my mouth. The buzzer sounds and I stand, ready for round three. From the little I've learned, these battle competitions are how the Amazons judge their warriors. If that's the case they should pick some more competent ones. I easily slap away a roundhouse kick, sick of playing with this woman.

A flash of blonde and ice blue catch my attention and for a second I'm lost as I stare back. Elle nods, her sensual lips curling into a slight smile.

A fist hits my jaw, knocking those thoughts right out of my brain. I land with a heavy thump, the impact forcing tremors up through my ribs.

The crowd erupts into a deafening cheer. I pace my breathing and blink away the bright ceiling lights as the Amazons goad their champion. I lie there as my pride stings.

Palms plant on the canvas and I push up a little, taking it slow, thankful I didn't get all of my brain knocked out of my ears.

I glance over to the only spectator who matters. Elle's concerned face relaxes as our eyes connect. She sits back in her seat. I don't expect what she does next. It almost knocks the same amount of air out of me that punch did. Her lips form a lazy smile and she mouths.

"Sorry."

It confirms what's happening here and whenever we've met. It wasn't just me in the meeting room when our eyes locked a little too long. It wasn't just me when she watched me in the training area. And it wasn't just me any of the other times we've run into each other.

I flip up, arrogantly spinning three-sixty degrees on my heels. It usually, and I'm
right again as this Amazon seethes at me, infuriates these girls. Control is a fragile animal and the best way to annoy a warrior is to make them lose their grip on it. I read that on a laminated card in week two.

She throws a punch and I duck. Another and I do the same. I let my arms hang by my sides, watching her movements, determined not to be sent down again. I catch Elle's eyes for a fraction of a second. Not if I have such an important spectator.

The fight slows as I hit my zone. I always thought it was fictional but then I never had a sufficient hold on my temper to reach the place where you don't have to think or plan your reactions, they just happen.

The Amazon's movements are fluid and graceful but I easily dodge a slow fist. Another cuts through the tar-like air. She leg sweeps me. I jump, feeling as if the air is holding me up. Now is time to end this; it's rude to play with an opponent. Combat training has taught me respect.

I grab an incoming fist as she becomes angry, sloppy. I twist it. It cracks like a dry twig. She cries out and the fierce roar of the crowd dulls. I pull her in sharply, whispering, because no matter what zone I'm in I don't need the entire Nation on my back.

"You're a good fighter."

I push her away, slamming a roundhouse into her head. She spins in the air and it's like an old war film where a damaged fighter plane funnels towards the ground. What should take a fraction of a second stretches as my zone keeps me somewhere else. My whole body feels her hit the canvas as the hard echo travels up the bones of my legs. A deafening silence spills around the arena. My competitor doesn't move. She's out cold.

I turn around, searching the crowd, trying to find what I'm looking for. Warmth radiates as ice blue eyes smile into my own. This victory isn't important. This woman is. I drop to my knee, not looking away.

Someone hits the reality switch and time resumes with a bang.

The crowd in front of her rises unexpectedly. A roar fills the arena. The referee pulls me to my feet, holding my hand up in victory. I lose sight of my prize. When the crowd parts she's gone. I scan bodies, desperately trying to find her again. I drown in a sea of strangers.

Warm fingers glide across my shoulder which brings up the question of who's stupid enough to be laying their hands on me. My glare doesn't last more than a second. Elle tucks a strand of blonde hair behind an ear. Glistening pink lips move and I lean closer. I grit my teeth, inhaling a fragrance I don't know yet. It's a light mix of citrus and something else I can't figure. It makes my stomach flip and eyes close.

"I feel I should have given you my handkerchief before you went in to joust for me."

Her laugh tickles my ear. I fight the urge to touch her. Arms stiff, my hands stay clenched by my sides. Every other person fades away as I whisper my reply. Even with a handful of butterflies bouncing around in my stomach I manage something intelligent.

"Is that an offer to be your champion, Your Eminence?"

A little thing like her brings this giant down with six words.

"I'm offering more than that, Discord."

She walks away as if we'd just talked about the weather or the canteen menu. She stops by a dark haired woman in a well pressed suit I recognise from our first meeting. Elle looks at me as she listens to her. It's not an innocent look either. It's loaded, but with what I'm not exactly sure. The corners of her lips curl into a soft smile and her hand goes to her pocket, pulling out that promised handkerchief, holding it up, turning so the crowd can see it. Even amongst the commotion in the ring it's her heels I feel walking back towards me. She holds the pristine piece of white silk out. There's an 'E' embroidered in one corner. I'm careful not to let our fingers touch because my reactions would be kind of obvious to the arena of attention we're holding. I'm surprised no one's thrown a bucket of water over me already.

Miss Well-Pressed lures her back with a microphone and Elle's hypnotizing voice echoes.

"To my champion, Discord Knight."

Wild applause resounds like a hammering ripple that reminds you you're alive...even if you're not anymore.

She retreats and with one last glance she disappears into the throng of moving bodies. I slip the silk into my pocket.

In the safety of the empty locker room I do what I've ached to. I take the handkerchief back out and smell the same perfume as earlier. It's weird what the scent of a person can do. The mind an amazing computer opening secret places when you feed it the right key. I just have to figure out exactly what to do with those places.

I dry off after my well-earned shower. My thumb rubs the one raised letter. My thoughts begin to confuse me. I'm not a gangly adolescent. I'm a grown woman. I've loved and lost. I've even loved and won for a short time. But this woman is something else.

A knock on the door and I stuff the silk into my bag. The Amazons obviously don't lose a lot so I guess everyone is taking this opportunity to celebrate; the congratulations and flowers have been coming in since I left the arena. I catch my reflection and pull a top on and do the buttons up on my pants.

"Come in."

I bend over, covering my head with a towel as I roughly dry my hair. The door clicks open.

"Leave them by the bench, thanks."

The door clicks shut, then another click. The lock. I pull the towel away quickly, getting into a fighting stance. I know the Amazons are fierce but I didn't expect such low vengeful tactics. Except it's not an Amazon who's in front of me.

Elle leans on the locked door, tucking a strand of hair behind her ear. I'm not incredibly experienced with women but what's been building between the two of us is obvious. The subtleties and nuances haven't been obscure they've been right out there, screaming in my head even when she wasn't around. I drop my towel on the bench and drown in sparkling pools of blue.

Words purr out of glistening lips.

"Hello, Dizzy."

My brain hits a wall as I stand and stare. And then, suddenly, as if I jammed my foot on the accelerator, it kicks back full throttle.

"Dizzy?"

She smiles and shrugs.

"After your magnificent trip to the canvas I thought it'd be fitting."

A part of me likes the fact I got a personal nickname. The rest of me hates why I earned it.

My voice stays even but my pulse hammers in my chest, like a rhythm carrying me on and on and on.

"In future I'll try to keep punches to my face to a minimum. I don't want to spoil my looks."

My joke makes one of her eyebrows raise slowly.

"I know I'd hate that to happen."

She walks away from the door. I track her. I turn, she moves.

"You fought well tonight."

We slowly circle each other, neither willing to make the first move yet, I guess. It's like being in a toy store and finding just what you want; you're still going to take your time over picking it up and buying because choosing is half the fun.

"Thanks. I saw you watching."

Her slow circles decrease. She gets closer. There's a buzz in the air, a charge as if a storm is on the way.

Her lips lift into a smile.

"I noticed."

She bites her lip for a moment before letting it slip away. That does it. I stop playing.

"You've locked the door."

That just gets a slow nod. Her ever-decreasing circles almost bring her close enough to touch. My fingers twitch, trying to feel her on their own.

Her answer punches me square in the chest.

"I didn't want to be disturbed."

She stops moving and I get dragged into those eyes again. Blue, bright, and so light
they sparkle.

A knock at the door makes us freeze. I hope whoever interrupted us stays outside of this room. I can't guarantee their safety if they come in. I sit, a little dazed, as she answers it. I don't listen to the conversation. I'm not interested. When she's done she turns and smiles.

"We have very unfinished business. Have dinner with me?"

I nod.

"I'll send my car at seven?" Her eyebrows furrow as she cocks her head. "Seven, yes? If you want to, that is."

My voice finally returns. My body stays where she sent it.

"Sorry. I.... Yes. Seven is good."

That door clicks shut, leaving me alone.

The hours until darkness falls seem to crawl. Whatever I try to tell my head fails because I want to see her. No negative thoughts, just an up beat. I'm in the Heavens now, what could go wrong?

An executive car pulls up in front of my building. It's not exactly in disguise but all of the senior staff get one. For all my neighbours know I could be going to see anyone.

I shift on the leather seat feeling like a teenager going on a first date. I smooth my top down and pick some lint off of my pants. We drive along the gravel path to what I assume is her place. Hidden lighting shows off tall columns and angles of a huge sprawling mansion. It's an impressive sight. The car stops and before I know what's happened I'm at an intricately carved wooden door. I take a deep breath. The door swings open. Framed by the light behind she looks amazing. Her hair is pulled back emphasizing strong cheekbones and full lips. A simple ivory dress makes her eyes bluer than I thought possible. She smiles and it feels like a caress.

I fight the urge to overstep everyone's boundaries. Elle takes a step back and I take a step in, like a weird dance only leading to one place. She closes the door and we stand in her hallway, in silence. The charge between us is amazing. It's thick, heavy, and, as I know, hard to contain. I quit playing games. If I don't act now my nerves will crucify me. I take two steps forward. Her delicate hands slide up my arms as I cup her face. I kiss her.

We manage to make it to the bedroom. I'm barely able to take in its grandeur before I'm undressed by teasing hands. We make love in a fever. Any fears about us not clicking fade to black. Any fears about me not being able to relax enough also disappear. My nerves can be a killer.

Of all of my lovers, Elle is very capable. She knows how to touch me, where to touch me and any other combination I can think of. Her fingers are...well, Godlike. I actually have to take a moment to catch myself before I turn our tables. I get to do everything I fantasized about. Her skin tastes salty and sweet. She tastes heavy and musky. It's something I can't get enough of as my tongue runs over her curves, taking control of them.

Her mouth allows a low purr, almost a throaty chuckle, to escape. Finally, she says the first words that night.

"Any more and I'll die."

I kiss her and hands tangle in my hair. She doesn't die.

The rest of the night is a blurring mix of light sleep and making the most of being awake. You see, when you die and everything is ripped away you make sure of one thing: you use your time a lot wiser. But even clever use stops with exhaustion. Finally we rest as annoying darts of sunlight begin to slip through her blinds. A hand slides over the sheets and rests itself on my stomach. I stop fighting and close my eyes.

# 5 CUPID'S INTRODUCTION

The night was long and full for the young lovers. In fact, the morning went pretty much the same way. That day they talked and generally started to get to know the simple stuff. Elle liked tea, Discord liked coffee. Elle took sugar when stressed, Discord never did. Elle liked the shower hot, Discord liked it cool. They settled on warm. It was a start, where everything comes from. I think at the back their minds was one thing: perhaps I'm not alone anymore?

## Chapter Five: Elle
## 16th June, Year 1 - 23:00
## Abstract Frames

I watch her as we descend the stairs, every powerful muscle working in faultless harmony. She reminds me of a big cat. Yes, a fearsome jaguar, padding along a jungle trail, sated after her meal yet still alert; she's stalked and caught her prey - or more like, I gave up our enjoyable play chase and was devoured. My hand trails down the balustrade and I snort a laugh at my choice of words. Devoured. Yes, I was.

I open the double doors to my reception as we keep a distance between us. She stops in front of my floor to ceiling windows, observing, watching, waiting for my car to magic her back to the real world. We remain in a state of suspended silence, neither comfortable nor uneasy. Dark eyes glance across and undress my body as she did last night. I wave a hand in front of my breasts where her gaze settles. With a cough and imperceptible blush she goes back to looking out of my windows. What an awkward dance this is, from complete intimacy to utter remoteness in less than an hour.

I accept this opportunity to watch. Layered charcoal hair shimmers as she shifts from one foot to the other. It represents a lot about Discord Knight. From a distance it's flat black, but, as I studied her while she slept, I saw it was a lot more complicated. Colours flickered through each strand like the faceted feathers of a Rook. It was at that point I decided it was safer if I went to make breakfast.

She moves, depositing me back into the here and now. Her tee shirt stretches across broad shoulders, the same ones I pressed my thumbs into leaving faint purple bruises I couldn't kiss away.

I watch as she stands, framed like a painting by my huge windows; they let the light in during the day - my driver arrives and headlights signal her imminent departure - they let reality intrude now.

I close my eyes, determined to be graceful and magnanimous. That is, after all, what I've been trained for. Then without a sound I feel her. Warm hands slide up my arms and my easily bribed body pushes back into her. I smile at my responses. Lips float over my neck and my muscles jerk. My head rests on her, allowing a warm mouth access to whatever it wants. Despite myself, I moan. She licks and nibbles at me. I reassess my earlier thought. She's like the junior version of a big cat, all paws and muscles, not understanding the strength at her disposal.

Powerful arms surround me like a protective barrier, keeping me safe. I turn in that embrace. Hot breath steams across my lips. Those sensations bleed into my coherent thoughts, leaving whatever train I was following far behind. We kiss deeply for what seems like eternity, only parting for...air, a moment to let our bodies cool, perhaps a million other reasons and perhaps none at all.

Headlights flash, reminding us of that presence. One that I'm not interested in, nevertheless, one I can't ignore. Intense eyes stare down as my hands hold on to firm biceps. I make my easy decision. I let go and lean over to my bag, pulling my phone out.

My driver answers.

*"Your Eminence?"*

"False alarm, I'm sorry. Take the rest of the night off."

*"Are you sure you won't need me?"*

I wonder how much of a risk I'm prepared to take with this woman. Should one risk anything at all for the unknown? Or is that it, should one risk everything?

I cover the mouthpiece and look up into abstruse eyes. They make my question pause before exiting.

"Stay with me?"

A slight nod is all I get from my confused jaguar cub. I remove my hand from the mouthpiece and answer my driver.

"Positive."

I snap my cell phone shut. Unaccustomed as I am to explaining myself, I offer a free one here.

"I wanted to spend some more time with you."

For a moment she looks at me and I look at her, both of us lost in our separate worlds. Mine is filled with a surreal need for more time. I wonder what hers is filled with because I'm not arrogant enough to believe it's the same.

The urge to move takes me to the other side of the room. I cover those fifty feet in what feels like an age. A button moves the shutters silently, revealing similar windows as before. Except there is a difference. I flick a switch bringing the outside lights alive, illuminating the single most comforting thing this colossal mansion for one has: my view.

I don't have to speak, we seem to be doing well without words, but somewhere inside I sense her unease. It's not directed at me but at the situation we appear to have fallen into. I try to lift the tension.

"Would you like a drink?"

An inane question for an indiscreetly obvious moment. What do you say when your lover is a stranger?

"Umm...maybe a soda?"

Her nervousness is agonizingly evident. I stop fighting through the dark and force myself to relax.

"You sound like you need something a little stronger."

Humour is our equalizer, because I want her to feel at ease with me, a person she knows inside out yet not at all.

The veil of anxiety lifts as a slight smile appears.

"Maybe a beer?"

"A beer it is." I tap the window pane. "This glass is one way. No one can see in. Not that many choose to wander by."

I gaze onto my stretching grounds. Then my body feels that charge again. Her warmth. I lean back, connecting, making the bond we've created real, and try to draw us together from opposite ends of this desolate plain we're standing on. We stare at my view. A shimmering lake almost twice the size of this house, floating like a saucer of ice, guarded by a select few mighty oaks. It was my main indulgence after being put in this empty palace. I always try to encourage inner peace, especially using Nature's own creations.

I watch her reflection in the glass, head turning, eyes moving, assessing, quantifying, qualifying. Her voice reverberates through me.

"I guess I missed this when I arrived."

My smile appears from nowhere.

"I don't give it up for just anyone, you know."

Her silent laughter ripples through me as a comforting hand rests on my stomach.

"I'm glad you gave it up for me."

"So you should."

I cover that strong hand with my own, matching her initiation of intimacy, very glad we have this closeness. Intimacy is a fragile thing dictated by many variables: fear, pride, even a person's past. Often we're too afraid of a possible rejection so we become the rejecters, keeping our distance, staying away from what intrigues us, what we crave. It seems we're dallying around those edges, dipping in to touch then moving away to check for wounds.

We stay like that, paused, for a long while. I enjoy her and my view. They're two calming things rolled into one.

My thumb rubs her hand, signalling my departure.

"Let me get you that drink."

She reacts instantly as if scolded. Her hand jerks away. I hold it, slowing her into a sensual glide across my stomach, one I feel even through my clothes.

Yes, what a curious little dance.

The chill from the refrigerator restarts all higher brain functions. I pull a beer out, staring but not looking at the label. I put it down and pick the phone up, dialling Charity's number. She answers after three rings with her usual.

*"Charity Nature."*

I lean on the counter.

"Hello, Miss Workaholic."

*"Hello, Miss Noticeably Absent. Well? Last night?"*

My finger plays with the sharp edges of the bottle top.

"Has turned into tonight."

I pour out some fruit juice as she thinks.

*"And you'd rather be speaking to me than doing whatever with her? Treating them mean does not keep sane women keen."*

I drop a coloured straw into my juice, stirring it into a frenzied whirlpool.

"I feel peculiar."

*"Do you want me to rescue you?"*

I let my straw go, allowing it to twist around my glass, out of control.

"I don't mean like that. I feel perfectly safe with her. Peculiar in a strange way."

*"You don't sound like yourself."*

What a massive understatement. I grab the straw, halting its manic journey.

"I'm not. I need you for brunch tomorrow. Can you give me an hour or three?"

The electronic beeping of her scheduler in the background makes my eyes roll. The obsessive use of that gadget has done obscene things to my sanity.

*"I have something on soul acquisition I'm dying to get out of. How is eleven until two for a start?"*

"Perfect. Thank you for rescheduling."

*"You're my one link to remembering sane women do exist and not just the ones I seem to date, Elle. I can't have you feeling peculiar."*

I've met a few of those women. They're empty vessels, but as Charity puts it, "They're suitable for work functions. Imagine if I brought along a stripper. Pretty Woman worked on celluloid but wouldn't in real life."

"Perhaps you need to move in circles less travelled?"

*"You mean for my next trick, date a woman who isn't a model? Elle, please, you're making me nervous."*

"You're not in a serious mood, I take it."

*"Sorry. We've been auditing Lucy's soul repatriation schemes and I think they've sent me insane. Bee and her...? A very efficient pairing is my only comment."*

"They're the proverbial sand under my fingernails."

*"Excuse me."*

There are muffled voices. I recognise her secretary's lilting Italian accent in the background.

*"I'm going to have to go. Work screams. I'll see you tomorrow for brunch. 'Night - as if you'll be getting sleep."*

"Have fun."

The phone clicks into a low hum. I pick a beer up for my guest. Walking back along the hall I catch my reflection in a mirror covering half the length of the wall. I stop, staring back. It all looks the same but it most certainly isn't. I turn, not prepared to get into a critical analysis of myself right now. After what I've gone and done I think any analysis may take some time and be very critical.

I push open the door to my reception room. Discord's head tilts. She's standing, staring at one of my more abstract paintings. I lean on the door frame, watching. Her head tilts the other way. I can't help but smile.

"It's called Decision. It's of a woman in the midst of an internal struggle."

Startled she turns, doing what I've come to find very endearing: hands settle in the back pockets of her pants as her flush peeks out from under tanned cheeks. I walk over, holding her beer out. She takes it, nodding her head back to the picture.

"If you say so. I'm not great with art. Not enough practice."

She shrugs, lifting the bottle briefly in thanks. She stares at the label, running her thumb over it. How can someone with such physical presence be so diffident?

"But do you like it?"

Dark eyes meet mine.

"Yeah, it's.... It makes you think."

I take her arm, turning us back around, feeling her muscles harden with the movement.

"What do you like?"

She takes a moment to answer.

"I like the colours. The strokes make her look powerful. Like.... I don't know. I guess it looks strong."

She glances at me for reassurance then attempts to take everything back when I stay silent.

"But I'm no critic. I'm not very good with art so I'm probably way off."

I lay a hand on her forearm, rubbing my thumb over the solidness. Her body leans into mine a little as we regain the footing with our closeness. Two steps forward, one step back.

"You're not. That's how it's meant to look. The figure's muscles are taught, arching away from the viewer; in front of you, but hiding. Giving but at the same time not letting you have what you want. The strokes are long, just like muscles." I glance at her once again tilted head. "I'm glad you like it. Actually it looks a little like you."

She snorts a laugh, relaxing as she sips some beer.

"Eye of the beholder."

"Eye of the painter."

She stares directly at me, her arm slipping from mine.

"You painted this?"

"When I used to paint, yes. Does it surprise you I have hidden talents?"

Obsidian eyes look distinctly unimpressed. This could be where the spell is broken. Never insult a person's pride.

"I know you have hidden talents. I didn't know they were so different."

"I have many skills, Dizzy."

She doesn't smile or change that blank expression. Her eyes stay just as intense.

"I bet you do."

Then after a pause that drags.

"I'm not great with words. The painting, it's really...good. I mean, the colours and - it all kind of matches." She shifts. "I should've just stuck with it's good."

Seems it was safe to risk my secret with her.

"I know what you mean. Thank you."

She takes a swig of beer then motions to the other pictures.

"Are all these yours?"

"No, unfortunately not."

I tell a short story for each: of the artist, the motivation, what the piece represents. Rothko, Kadinsky, a late Picasso. I like indulging my passions. We come to the last ones, the absolute favourite things I own: my Lempickas. We talk about St. Moritz and the sadness in her eyes, then the contrasting Madame M and the sensual intensity she has.

Dizzy glances across to me.

"These are pretty amazing."

I smile. It's always nicer to share.

"Yes, they are."


We talk about art. She might not be the most educated on the subject but she knows what she likes in this room and, more importantly, she understands why she thinks a certain way about a piece. It's a very attractive quality: a tempting mind cocooned in a persuasive body.

Her layers fascinate me. I've seen the fighter, the alluring warrior: strong, poised, resolute, absolute determination not to be beaten. It's what attracted me in the arena. I saw another side here. The child: hesitant, vulnerable, shy, unsure of the power she holds. Testing, trying, tentative. Finally, I experienced that last side. The lover: confident, sensual, considerate, hands ingrained with a power she'll never know the depths of. It's all juxtaposed to form an endearingly complex woman, one whose secret depths I will enjoy trying to reach.


As always, time slinks subtly by. We sit on the chaise in my lounge, the lighting dimmed. I sip my fruit juice; her, another beer. We talk about anything and everything. A seamless draw of information carries us towards leaving this room for another. Yes, I have a thirst for her but as I've now discovered it's not just sexually. I rub my thumb over the side of my glass wondering how this will all work out. We both have pure motives so I would hedge, well.

Her voice is quiet as she breaks my enchanted thoughts.

"Can I ask a question?"

She plays with the beer bottle, a thumb running up and down the neck.

"Of course."

"I'm here for eternity, right?"

I nod as she glances over, her eyes returning to her bottle quickly.

"What about my family, can I see them?"

I sit side on, laying a hand on her thigh. Her attention refocuses through dark eyes.

"It's not normal procedure to allow access to that area." She stiffens so I pat her leg. "But then we haven't rerouted a mortal in many, many years. Are your parents still alive?"

"Yeah."

"When the time comes I think we can work something out."

Her muscles stay tense but so would mine if I were in her position.

"Okay."

"You have a few year's grace, Dizzy. We'll talk about it nearer the time."

"I guess."

I change the subject from the harsh realities of leaving your loved ones behind to something easier on the soul. I lead her through her life as it was then and how it is now. Despite scant descriptions it's a joy to watch her eyes sparkle to life. It's not a joy to watch her deep sadness when we glance over the subject of her family. I make a note to have her mother and father's names flagged up on entry.

After a while the conversation lulls. I catch her eye and wink. She smiles. Our silence waits to...break? It's waiting for something. Then that something happens inside me. I lean over, taking the bottle from her hand, putting it on the floor where I leave my juice. I stand and tug her arm. The low timbre of her voice lilts.

"Yes?"

"Yes."

We just make it to the bedroom.

# 6 CUPID'S INTRODUCTION

That was some seventies style love-in they had going on. Bet you're glad we indulged in the flashback now.

Elle's very private with her life so she kept Discord as secret as she could, not for any other reason than to stop any chance of idle gossip. She had no idea how crucial secrecy was going to become.

They spent more and more time with each other. The constant sex turned into something much bigger than either of them expected or could've predicted. Days together turned to weeks, weeks to months and that slow slide happened. Passion grew into love. And with that came a whole lot of problems, mainly coming back to one issue.

Gods and mortals just don't mix.

We drifted out of summer, through winter and into spring. And here's where we come out of our flashback, to April. We're back to the present. And we're back to some real problems.

## Chapter Six
## 2nd April, Year 2 - 18:00
## Graduate This!

All of the Heavens welcomed an excuse for a celebration. The Amazons attended in ceremonial dress, other departments also came in uniform. Every senior official was there. Discord had earned her right to remain as an Angel of Vengeance. Row after row of staff flattered the newcomer with applause.

Discord's graduation ceremony started well enough. Michelle, Head of Combat Training, had designed Discord's Combat courses so she was ready for anything. Gabrielle, Head of Intelligence, had designed her basic training on covert information gathering. John, Head of Mission Procurement, had made sure she could work every gadget technology afforded them.

Elle looked around the room proudly, smiling at Charity.

"And Lucy says we can't organise anything. Shame on her."

"She's just annoyed she didn't get invited." Charity chuckled as she sipped Champagne, her gaze settling on a corner the Amazons had taken as their own. "Actually, I'm surprised the Amazons are so joyous. They're normally like separatists. What did you have to promise Electra to get the Council members here?"

"My soul." Elle joked. "No, I think they were intrigued more than anything else. They didn't think we'd get another mortal."

Charity arched an eyebrow.

"Hoped, more like. Electra's probably incensed you have an extra vote on your side to interfere with her little political war games."

"I won't disagree with you."

Charity clinked her glass with Elle's.

"The Council is an acquired taste I've yet to acquire. I'm just glad they keep their noses out of the Bank's business. I wouldn't be as forgiving as you are."

"They'd never be stupid enough to endanger the Nation's portfolio and go against you, El Presidente."

Both women kept their best fake smiles in place as Electra walked by. Charity whispered.

"We should make the most of it, I suppose. I'll mingle and see if I can engage the enemy."

The polite smile never left her lips as she strolled towards a mass of Council members. Elle watched, remembering one of Charity's favourite sayings: keep your friends close and your enemies closer still.

"Rather her than me," Elle mumbled.

She turned, catching sight of a familiar brunette with a plate full of food. It was quite some amount for someone who she'd never seen eating anything other than a salad in the canteen.

"Gabrielle. Feeding the five thousand?"

The brunette glanced at the food almost spilling over.

"Oh." Gabrielle cursed Michelle for sending her up to the buffet. "No, Your Eminence. This is Michelle's. I have my weight to watch and she has hollow legs."

Elle shot a look over to where Michelle was, watching her talking intimately with a shorter redhead.

"Combat courses must be good for her metabolism." At the mention of courses, Elle's brain joined the dots. "Which reminds me, I haven't had a chance to congratulate you on your good work with Discord."

Gabrielle cupped a hand around the edge of the plate, glancing across to her friend, willing Michelle to come and help with the uncooperative food trying to escape capture.

"All in a day's - week's - well, month's work. Not that I'm saying she was slow or anything. Just...." Gabrielle blinked rapidly at her verbal scrambling. "Thank you."

Elle hid her smile by taking a sip of fruit juice. She patted Gabrielle's arm, having had a lot of experience with her occasional momentary losses of brain functions.

"I know what you mean."

Twenty feet away Michelle caught sight of Gabrielle, plate stacked with food, shifting about with crimson cheeks. She sighed and muttered under her breath.

"Please don't spill anything down her."

A few pieces of corn tumbled off of the plate and sealed Michelle's fate.

"Listen, I've got to go." Michelle walked backward, sending a disarming smile to the redhead whose phone she'd just programmed her number in. "Call me, we'll hook up."

With a teasing wink she spun around and stalked over to save her friend - and food. She arrived with a courteous bow.

"Your Eminence. Gabrielle. Everyone seems to be relaxing. The ceremony went very well."

Michelle slipped the plate away from her friend's hands, deliberately ignoring the heated stare sent her way.

Elle nodded, taking in the room, watching groups of her senior staff relaxing.

"Yes it did. A mortal in the ranks is an admirable achievement." Elle turned back to her guests. "Well done to the pair of you. Thank your staff on their success."

Psyche ambled through the crowded hall, nodding and smiling whenever she encountered a familiar face. She stopped by a golden skinned woman who was politely conversing with the Council. Psyche tried not to shift about while she waited for a lull in the conversation. Finally. She bowed deeply to the woman.

"My Queen, may I have a word?"

Kreousa smiled, "Of course, Psyche," and nodded, speaking to the circle.

"We'll talk more of these matters at the next Council session."

Kreousa's smile stayed in place until they were far enough away for it to slide from her face.

Psyche quirked an eyebrow.

"No thanks for saving you?"

Kreousa glanced across, her expression quite unreadable.

"Do you think a Queen can not save herself from politicians?"

The corners of Psyche's mouth drew into a lazy smile.

"You always have an answer."

"That, my fiery lieutenant, is because you always have a question."

The pair walked behind a figure that elicited a low snarling growl from Psyche. She whispered when they were far enough away.

"That woman is planning something."

Kreousa nodded to another Council member as they passed, greeting her politely.

"Sister."

"My Queen."

When they were alone Kreousa finally answered.

"Electra is always planning something. Life would be easier if she..."

"Fell to the Earth like a brick?"

Kreousa's impassive expression remained almost in tact. Only the barest of smiles hinted at her lips.

"No, concentrated more on the political matters and less on false issues. But, I have no control over politics."

They stopped at the bar and Psyche ordered two drinks then glanced around, making sure they weren't being watched. A smirk tugged at the corners of her full lips. She held the glass out but, with a quirk of her eyebrow, moved it away when Kreousa tried to take it. She repeated it several times until, with a shake of her head, Kreousa sighed softly and wiggled her fingers.

"Bring it forth, thank you."

Psyche nodded, still with a playful twinkle in her eyes.

"I'm always ready to serve, My Queen."

"You're in a good mood."

"When Electra's troubled then I'm happy. I'm easy to please."

Kreousa quirked an eyebrow.

"I don't remember that. Quite the opposite, in fact."

Psyche smiled brilliantly as she watched another part of the room: Discord appeared, nodding a hello to Gabrielle and Michelle but omitted a formal bow to Elle.

Psyche leaned closer to Kreousa, her eyes never leaving them.

"Discord is something else. Not many could bow to mere departmental heads and leave out the divine ruler. Not exactly trained in the formalities of social occasions, is she?"

"We shouldn't hold it against her. When we first met I had to force you to kneel before me."

Psyche bowed her head, smirking.

"If she turns out like me we'll have nothing to worry about."

Kreousa turned, lifting her glass in a toast but Psyche's attention had been stolen already. Kreousa's gaze followed Psyche's, back to centre stage: Elle, Gabrielle, Michelle and Discord.

"You seem intrigued."

Psyche focused intently on the women, taking in every movement they made.

"Watch their body language."

Kreousa did, unsure what she'd missed but understanding it must be important to have struck such a chord with her companion.

"Whose?"

Psyche's head cocked to the side as her eyebrows slid into a frown.

A waiter appeared at Discord's side and she took four drinks, giving them to each woman in turn. Michelle and Gabrielle mouthed their thanks and Elle took hers, her left hand resting on Discord's forearm for the briefest of seconds before sliding off in a slow caress.

"Ah, shit," was all Psyche could say.

Electra stood in the shadows, her attention magnetised. She sipped her drink, eyes boring into centre stage, engrossed in the view of a God holding court. With a tilt of her head she whipped around, signaling with a hand to a tall woman dressed in her own livery. The woman bowed discretely and slithered through the throngs of Amazons to Electra's side.

Electra's thoughts built themselves into a plan.

"What do we know about Discord, Jude?"

"In what respect?"

Electra waved a hand dismissively.

"Who is she partnered with here?"

"No one, to my knowledge."

Electra's lips slinked into a dangerous smile.

"Perhaps I should go and update that fact for you, Jude."

Psyche sighed at the public display between Elle and Discord. Suddenly a trip-wire went off in her brain. Her head snapped to Electra jolting into motion. Instinctively Psyche followed suit, Kreousa joining as well. The three headed towards Elle's command.

Kreousa whispered as they marched quickly.

"Are Discord and Elle in a relationship?"

Psyche frowned, replaying what she'd seen and if it could've been misinterpreted.

"Not that I know of. If they are, they need to operate with more discretion."

They arrived in time to hear Electra speaking to Elle.

"Your Eminence, my most worthy sisters. I congratulate you and your efforts to bring a fresh soul into the ranks of Vengeance."

Electra saluted Elle with her glass, making everyone follow. Elle's nostrils flared imperceptibly and her tone was flat.

"I'm glad you approve of our choice."

Penetrating eyes matched Elle's gaze.

"The Amazon Council will always support anything Your Eminence does benefiting the Heavens as a whole. I wish you luck with your attempts at training Discord. It must be difficult for her trying to achieve perfection."

Psyche made eye contact with Kreousa.

Discord uunconsciously shifted closer to Elle and they exchanged looks. Discord scowled; Elle half-smiled as she picked up the pace with the verbal jousting.

"Well, Electra, this is a celebration to mark the end of that training. However, it was admirable of you to allow your personal champion to help with the physical side. It was a shocking Arena defeat for Jude but beneficial never the less. I thank you for your graciousness."

The Amazon bowed deeply then straightened, adjusting her leather tribal cuff before speaking.

"We like to fix such fights to give your Angels confidence, Your Eminence. Another example of how we prostrate ourselves at your mercy in gratitude for your magnanimous generosity. I dare say in a real battle, not these play ones your ranks amuse themselves with, your Amazons would be your only worthwhile guardians. As ever, we are at your service."

Discord made a sudden move forward. Elle glowered at Electra as her hand went out, connecting with Discord's chest, stopping the tall woman instantly. Discord took a growling breath, her chest rising and falling quickly, teeth gritted in an obvious snarl. Her hand moved over Elle's, holding it tightly. All three Amazons stared at it. Psyche's eyes flicked to an ecstatic looking Electra, and Kreousa closed hers for a second, expelling a held breath. Elle's hand slowly dropped away.

Electra's lips formed a beaming smile.

"Your Eminence, may I beg your indulgence. I have what I came for."

She turned to Kreousa, bowing deeply.

"My Queen." She then barely dipped her head as an after thought. "Psyche."

Psyche mirrored Discord, her feet moving towards Electra in an instant. Kreousa held a finger up, shaking her head. Psyche's hands clenched tightly as she reluctantly stood down, glaring at Electra striding away purposefully.

Elle regained the circle's attention with a soft sigh.

"It's always a joy to speak to your Council members, Kreousa."

Kreousa should've been embarrassed but her mind was on other things. She was eager to discover what Electra planned to do with her suspicions. One thing she knew above all else - this was not a good turn of events.

"Your Eminence, I apologise if any offence was incurred. That was not our intention. I wish you a successful evening. I must deal with an urgent matter. Forgive me."

She bowed then turned to Psyche, glancing discreetly towards Discord. At the door Kreousa, now flanked by Royal Guards, set on following the route Electra took.

Psyche shifted, feeling as uncomfortable as she looked.

Michelle's tone was icy.

"Your Eminence, I know John had some points he wanted to raise about the training procedure."

She directed Elle and Gabrielle away. Discord went to follow but Psyche grabbed her arm. Discord eyes flashed menacingly. The fingers loosened but didn't let go. Psyche took a step closer, her voice low and measured.

"Don't ever touch Her Eminence again in public. It's a clear sign as to what's going on between you."

"What are you talking about?"

Psyche's nostrils flared, annoyed at having to explain the obvious.

"I don't care what you do in your spare time but use more discretion or the consequences will be on your shoulders. This isn't a threat but a warning. Don't be careless again."

She let go of Discord, walking away quickly towards Kreousa's chambers.

The turn of tides had been set in motion.

# 7 CUPID'S INTRODUCTION

With all of that going on Luce was having her own problems, mainly with the safety net installed around Hell. Let's face it, given her track record it wasn't likely that Elle would trust her.

Let me explain one thing, Lucy has a lot of respect amongst the old money brigade: Ares thinks of her as the daughter he never had; Artemis baked her last birthday cake; even my Ma saves her a seat on our table at big functions. In the Hierarchy stakes she's high, not just a naughty little black-winged Angel Elle got pissed off at. So, although Lucy is one of Elle's girls, to us she's more of a God. She has the powers, her own turf and lots of influential fans. And with her personality, it's a wowzer of a mix.

## Chapter Seven: Lucy
## 3rd April, Year 2 - 16:00
## Stats All Folks

The elevator doors open with a cheery, chirpy ding. My heels click loudly and annoyingly on the wooden floors and my coffee is too hot with not enough foam. I slip my sunglasses on, blocking out my brighter than bright halogens, wondering when I sanctioned this level of illumination.

Bee is disgustingly happy.

"You have a visitor." She nods to my ball and chain, Stats Man, sitting in the corner, resplendent in a horrible off the rack grey suit. "Also, I have some things for you."

I weigh up making a dash for my office and locking the door but if there's one thing about Bee she's persistent. There'd be no escape.

She picks up a pile of paper, walking over, her tone crisply efficient.

"I need you to sign this one." She keeps flicking through her pile. "These two. These six need initials on the top as well as at the bottom. The outbreak of Ebola last week, seven forms for that. That's it. Oh, except these five and..."

I interrupt, feeling it only fair to warn her.

"Bee. Are you noticing anything different about me? It might be subtle, it might not."

She glances at her watch.

"It's before midday so the bad mood is explainable. The sunglasses; late night?"

"Not exactly, Bee. Not. Exactly."

She pauses and removes the paperwork. Bee learnt my moods quickly. It's why she's lasted so long. I slide my sunglasses on top of my head. She takes a small step backward.

"I spent all last night going over my..." I stare at my visitor in the ill-fitting suit, shouting my last word. "...stats!"

Elle's spy jumps up and smiles the smile of a man waiting to be fed to the lions.

Bee glances over at him. She leans closer, whispering.

"I have a bet you'll give him a nervous breakdown in the next year. I.T. is in the syndicate. They're betting against you."

The thought brings a smile to my lips because I detest I.T. with their clashing sweaters and horrible shoes. Something that also brings a smile is the low V of Bee's shirt. I glance down catching a glimpse of a black lace bra. Without even making eye contact her hands move her jacket, closing that gap in a second. We carry on as if nothing happened.

"How much is in the pot?"

She leans closer, refusing to be put off by my behaviour. Bee is stubborn.

"We've all put up a week of annual leave. There are twelve in total."

Our shoulders brush as I lean closer.

"You smell edible, Bee."

"I just had a pastry. It's probably that."

"No, you're more alluring than a Danish."

She glances at me, narrowing her eyes. I wink, taking my hint.

Stats Man's finger pulls at his collar. He smiles nervously. It falls as I glare back.

"Twelve weeks of holiday is a lot. What would I do without you?"

"I hate to think."

"I'll let you have all the holiday you want if you let me have all of y..."

"Thanks, but I prefer to take it from those that really need it, like Carl in I.T. It means more that way, like I've really earned it. Anyway, it's a matter of principle. They can't bet against us."

I feel very proud of her at that moment.

"Us?" I tap the tip of her nose gently. "That's what I like about you, Bee, your loyalty. Give me that paperwork before I change my mind."

She hands me the pile of files. I wink, shouting his name out, *"Stats!"* then whisper. "Come on. Let's see if we can win you twelve weeks holiday."

I put my files down on my desk. Bee sits, getting her pad out. He almost falls into the chair, looking like we'll kill him sometime soon. Very possible.

"How many points ahead is Her Subtle Brightness?"

Paperwork tumbles off of his lap as he searches for his notes. I pace up and down then start clicking my fingers, trying to impart some speed into

Elle's little man. I stop in front of Bee.

"Come on, figures boy, how many points?"

"Um..."

"It's not a hard question."

Papers rustle behind me as I smile at her.

"I'm trying to find..."

"Come on, Stats Man, how many points?"

I catch another glimpse of cleavage. She looks up emotionlessly, pulling the V of her shirt closed.

I mouth silently, "Nice breasts."

She doesn't bat an eyelid but mouths back, "Thank you."

"I think you're eighteen points behind...."

My head snaps around and all the papers he managed to collect tumble to the floor. His face pales, he fidgets. I notice the start of a facial twitch.

"You think? Guessing may have cut it with her Holy Shinning Brightness in the Garden of Eden but in my house that just isn't good enough. I suggest you look through your paperwork again and make your next statement accurate."

I bend down, looking at the chart on Bee's lap. Her work is always correct and we are eighteen points behind but he doesn't have to know that. My finger runs off of the chart onto her tightly fitting skirt and toned thighs beneath. I look directly into her eyes as I move it across her leg.

Panic fills his voice.

"I'm just looking for the figures. Hold on, please."

"I'm holding."

Her gaze is unflinching as she glances over at him then leans closer, whispering.

"I think you're touching on the wrong figure, Lucy."

A warm hand gently takes hold of my finger and moves it back onto the cold of the paper. I can't help but smile. She sits back in her seat, tapping her bottom lip with her pencil. I whisper quietly before standing up straight.

"You're so dastardly to me, Bee."

Her facial expression doesn't alter. What a tyrannical little minx.

I spin around on my heels, clapping my hands loudly. My number cruncher jumps and squeals. Unnerving the Godly is so easy.

"Come on, I don't have all day. Okay, just tell me how many points we each had last week."

I take a step closer as his shaking hands flick through a black folder.

"Actually, what's the average gap been over the year?" I take another step closer. "And what is that pro-rata per week?"

Another step and I can see sweat glistening on his thinning hairline.

"No rush but I do have somewhere to be in three minutes."

I fold my arms and tap my foot noisily.

"I...I need a minute to work this out."

I glance around at Bee and blow her a quick kiss.

"You only have two and half now."

After about a minute I start to quicken the tempo of my tapping. I then begin to pace. I know I'm being annoying. It's nothing personal. My main peeve is Her Highness and this intrusion. Do I get to check her paperwork? Oh no, that's all private, yet everything I do is scrutinized twenty times over. And people wonder why I'm slightly bitter? It's because I'm the eternally picked on fallen Angel.

I walk back to my little spy and slap the paper out of his hands. It flutters to the floor slowly. He recoils in his seat as I begin to rant.

"Time's up. Why would Elle send you if you can't even organize two files of papers? I've asked you about your job, nothing more, and you can't even answer that. What's the point in having you here?" My voice creeps up in volume. "Out." He looks like a rabbit in headlights. "Did my command vanish into the ether? I said get out! Now!"

His hand blindly pats the floor, searching for his papers as his eyes lock with mine. In lean in, he leans back. He scrabbles to his feet, bowing very quickly and almost runs out of my office.

My rant doesn't stop.

"Why am I, the boss of all this greatness we're surrounded by, ruled by that little fluffy cloud of goodness?"

Bee looks perplexed.

"Lucy?"

"Who does she think she is telling me what to do? Why am I always scrutinised?"

"Lucy?"

"And what do I think I'm doing following her orders?"

"Lucy!"

"Do this, do that, jump. How high, Elle? Of course, I'm obviously your humble and most obedient servant."

*"Lucy!"*

"I feel like her Chihuahua on a lead being dragged obediently around. I could..."

Bee pulls up her shirt quickly, flashing beautiful lace covered breasts. My mouth stays open. My brain loses comprehension of what it was ranting about. I'm shocked into complete silence. She pulls her shirt back down, tucks herself in and picks her papers up.

"I don't win anything if you have a breakdown. I'll be at my desk if you need anything."

The door clicks open then shut. I close my mouth. And this was the day when I was silenced by a secretary. Wonderful.

# 8 CUPID'S INTRODUCTION

Back to the vicious reality of the flipside of that coin: Elle and the Heavens. May was in full swing, the seasons kind of signifying what was going on. Spring had been alive but on the horizon was summer and it was set to be a boiling mass of snakes. As for autumn, some things weren't going to see it through.

The Amazons, or more like it Electra, sent her spies out to confirm what she saw at the graduation. Her spidery intelligence network had eyes and ears everywhere. Six weeks of close observation got them the info they needed. Elle and Discord were officially caught out.

Buckle up because on this rollercoaster we're about to go from the high to the low. Let me take this opportunity to introduce you to my ex-girl. As fate would have it Psyche and Kreousa held the happiness of our God in their hands.

## Chapter Eight
## 15th May, Year 2 - 13:00
## Take Away My World

"A sealed note requesting my presence? I'm intrigued, My Queen."

Psyche's tone was playful as she closed the doors of Kreousa's private chambers but her smile didn't last long.

Hands clasped tightly behind, Kreousa stood in the middle of the room, elegantly poised, expression set in stone. Psyche recognised that look. Something bad was on the horizon.

"It has started," said Kreousa.

As usual there were no preliminaries, no, 'How are you doing, Psyche? Is everything okay with work? Did you see that special on sharks last night, wasn't it great?'

Years ago she'd pulled Kreousa up on this skill - she called it a skill because there were no other words to describe it. Kreousa had just stared and with a slightly amused tones, said, "Would you rather we talked of kittens or needlecraft before I told you the world was about to end or get straight to the point?"

After that Psyche left her aversion to making a bitter pill taste better with a teaspoon of sugar.

"Care to elaborate?" asked Psyche.

Kreousa sighed.

"Elle's having a relationship with Discord as we suspected. Electra gathered her evidence and called the Council together last night to hear it."

Psyche tried to work through this sudden influx of news. She understood the problems associated with a God and mortal mixing but Electra had to be crazy to try and apply this to Elle.

She massaged her temple, tension immediately biting hard.

"What stage are they up to?"

Kreousa answered quickly as if every second mattered.

"Last night was the preliminary hearing. In an hour they make their decision on what action will be taken. I fear they'll hold a private vote of no confidence and overthrow her."

That hit Psyche like a sucker punch.

"What?"

Kreousa's focus seemed to drift as she muttered an obscure little statement.

"We have a heady storm approaching."

"Understatement. Can we persuade enough voters for a hung decision?"

Psyche caught Kreousa's slight frown, the almost imperceptible shift - the only thing giving away the fact this had thrown her. In the years as her Lieutenant, Psyche could never decide if this apparent ambivalence was good or bad; it'd made her an expert on body language, nuances and subtle instances, sure, but at the same time she had to pay maximum attention in case she missed something.

"Not on a matter such as this. It'll be unanimous."

Psyche's gaze snapped up. She stared at Kreousa.

"Even you?"

The hard planes of her Queen's face softened.

"Well, perhaps not unanimous but you know I can't veto the Council."

*This was insane*, thought Psyche. She wracked her brain trying to come up with a plan.

"Denial?"

"Too late, the witnesses have sworn their testimony. They'd never believe it."

"Can we persuade them to retract their statements?"

"No. I've tried but they're Electra's cronies."

Psyche fell into a chair, leaning elbows on thighs. She stared at nothing and tried to think of any tactical scenario to derail Electra that her tone slipped. Still deep in thought, her question fell from full lips.

"How hard did you try?"

It sounded horrible like an accusation. She shifted and didn't even have time for an apology before Kreousa turned and speared her with a look normally saved for times the Council annoyed her to the point of insanity.

"Very hard."

Psyche frowned, backtracking at that carelessness.

"I didn't mean that the way it sounded." Her shoulders sagged and bad mood retreated. "I wish we could get rid of Electra. Years of making everything so difficult...."

She trailed off, not wanting to go over rutted ground. Despite being pointless, it was also getting boring.

"Electra has skills that, at times, outweigh her deep need to act inappropriately."

"I'd love to hear about those skills because all I see is that need to be inappropriate."

Kreousa sighed, shaking her head.

"There's no love lost between you, I understand that, Psyche. We both know why. But with Electra, a promise of ultimate power never realised is worse than all the power in the world corrupting you."

"And we're back to your infuriating need to cloak every statement for fear of me actually understanding what you're saying!" Psyche got up and started pacing then whipped around. "Electra is scheming - like the venomous snake she is - and you're playing, guess what I'm talking about. Why don't we play 'Let's not defend Electra' for once?"

"I'm not defending her. I'm explaining her reasons. There's a difference."

"Is there?"

Kreousa didn't look away.

"We're on the same side."

Psyche's eyes squeezed shut and she exhaled a deep breath. Her anger slowly leeched. She was taking this out on the wrong person. Her brain changed directions.

"I know we are, Kreo."

The private nickname soothed the moment.

Kreousa seemed to star for a long time before finally commenting.

"You haven't called me that in a long time."

Psyche sighed.

"Yeah, well, you never know who's listening."

They both knew who that sentence referred to. The silence stretched until finally Kreousa walked around her desk, stopping inches away, the normal barrier of furniture, guards, or just herself, being left for the moment. She brushed a strand of hair from Psyche's shoulder.

"Why does history have to keep repeating itself?" Psyche asked.

"Because there are only a finite number of stories and a finite number of endings."

"Doesn't Elle deserve someone to fight for her? Doesn't she deserve more of a chance than we had?"

Kreousa's whole demeanour seemed to stutter as those words lingered between them. It took a moment but finally she stepped back, away, shutters dropping, her stoic expression resuming its guard. And the intimacy fractured.

"Elle does deserve better and perhaps if it's meant to be then it will - one day. If they don't find their way back to each other then Fate has had her say."

"Like us?"

Kreousa retreated to the large window behind her desk, turning her back, looking out onto grounds that only an hour ago, Psyche had been sunning herself in.

"I was speaking in general."

Psyche's emotions tore her composure. Annoyance, stress, frustration, it all exited as a hot blast of anger because some things just shouldn't be allowed to happen - repeatedly.

"I can only stand for what I believe in, in my heart, Kreousa. And I won't believe in a vote to overthrow Elle. Stand up for the Council who've dictated to you if you want. I can't."

Psyche turned on her heels, needing to get some distance before she started venting again.

"Psyche!"

But her body was clearly better trained than that mouth. Her legs stopped dead, keeping her inches away from the safety of Kreousa's chamber door.

A solid grip took hold of her shoulder, squeezing.

"Your words are well chosen, your assessment sound. I'll help Elle but you know my power is in battle and ceremony and not politics." Kreousa's thumb rubbed softly, her actions for once matching her words. "I'll protect you and your choices as much as I can, my fiery warrior."

"Thank you," was all Psyche said before pulling the door open and heading toward the bitch that'd started playing games again.

# 9 CUPID'S INTRODUCTION

Elle was the happiest she'd ever been with Discord, but she was completely unaware of the tidal wave of treachery hurtling her way. All of her defences were down when Electra took her best shot.

My ex-girl went in to bat for Elle. Psyche stood up on the plate facing a ball machine stuck on fast pitch. Basically, no matter how many good intentions you have sometimes it's going to be a tough fight.

## Chapter Nine
## 15th May, Year 2 - 13:30
## Organised Duplicity

Psyche stood outside the Council's palatial rooms waiting for security to allow her clearance to enter. Two thousand years of being Second in Command and the Council still wouldn't give her the rights she deserved. To them she'd always be an outsider, the woman who'd tried to steal their Queen's heart. Talk about hitting a career ceiling.

A red light flicked on, then a green, and the security doors opened.

Psyche doubted this separatism was quite what Elle had in mind when they were invited, en masse, into the Heavens. Of course, it wasn't as if Elle had a lot of choice. Society on Earth had expanded by billions with the guardian numbers staying static. Caretaking couldn't work like that.

She walked along the wide hallway. Guards in ceremonial dress flanked each side. Against Council orders they saluted with their swords, bringing them to their lips, kissing the hilts. As she reached the end she turned and bowed, showing them the same respect.

The heavily carved wooden doors to the main assembly halls opened and Psyche walked into the lions' den.

The Council was seated around a huge oak table at the end of the room. Large metal discs held flames that cast a flickering glow over everything.

She always found these chambers hauntingly beautiful. Shame they had to be filled with such a mass of snakes.

She got straight to it.

"It seems you've started without summoning Kreousa and I. Can someone explain?"

Psyche walked to the head of the table, to her seat next to Kreousa's empty throne. Her eyes flicked across impassive faces. This wasn't good. Not if they were all in attendance.

Psyche had invested a lot of time learning the Council's ways. Her early years were hard. She'd been hot headed, going to each meeting looking for a fight. On a lot of occasions she got one, both verbal and physical.

The decades passed and her temperament calmed. She benefited greatly from the discipline and structure the Heavens held. Instead of getting incensed with Electra and the others she decided to play them at their own game: she researched decades of rulings, laws and precedents, spent years pouring over ancient scrolls because, after all, what she had most of was time.

The Council and their ancient rules didn't change but she had and so had Kreousa. However, on the Council's board of play the most powerful piece wasn't the Queen, therefore she knew they could only do so much. Sometimes it was enough, sometimes it wasn't. And that was what she feared today, that the eleven people in front of her were unstoppable.

"Psyche." Electra motioned for her to sit. "We waited as long as we could but our courtiers couldn't find you."

Psyche remained standing and smiled graciously at those empty lies.

*If it's a game you want*, she thought.

She used her height and presence as a distraction and strolled around the table, moving behind the members' chairs. She caught their resistance to turn; in battle nothing raised your hackles more than an enemy sneaking up behind you.

Psyche kept her tone pleasant. Her power here was limited.

"Why has the Council been summoned, Electra?"

"We had news. The bloodline of our leadership is at risk..." Electra's lips slithered into a smile. "...again."

Electra's dagger was delivered and it hurt as intended. But Psyche had experienced worse wounds than that. The most severe delivered her into the arms of the Heavens, something Electra often forgot, it seemed.

Psyche highlighted those lax choice of words, taking any victory, even a small one.

"Bloodline? Kreousa?"

"No, Psyche. Elle."

She carried on circling the table.

Kreousa had once said the weapon of a warrior had changed from that of a sword to a pen. And she was right. In battles of old their orders were never questioned, but this cowardly attack with paper and words? Psyche knew the best they could hope for would be a stalemate.

"Elle's not from our bloodline, Electra."

Psyche knew the retort coming. She'd heard it a thousand times. She paused at the head of the table and mouthed...

"Neither are you," said Electra.

...at the same time.

"I was accepted by a clan and passed my battle trials. I've earned my status not acquired it without tests like some of our less noble sisters."

The Council bristled at the barely camouflaged insult. Psyche finished her sentence, knowing how to play them.

"Easy, sisters. Present company excluded of course." She bowed, avoiding their arrows of irritation. "But enough of us, what's the problem with Elle?"

"She's having a relationship with the mortal Discord Knight."

Electra sat back in a smug glow. Psyche stopped behind her chair, digging her fingers into the carved channels of the high wooden back.

"I'm happy for her. Now onto the business of why our Nation's Council was summoned today. Can we move onto that?"

Electra straightened. Psyche knew most of the buttons to provoke her. They were all fun.

"This does affect the Nation. Surely you remember the rules about bloodlines and relationships outside of the hierarchical system?"

Electra could battle with words as well as Psyche could with a sword. The rules were ancient and should've been voted out, and it would've happened had they not carried the same Council members over from Earth to the Heavens. They were impossible to oust with the gift of immortality.

"I don't find them relevant to Elle. She's a God, not from Royal bloodstock."

Electra cocked her head, her sun coloured hair framing her face.

"When we took our invite to work and reside in the Heavens, Psyche, we asked for several concessions. We wanted to retain this ruling Council for laws and decisions regarding the Nation." Electra pushed her chair back and Psyche with it. "And Elle wanted one thing."

Electra's expression was as hard as ice. Her voice condensed into a thin hiss.

"Her people asked she be treated with the same privileges our Royal bloodline were." Electra's index fingers slowly lifted Psyche's hands from the back of the chair. "I assume she wasn't very well advised on what that entailed."

Psyche knew that Elle's advisors recognised the potential military threat so they covered the battle command angle. Amazon troops could never easily overthrow their Queen or a member of the Royal bloodline. But politics didn't work that way. Psyche's stomach sank as she saw how devious this plan was.

"Your silence means we have your understanding, Psyche? No clever interpretations of law come to mind I take it?" Electra's smugness was explicit. "So, if you have no smart answers then..."

The main door opened. The flames flickered. All heads turned. Kreousa and the Royal guard entered.

Kreousa's commanding voice boomed throughout the chambers.

"I can't believe that. You always have smart answers for me."

Kreousa strode to the opposite side of the table. Her guards stayed close, their full battle armour glinting under the glow of the flames, ricocheting light like glittering gold.

Psyche frowned as she counted Kreousa's escort. There was double the usual amount. The Council members glanced at one another, too. Kreousa nodded to her guardians. They fanned out quickly and, without a pause, lifted their swords by the hilts, dropping them with a synchronised echo that travelled through the room and everyone in it. The message was received loud and clear.

Electra's fist slammed down on the table, her show of strength.

*Not impressive, considering*, thought Psyche.

"What's the meaning of this?" Electra seethed.

Kreousa's head turned slowly.

"You'll address me with respect. I'm still your Queen."

Kreousa's expression didn't change. She stayed completely calm - on the outside. Psyche had to wonder what Electra needed to do to get a reaction from Kreousa.

The battle of wills started except on Kreousa's side were ten battle ready guards, hands paused over their weapons. All attention focused on the two women who controlled opposite sides of the coin: one held the army, the other the laws.

Kreousa said one word, "Electra," with an air of authority that no one could ever match. There was a static pause as the flames flickered across beautifully armoured warriors. Electra sat back down. She glared at Kreousa.

"Forgive me, My Queen."

Vestra held her hands out, attempting to calm the situation. Someone needed to before this turned bad.

"This armed intrusion is hardly warranted. We're no threat to you, My Queen."

Psyche watched. Vestra was one of the few Council members who'd used her time as an opportunity to learn and evolve. Over the centuries she'd changed into something resembling a human being - a disclaimer: compared to the rest of the Council.

Kreousa, as usual, got right to her point.

"If you're a threat to my bloodline then you're a threat to me. I won't have Elle deposed and she is, after all, the reason this Council was convened, yes?"

Electra's lithe body shot up.

"Guards? Guards!"

The warriors in the hallway entered. Psyche's hand went to her side but her weapon wasn't there. She dug nails into palms at her lack of preparation. She took a step back, ready for the fight that was bound to occur. Council members shifted in their seats. The only person who looked calm was Kreousa. Her voice was as unassailable as her demeanour.

"Thank you. Guards?"

They bowed, taking positions next to the Royal warriors. She repeated her last statement.

"I will not have Elle deposed."

Electra's eyes darted around the room as she realised the potential for a coup d'etat. She sat back down slowly. Vestra took over as speaker; the wisest move the Council had made in a long time.

"And the Nation cannot have the Royal bloodline compromised, My Queen."

Kreousa nodded.

"I understand that, Vestra. The relationship will end."

Electra's hands balled, her knuckles whitened, but she remained quiet as her chance fell away.

Vestra whispered to her neighbour. She nodded and whispered to hers. The vote went around the table. Vestra took the count.

"Those for the motion of non-intervention?"

Ten hands rose. Vestra stared at Electra.

"I assume you're abstaining?"

Electra nodded, a half smile, half sneer on her lips. Psyche knew this trick, too: keeping her name off of a no vote.

"I am."

Vestra turned to Kreousa, bowing slightly.

"We graciously offer you twenty-four hours to end the relationship, My Queen."

And a suffocating weight lifted from Psyche's shoulders.

The Council was dismissed and 'escorted' out by the warriors. Psyche stayed on her side of the room as Kreousa took Electra aside. She couldn't hear what they said but the gist was obvious. After less than a minute Electra stormed out, clearly not happy - when was she?

Kreousa's boots echoed as she crossed the room, hands behind her back, head held high.

Psyche reminded her of a relevant point.

"Electra won't forget what happened. There'll be repercussions."

"When aren't there? Elle is the Heaven's linchpin. They don't understand that as we do."

One thing Electra always did was annoy Psyche to the point of no return. Like earlier, she was finding it a little hard to contain.

"Is Electra going to have free reign for the rest of eternity?"

Kreousa shrugged, her face a picture of concentration.

"I have very little power over her and I'm surprised today didn't end badly. She'll come back with something else. Elle isn't out of danger."

Psyche tried to ignore this avoidance tactic but couldn't, her mind wouldn't let her.

"So when is she going to be put in her place?"

"I'm not able to do that. She controls the fortress here, I the army. Our fight must be controlled, you know that."

"What they're doing to Elle is wrong."

Kreousa shrugged with a sigh.

"The Heavens are pervaded with wrong. It's the way of all existences. Good and bad have to learn to live together."

Psyche's fists clenched at her infuriatingly philosophical mood.

"I'm helping Elle because I respect her personally and professionally."

Kreousa's warm chuckle dissipated some of the tension; Psyche relaxed a little. It was nice to be reminded every so often that Kreousa wasn't a robot.

"There's that, too. She's a good leader and they shouldn't be tossed away on a whim."

Psyche shrugged, slightly placated as Kreousa continued.

"I understand your stance, how could I not? If it helps I agree with you, but I have a Nation to represent. I'm not one person but a figurehead. My actions are dictated."

"I get that, I do, but it doesn't stop me hating it."

"Then you like it more than me." Kreousa sighed heavily. "And now it's time I delivered my bad news to Elle."

Psyche moved closer, keeping a safe distance, whispering so they weren't overheard.

"I know what you risked. Thank you."

A hand slipped onto Psyche's. Kreousa's words came from glistening lips.

"I said I'd protect you and I'd do it a thousand times over."

The hand slipped away. Kreousa turned and exited, flanked by guards.

Psyche concentrated on the flames jumping and flailing in the metal disks. Losing the person you love is hard enough but having to force that separation? She didn't envy the next few hours for Kreousa, Elle or Discord.

# 10 CUPID'S INTRODUCTION

Kreousa had the most valuable of commodities: knowledge - and it is power. But with that comes more responsibility than I've ever been comfortable with. I wouldn't like to have been in Kreousa's boots when she delivered the Council's ultimatum to the Heaven's supreme ruler. Remember, even the most solid of coalitions comes with conditions. Gods aren't exempt from the rules. Still, all this sucked. Elle falls in love and some bitch wants to steal it away? How is that ever right?

Elle and Discord had managed to get almost a year of happiness. And they were happy. Until it was all buried under a ton of betrayal.

# Chapter Ten
## 15th May, Year 2 - 14:30
## Visitor from Out of Town

K reousa stopped at Sam's desk and motioned for her guards to leave. They bowed, giving their Queen the privacy she requested. Kreousa stared at the blonde.

"Hello, Samantha. Is Elle available?"

Sam looked up, pulling her copy of Harry Potter closer. Her eyes darted to the guards waiting outside of reception's large glass doors.

"Samantha? Is Elle available?"

Sam jolted, eyes blinking rapidly as she put her headset on. She stared at the box then slapped it hard, explaining with one word over the crackle of electricity.

"Lucy."

After a moment, she spoke into the mouthpiece.

"Your Eminence, Kreousa's here to see you. Yes, Queen Kreousa. Yes, here." She unsuccessfully whispered the last sentence. "And she has guards with pointy things. No, not at me. No, they're outside. Okay."

Sam pulled her headset off, smiling.

"She's free. In you go."

Kreousa quirked an eyebrow, wondering how Elle managed to do anything with this woman as her assistant.

"Thank you, Samantha."

Kreousa shook her head and knocked on Elle's door.

"Come in."

It was the first time Kreousa had been in Elle's office. It was different to her own, that was for sure. Light in colour, it was furnished like a cosy den. Kreousa quickly scanned the room. There was a plasma TV on one wall and a spiralling abstract picture the other, with a knurled fig tree and comfortable looking sofa opposite. Elle was sitting there, legs folded underneath her, book in hand.

Kreousa bowed. Elle smiled.

"It's a nice surprise to see you, Kreousa. Don't tell me, you were in the neighbourhood and decided to pop in? Do you need a cup of sugar?"

"No. I've come to talk to you, Your Eminence."

"I see. That sounds ominous."

Elle dog-eared a page, laying the book down as she stood. She walked to the window, lowering the blind.

"Today's a little bright." She said with a long sigh. "Now, what can I do for you?"

Kreousa took a deep breath, readying herself for the dirty task. As always, she didn't dally.

"The Council know about your relationship with Discord."

She watched Elle's controlled reactions. They were almost perfect except for the telling jaw clench.

"Excuse me?"

Kreousa thought back to the time she'd been in Elle's shoes, when she'd realised what she treasured had to be given up. The pain had been so intense it'd made it impossible to eat, sleep, talk or even breathe at times and for months she was crushed under a weight of sadness. With a quick shake of her head she resumed the task at hand because this wasn't the place for tired memories of what could've been. No, this was the place to crush another set of dreams.

"The Council know about your relationship with Discord."

"I don't understand what you're talking about."

"The Council is set to depose you in twenty-four hours unless you bring your relationship to an end. Unfortunately it's fallen to me to bring you this news." Kreousa sighed as she shook her head. "I'm sorry."

"This is nonsense."

Kreousa crossed the space between them, staring into cold blue eyes framed by fluttering eyelashes.

"I don't have time for this, Elle. They know."

She watched as Elle moved unsteadily towards her desk, putting a hand backward as if to brace herself. There was silence for a moment before she withdrew her prop, her rigid body regaining its regal poise once more.

"I'm a God and you're a mortal. You can't tell me what to do. You and your tribes have been given refuge at my invitation, let's not forget that."

Kreousa wished things could be different. A desperate feeling of déjà vu descended, taking her by surprise. She readjusted her leather wrist cuff.

"And the Council holds the attention of three thousand of your *guests* here in the Heavens. We have the same rights as your blood Angels."

Elle held her hands up, closing her eyes for a moment.

"I didn't mean that the way it sounded. You're as much a part of here as anyone else."

Kreousa glanced at the clock, aware that every extra minute this took meant Elle would have less time with her decision.

"I'm glad you realise that because you need my help at this point."

"Do I?"

Their eyes met and Kreousa ignored the pointed glare attempting to dig its way through her armour.

"Elle, Electra is set to ask for a vote of no confidence and she'll win. She'll take a ballot of our three thousand warriors and she'll win that, too. You will be deposed and the Council will gain control. If you resist...."

Kreousa knew exactly what would happen and she'd rather her warriors weren't instructed to bear arms.

"If I resist, what?"

"Resistance is not an option."

Elle walked up quickly, jabbing a finger into her chest. Kreousa instinctively tensed, barely managing to control the urge to deflect it with a swipe of her hand.

Elle's words hissed.

"Don't you dare threaten me!"

Kreousa took Elle's finger in her hand, holding it carefully as if made of fragile glass. She tried to explain the decision to the flushed woman.

"I've bought you time. That's all I can offer. I can't stop them, not without a civil war and I'm not prepared to kill my sisters. Elle, I didn't make the law. Also, I didn't sign the concordant between my nation and your Heavens, you did, my friend. My hands are tied. I'm sorry."

Elle snatched her finger away, taking a few unsteady steps backward, eyelashes fluttering.

"How gracious of you to feel sorry for me."

Kreousa feared nothing she said would be listened to. However, she had to try. Later she knew Elle would remember. She hoped she'd understand.

"We have a very strict caste system. She's a mortal, you're a God..."

"A point you've all forgotten about. I am a God!"

The door opened and Sam peeked in.

"Is everything okay, Your Eminence?"

Elle closed her eyes for a second and when they re-opened the switch was immediate. Despite herself Kreousa was impressed at the mask of officiousness.

"Yes. We're having a very heated discussion but we won't end up killing each other." Elle turned to Kreousa and mouthed. "Yet."

Sam clicked the door closed.

Elle's voice was threatening as she held a palm up, wiggling her fingers.

"I could kill you all with the power I hold in this one hand. You come in here telling me who I can and can't see?" She hissed. "How dare you!"

Kreousa covered that hostile hand with one of her own. She squeezed it gently, stepping closer, laying it over her heart.

"I'm hoping you won't kill three thousand warriors who would die for you because of one woman. I'm hoping you'll see the bigger picture, Elle. They see you as they see me. You're their Queen. The bloodlines can not be influenced."

Elle's mask slipped as her face became pained for a brief second. Kreousa clenched her jaw at the words truthfully whispered out, as Elle struggled with her emotions.

"I'm not giving her up for a bloodline, Kreousa."

The Amazon prided herself on staying detached, but not here, not as she stared at Elle's face. She softly whispered her answer as she held that hand to her chest tightly.

"My power is with war and death not words and edicts. I can't stop this, but you have one day. I can't decide for you. That's something you must struggle with. Believe me, I understand how unfair and difficult this is."

Elle shrugged off the comments, pulling her hand away and pointing to the door.

"Get out."

Kreousa didn't argue. There was no point. Whatever had to be decided upon was not her business now. Her fingers paused on the door handle as she glanced back.

"Make your decision wisely. Nevertheless, believe me I know what you're going through."

Elle spat her answer out.

"Don't patronise me."

Kreousa simply nodded and left. As she shut the door she took a long deep breath then exhaled slowly, her shoulders lowering as a fraction of the tension exited. Sam looked up from her book and managed a weak smile.

Kreousa strode across to her desk. She glanced at the clock. The working day was almost over.

"Does Her Eminence have anymore meetings today?"

The wide-eyed blonde shook her head. Kreousa glanced back at the closed door, wishing there was more she could do.

"Good. She's...very busy now. Don't let anyone disturb her."

Kreousa made her way back to her chambers, flanked by her guards. She knew what she'd be doing tonight. The same thing she did when Psyche had been forced to leave her so many years ago. She was going to sit in her palace, alone.

# 11 CUPID'S INTRODUCTION

Put yourself in Elle's shoes. You find your perfect sex bomb everything, then a crowd of people you invited into your own home start telling you to dump her? Personally, I would've swung for all of them. I guess that's why I don't get put in charge of worlds. Anyway, back to the story. This was hard on Elle. All she did was fall in love and look what happened.

## Chapter Eleven: Elle
## 15th May, Year 2 - 14:59
## Soured Paradise

"*I* *can't take your call. Leave me a message and I'll get back to you.*"

Charity's voicemail clicks off. I stare at the receiver then throw it against my wall. It smashes a picture and drops down into a broken heap.

My door opens and it's Sam again. My responsibilities don't include being seen as weak so I turn away, but my mirror shows I can't run: my eyes are red, my eyeliner has run, I look terrible.

"Are you okay?"

A lie would be easy but I don't have the strength.

"No. Cancel everything else I have today and for the rest of the week. Only put Charity's call through."

"What happened?"

I turn, forgetting myself, my body desperate to move, pace, do something, anything.

"Leave."

Innocent eyes widen as they flick across this sorry God.

"I'll get Charity."

Are her last words as she backs out of the room. The door clicks shut.

Each dragging moment makes my heart pound and my palms sweat. A void stretches out before me. My life feels like a desert waiting to kill anything wandering in.

My distraught brain makes a snap decision. I wipe my eyes and slip my sunglasses on. Everything blurs as I walk by Sam, calling over my shoulder as I go.

"I'm going to see Kreousa. Keep trying Charity. Tell her I'm going straight home after."

Hallway lights flicker and dim, darkening my path; Lucy and her tricks. But this time I don't care. I ignore everyone I pass, focused only on sorting this terrible mess out.

Amazon territory. Their space. A heady mix of incense, crackling flames and ancient rules. As I near, two guards block my way with their bodies. Suddenly they realise who I am and their movements stutter. They bow but do not move. My tone reflects my day. It is not amused.

"I want to speak to Kreousa."

They glance at each other, and the shorter guard hastily goes to her booth, picking up a headset. I glare into two eyes that dart away quickly, and that brings forth a revelation. Am I willing to go to war with these women because they hold me in such high esteem? Kill them, hurt countless others, destroy more lives than during the split with Lucy? Because that's what this boils down to. What am I prepared to risk? Everything could lose me everyone.

With a tap on the glass my path is unimpeded.

The corridor to Kreousa's chambers stretches. Dark red walls close around me. Dancing flames haunt my path. And so I go on.

I open her door and walk in without knocking. Psyche turns quickly, her expression pained. We stare at each other for a brief moment before she turns away. I wonder what they've done to her. Perhaps the Council are on another course of destruction?

Kreousa speaks in hushed tones I struggle to hear.

"I had no choice, Psyche. We'll speak later."

There's an urge to tell her what having no choice really feels like but I bite my tongue instead. Psyche walks by quickly, slamming the door as she leaves.

My tone is harsher than I've heard it in a long time.

"Another unhappy customer, Kreousa?"

She looks out of the window as darkness dims this terrible day. Silence reigns before her intervention. Her tired tone takes me by surprise.

"Have you made your choice so quickly?"

"I don't appear to have one at the moment. That's my problem."

She takes her leather tunic off, laying it over the back of the chair. Networks of thick scars adorn her arms.

As always she's painfully succinct.

"You're right, you don't. I wish it were different but it's not."

For a moment I lose sight of why I came here. To shout and scream, maybe hurt her like she's hurting me or just to voice my frustrations?

"I don't understand why my relationship is a problem."

She leans back against the glass.

"Our way is our way. At times it doesn't seem to make sense but eventually it rings true."

I'm not comfortable talking like this to her and I'm sure she knows it, but unfortunately she's the closest thing to a chance I have.

"I'm not an Amazon. I'm not a Queen. Your rules can't be applied to me. This is the Council trying to use my choices as an excuse to get their own way."

She shrugs.

"Perhaps it is. It doesn't change the fact every warrior views you as part of the Royal bloodline. Anyway, you signed the concordat, therefore the Council expects adherence." She raises a hand, stopping my question. "You asked us to join your ranks, Elle. And you asked to have the same rights as my bloodline. Well you have them. Welcome to my life."

The last sentence is vitriolic. It's the first time I've ever heard her speak with such emotion.

I fall into one of the chairs. She walks around and sits in the other. I don't face her. I can't.

"How can I rule effectively when they can hold a vote at any time? There's always that threat, hanging."

Her hand touches my arm, making me turn. The scars I saw earlier are glaringly white against her dark skin. I marvel at the ferocity of violence for it to have lasted this long.

"Their power is in ancient rules, nothing else. You have the backing of our warriors in every other matter, Elle, just - not this. They won't send this out as a message. If nothing else, at least we're consistent in our decisions." She pauses, smiling wearily, her voice soft. "Please don't hold this against us as a nation. We mean you no harm."

I can't help the laugh snorting out.

"Harm? What do you think you're doing, helping?"

She looks away.

"The Council have made their decision."

I stand, realising the futility of this meeting.

"How am I meant to tell her? Should I say it with flowers, maybe a trip to a nice restaurant?"

She stands, and for a moment I think I see a crack in her ironclad battle armour but it shuts as swiftly as it opened.

"Tell her quickly. It's less painful."

"I'm sure she'll thank me in the end, maybe in a hundred or so year?"

I begin to walk out but her answer stops me instantly.

"She'll never thank you. Ever."

She walks to her window, staring out, a hand resting against the glass.

I consider her words and the flat sadness they held but I have my own problems to face. I leave her office, heading straight to my house, with, I look at my watch, twenty hours to find a way out.

# 12 CUPID'S INTRODUCTION

I normally dump my girls by text or e-mail. Elle planned to do it the hard way, face to face. With a decision like that comes a lot of alcohol. All I can say is good thing Charity was there to hold her hand. Lucky really, because in times like these your friends are all that matter.

## Chapter Twelve
## 16th May, Year 2 - 00:15
## Intoxicated Couplings

C harity's key stuck, refusing to turn. She gave Elle's door a shove. The cylinder finally twisted and in she went. Her hand brushed the wall. She flicked a switch. The halogens buzz to life, illuminating the cavernous, oak-panelled hallway.

Her cowboy boots echoed and she couldn't help but smile. Elle wanted rugs to make the hall warmer. She liked the sound her boots made. Elle kept the hardwood.

Charity knew where she'd be, the library, her sanctuary. And if their last phone call was anything to go by Charity expected her to be very drunk. She opened the door. She was very right. Elle was at the drinks cabinet pouring a large glass of whisky out. Charity frowned at the amount. Now she knew it was serious. Elle rarely drank, she preferred fruit juice. The few times she did it was not whisky anymore. The last time Elle had drunk - Charity glanced at the label as she walked across - Aberlour, was when Lucy almost crucified them during the split. It was a long six months, a lot of them filled with alcohol on Elle's part. It was the last time Charity had seen her significantly drunk.

She rested her chin on Elle's shoulder, watching what she was doing from behind. From the smell of liquor this obviously wasn't her first. Three ice cubes slip from Elle's fingers, clunking into the heavy crystal glass. Elle took a long sip before speaking.

"Want one?"

One of them had to have her senses tonight.

"No, thanks. What happened?"

Elle stared into her glass as Charity crooked her head to look at her friend. Elle could hide many things but there was one giveaway. Her eyes. They always held the truth. It was a curse and a blessing.

"What happened? The truth hit and my house of cards came crashing down."

Another slow sip and Elle grimaced. Charity took hold of her shoulders, turning her around. Charity was taken aback. Elle's eyeliner was blurry; she'd been crying. Her eyes were red; for a long time, it seemed. Elle blinked heavily; the same amount of time Charity would say she'd been drinking for.

Elle downed it in one which was a feat most accomplished drinkers would find hard. Charity drunk Scotch, and Aberlour was a powerful malt.

Elle retreated, her movement sudden, and the doors to the cabinet re-opened. Elle might not indulge but her stock was well rounded for those who do.

"Are you sure I can't tempt you? I'm having..." The bottles dinged and she turned, holding up one Charity recognised. "...Glenmorangie, cellar 13."

Charity didn't argue or try to persuade her otherwise. She just allowed the current to pull her along.

"A connoisseur's choice."

Elle snorted a laugh.

"I have to be a connoisseur at some point. Best it's all in one night."

Elle poured two large glasses out, handing one to her friend. Elle toasted.

"Here's to the regretful job of being a God."

Charity jumped in with both feet. She took a step closer, cupping her friend's cheek, looking into clouded blue eyes.

"What happened?"

This wasn't work. Charity knew her friend too well.

Elle's hand touched hers and lingered before slipping off. Her voice was almost silent.

"They know about Discord. There was a meeting today - of course, I wasn't invited to defend myself. Our relationship was tried and condemned in an afternoon."

"Who did this?"

Elle's eyes closed for a moment. Her glass banged down.

"Kreousa was the messenger. It was the Council."

This wasn't the place for anger. For now Elle needed her to be composed. She unclenched her fists carefully, slowly.

Elle continued, slurring slightly.

"Did you know they see me as part of the royal bloodline? Sounds impressive but the downside is, I have to tell Discord we're over or they'll hold a vote of no confidence in my leadership."

Charity rubbed her temples as she put her glass down, trying to follow everything, trying to find a foothold on this icy impasse.

"They can't do that. You're a God, they're mortals."

Elle's fingers played with the rim of the glass.

"They can and they have."

"Call their bluff. Let them have their stupid little vote..."

Elle picked up her glass and threw it at the wall. Charity flinched as it hit, spraying, shattering into sharp painful pieces that settled like iced snowflakes. She took hold of Elle's hands, making sure she didn't hurt herself. This wasn't like her. She was calm even under pressure.

"There is no bluff to call! I've been thinking of nothing else for hours. There's no way out. If I don't adhere to the vote, Electra will issue a challenge that must be met. We'll end up with a battle royale and mass bloodshed."

Charity knew they couldn't take another Hell.

Elle twisted from Charity's grasp, holding her forehead as she continued.

"I could have my Angels draw up battle lines. We could kill off a few hundred of each other. We'd drive them out to set up an alternate existence a la Lucy but with no controls on their territorial acquisitions.

"I have no options, none. I'm in a corner and I'm not prepared to authorise that sort of killing. There's also the Earth to think about. We can't function with such a loss in numbers.

"As for being considered royalty, seems like there aren't many plus points to it."

Elle wiped her eyes violently, as if ashamed of those tears.

"Don't try and fight an invisible enemy, Elle."

Charity led Elle to her favourite leather couch. They sank in to that dark brown safety. Charity patted her lap. When they were growing up, any time Elle was upset Charity would sit with her like this, and stroke her hair until she either calmed down or fell asleep, which ever came first.

Her blonde head sank into that comfort spot. Charity ran her fingers through Elle's well-kept blonde hair, over and over and over, relaxing them both. Minutes drifted and finally she heard heavy breathing as Elle faded out of fear and sadness, and in to - she leant over - a peaceless sleep. She planted a soft kiss on her head. Elle murmured, snuggling in closer.

The amount of alcohol preceding her arrival helped the decision Elle would have come to, and Charity knew it was the correct one. Leaving Discord was the only option Elle had left.

Charity flicked the switch on the lamp and it all went dark.

# 13 CUPID'S INTRODUCTION

Imagine you're a God. You have more power in your little finger than the whole of a planet, yet you still can't pick who you want to play naked twister with. Sometimes I wonder what Elle gets out of the job. They must have pulled a fast one in the interview. Picture it.

"Caretaker for Planet Earth wanted. Must be able to rule billions but never have any sort of social or love life and needs to subserve to underlings well."

Even being born into it doesn't make it any better; her mom, Fate, did it before, her mom before her and so on. Personally, I'd be telling them what orifice they could stick it up. Course, Elle's a good girl and I'm not.

Back to the story, as with any drunken spree, and I have plenty experience, it's always the next day that hurts.

## Chapter Thirteen: Elle
## 16th May, Year 2 - 10:00
## Mixed Blessings

I cradle my poor head as Charity gets me some liquid vitamins with my juicer. The sound reverberates through the kitchen like a pneumatic road drill. I keep my eyes closed because I feel disgusting.

When I woke I was confused. For perhaps a minute or two I couldn't remember what'd happened. Then the thoughts in my head began to weave back into a distressing pattern, the one I'd attempted to obliterate with a horrible amount of alcohol last night. It hit me so hard I had to lie back down.

A bang makes my eyes re-open. I stare at the glass of fruit juice in front of me.

Charity whispers.

"Drink this for me?"

The bright colour threatens to give me even more of a headache. One saving grace is that the familiar taste masks the other that's vilely evident in my mouth.

A hand strokes my head. My voice stays low because the possibility of the noise exploding my skull is high.

"Tell me about who you're dating now?"

Charity never dates the same woman for more than a month. The day she does is the day she falls in love.

I look up into refreshingly honest eyes. She nods, understanding I need to be taken away from my threatening mind. I listen to a short tale of another beautiful model who: can't use cutlery correctly, examines her fingernails when she speaks, is always worrying about split ends and knows the dietary content of the food she eats even though she'll vomit it back up later.

"President of First Fidelity Bank and I can't get someone with an I.Q. more than the number of pencils on my desk. And for the record I only have six of those."

I do not make a willing participant in the conversation. She rubs my hand as she speaks, reminding me I'm not alone. Still, there's a feeling deep inside of me that says with this decision I am.

Before I know I've spoken I hear my very own words as if from afar.

"I have to tell Discord."

The subconscious is such a powerful thing. It can't be silenced or diverted. You'd think someone who's been around as long as I have would realise that.

"Yes, you do."

Is her simple answer for my one-way statement.

I have no choice, I realised that last night when I tried to drink the knowledge quiet. Alcohol can delay the inevitable but it can't stop it.

I get up, unsure of where I'm going, definitely unsure of where I've just been, only sure of where I am now. It's not a nice place, not when I realise what I have: all of the power in one hand and Discord's heart in the other. One of them has to be sacrificed and my responsibilities are screaming for one thing only. To let her go.

## 14 CUPID'S INTRODUCTION

Elle had eight words she'd used in her relationship with Discord. Bury - head - in - sand - and - hope - for - best. But you can't do that with life because it has a way of finding your hide out and kicking you in the teeth.

Two days ago everything was great, then real life dragged Elle and Discord away from each other. Just goes to show what happens when time isn't on your side.

## Chapter Fourteen: Elle
## 16th May, Year 2 - 18:00
## Tragic Foreclosure

I pace the length of my office, waiting for Discord to arrive. I take a sip of water and swallow two more headache pills, hoping I've overlapped the benefits of my previous dose. I flick through various magazines, putting each down before I get further than the adverts. I open one of my favourite advisors: Coelho's little blue book. I read what his 'Warrior of Light' suggests: "Every warrior of light has felt afraid...has hurt someone they loved...or betrayed someone." I slam it shut, jamming it back into its space, wanting less pertinent thoughts.

My fingers play with reams of paper on my desk as I try and take comfort and strength from the familiar. That's why I called her here. I couldn't go to her apartment or my house. I can't be somewhere we've been lovers and make this work.

I take the thin band off of my wrist, tying my hair back. I put my suit jacket on. I sit and wait. Time hates me and I hate time. The minutes drag.

The intercom makes me jump. Sam's words knot my stomach.

*"Discord's here to see you."*

The intercom dies. So do I. A pause before it buzzes back to life.

*"I mean, Discord's here, Your Eminence. Sorry."*

My finger hovers over the button, my last chance to stop this.

*"Hello? Your Eminence?"*

My eyes squeeze shut. My finger presses down.

"Send her in, Sam."

That finger slowly slides off.

I stay behind my desk. Discord closes the door, keeping the outside world away now it's too late.

My stomach lurches because she looks enthralling. Head to foot in black, it suits her. She stares at me. One of her most captivating features is her intensity. I can feel it right now, covering me. It's a very alluring quality.

She smiles and my heart sinks. I grip the edge of my desk, trying to stop myself walking over and falling into those arms and telling her the truth, but I know my duty to my grateful subjects. I stay where I am. Truth has no place here.

She may be many things but she's no fool. Her expression changes as she does what she's best at. Watches.

"What's wrong?"

My laugh dies before it gets a chance to sound.

"Sit down please, Discord."

Now she knows there's a problem. I never call her that in private, only Dizzy. Her shoulders tense and she takes a moment before doing as I ask.

Onyx eyes bore into my cowardly soul.

"Whatever it is, just say it."

I look at her, the woman who worships and protects me, who's gentle despite the strength she holds. Well, neither of us holds the power today.

My mouth begins as my head refuses to take part in this sham.

"A situation has arisen with the Amazon Council. Issues have been brought to my attention leading to the un-sustainability of our relationship."

She blinks, eyebrows furrowing.

"Un-sustainability?"

I don't explain, just keep going through this snake pit of lies covering the truth. Each word tears itself painfully away.

"I'm afraid we can no longer see each other. I'm sorry, Discord. I have no choice."

Her jaw grits, fists ball and knuckles whiten. Unblinking eyes stare as the stunned silence becomes unbearable. Her voice is off key when she finally speaks.

"No choice? But...you're a God. You're in charge of them."

That ironic arrow finds its target and knocks the air out of me. I stare at my desk for a moment trying to regain my hold on this disgusting reality.

"It counts for nothing. I'm sorry."

"You're ending it, just like that?"

"I'm sorry, Discord."

Any warmth in her tone disappears. Her voice slides: distant, devoid, despising.

"I see. Is that all, Your Eminence?"

I nod, unable to say more without betraying myself. My finger traces the almost imperceptible cracks in the wood of my desk. She stands at the same moment I glance back up. Her dark eyes, frightening, afar, bewildered, catching mine for a moment before leaving to stare into nothing.

It feels like a terrible film, when the hero loses everything, especially the girl.

"Can I go now?"

"I'm..."

"Don't."

What did I expect, soft soothing words, a hug and a nod of understanding, a pat on the back for putting the Amazon's first? I'm surprised I haven't had a slap in the face.

The next ten seconds becomes one of those times that will replay itself, imprinting forever and a day in your mind. Like a favourite part in a movie you watch over and over until you know every word, look, pause before it happens. Discord stares and her mouth opens but silence remains, haunting the space between us. Then with a deep breath she turns and disappears with my heart.

## 15 CUPID'S INTRODUCTION

Listen, don't judge her too harshly. It was a tough decision to make. Anyway, at least Discord didn't go mental. But isn't that always the way those silent types: they stay quiet and hold their pain close. This time was no different - kind of. I mean, there has to be an explosion of sorts, right? Right.

Remember, sometimes, even with the best of intentions, you forget, when the love train derails the injured are everywhere.

## Chapter Fifteen: Discord
## 16th May, Year 2 - 18:59
## Like A Hole In The Head

I break another wooden toothpick, adding it to a growing pile in front of me. The bartender puts a small glass of Bourbon down. I stare at it. How hard can it be to get an order right?

"I asked for the bottle."

He leans over, trying to be my friend. I don't need any more, not if they're like the ones I've had so far.

"Is it really that bad?"

He says with his perfect smile and his perfect hair and his perfect little suit. I grind my teeth and glare my answer. He takes a step back, nodding, then reappears with a half bottle of what I originally asked for. I lay my credits on the bar. I've been saving them up for a rainy day and today it's pouring.

The next two hours are a successful blur.

My new best friend, the bottle of Bourbon, and me become pally. I listen to how people only use her to get drunk. I tell her how people only use me for a cheap fuck. As I pour out the last of her contents she accepts I won the, 'feeling sorry for yourself,' contest hands down. I raise my glass in a toast, of what, I'm not sure.

I lean back in my booth, watching the others here. They laugh, joke, and have a good time. Perhaps they haven't had the rug pulled from under them yet? Well, we have eternity, there's enough time for everyone's dreams to be shattered.

I lean across the table to get a napkin and I'm banged into. My hands splay to keep upright. My teeth grind, my shoulders click, my head turns. My mood, even drowned in alcohol, isn't as rude as this woman's is.

"Hey!" She glares at me then turns to her friend. "She was drunk and knocked my drink, honey."

Her voice bangs around the inside of my skull like a rubber ball. A small pathetic woman tries to, "Shhh," her.

I'm not stupid. I know how I'm viewed up here. I've been given a wide birth from day one. It's not something I'm happy with but I can't seem to change it so today I'll use it to my advantage.

They glare but stop when I straighten up, towering over them. Whiney girl mutters some insult and the Bourbon places a foot on my temper accelerator. I move my face close to hers. I must reek of booze but I don't care.

"Problem?"

When someone thinks they have support they're often more confrontational than when alone. This girl proves that perfectly as her leash slips. She hides behind the shorter redhead, barking her answer.

"Yes. You. You're rude and drunk. Go home, sleep it off and leave real Angels like us alone."

My temper has been pushed to breaking point. First I lose Elle and now a scrawny little runt is shouting at me. I drag Red's girl closer, growling.

"Real?"

She recoils, Red hangs off of my forearm and everything deteriorates. What happens next is not something I'm proud of. I'm not violent no matter what my job is, how I look, or what other's opinions are, but I'm also not made of stone. I'm real all the way through and as sensitive as the next person. Even more so now because here I have nowhere and no one to run to when things get tough.

All of a sudden an iron grip locks around my arm and I come face to face with a sighing member of internal security. My temper takes over as her grip digs into my flesh.

"You're out of here."

I react badly, elbowing her in the face. Blood sprays as her nose shatters and she hits the floor. That's when I see the leather wrist cuff. She's an Amazon.

I drop the woman who started all of this, and her girlfriend stops hanging off of my arm. They have enough sense to haul ass.

Things go from bad to worse as my perfect ball of anger grows bigger with each additional security member - and there are a lot of them. The only thing running through my head is what Elle told me earlier, that the Amazons were involved in us splitting up.

Getting my aggression out on the bitches that have screwed my life up is one way to look at it. An unacceptable loss of control is another.

A punch to my jaw literally knocks that line of thinking clear out of my head. The rest is a spinning blur of violence: a push to a tall brunette, a blonde crashes over the bar, a redhead takes out a row of tables. That's when they bring me down. You see there's one thing about the Amazons. They might not be great individually but they work very well in packs.

I steel myself for my beating. Something - a boot I guess - connects with my ribs, then my stomach. My spine and kidneys aren't left out, either. Each hit knocks more air out of me until I'm gasping. Suddenly I'm dragged to my feet. I don't struggle. I wait for what I know is coming. This is the bright side. A beating with this much alcohol will knock me out tonight. I hope it'll be enough for me not to dream of what I've lost.

I barely stand on my own two feet as I'm let go. I blink at who stares back at me. The blonde Head of Combat Training. My alcohol soaked brain goes blank for a second. Blondey...no, Michelle, yells at security.

"Enough! Back off!"

The Amazons stare at her then me. Two more arrive. My tongue feels around the inside of my mouth checking for missing teeth. None - I glace around - yet. Then things go from worse to awful. One tries to move Blondey out of the way and we spiral out of control. A push becomes a shove. A shove leads to a punch straight in Blondey's stomach. She doubles over, grabbing the bar to stay up. The Amazons move away but she gets into a fighting stance making the pack reform and head in for the kill. Me, I don't move. What's the point? I'm looking forward to some real pain to take away the one that's gnawing inside.

That's when we both get a break. The main door opens and in walks one of their top women, the one with the nice eyes, Psyche.

"What's going on?"

And those nice eyes go wide when she sees what's happening. The broken chairs, upturned tables and smashed glasses don't paint a great picture.

"Stop this, everyone out."

The mass of security surrounding us like hungry panthers doesn't move. She barks her words out again.

"I'm not asking!"

The room empties in record time. They salute her as they pass. I lean on the bar, trying to get my breath back.

Blondey fronts up to her, using the few inches she has to prove her point.

"What is it with you lot?"

"Don't shout at me. I didn't hit her, Michelle."

"No, but your animals hit me."

"I'll deal with it."

I'm relegated to what I am: an outsider. So I watch. Psyche frowns, a thumb tapping her lips. Her eyes move around the room.

"They did all of this damage, too?"

I feel Blondey's eyes boring into me as she answers. Mine stay focused on Psyche, the safer of the two.

"Not exactly."

Psyche stares intensely so I stand my ground. Her hand drops and she turns to Blondey. At the same time my hearing begins to buzz.

"Let's make a deal, Michelle. Neither of us wants the paperwork..."
I butt in as a cold clammy feeling drifts over me. I'm going to pass out.
"Can I go?"
Blondey turns with a hand on her forehead, and laughs. Except I don't think she finds it funny. I don't blame her. It's not high on my list of comedy moments either.
"Go? You'll be going to the brig unless you tell me what this performance was all about."
Nausea sticks her claws into my stomach lining. I lean back on the bar and take as deep a breath as I can seeing that my ribs will soon be a nasty shade of purple.
"I wasn't performing."
Her boots pound on the floor as she walks over.
"Okay, the brig it is then."
She grabs my arm and my perfect ball of anger begins to reform. I peel her fingers off - which isn't easy, proving there's a reason she heads Combat. Her eyebrow spikes and everything slides backward again. I stare into the scowling face of a scowling blonde, but, and it proves help comes from funny places, suddenly her face moves away. Psyche's hand sits on her shoulder.
"Michelle, can I talk to you?"
With a look designed to turn me to stone, Blondey narrows her eyes. After a moment she follows her to a table a few feet away.
Little black squares take over the space in front of my eyes. My head swims. I pick a chair up from the floor, righting it, sitting my sick feeling self down quickly. I rest my elbows on my knees and hold my lava hot neck with my ice-cold hands. I catch parts of their conversation, mainly phrases, but my focus is trying to stay conscious.
"...I don't care what's happened, Psyche.... Tell me who..."
My hazy shade of sense blurs and fades in time with the ringing in my ears. Suddenly two legs fill my dwindling field of vision. I make the effort to look up, wondering if I'll be walking or being dragged to that brig. Psyche stares down.
"You don't make things easy on yourself, do you?"
I give her my shortest response designed to end all conversation, mainly because looking up is making me feel dizzy - the name punches me in the guts. My teeth grind.
"Fuck off."
She raises an eyebrow and lowers her voice.
"An expert on how to win friends and influence people. You're lucky I know what you're going through."
A desperate need not to speak takes over. One word is all I can manage.
"Doubtful."
She shakes her head and looks unimpressed.
"I'll get this place tidied up, Michelle." Her words drift as she walks away, hooking a thumb over her shoulder. "You get to look after her. Tough break."
A steadying breath and I stand and concentrate on stopping the room

from sliding off at an impossible angle. I take a moment out of this
madness and manage three painful steps to the bar. I knock the lid off of
the ice bucket and grab a couple of cubes. I crunch quickly, hoping they'll
stop whatever my body and mind have planned. With a shake of my head
and a puff of breath I'm better than before and ready to get this over with;
best thing to do when trouble is heading your way is to face it head on,
that's my theory.

"How long am I going to the brig for?"

My trouble stares at me as if I'm talking French. Blondey frowns.

"What?" Suddenly her frown lifts. "Oh, right. No, you're not heading
there."

My hand grabs a chair as black squares revisit, big time.

"Come on, let's get you sitting down."

She leads me back to the booth I sat at before I screwed up, then walks
to the bar, returning with a wad of paper napkins. She hands them to me,
but my coordination is off and my fingers aren't quick enough. They spread
over the table like a newspaper blown in the wind.

"They did a good job. Your lip's bleeding."

I struggle to pick one up but between the drink and my beating I can't
reach out. I give up, licking the corner of my mouth instead.

The sound as she pulls a chair up could be used for torture. She picks up
a napkin, bringing it to my face. I can't help it, I recoil automatically. Her
hand stays still, waiting for me. There comes a time when a girl has to give
up going it alone. My eyes close and I try to relax but it's easier said than
done. She touches the side of my mouth, then my cheek, forehead and chin.
Stabbing pains shoot through my entire body. I open my eyes as she screws
the napkin up, shaking her head.

My voice slurs.

"What was the brig, a threat?"

She puts the rest of the napkins into a pile as she answers.

"No, it was a certainty but.... Listen, I'm not adding to your bad day. I
don't want that kind of karma. Anyway, I'm the perpetual good gal so I can't
leave you like this."

I shake my head, trying to clear it. It's then I realise how I must look:
drunk, bloodied, bruised. I'd sigh if my ribs could stand it.

"I don't need sympathy."

I do need some strong painkillers. My body lets out a long scream as I
clutch the edge of the table. I lower my forehead to the cool wood, closing
my eyes, trying to control the pain. A warm hand softly squeezes my
shoulder.

Her low tone is like a calming lullaby.

"I'm not giving you sympathy. Stop being a tough girl."

It's as though my brain only needs to hear that request once. The last
day crashes down, enveloping me in a painful black cloud. It breaks
through my battered and alcohol-soaked defences, tugging at my self-
control. Tears well up. I grit my teeth, barely managing to keep it together.

After an eternity I lift my head back up. She's sitting patiently, watching,
waiting.

"Let me help you."

I snort a laugh as the alcohol lies for me.

"Keep your help."

I glare as she takes a deep breath then shrugs.

"Right, stay here. The Amazons will be back soon. They'll enjoy taking their angst out for having to clear this place up."

She stands, turns, and starts to walk away. I look down at the bloodied tissues on the table. My choices float to the ground like confetti.

"Wait. Just.... Okay, I'm sorry."

She walks back, not saying a word. Her hand takes hold of mine, pulling me up. My ribs spasm painfully as I force out words.

"Where are we going?"

I resist taking her arm to lean on. I'd rather be in severe pain, like now, than owe anyone in this place a thing.

"I'm taking you back to yours. I'm cleaning you up, putting you to bed then leaving you to your bad mood and restless sleep."

Even in my semi-drunken haze something occurs to me.

"Why go against your own people for me?"

There's a long pause before she answers.

"You haven't done me any harm, Discord. Anyway, they're not my people. I'm an Angel not an Amazon, don't mistake us. We might wear the same wings but our allegiances differ."

I file that statement for when I can concentrate.

My apartment is onsite. I can't live back on Earth until everyone who knew me dies - a safety feature I'm an expert on not thinking about. Some things you have to forget to function, no matter how hard it is.

The five minutes it takes to walk to my housing section is filled with severe pain. I don't let on, it doesn't let up. I do match her pace, even if it's quick and painful. I nearly groan in relief as we get to my door.

I try to pull my keys out of my pocket but my mobility is almost zero. Frustration wells up as I fail miserably.

She speaks softly.

"Let me?"

I nod, annoyed at the state I'm in. Her hand squeezes into my jeans pocket. She glances up and smirks at her fumbling.

"Sorry."

Any other time it'd be funny.

We finally get in. Half an hour later my cuts are bathed in antiseptic, I'm in a fresh top and loose bed pants that took me ten minutes to put on, and I've had two strong painkillers and a glass of cold water. I don't feel any better.

We make it to the bedroom. I haven't fought her once. I'd say she expected it to be harder but I don't have the will. I want to lie down and sleep this off because I feel like I've been run over and left for dead.

I sit on the bed, my hands sinking in the soft comforter. The painkillers have made everything slow down. Her face hazes into view, lips mouthing words I hear a fraction of a second later, like a badly dubbed movie confusing your senses.

"You need to lie down. I'm leaving two more pills and some water. It's a good opportunity to try out some of those newly learnt healing skills of yours. Your body will take a couple of days to sort this out. Don't panic if you feel shifting. It'll be your bones resettling. They must've broken something. Relax and go with it."

The pills suddenly kick in full force, taking me by surprise, washing over me and removing my ability to move. I stare at her lips, not able to say anything.

"Discord?"

It's a fight to keep my eyes open. A hand touches my forehead. Her eyes open wide; light green, like beacons beaming. I blink, and when I refocus she's reading the pill bottle. Her mouth drops.

"These and alcohol? Dumbass, Michelle. Okay, just...don't fall into a coma."

Warm fingers open my eyelids fully and the contact makes me fall back on the bed. Nothing seems important anymore. Not Elle, not the Amazons, not the fight at the bar. I stare at my ceiling fan as it turns slower than normal, sending a deep throb through my bones. I try to move my arm but it doesn't work so I give up, not able to remember why I was doing it anyway.

The bed shifts and her face appears. She grunts, lifting my head, putting it on a pillow.

"You'll be spaced out for a while. I'll stay until morning to make sure you don't die in your sleep."

I try to nod but fail, not sure what the problem is because I'm feeling better than fine. I don't even panic when those black squares begin to swallow everything up.

My hearing dulls to a low buzz. My eyes slide shut. Today is finally over.

## 16 CUPID'S INTRODUCTION

Blondey, a.k.a. Michelle, stayed the night. Discord didn't die, no thanks to Head of Combat's choice distribution of booze and medication - her heart is in the right place. The bar incident was covered up by Psyche who was doing her own damage limitation after what Electra had started. Discord seemed to have a lot of people looking out for her. Shame she didn't realise, would've made the next few months a lot easier.

Elle, on the other hand, had been balancing on the slippery slope of breakdown. Her concrete defences were cracking left, right, and centre. You have to understand, this wasn't just some affair, it was the first time in the Heaven's history she'd fallen in love. After all, in her position you don't give your heart up to anyone. But now, with all of these problems with the Amazons, Elle had realized that superficial flings would be all she'd get out of this gig.

It took weeks after the initial break-up but eventually it happened. She fell apart. It wasn't a full on weeping breakdown - I can't handle those, they give me hives. Instead it was a slow and silent slide into herself. That was harder for Charity to watch. Your first instinct is not to want your friends to hurt, but Elle's damage was too great. A band-aid, some lipstick and a hair ruffle wouldn't mend this. Nope, sometimes the best medicine is to let it happen.

Isn't it a bummer when you find your soul mate but get to spend the rest of eternity with her, but apart?

# Chapter Sixteen
## 1st June, Year 2 - 15:00
## One, Two, Three...

"Can you reschedule this afternoon?" Charity pushed the phone to her ear, trying to block out the hum of conversation. She glanced around the restaurant looking for Elle. The clicks of a keyboard sounded on the other end of the line as Vanessa, no doubt, rolled her eyes at having to shift things around.

*"How much of a reschedule?"*

"Everything."

Vanessa sighed and the line hummed.

*"Tomorrow will be packed."*

Charity saw a familiar blonde in the dark recesses of a booth. She should've guessed. It was the most private and looked out over the gardens.

"I know, but I've hit something unavoidable. I'm turning my phone off so if it's urgent leave a voicemail and I'll pick it up later."

Vanessa's tone was crisply efficient, but nevertheless, not impressed.

*"I'll send your new schedule via email. If you need anything I'm here until seven."*

She put her phone away. She slipped in-between tables, saying a quick hello to familiar faces then finally got to her best friend, laying a kiss on top of her head. She sat opposite.

"Sorry I'm late. Work was a terror."

After a long pause Elle finally dragged her attention from the blackened glass. Her mouth twitched into a terrible excuse for a smile.

"It's fine. I thought it was one of your girls being demanding."

"No woman could come between us." Charity tapped the wine list. "Pick a nice summery white."

Elle ordered in a monotone, giving that same sad excuse of a smile to the waiter. Charity slipped the menu from docile hands and picked her friend's favourite finger foods of olives, capers, and asparagus. Almost instantly, square ceramic platters of nibbles appeared with delicious offerings Charity knew she'd have to work hard to get Elle to eat.

She moved a hand across the table, stroking the tips of Elle's fingers.

"How are things going?"

A flash of evening sunlight fought its way through the glass, casting bare shadows over their table, and Elle. Gloomy eyes stared back. Elle's hand retreated and speared an olive with one of the small metal picks.

"Things are fine, nothing new to report."

Some points were worth being gentle with but not this one. Weeks of deterioration meant that time had come and gone.

"How's Discord?"

Elle's metal pick harpooned the olive fiercely and she left it sticking out. She sat back, crossing her arms. Her tone was harsh.

"I'm not allowed to speak to her, don't you remember?"

Charity raised an eyebrow and glanced down at Elle's awful body language.

"Sorry." Elle uncrossed her arms and sighed heavily. "We haven't spoken. I assume she's coping." There was a terrible pause. "I hope she's coping."

The waiter rejoined them and Charity motioned for him to fill the glasses and dispense with the tasting ritual. She knew the wines here, they were all good. He leant over, rattling a matchbox, moving a candle to light. Elle's hand quickly lay flat over the little wax circle, her instructions short and sharp.

"No."

"Forgive me, Your Eminence."

Elle waved his apology away dismissively. Shaking hands slipped the match back into the box. He bowed, leaving quickly. Charity watched him politely tend to others She looked at her usually congenial friend. She reached across, moving Elle's rigid hand away from its hovering position, laying it gently on the table.

"At some point you're going to have to talk about it because if you don't it's going to fester."

Iced eyes stared, making Charity wonder who exactly was sitting across the table. To say Elle was not herself was an understatement. Even her tone was vapid.

"It already is. Let's talk about something else."

"Elle..."

"No."

It was going to be a long night.

Charity spoke of light-hearted matters for the rest of the evening. Any attempt to broach the subject of Discord was batted away swiftly and forcefully. It showed, in no uncertain terms, it was a line not to be crossed. But Charity didn't give up because wasn't that what friends were for, to tread dangerous ground? If she needed to fight through this little minefield Elle had laid out then she would.

Evening approached and the late lunch ended as uneventfully as it had started. They left the bustling restaurant for the hush of the semi dark street. Lamps cast an eerie glow as their cars pulled up. Charity looked at a woman who was slowly ceasing to exist as the person she knew. Seeing her in pain was bad enough, but not being able to do anything was torturous.

She adjusted Elle's dishevelled scarf and pulled her into a tight hug. Elle's arms draped limply across her shoulders.

"It's okay to fall apart a little, just a little. I won't tell anyone."

Elle's breathing stalled and body stiffened, and with a shaking hand, Charity was gently pushed away. Charity took hold of that hand, gripping tightly.

"Elle..."

It wrenched away as Elle's face took on a terribly pained expression, the first real sign of what was happening inside that head of hers.

"I can't. I'm sorry."

Elle's driver opened the door and she moved along the back seat to the far side and stared blankly out of the window. The door closed. Her car slowly crunched gravel until Charity couldn't see it anymore.

The next week went along similar lines. Charity rescheduled her entire working life and even paused her woman of the moment in favour of seeing Elle every night. She hired the latest movies, they ate at the most exclusive restaurants; Charity made sure she didn't waste away, kept her fluid level up and was lying down at a reasonable hour - she was certainly not sleeping. The first few days showed zero results. Elle cast a ghostly figure at work and it didn't change in private. The next few, however, showed a mild transformation from a washed out grey to a muted version of her old self. A broken heart wouldn't mend in such a short time but it would resume beating.

The weekend and Charity decided on a new tactic. Mother had been hounding her to bring Elle around for some T.L.C.

"The Nature household has a new addition."

Charity cradled the phone with her shoulder, loading her bag up in anticipation of the yes she'd need to argue out of Elle.

*"If you're going to tell me Hope is pregnant and I have a half-sister on the way, I'll slit my wrists right now."*

"No, Elle. The addition is a new sauna and steam room. Want to indulge in sweating with a purpose?"

*"I don't know."*

"There's that enthusiasm I know and love."

The banter fell flat as Elle sighed heavily.

*"I'm not exactly fun to be around."*

Charity pulled her trump card out. It was the same as business, to close the deal you exploited every opportunity.

"But Mother was so looking forward to...." She paused and counted to three. "It's fine. I'll make an excuse. I'm sure she won't be too disappointed."

The line fuzzed.

*"Just...don't expect sparkling conversation."*

She blew her successful self a kiss in the mirror opposite.

"I'm coming around to get you now. Be ready and waiting."

Charity grabbed her bag and dashed out front to her latest present from herself. The sleek lines of her new Aston Martin convertible glinted in the sunlight. Her fingertips caressed the silky smooth paintwork of the beast she'd waited a year to get. She flicked a bug off of the windscreen and carefully got in. The key turned and the Aston Martin burst into a fierce roar. Birds vacated the nearby trees. Charity patted the wheel and grinned like a kid who actually got what they wanted on their birthday.

"Be gentle with me."

She donned her sunglasses and headed to Elle's, ready for mission impossible.

The journey didn't take long but that could have been her total disregard for all speed limits. What was the point going slowly if it was a clear day and there was a wide open road ahead, teasing you?

She shifted the car into third to keep the revs down and slunk up Elle's driveway. She parked, jumped out and tried not to look at the numerous bugs she'd no doubt collected in the grill.

She knocked on the door. It was finally opened by Elle's, now part-time, butler. He bowed slowly and Charity actually thought she could hear his joints protesting at the movement.

She smiled.

"Hello, Davis."

His face remained impassive.

"Do come in. I shall tell Her Eminence you are here, Miss Nature."

He walked away at a snail's pace - which was as quickly as his legs would carry him. Even when Elle and her were children he moved the same way. He never could catch them when they were doing anything wrong - didn't stop him trying, of course. The amount of times they ended up skittering through the bushes out back while Davis hunted them at Fate's beckoning.... Charity smiled. They were good days.

After an age, a door upstairs slammed and Elle descended the stairs, stopping lifelessly in front of Charity. Elle looked awful, but worse still, she knew it. Her hand waved over her outfit.

"Don't mention my lack of coordination." Elle fumbled with a handful of accoutrements, dropping her keys. "Literally, my lack of coordination."

"Your outfit is fine, but...." Charity stared at her gaunt face. "Elle, have you had any sleep at all?"

Elle scooped her keys up.

"I was working late. There's a lot to do."

"There's always a lot to do. It's no excuse."

Elle glared.

"You sound like my mother, Charity."

Cheering her up today might be harder than anticipated, but Charity was always up for a challenge.

"No snapping at your best friend."

Elle sighed and scraped her hair back severely, putting it in a ponytail.

"If my best friend sounds like my mother then I think I'm justified." Elle's eyes squeezed shut. "I didn't mean that. I'm sorry."

"I take it she paid you a visit."

Elle knelt down, sorting through the contents of her bag. Charity knew every one of her tricks and that was one of them, fiddling with things. She also knew how affected she could be by Fate's unforgiving words.

"She came around earlier, criticised everything and then left. Nothing out of the ordinary."

Charity stroked her hair. Elle just let her.

"Elle you don't look well."

Elle's hand gripped her bag, banging it down, making her friend jump.

"Stop hounding me! If it's not you, it's Sam or Mother or.... I'm working very hard and...." Elle's head hung as she took a wracking breath. "Please, Charity, don't keep on at me."

She looked utterly dejected.

"Of course. Come on, let's go to my Mother's and we can talk - or not."

"I'll take not."

Elle slammed the door as they left. Charity hoped it hadn't given Davis a heart attack.

Charity took a silk scarf out of her pocket.

"You'll need it."

Elle stared forlornly.

"A present?"

"Functional and fashionable. Think the fifties - nineteen, not eighteen. No wigs for us."

Charity took her bag and hooked arms. Elle's footsteps stuttered to a stop.

"What have you gone and bought?"

"A monster and we're going for a spin in its jaws." Charity ran around the car and opened the passenger door with a sweeping bow. "Your Eminence, your chariot awaits."

Elle got in, eyeing the interior suspiciously, her hand slipping over the dash. Charity closed the door and got in the other side.

"Your enthusiasm does not detract from the fact that I want to arrive at May's in one piece."

Elle put on the scarf then dark glasses, looking every bit like a nineteen-fifty's movie star.

"Your Eminence, as if I, your driver, would do anything to endanger you."

Charity wheel spun out of her driveway.

"And you're getting those tyre marks erased from my paving, too!"

Charity took the long way around, through the back roads, testing out the ground clearance. From the scraping sound as they hit several bumps she'd say it wasn't too good.

They pulled into her mother's driveway. The rumble still echoed in their bodies even after Charity switched the engine off. Elle turned, removed her sunglasses and hooked them in her shirt. She wordlessly pushed the door open and walked towards the house. Charity was left bewildered by her re-enactment of a silent movie.

Charity pulled herself up by the top of the windshield.

"What?"

Elle stopped, pivoting slowly, her cheeks puffing in an exhale.

"It took a moment for my words to catch up because..." She threw her hands up. "...we were going faster than the speed of sound."

Charity vaulted the door and grabbed her bag, throwing it over a shoulder. They hooked arms.

"I bet you're ready to relax now."

"I have dust in places I didn't know existed." Elle's eyes rolled and Charity knew her exuberance was finally rubbing off. "Come on, Miss Nature. Let's do some of that sweating with a purpose you promised me."

Two hours of soaking, steaming and general pampering might have relaxed Elle's body but not, Charity feared, her mind. That couldn't be accessed so easily. Weeks of changing subjects and flat refusals to talk about Discord had left Elle looking weary and it was not a way Charity liked to see her.

They went to the heart of the house: the kitchen. Elle flicked through a magazine, her eyes not moving from the same spot despite pages going by quickly. Charity watched closely and squeezed her some juice, knowing damn well she was thinking about things she shouldn't. She stopped the juicer. Or perhaps things she should? She was getting confused about this whole thing, too.

The door opened. Charity's mother, May, burst in, stopping when she saw Elle.

"I haven't seen you in so long, darling." Elle was enveloped in a tight hug. "Is this a new haircut?"

May ran a hand through Elle's now slightly shorter locks. Charity dropped a straw into the fruit juice and left it on the table.

"I had it done yesterday. I needed a change."

Charity was with her as she sighed at the hairdresser, telling him to do what he wanted as she didn't care. Charity made sure it wasn't multi-coloured highlights.

"And you look wonderful." May took Elle's face in her hands, smiling widely. "I'm glad I rescheduled my meeting with Poseidon now. Anyway, his innuendos about how my tidal laws are ruining his 'foaming waves' were driving me mad."

Charity sat on the counter, pretending to read a magazine but secretly left her mother to what she did best: cheer up the broken-hearted. May had enough trauma with Charity's ever changing round of women to know exactly how tactful to be. But, like she'd done repeatedly, Elle skilfully diverted each attempt on to something less hazardous. It begged the question, how exactly could they help Elle of if she wouldn't even help herself?

Charity watched her friend's fascination with the same magazine she'd been staring at for the last hour. May deposited their glasses in the sink.

"Your sister's coming over in twenty minutes."

Charity jumped off of the counter, getting their things together.

Elle spoke in a monotone, closing her magazine.

"I'm not in the mood for Hope today."

"Me neither. Let's go."

"That's why I mentioned it, dear." May kissed Charity's cheek noisily. "Remember, we have the annual All Souls Fund Raiser at New Year. I need you to attend this year. You have enough notice to clear your calendar." May took Elle's hand. "You'll come won't you? Charity can't bring one of her insipid women if you do."

For the first time in over a week Elle laughed. It was sedate but Charity's heart lifted at the sound. Elle threw her arms around May's neck in a hug.

"I'd be delighted. I'd hate to think Charity would get to stretch the numbers of her harem any more."

Charity rubbed Elle's shoulder, grabbing their bags, signalling their departure.

"Thank you, ladies. I can't help if I'm irresistible. Come on, let's go before Hope arrives."

With a hug and kiss for her mother, Charity took Elle's hand and they left.

An overcast sky greeted them and Charity flicked a switch, turning the open top into something much more sensible. The roof smoothly unfolded, the only sound being the click as it secured in place.

Charity took the long way back but kept the speed sensible. Elle didn't say a word, just stared out of the window as rain delicately began to slash the glass.

Charity glanced over and Elle's eyes were squeezed shut, fingers gripping the arm rest.

"Elle, you have to let it out."

And it was that easy. That simple sentence penetrated every one of Elle's well constructed defences. She finally broke. A visible drop of the shoulders accompanied a quiet sob as a hand splayed across the glass.

"I hate them for what they made me do." Tears dripped down her cheeks. "And I hate myself even more for doing it."

Charity pulled the car over, Elle's wracking sobs filled the car. Charity kissed her cheek and did the only thing she could. She held her close.

## 17 CUPID'S INTRODUCTION

Elle isn't Earth's caretaker for nothing. She's strong, sexy, intelligent, and able to keep her mind together in the toughest times - and they had been tough. That night was the worst of it. It was spent in tears, but the downhill slide stopped there. Well, love wise it did, but Elle wasn't coping too well with other things either. If it were up to me I'd have gotten her some babes to massage her cares away. Charity and I clearly don't think along the same lines.

Things went from awful to disastrous to downright maniacal at work. The Amazons Council were like Piranhas. They almost ripped her to pieces, first mentally with Discord and then physically with day after day of meetings holding zero importance. It all mounted up into a nothing nightmare. You know, a great big pile of nothing with a side order of nothing followed by a dessert of nothing. You get where I'm going with this.

I'm not going to comment on the fact Kreousa gets all this time dedicated to her. No mention of me and the fact Psyche lost her virginity right here. Yeah, we blanked her memory but she could've retained something.

# Chapter Seventeen: Elle
# 14th June, Year 2 - 19:00
# History Boomerang: The Queen's Fable

"I'm delighted to say we're successfully convened."

Vestra bangs the gavel down and ends this travesty of a meeting. Funny how the most important subject we had to cover this month is rescheduled to today, when Charity calls to say she can't make it and I'm alone, facing a pack of rabid dogs.

I glare at Electra as she gathers her papers. Sensing me she stops, head tilting, eyes meeting mine. A wisp of a smile levels before she bows, then turns sharply on her heels and leaves with her staff.

I run a finger down my glass of fruit juice soured by the vitriol that woman delivered while she stripped me of more land and voting rights for her damned Nation. I take a deep breath, willing my battered body to move and get out of this viper's nest. A familiar face stares back at me from the other end of the table. Psyche bows her head. I glare at her and her eyes slide away.

I snatch my bag off of the table and drag myself away from the biggest influx of mistakes I've ever allowed entry.

Each step carries me a little closer to my offices but also brings forth the physical toll of that six hour meeting. Finally I stop at a drinks machine, pressing a button for some tea; coffee would kill me at this point. The brightly lit front feels cool against my forehead. My eyes close and I take a moment to steady the tiredness creeping into my bones.

Footsteps and a cough make me straighten instantly. Psyche smiles and bows her head. My mouth refuses to offer up a smile and my words form an out and out betrayal of the position I hold, because a very big part of me is sick of this charade it's forced to perform with these women.

"Is six hours with me not enough? Would you like this as well?"

I grab a handful of my top as her eyelashes flutter in surprise.

"I don't understand, Your Eminence."

The more I look at her the angrier I become. It spills out, covering the distance between us.

"The shirt off of my back, do you want that too?"

A happy ding signals something going right. I blow on the steaming liquid, taking a small sip while I watch the woman who chaired the meeting today. She shifts.

"I was doing my job, Your Eminence."

I have to admire the fact she's willing to face me after today, but then she must be ecstatic at the new acquisitions gained. I know I would.

Watching her through the haze of steam from my cup, I realise something.

"This doesn't have any sugar in."

I drop it into the bin and tell my brain to pull itself together. Suddenly it catches up with the time delay my mood has forced it into.

"I thought your job was to be my Angel, Psyche?" I turn sharply, not wanting to be in the same hallway as her. I shout into the space. "Not use every dirty trick to extract more goodies. It seems you won't be satisfied until you have more voting rights than me."

The elevator doors seem so near yet too far. Her long legs bring her in step with me effortlessly.

"I am your Angel. I walk by your side, Your Eminence. With you, under your command. But I also have my Amazon commitments. If it's any consolation, sometimes it is hard to justify our timing."

My eyes dart across.

"Meaning?"

She stops and holds on to my arm. Her hand slips away.

"Permission to speak freely?"

I cross my arms.

"Why would my permission mean anything to you? Let's stop playing games. Spell it out for me."

She inhales deeply then spears me with an intense look.

"Your mental state at the moment has been noted..." Her hand touches her chest. "...by me, as less than perfect. That's what I meant about timing, Elle. I'm speaking as a friend now."

I almost explode at her assuming she should even be in the same category as Charity.

"A friend? I'd hate to have you as an enemy!"

I spin on my heels, signalling an end to this insane conversation.

Seething, the elevator button gets my anger repeatedly. Her tall figure stops by my side.

"I've ended our conversation, Psyche."

The doors open and I get in, staring at a serious face of a woman who is trying hard to push me too far. The lift doors begin closing, and with a jump, she slides in-between.

I slap the button to my floor.

"Please, Your Emin..."

"A friendly word of warning you don't deserve. Be careful of the ice you walk on, Psyche, because it may not take the weight of your words."

Her mouth opens then grits shut. Her hand shoots out and she bangs the red stop button. We jar to a halt. Slim fingers stop me pressing the emergency call button.

"What do you think you're doing?"

"Please, I'm trying to make amends."

I divest myself of that grip as intense anger ripples through me.

"By behaving like you did in the meeting room? All you didn't do was ask me to perform a little dance, or is that next week?"

"I'm not responsible for you and Discord."

My fists ball as I try to remember I'm a God and shouldn't use my powers to crush her.

My finger jabs the air in front of her face.

"It was your sisters and your Council who let me know in no uncertain terms they'd withdraw their support if my relationship continued. What was I to do? I can't have another split of the Heavens. I don't think your sisters gave me much of a choice. It was tow your line or end up with another Hell!"

Deep breaths do not calm my bubbling rage.

"I may have trusted you, Psyche, but don't mistake that for the right to speak to me anyway you see fit. You negated any trust I had in you when you stabbed me in the back."

She shifts in a halting pace then whips around.

"Stab you in the back? I defended you over my own Council. I risked my position. Why do you think they picked me to head the meeting today? It was to punish me for taking your side and to try and drive a wedge between you and your supporters."

Any words I have fall away as that sinks in. She moves closer, tense and angry by the sounds of her frustrated delivery.

"And do you think it was Electra's doing to give you a chance to end your relationship with Discord? It was mine and Kreousa's. We fought for you. We bought you time and we held them off, nearly at the risk of a coup d'etat in the Council chambers." Her hand lays over her chest, clutching at the leather of her tunic as her voice drops to a bare whisper. "You talk about trust? I have *never* failed you."

I lean against the elevator wall, trying to cope with this influx of information. Silence bounces around our small space.

Finally my brain produces a useless sentence.

"I didn't realise."

She massages her temples slowly.

"You know about our class system, it's everything to us. They can't watch you, basically their second Queen, with a woman who..." She counts reasons off on her fingers. "...isn't a warrior by birth or upbringing, who doesn't have the kudos of a blood Angel and who's been here for five minutes and has almost compromised the power behind the Heavens. It's not acceptable..."

"Don't tell me what's..."

She holds my hand, squeezing it tightly.

"Wait. Let me finish. It's not acceptable - to some of us. Elle, we're not all your enemy."

The ounce of composure I held drips away as the truth leaks out.

"She was the person I chose, my consort. She was the one."

Her eyes shut as she nods slowly. When they reopen they're filled with terrible sadness.

"Do you think Kreousa hasn't experienced what you're going through?"

I blink obliviously back as she slides down the elevator wall, sitting on the floor heavily, her body not holding its usual poise but instead her long legs splayed messily. She pats the metal floor. When I don't move she hits me with that terrible sadness again.

"Please, it might help you understand."

I sit, keeping my distance.

"What I tell you has to stay in this elevator."

Her expression makes me agree.

"Very well."

"Thank you."

She sighs as she stares at some place I can't yet see.

"Kreousa's clan always held the main control of our Nation."

The corners of her mouth twitch into a smile.

"She comes from an influential family. She's a fearsome warrior, a magnificent horsewoman. She can kill an enemy at a hundred feet with a dagger. On Earth she was revered."

I shift, getting comfortable, watching her striking features twitch as that smile falls.

"One day the sentries captured a young woman who'd wondered in to Amazon territory. I'm sure it won't be hard to believe the ground was marked very carefully. All they didn't do was piss in the corners of the land. Passing boundary markers was a serious charge.

"She was brought before the Queen and the Council for judgment. Death wasn't unheard of if a person held no use for the Nation. I remember the way Kreousa looked at her during those first moments. It was more than just a meeting of the minds.

"Throughout the trial Kreousa's eyes never left her. An hour later Kreousa simply stood up and dismissed a surprised Council.

"I don't need to tell you what happened next. Use your imagination. Suffice to say there was something strong and intense between them.

"After a few months of illicit meetings, word spread about the lovers. The Council weren't going to allow it. There were..." Her voice becomes authoritative and lower. "...'brides from suitable families ready to be chosen by the Queen. No little half-breed can interfere with the bloodlines.'

"It might help you to understand, Electra was one of those brides. She was expected to be chosen. She came from a very influential political family and it was seen as a way of aligning the tribes. We were steering away from the use of force to decide matters and towards the use of reason. Electra was set to have it all: power over an entire nation of warriors; her very own army."

She pauses, tapping fingertips to the metal of the floor, sending a rhythm out. Suddenly that tapping ceases.

"Kreousa may have been Queen but she had no control of what happened next. Warriors loyal to the Council were sent to kill the woman under the guise of escorting her out of Amazonian territory.

"Kreousa found out what was happening. She ran as fast as she could to the woman's hut. She killed two of them with her bare hands. The others fled, not willing to harm her. Kreousa tended to her lover's wounds but they were severe. Six agile warriors against one unarmed woman will never end well."

She draws a leg up, hugging it with her arms and rests her chin down. The truth flutters into place as I realise who the woman was.

"They'd broken one of my arms. I had dagger wounds all over. I could hardly walk. I was a solid warrior, I'd managed on my own for so long but...they came in the middle of the night. I couldn't defend myself. And Kreousa tried so hard to help me, but...."

She sighs, deeply.

"But we knew it'd keep occurring if I stayed. After a heated discussion I left. She begged me not to go, to wait until she'd healed my injuries at least. A Queen on her knees for someone who wasn't even an Amazon by birth. Ironic.

"I took her horse and rode for a day before I must have passed out. I woke up far from Kreousa's clan, on the edges of the territories. The clan that found me was more peaceful. They took me in and after a few years I earned my place in their society. I was allowed to call myself an Amazon.

"Years went by. I didn't forget about Kreousa. She looks the same now as she did then. You can't leave her behind easily. But time moves on so I knew I just had to get on with my life.

"Nothing stayed the same in the time that dragged by. The Romans had spent years invading our land until even peaceful clans like my own had to take arms."

Her hands stop hugging her leg and rest on the floor with the barest thud. The sharp planes of her face set as a tragic smile falls on full lips.

"It was a blazingly hot day. We'd spent the morning preparing ourselves. Those who had loved ones said goodbye. I rode into battle with my sisters. You could smell death and blood in the air. Only being in a battle can prepare you for those smells, the noise, even the rumbling of the ground under the horses' hooves.

"The soldiers took us by surprise. They cut us down with hail after hail of arrows, but we took out as many Legionnaires as possible. We made sure the Romans didn't forget that day.

"My horse, the one I'd taken from Kreousa, had been hit. It careened down, sending me skidding across the dirt, knocking the air out of me. I remember struggling to my feet, pulling my sword out as quickly as I could. We were so out numbered. It was a massacre. My friends were being cut down in front of me and I didn't know who to help first.

"This part I've never forgotten. I'd struggled through three Romans to the centre of our battlefield. I turned, and looked straight into Kreousa's eyes. She'd brought her army in to defend our land. I knew she'd found out where I'd settled as we were always privy to many trade gifts from other clans."

Her voice slips to a whisper as her eyes glisten.

"She wore full ceremonial battle dress and looked as regal and beautiful as the night I left. I was so happy to see her. I smiled..."

Her expression hardens as her fists clench.

"...as her mouth opened to scream at me. A sword found its way into my back, all the way through to exit out of my chest plate. Blood bubbled in my throat as it pulled back out.

"It was all so sudden, everything in a few seconds. I looked up to see Kreousa being surrounded by Legionnaires. She smiled sadly and pointed up to the sky, up to here, the Heavens, with her sword.

"I felt myself fall. I could still hear the battle all around me but all I could see was that I'd turned the Earth red. I closed my eyes tightly and prayed. I prayed they'd kill her quickly. It was the last thing I remember of that day."

I stare into red rimmed eyes, completely shocked. I might be a God but a soul's journey into the Heavens is its own private business.

"They didn't kill her quickly. They recognized her battle uniform as that of a Queen.

"I waited for her here. Hours turned to days. Days of pacing, imagining her fate, trying to think of anything else. She didn't come. Michelle got the brunt of my rage. I'm grateful she doesn't hold grudges.

"It was two days before she arrived. Two days. That's a lot of time for Roman soldiers to amuse themselves with a beautiful Queen. When they got bored they slit her throat like she was an animal. If you look closely you can still see every wound they gave her. They cover her like a second skin. She calls it her 'Suit of Death'. Perhaps naming your pain gives you power over it, I don't know.

"Anyway, I was recognized in the commotion as I waited. I wasn't allowed near her when she arrived. It was a hard time for both of us. Kreousa's physical wounds healed by default of coming here, but mentally.... For a long time I didn't think anyone could save her from her own memories. Not even I know everything that happened.

"But time's a great healer. Kreousa's a fitting Queen. She dealt with the pain and came back stronger than ever. The End."

I sit in a shocked silence, finally seeing the puzzle as it really is, not how I first perceived it. I turn to an incredibly brave woman.

"But what about the two of you?"

She shrugs.

"Electra was made Head of the Council." She laughs sadly. "Even in death there was no freedom. But Kreousa is a strong woman. She made me her second in command - and she had to shout over the objections for decades and still does on occasions."

I raise an eyebrow at her avoidance tactic.

"But what about the two of you?"

Her lips curl into the barest hint of a smile.

"I'd be lying if I told you we've always been just a Queen and her Lieutenant. For a time...."

She trails off of that sentence, starting with a fresh one instead of speaking the last aloud.

"It's not a healthy relationship. You can't exist in secret forever. It's too hard..." She touches a hand to her chest. "...in here. Time healed her and it healed me. She'll always be my Queen. She'll always be the person I protect over everything else. So you see we're better qualified than you think about this situation."

My voice is a bare whisper in our confines of the elevator.

"It doesn't make it any easier."

She slowly gets to her feet, extending her hand out.

"It's never easy, Elle, but some of us are destined to sacrifice what we love the most."

She pulls this God to her feet.

# 18 CUPID'S INTRODUCTION

Told you it wasn't a nice story. Listen, Gods aren't immune to the lines of Fate and Destiny - Elle even more so, after all they're her parents.

Fate almost imploded when she found out about Elle's "Personal choices" - her words not mine. Her mom is a tough crowd to please, probably why they don't get on. Lucky her Dad is relaxed.

A little about her mom and her job; Fate and her all important lines. They glue our destiny together. You know, keep A from sliding all the way into C when it should be hooking up with B. In fact, what a great analogy. People are like the alphabet. When you put people together, like friends or lovers, you get words. When words link into sentences you get life. And when you put sentences together you get.... Well, sometimes you get garbage, other times an epic novel. You can see how some people and relationships will never work out no matter what.

So, Fate's lines stop chaos from slipping in. She retentively keeps order the heroine of the day because, remember, the balance has to be maintained.

Now, one thing to know, these lines were automated centuries ago; there's not much hands-on meddling anymore. Nope, it's all run from a central computer that fights the battle of choice versus fate and destiny. You make a choice and the computer will re-route you back onto the path you've been assigned. Sorry to burst your bubble but you can fight the tide but it'll always come in.

Either way, Elle dug her nails in and refused to be beaten by the Amazons. She formed a little diversion tactic. Psyche risked everything she had - as she would wanting to make amends - and with the backing of Super Perfect Queen Kreousa they placated the Council members with some flashy, but not dangerous, freebies. You know, a few more investment perks here, a couple of medical insurance upgrades there and some exclusive Vegas condominiums. It was like throwing treats at barking dogs; it shuts them up for a while.

Days turned to weeks and the Heavens got back to running the way they always had. Don't get me wrong, the waters were still stirred up. Lucy continued to be her sneaky self, there was the odd Angel/Amazon fracas, but in the great big scheme of things the creases had been ironed out.

Just over a month had passed since Elle had split with Discord. They'd successfully managed to avoid each other. Still, absence can numb the pain but it can't stop it. As much as we'd like to think differently sometimes two people aren't meant to be together. You can kick and scream, plead and beg all you want but Fate has her fingers in her ears and just isn't listening. Elle and Discord's paths veered away from each other.

A new face came on the horizon for Discord. It was the blonde who saved her ass in the bar: Michelle. Michelle is your classic beach volleyball player: tall, athletic, blonde and tanned. She's a spark of energy who always keeps on a happy slant. That's not to say she's an idiot, she's not. She's clever enough to want to live to the max. I have a lot of respect for that kind of 'tude. She's also great fun at parties and those girls are hard to come by.

Where Michelle is you can normally find Gabrielle. Gab is Michelle's best friend and solid sounding block. Their styles contrast each other very well, as do their looks. Gab's more of a woman's woman: beautiful breasts, gorgeous firm ass and a killer smile. I could eat her up in one sitting.

Back to the story. On the new girl's travels she'd picked something up along the way. An admirer.

# Chapter Eighteen
## 21st June, Year 2 - 21:00
## Warning: Road Narrows

"Y ou may as well be carrying a big sign saying, I heart Discord." Gabrielle stared at the muted TV, not really watching it. She pushed the bowl of chips over to Michelle who took a handful and pushed it back.

"Thank you for your input, Gab. For the record I don't heart her but I do want to..."

She leant over, quickly pressing a finger to Michelle's mouth.

"Stop it right now."

Michelle pursed her lips, kissing her finger.

"Okay, I'll reword for your sensitive self. I'm helping her. She's a friend."

Gabrielle couldn't help snorting a laugh at the excuses she wheeled out at times like these.

"You don't even know her."

Michelle's index finger shot up.

"Yet. And I may not know her as intimately as I'd like but I've been watching her training, and in the gym, and she strides by my office every morning."

Gabrielle looked down at her handful of chips thinking of the calories she'd be ingesting. She pulled a face, emptying them back in the bowl. Only then did she digest Michelle's words.

"Strides? Did she also swashbuckle her way through reception? It's all this Sandra Bullock we're watching. Turn her off."

She glanced over to Michelle whose first answer was a sarcastic smile before crunching down loudly on a potato chip. Gabrielle tutted and snatched the remote, stopping the player.

"How can you like..." She motioned towards the now black screen. "...her, yet be fluttering your eyelashes at Discord?" She held her index fingers up, moving them apart at arms length. "Poles apart."

Michelle shrugged.

"I know Discord's not Sandra Bullock but I like her personality."

Gabrielle thought over that response, her personality?

"The minimal time I've spent with her I've seen more lone contemplation than a roaring party girl. In fact, I can't think of a time I've heard her say more than two long sentences in a row."

Then she noticed Michelle's grinning face. She grabbed a cushion and threw it at the blonde. It was blocked with a forearm.

"Remember my speed and skill, Grasshopper. You must disguise the use of a cushion as a weapon."

Suddenly an electronic song started playing. Gabrielle jumped, glancing around quickly. Michelle grinned, grabbing her bag.

"It's a call for me. Because I'm popular."

Gabrielle sighed.

"And so very modest, too."

Michelle wiggled her eyebrows and held the phone up, staring at the thin sliver of plastic. She smirked, leaning back, her voice dropping an octave as she took the call.

Gabrielle took their glasses out to the kitchen not bothering to hang around while her friend entertained one of the streams of women who passed through not only her mobile but her bedroom, too. She did the dishes, tidied the kitchen and watered the plants. Twenty minutes later she glanced back in to see Michelle finally slipping her phone back into her bag.

Gabrielle resumed where she'd left off, determined to corner her on this subject.

"Back to my comments before another one of your endless women calls."

"They are kind of endless, huh? You'd think I'd run out of them, but here we are, quite a way into eternity, and there are plenty left."

"I've always thought of Discord more as James Dean than Einstein."

Michelle blinked rapidly, her face a picture of confusion.

"What are you talking about? Discord is...." The blonde's smile turned naughty. "Okay, she's not a talker, but that time she walked by in the hall she smelt really nice."

"That's no reason to want to set your crosshairs on someone, Michy. 'I fell for her because she smelt nice.'"

Michelle threw her arms over the back of the couch, stretching her long legs out. Her phone beeped and she picked it up, glancing at the display.

"But you only spoke to her two minutes ago."

"This is a different one."

"Michelle, please concentrate on what I'm saying."

The blonde sighed and put her phone back down.

"I am. You were saying how I don't have a reason to set my crosshairs. See, I am listening. And my answer is this: I dated Jo at the Bank because she smelt nice."

"That wasn't dating. I walked in on you two, remember?"

Michelle grimaced and patted Gabrielle's leg.

"Awkward moment. Alright then, that time in the bar when..."

Gabrielle burst out laughing.

"When you almost killed Discord? I don't like being called at three a.m. because you can't read the back of a bottle of pills. In fact, I can't believe she even wants to know you after that."

"Know me? She thanked me. Picture the scene. I'd just come out of a ball-breaking meeting with the Council over their training needs - retentive a-holes - and I bump into Discord. She mumbles, with a cute blush for someone who's..."

Gabrielle shook her head, knowing that this could end up being so drawn out that Michelle would forget her actual point.

"Michy?"

The blonde rolled her eyes.

"The point, I know. 'Thanks for helping out.'" Michelle wiggled her eyebrows. "It's just a matter of time now. And you know what'll be nice? She's only slightly taller than me. I'm sick of never being on top."

Gabrielle's finger pushed down on Michelle's mouth a moment too late. The blonde raised an eyebrow and kissed it again.

"You just want me to kiss your finger all night, huh?"

"Stop diverting. I need you to try something new for me, Michy. Can you think with your head instead of your hormones?"

"I could but not with her. I want her and I'm going to get her. She makes me think bad thoughts when we're near each other. Bad, bad thoughts."

"And why this sudden fixation, it's not like she's all that new up here?"

"I didn't really notice her before. She's not into the party scene."

Gabrielle ruffled her hair playfully, but her tone was serious.

"Michy, this is problematic. Do you know where she's come from?"

Michelle snorted a laugh.

"Yes, Gab. Discord has come from Earth."

If only she'd engage her brain some of the time, thought Gabrielle.

"I meant where, as in who, has she come from?"

"Can you speak in English? I'm not one of your flaky assistants taking shorthand."

She slapped Michelle's thigh and grabbed her knee, getting a yelp from her friend.

"Who did Discord date before you?"

Michelle raised her eyebrows as she leant across her friend to get a soda.

"Don't you know? You mean I know something before you?"

She refused to rise to the bait of Michelle's gaping mouth.

"No, I know who Discord was dating. I'm seeing if you do."

Michelle slowly raised her finger.

"A test? Aha. I can assert my supremacy because I know the answer to this. Discord was seeing the big boss."

Gabrielle shook her head.

"The scrapes you get in over women."

"At least I get into scrapes. You're going to forget what to do soon. Let me set you up with James. He's your type. Muscled, tall..." Michelle tapped her temple. "...bit stupid."

Gabrielle sighed, deeply.

"None of your diversion tactics. I'll date when I get more than one evening a month to relax. Back to the subject at hand. You know Discord was involved with Elle and you're still going after her? Are you insane? What happens when she finds out what you're up to?"

She watched Michelle study the cushion fringing. She hoped her friend was thinking about the question and not just shooting from the hip like normal. Eventually she banged the cushion with her hand, making Michelle jump.

"A.D.D. playing up again?"

"No, I was hoping if I ignored you you'd go away."

"Don't tell me then. See if I care - which I don't."

Michelle sighed and took a moment.

"Yes you do, you're gagging for info. They've split up. I haven't stolen her from Elle. In fact, I haven't done anything..." Michelle's index finger shot up again. "...yet. Anyway, the way I heard, it was a casual screw."

Gabrielle frowned, putting a hand on Michelle's head.

"The way I heard it, they were serious."

She gently pushed a handful of hair into her face.

Michelle slapped her away, pulling strands out of her mouth with a laugh.

"You heard Samantha was having an affair with Bee last month. I'm not listening to your sources."

Gabrielle cringed. It was a rare instance of gossip forwarding she'd like to forget.

"Moment of madness brought on by excessive paperwork. I retracted as soon as I thought about what I was repeating. Who told you about Elle and Discord?"

Michelle grinned and stared at the bowl of chips for a moment, taking her time to pick one out, making her wait.

Gabrielle poked her.

"Michelle?"

"Okay. Psyche hinted in her usual secretive way. 'She's broken up with someone, don't repeat that.' Which had me thinking, why wouldn't I be able to repeat it? So, I followed it up.... Ah, don't give me those puppy dogs, you were off on your course and, stupidly, didn't leave your mobile on and weren't online, and didn't check your emails - and obviously still haven't."

"I don't like technology so...hey, don't try and get off the subject of you doing your usual and not looking where you're going."

Michelle put a hand to her chest, eyebrows knitting together.

"What are you insinuating?"

Gabrielle rolled her eyes and shook her head.

"That I've seen this a hundred times over. Why don't you try and get Miss Right instead of Miss Right Now?"

"Because Miss Right doesn't exist. You remember setting me up with Eve from Resources? You said she was Miss Right and she turned into a magnet."

Gabrielle thought back to Eve who was an intelligent, cute, athletic woman but her fate had been sealed when she tried to pressurise Michelle into the slightest amount of commitment. Gabrielle just sighed, dragging her hair back.

"A magnet and wanting to see you for more than a month are not the same things."

"Okay, what about Deb from...?"

Michelle clicked her fingers as she tried to remember. Gabrielle grimaced knowing where this was going. She elaborated as the sounding of clicking quickened.

"Transportation."

"Yeah, transportation. You remember Debbie from transportation?"

Gabrielle frowned, trying not to actively encourage any associated memories.

"A bit. Everything's vague."

Michelle waved her hands around as she recalled.

"In the middle of a Vengeance case she appears, asking why I hadn't called her. I had to abort the entire mission and fill in about..." She held up all of her fingers close to Gabrielle's face. "...this many forms afterwards. So, from my experience, I'm staying with Miss Right Now, and that's Discord."

That was the last time she'd seriously tried to set her up. After that she didn't risk it. Michelle always seemed to bring the most possessive side out in women due to her nonchalance.

"Just be careful. Whatever happens, Discord's come out of some kind of thing with Elle. Don't tread on toes."

Michelle put a potato chip on her friend's thigh. Gabrielle blinked, glancing between that chip on her leg and Michelle.

"What are you doing?"

Suddenly a hand slapped the chip hard, shattering it all over her pants.

"Annoying you like you're annoying me."

Gabrielle corralled the pieces into her palm, frowning as her friend continued.

"As for treading on toes, for Head of Intelligence you obviously haven't thought this through. When have you *ever* known Elle to be serious about anyone? Never. Ever. Ev-ver. If she was going to get all gooey-eyed it wouldn't be one of us. Gods have relationships with Gods. It's a simple fact of life for a member of the burgeoning Angel underclass."

"Sometimes you have moments of such intelligence that I wonder if the rest of the time you're just kidding." Gabrielle used a napkin to wipe her pants. "Okay, point taken, but I'm researching this some more."

Michelle smiled, grabbing the napkin, balling it and throwing it into the bin with pinpoint accuracy.

"Of course you are which is why I love you."

Gabrielle paused for a moment. She suddenly had visions of what could happen if Elle found out.

"A woman's scorn is nothing compared to a God's. Promise me you'll back off if Elle tries to melt you."

She ruffled the blonde's hair, dodging the hand trying to slap her away.

"You don't have to worry about your master, Grasshopper. I am experienced in the way of the woman."

"That's what I'm afraid of."

## 19 CUPID'S INTRODUCTION

The lines of Fate kept the barricades up between Elle and our lonesome cowgirl. Elle continued the numbing routine of throwing herself into work. Discord took the other route, throwing herself into anything physical. Dis lived the mantra, 'an exhausted brain doesn't have the energy to be a depressed brain'.

Discord had her admirer on standby. Michelle was unused to having to fight for attention. She'd used her looks well over the years and was never short of lovers. Women fell over themselves for her. Either way, no matter what she tried Discord didn't notice her. You wouldn't think it'd be possible to be oblivious to a beautiful blonde trying to get your attention, but Discord was grieving for her loss and, to be fair, still way out of her depth in the Heavens. But Michelle wasn't giving up. She formed a plan.

## Chapter Nineteen
## 21st July, Year 2 - 15:00
## A Little Preparation

"I'm here to help you out, Michelle. Don't kill me in the process." The tall blonde smiled and ushered John into the gym with a quick shove.

"I'd never hear the end of it from Sam if I damaged her Coochie-Smoochie."

John's face paled at the use of what he thought was a private nickname. Michelle quirked an eyebrow.

"Relax. I won't tell anyone."

"Good!"

"I mean there's no one left to tell, anyway."

John's mouth almost clanked as it hit the floor.

Michelle laughed and added, "Not."

She patted his shoulder.

"Come on, I'm not a blabber,..." She leant down quickly and blew in his ear. "...Coochie-Smoochie."

Her eyes darted about the busy gym, stopping for a moment on a familiar petite brunette wiping her shoulders off with towel. Michelle wracked her brain trying to place her. Suddenly their eyes met and the brunette sauntered over, body moving seductively. With a wink the mystery woman stopped barely a foot away, her voice showing her obvious pleasure at what her eyes were taking in: all of Michelle's body.

"Hey, stranger. Good to see you again."

Michelle leant over, buying some time by planting a kiss on each of the woman's cheeks as her brain tried in vain to remember her name.

"You, too."

The brunette leaned closer as she breathed her question.

"Are you going to Theresa's party this weekend?"

Michelle's eyes roamed over what she could see of the smaller woman's barely clothed body: an extremely small top exposed a glistening chest. Her eyebrows scooted up as she remembered the pool party where she'd seen a lot more of that cleavage - and a few other things.

Michelle smirked.

"I am now."

"Good. It'd be nice to get reacquainted with you."

The brunette backed away slowly, keeping their eyes locked until, with a graceful turn, she sashayed her hips and exited. The door banged shut.

John blinked, astonished.

"How many women do you want?"

Michelle shrugged, getting back to the task at hand. She looked around the room.

"Ah, all of them I guess."

Her mouth broke into a wide grin as she sighted her target. Discord adjusted the cycle seat to her height then ran a hand through thick jet black hair, pushing it back.

Michelle nudged John in the side, getting a girlie, "Ow," in response.

"We're going to cycle."

Two steps forward and she stopped, wondering why she was walking alone. She glanced over her shoulder to her immobile friend. She leant back and grabbed the bottom of his tee shirt, tugging sharply to get his little feet to move.

"Hey, careful."

"What is this allergy you have to exercise equipment?"

His shoulders tensed as he glanced around the gym with a grimace.

"Do you remember the Spanish Inquisition? These machines are based on that time, you know that don't you?"

She slapped the back of his head lightly, not wanting to give him any permanent injury that would mean he'd get to leave. He yelped. Michelle rolled her eyes with a groan.

"You sound like one of those miniature dogs that Artemis has running around her house. You step on one and all the glass within a forty mile radius shatters."

He blinked, raising both eyebrows and crossing his arms over a puffed up chest.

"How do you know what Artemis has at her house?"

Her eyes darted about as she processed a quick lie to cover up the weekend of naughtiness that had left her aching for days after.

"Everyone knows."

She pulled him towards the cycles, hoping to divert his thought process with the shock of imminent exertion. But to no avail. John had his bone and wasn't going to let go easily.

"You slept with Artemis?"

Michelle grabbed his collars, gently pulling him in and off-balance. His eyes widened with the unexpected movement.

"Are you trying to get me frazzled? Hello." She tapped his head with a fingertip. "Artemis - God. Me - Angel. Where are you putting those two together and coming up with sex?"

He grinned and started a repetitive high-pitched yapping sound just like Artemis' annoying little dogs that followed her everywhere. Then a loud beeping from a machine filled the air. It obliterated John's need to be annoying and captured Michelle's attention. She glanced over her shoulder and got a great view of Discord's lean muscled form slipping up a gear on her cycle. Thick strips of muscles in the backs of her legs pulled tight as she powered each downward stroke. The blonde's arms dropped, banging against her thighs lifelessly. A thud and cry made her turn back around. She stared at the heap of man at her feet. She grabbed a handful of his shirt, pretending to help him up but gave him a sharp shake instead.

"What are you doing? You'll draw attention to us."

His voice went decidedly whiney as he peeled her hands away from his top.

"Then don't drop me next time. I'm small and damage easily."

He blinked, eyebrows furrowing as his brain figured something out. He leant to the side, looking directly at the sweat covered back of the familiar shadowy form. He straightened up, mouth dropping in a comical gasp.

"No wonder you didn't name names with your new five minute thing." His body leant to the side again, glancing around his friend then back. "Not her. Please."

Michelle ignored his grimace and shrugged. She walked to the bike next to Discord, got on and pressed the buttons on the computer screen, setting her routine. A hand slapped over the screen.

"We should start off with some rowing. It's better for your upper body."

John patted a firm shoulder. She stared at his hand, raising an eyebrow with a smile. It slid off.

"I thought we discussed cycling, John?"

He stood close, speaking in hushed tones as Discord, oblivious she was the centre of the intense discussion, carried on her routine.

"Do you know who that is?"

Clearly they needed a talk, Michelle realised. She dismounted, walking to the cooler with John close on her heels. Her hands gripped the water bottle, needing something to throttle.

"Yes. Discord Knight. New girl in town."

"But do you know who they say she's seeing?"

Michelle sighed. It was like talking to Gabrielle.

"Yes. Elle."

"You know and you're still trying to put the moves on her girlfriend? Are you mad?"

John's palms started to sweat at the thought of the trouble they could get into.

Michelle corrected.

"Ex-girlfriend."

"Nothing's been confirmed."

Michelle sighed as she watched Discord in the mirror, trying not to listen as he continued.

"So you can't slide a move on Elle's girlfriend or...ex, or whatever you've heard because, let's face it, if you had good contacts you wouldn't be stalking her in the gym. Elle's your boss." He pointed at Discord. "That's her girl. Admire from a long distance but do not touch."

Michelle took a step closer, towering over John's smaller frame and patted his head. She loved him to death but sometimes he was really infuriating.

"I know they're not - not - not together. They haven't been for months."

John wagged a finger.

"You can't buy gossip on those two. This is dangerous territory."

"My sources are always reliable. Listen, I don't want to marry her, I want to - speak to her. Are you going to help me or not?"

He shook his head vehemently, crossing his arms.

"Not."

Michelle shrugged.

"Fine. I'm going to cycle."

Michelle walked back to the cycles and sat down. She glanced at Discord's routine, determined not to let her chance slip by. Her eyes widened as she saw the level: Tour de France, hill climb? That was designed to hurt and nothing else.

She turned at the tutting of the person next to her. John sent her a hard stare as he got on the cycle. He leant over, his words whispered harshly.

"I'm here to prevent you getting in too much trouble. I'm not here to help and I'm not responsible for anything going wrong."

Twenty minutes later the sweat cut a cool path down her back. She glanced across at her neighbour. Discord's intensity was magnetic as she pumped the peddles, not slowing, not losing the rhythm she'd built. Michelle let her eyes roam over rippling muscles as Discord's hands gripped the handlebars tightly, rising up to drive harder. Michelle turned back to her computer screen and frowned at her own progress - or lack of. She blew a drip of sweat off of her top lip, grit her teeth and quickened the pace.

Ten minutes later her thighs were screaming and lungs on fire. She snuck a look at the steady, but still maniacal, pace the other woman was setting. A whimper broke her rhythm. She glanced over at John's beetroot cheeks.

"What are you, a ten year old girl?"

He panted his answer out, practically slumped over the bars.

"No. But I'm not an Amazon either."

His screen started to beep loudly showing he wasn't keeping up with the pace. His eyes went wide as his hands covered it, muffling the sound. Michelle leant over and took his program down two levels. He sighed audibly and mouthed, "Thank you," in a little airy burst.

"I didn't know you were so unfit, Doughboy. I'll get you in a course next week."

His answer panted out.

"Err...no. Thanks."

Michelle turned back to an empty cycle next to her, the pedals still spinning ferociously. She jumped down, glancing around the room, trying to see where her target had gone. Jet black hair shone under the halogens as Discord grabbed a towel and pushed open the door to leave. Before Michelle was halfway across the gym a squeaky voice called out.

"Help!"

She turned to see a tearful John covered in sweat, pulling at his legs. Her shoulders dropped and she walked back and untangled the foot straps from his laces. She stared at the swinging door. Her plan had failed. Discord was gone. She sighed, helping John off of the cycle.

"I can't believe this." She stared down at herself. "You can see me, right? I am here?"

John mopped his wet face with his wet top.

"What ever amount of exercise you're doing it's too much. Lessen it for your own sake."

"Sure thing, Doughboy." She poked his soft stomach a couple of times. "Come on, let's go before you have a heart attack."

She slammed a hand into the door, pushing it open, annoyed that nothing she did was getting this woman's full attention. She stood in the hallway and waited for the panting Girl Scout to catch up. John hobbled out, doubling over, hands on knees as he gulped air into a set of burning lungs.

"Okay, that workout is just hitting me."

The changing room door opened and out stalked Discord, all muscles and tight lean body moving with a fierce grace that made Michelle's mouth drop. Without breaking her stride Discord side-stepped the perplexed blonde and entered the martial arts section. Michelle threw her arms up.

"Is that woman blind?" She grabbed a handful of her top and pulled it to make her point. "Why is she not seeing me?"

John fanned his flushed face with a hand.

"I'm sorry to interrupt the fact that someone hasn't paid you attention, Michelle, but I need to go and vomit my internal organs up." He puffed his cheeks out, backing towards the changing room doors. "I'm leaving you to your prey."

The door opened, smacking him in the back of the head. He swung around holding his skull. Michelle snorted a laugh. Gabrielle smiled and ruffled his hair. He backed away, batting her hand from his now pounding head, almost in tears.

"Are you trying to finish the job?" His hands waved frantically over his body. "I'm only small! I damage easily! Do I need to get that on a tee shirt? You giants don't understand my level of fragility." He held the door open, glaring at Michelle. "I am not helping you get girls again."

She smiled.

"I appreciate you almost killing yourself."

The door banged shut.

Michelle turned to Gabrielle, waving a hand extravagantly at the changing rooms.

"He's a bad luck charm. I thought I was going to have to resuscitate him - and that was just because he went into shock because I made him step foot inside the gym."

Michelle turned and looked through the small glass circle in the door separating Discord and her. Gabrielle stood next to her, sighing at her best friend's persistence.

"Are you still chasing her?"

"Do I look like I'm chasing her?"

"True. It looks more like stalking."

Michelle smiled, watching Discord towelling down.

"I'm not stalking her. I'm lusting her - from all the way out here, through the door and right into her..."

Gabrielle slapped a hand over the blonde's mouth and whispered in her ear.

"Thank you. Why don't you engage your brain for a few minutes, just for me?"

Michelle nodded, the hand still firmly attached to her face.

"For once look at the person you're chasing, Michy."

Michelle split those fingers with her own, staring at her friend.

"What do you think I'm doing?"

Gabrielle tapped the side of Michelle's head, tutting loudly.

"Look at her. Look - look - look with your eyes not your libido."

Michelle turned back, almost pressing her nose against the glass.

"I'm not sure what point you're trying to make. I've looked which is why I want her."

Gabrielle blew in her ear, smiling.

"Michelle?"

The blonde sighed with a grin.

"Okay, I'm look - look - looking."

Her forehead rested against the cold glass. She watched Discord grab the chin up bar and pump lifts out. Her skin glistened with a heavy sheen of sweat. Michelle's eyelashes fluttered in a languishing blink as she devoured the body moving fluidly in front of her. She sighed, misting the glass up.

Gab poked her in the side, shaking her head.

"You need help."

Michelle missed the barb as her mind floated elsewhere.

"Yeah, and I picked John. What a mistake." She turned to her friend. "Can he even walk up a flight of stairs without needing to take a day off?"

Gabrielle rolled her eyes and leant over, her hand squeaking down the small circle of darkened glass as she wiped the remnants of steam away.

She turned Michelle back around.

"Concentrate."

"Relax, mom, give me a chance."

Tanned hands loosened on the bar and Discord dropped heavily to the floor. She sighed, slumping down onto a bench and closed her eyes, her muscles quivering from the exertion she'd put them through.

Michelle glanced around the empty martial arts section before something occurred to her. Her mind ran back to almost every time she'd seen Discord. Walking through her offices - alone. Numerous times in the gym - alone. In the canteen - alone. On the running track - alone. And for the first time she realised how desolate the woman's life really was.

"She's always on her own."

Gabrielle sighed softly, thankful her friend's brain was finally switching itself on.

"Always."

Michelle glanced back in.

"She doesn't look happy, either."

"Exactly, that's not the face of someone who's come from a casual relationship. I'm standing by what I said. Elle and her were serious." Gabrielle ruffled her hair and kissed her cheek before continuing. "So think about your plan? I have a meeting I'm late for."

Michelle grabbed her friend, stopping her from going right way. She needed Gabrielle's unique way of thinking a moment longer.

"I understand what you're saying but I still want her."

"I know, but I don't think she's anyone's to have at the moment. Why don't you try to be her friend? I think she needs one."

A finger pushed onto Michelle's lips, stopping any comments. Gabrielle carried on, reiterating the thoughts in the blonde's mind.

"Like you said, she's always alone. She's come up here and we've all pretty much ignored her. Why don't you at least take her out and show her a good time?"

Michelle pulled the finger away.

"I think that's what I was trying to do."

"Yes, but minus the sex. And I know you want her. One consolation, you have eternity to get her."

The changing room door opened and out walked an olive skinned woman. Michelle wiggled her eyebrows. The woman winked.

"Hey, boss."

"Hey, gorgeous."

The main gym door opened and the woman disappeared in. Gabrielle frowned.

"Doesn't Jen have a boyfriend?"

Michelle snorted her answer.

"Duh, yeah. And she's my assistant, like I'm going to touch her."

"Silly me, I forgot you have some rules." Gabrielle began walking off. "Think about what I've said, okay? I'm late, speak to you later."

Michelle stood and watched Discord, head hung, black tendrils of hair hiding her face. She tutted. That was the thing about Gabrielle, she always brought fantasies back to reality.

She pushed the door open and walked to the water cooler, pretending to get a drink but in reality watching Discord slowly wrapping her knuckles up in tape. She crushed a paper cup in her fist and leant on the bottle for a few seconds, gritting her teeth as she shelved her grand seduction. Gabrielle's words echoed, *"Why don't you try and be her friend? I think she needs one."* She walked over, sitting next to the dark woman she'd spent too long watching. Discord didn't stop taping her knuckles. Michelle took the plunge.

"Why hit a bag when you can try and hit a moving target?"

Discord glared through damp strands of hair.

"I wouldn't want to hurt you."

Michelle smiled angelically.

"I said try and hit a moving target. You'd have to get me first."

Michelle knew a challenge like that wouldn't be refused and she was right. Discord got to her feet and clicked her neck.

"Come on then, Blondey."

Michelle bristled instantly at the use of her most hated nickname. She stood, her voice low and considered.

"My name's not Blondey, it's..."

Discord threw a punch, narrowly missing her face. Michelle jumped, shocked despite herself. The edges of Discord's mouth twitched.

"I know your name. You introduced me to El...." Dark eyes disappeared momentarily in a stuttering blink. "Her Eminence. And you're the signature on the bottom of my combat certificates."

Michelle shifted directions hearing the catch in Discord's words.

"And I saved your ass in the bar when you'd picked a fight with the entire Amazon Nation."

"I said thanks."

"With a blush. Cute."

Discord's face hardened and nostrils flared.

"Not how I remember it."

Michelle grinned as Discord tied her hair back. Her eyes lingered on the firm biceps visible during the action.

"You have a bad memory. It's okay, I forgive you."

Discord glared, obviously not amused. Michelle didn't care, she was ecstatic, she'd finally been noticed.

"Fine. Let's see if you deserve that title - Blondey."

A sudden kick swished through the air, the sole of Discord's sneaker stopping millimetres away from her cheek. Michelle didn't flinch but folded her arms and yawned, happy to bait the woman who'd made her run around after her for weeks.

"What, Head of Combat? I think you have your answer."

Discord threw another punch and Michelle dipped her body, avoiding the move easily. She took the unguarded opening and slapped Discord's stomach hard to prove her point.

"Come on, you'll have to try harder than that to make an impression, Discord. I wrote those tactics you're using."

They sparred for a few minutes, sizing each other up, determining strengths and weaknesses. They were surprisingly well matched, much to Michelle's annoyance. She assumed this was going to be easy, and the realisation she'd actually have to put some work in rattled her plans yet again.

Michelle competently blocked a right hook that came whizzing at her. She held the wrist and twisted it sharply, sending her opponent plummeting down to her knees. The blonde threw the wrist out of her grasp and circled the seething woman.

"Is this all my girls taught you? I'll have a chat with them tomorrow. You should be using your forearms more defensively."

Michelle backed off. Discord got to her feet, rubbing her wrist, her face flushed, eyes intently focused. With surprising speed and agility Discord darted across their gap, taking Michelle by surprise.

"No need," Discord said.

A knee connected with Michelle's ribs with a little too much energy, making her muscles spasm and bones jar. A sharp and heavy force landed between her shoulder blades, sending her down, knees banging painfully on the thinly matted floor. The addition of a sideways push to her shoulder sent her sprawling to the ground. Michelle blinked, staring up at the ceiling, chastising her brain for not paying enough attention. She sat up, annoyed she'd misjudged her opponent.

Two menacing eyes glared at her, closely.

"What's up, Blondey, can't take the pace? Looks like your tactics manual needs another chapter."

Michelle touched a finger to her ribs, wincing. Bruised not broken. Her libido had been knocked clear out of her, that was for sure. She looked up and deliberately smiled, trying to annoy her opponent.

"The test of a real fighter is the ability to take a hard hit and keep coming back, Discord. Didn't you get your laminated wallet inserts when you graduated?"

Discord's tanned face tilted as she blew a strand of hair off of her face, her hands settling nonchalantly on her hips.

"Yeah, but I binned them."

Flipping up, Michelle then dropped back down instantly, ignoring her painfully throbbing knees and leg swept Discord; a move avoided with a graceful jump. When Discord floated to the ground she pivoted and Michelle watched a sneaker coming towards her at a speed she knew was unavoidable. It slammed into the side of her head, making her crash to the floor. Her vision blurred and ears rang as the gym momentarily went hazy.

Enough of Michelle's instincts remained to try and roll out of harm's way but she was stopped by rough hands grasping her wrists tightly, and a sudden weight descending on her ribs. From this angle she couldn't get any leverage and her struggling arms were forced above her head.

She looked up as all of Discord's weight shifted. Eyes as dark as night stared intensely down as a lightly bronzed face lowered, stopping inches away. She felt hot breath on her lips. Her mind raced through every conceivable option she had. After three seconds it stopped. She growled fiercely and ceased struggling.

Michelle expected a harsh taunt but instead the face softened and words whispered.

"I could mix some pills and alcohol before we spar next time to give you an advantage?"

The hands gripping her wrists loosened slightly and she took her opportunity; she wasn't Head of Combat for nothing. Twisting suddenly, she managed to swap their positions so she was on top. After a brief struggle she forced Discord's hands above her head and slowly stretched her body down fully onto the prone woman's form. The heated skin of their arms connected as she stared into the guarded face of a very worthy opponent.

Michelle smiled, squeezing the wrists hard.

"No, I'm doing fine with you just like this."

## 20 CUPID'S INTRODUCTION

It all has to start somewhere, people. Michelle started to spend time with the lonely cowgirl. A few hours in the gym, extra combat proficiency lessons, just sparring. At the heart of it Michelle was torn. She was attracted to Discord but with Gabrielle's sensible voice sounding in her head she also saw the trouble she was in. It was interference to her plans and her conscience.

While all this was going on, my constant, Luce, was just being her perpetually naughty self.

# Chapter Twenty: Lucy
# 30th July, Year 2 - 12:00
# One Day In Those Shoes

I carry my heels because I can't face Choos at this point in my day. I was up all last night pouring over figures, trying to make them add up to what I want. After several millennia you'd think I'd learn it doesn't work that way. They'll add up to whatever they damn well please.

I stop and lean on the doorframe leading into reception, watching Bee work. Her cordless headset means she's watering the plants as she talks.

"F for fire, D for dead, S for soul, seven, two, nine, eight. Sent on the fifth of this month. I didn't get a proof of delivery on it." She slams the watering can down. "I paid for a signature, that's my point."

She wipes the large leaves of her cherished Banana plant with a cloth. Her voice isn't raised but her tone is masterful.

"Because when I pay for one then I have to insist on getting it. Yes I'll hold."

Her rear moves in the tight, but suitably knee length, skirt. She goes to the filing cabinet, still facing away, pulling out a drawer.

"If you have a spare few minutes, Lucy, I have some things you need to sign."

I blink, still not having made a sound. She answers my question before I ask it.

"I can smell your perfume."

I actually laugh out loud, making her turn. I pull a face.

"Am I wearing that much?"

She just shakes her head.

"No, it's one of my favourites." She points to her headset. "I'm still here. That's right. Can you email it and send me a hard copy in the post? Good. Thanks."

She walks over, pulling the headset off. Her fingers take my shoes, replacing them with files.

"Unspecified outbreak killing a few thousand. I was thinking we could sneak this final authorisation form in with some trivial paperwork, that way we've technically let the Heavens know in good time. Up to them if they can't find this one piece of paper in amongst seven hundred others."

I've come to realise that Bee is full of wonderful surprises.

"Naughty. I like it. And that's why you were being so efficient with our courier firm..."

She finishes my sentence.

"Because we need to get proof on the delivery of these seven hundred - and one - pieces of paper. They can't deny getting them."

"Anything that buries Elle in her own paper is a great plan."

My stomach twinges saying it's almost lunchtime. Bee's stoic expression doesn't alter.

"I had your lunch delivered. Smoked salmon and cream cheese bagels, and soda water - no alcohol before three. It's on your desk."

Her raised eyebrows ask if there's anything else. I shake my head. She rests my shoes on the outstretched files I'm carrying.

"What would I do without you, Bee?"

"Fall apart at the seams, most probably. Or never get out of bed, not have any dry cleaned clothes, definitely try and survive on Champagne and sex. Be liquefied by Elle regarding your paperwork..."

I hold a hand up quickly.

"Well, I'm glad we have that sorted."

"One more thing. I need you to authorise a transfer from I.T. to Doom."

She pulls out a booklet of more paper for me to deal with. I scribble something resembling my signature in somewhere resembling the right places.

"He passed all of his exams?"

"With flying colours."

"Then why was he placed in I.T.?"

"Because he passed those exams with flying colours, too."

I hand all the forms back.

"What is he, a genius?"

She drops them into an internal envelope.

"Yup."

"What does a person do with a genius?"

She seals it up and drops the internal envelope into the post bag.

"Not put him in I.T."

Her headset goes back on and she holds a finger over the phone buttons. "Anything else?"

"No."

She gets on with her calls.

"I didn't put him in I.T." I head back to my offices. "It's not my computer system that scans them." I open the door and turn back. "As soon as I saw him I said to put him in Doom. I mean, he's almost seven feet tall and completely odd looking. He's made for that section."

She sighs, covering the mouthpiece with a hand.

"I know, Lucy, and a very good decision it was, too."

I wouldn't give her up for the world but at times she's such a little minx.

I pout in my office. After five minutes of picking through my lunch, which was extremely nice, I'm bored again. Everything is uninspiring at the moment.

I press down on the intercom.

"Bee?"

*"Yes, Lucy?"*

"I don't have anything to do."

*"I have about forty files of things you need to go through so we can proceed with various cases."*

That thought is not as appealing as me sitting here doing nothing for an hour.

"Oh, I forgot about the...things I have in here."

*"I don't let you have things because I never see them again."*

"Ye of little faith."

*"I have faith in your ability to shred even the most important of..."*

I scrunch some paper over the intercom.

"You're breaking up." Scrunch. "Bee? Bee?"

My finger pops off of the button and I fall back in my chair. I swivel around, utilising the pneumatic air system, then go up and down, then recline fully. Three minutes later and I'm bored again. I did not anticipate this level of inactivity when I left Elle and got my own place. I thought it'd be fun. It's not when I can't do what I want.

I flick my chair back up knowing what I'll do. I throw my door open and it bangs loudly. Bee doesn't flinch.

"Have you come for those files?"

Not likely.

"I'm going to do a departmental walk around."

One of her eyebrows rises slowly.

"What departments are you going to visit?"

And we hit my first problem. I'm not overly sure what ones I have.

"Doom."

"They work nights. Any others?"

"I.T."

She puts her pencil down and sits back in her seat.

"And?"

"And...several others. All of them, in fact."

"Sounds like a great idea. Your day is, as always, completely free, so have fun."

She nods and gets back to typing. I perch on the edge of her desk, fiddling with her pencils.

"Aren't you coming with me?"

"I don't have cover for reception."

"But I might get lost and then who would fill your day with naughty?"

She carefully pulls her headset off, her calm exterior still very much in place. I know I'm annoying but if I wasn't it'd throw her.

"Lucy, I have a lot of work to be doing. Hell does not run itself."

I slowly jut my bottom lip out. She sighs.

"How about we just tour one? That way I can...*we* can get back to work so *we're* not too behind?"

I have the attention span of a fly so sounds like a great idea.

"I'll savour you for the full ten minutes, Bee."

She stares at me, her eyes closing for a moment.

"Give me thirty seconds to put reception on standby and I'll be right with you."

And thirty seconds is all it takes her efficient self to bring the area into automated bliss. The lights dim, the computers die to a low hum and the phone lines are for once silenced.

"Where are we going, Bee?"

"How about disease requisition? They have some new strains in development that might be educational."

"Lead the way."

And she does. We walk down corridors I never knew existed, until we arrive at a huge metal door with the smallest of windows in. I get on tiptoes and peer in, expecting to see airtight chemical-suited staff walking around. What I get are two people in garish Hawaiian shirts playing football in a corner, a woman making cocktails, and the whole place lit by fairy lights. It is not quite what I'd imagined.

I look at Bee, then back in, then at Bee. She shrugs.

"It makes them happy and when they're happy they make diseases. Who are we to judge?"

I peer in again and am spotted by a short man in the corner. He squints at me. A football smacks him in the side of the head.

The door slides open. They all stare, paused. The short man holds a hand to his head, the cute blonde clutches a cocktail umbrella and a taller man is unmoving now his projectile has left his hands.

"Afternoon, staff."

Silence. I lean closer to Bee as I watch my frozen disease creators.

"They do know who I am, yes?"

"You're slightly mythical. They're probably surprised."

"They're surprised? I'm the one who's found out her most lethal department is one long party."

Bee walks over to the lights and turns them up fully. She points at me.

"Lucy."

Mouths drop, faces look shocked and finally I get some bowing. This is what being in charge is all about: subservience.

I bend, staring at an impressive looking jar of liquid. I tap it with a nail. "Ebola?"

The woman cracks the lid off as I scamper back to Bee.

"Martini with lemon and lime juice." She hands me a taster glass. "All of the real diseases are..." She points to a thick metal door. "...behind there."

I take a sip. It's very good.

I peer through the thick glass of the door. It looks like a mad scientist's lab: coloured liquids drip through long glass pipes, filtering into rows of vials. Now this is what I expected.

I get a short tour of the diseases in preparation: new ones, modified strains and others that I would never have guessed we'd be wasting our time on, but as the woman explains.

"The biggest killer is influenza. It's simple yet effective. Wipes out thousands in one go and doesn't raise suspicions, so no one really bothers with a cure."

Bee closes the door and I assume the partying resumes. I follow to the elevator, excited about our venture into the unknown. Bee presses the call button then we get in. The doors close with a squeak. Numbers whiz by.

"Did you enjoy that?"

I move closer. She refuses to budge and stares blankly at the doors.

"Not as much as I'd enjoy..."

The doors ping open and she marches out. I keep up.

"Bee, we're always being interrupted."

"Perhaps someone is trying to tell you something?"

I go towards my office and she regains control of reception in that smooth effortless way I've grown to admire.

"There's no one higher up than me, Bee."

I wink and close my door.

## 21 CUPID'S INTRODUCTION

We'd clawed our way into the baking heat of summer. About three months had gone by since their split. Dis and Elle got on with their separate things. Don't read that as felt any different for each other. Moving on isn't that easy. Okay, it is for me but I think I got all the genes with that one.

You remember that little chat that Michelle and the Gabster had? What they said was dead on. Discord did have more than one admirer. Gabrielle was right, ex-wives do find it hard to let go.

## Chapter Twenty-One: Elle
## 7th August, Year 2 - 17:00
## Tell Me Once, Twice...

The Council meeting drags, digging its nails into my day. I've counted the hours, then minutes, now seconds. Time has not been cooperative.

Charity makes a point about the administration of our soul tally and everyone looks for my approval. I glance around at the Council then at the document I should have been reading. My eyes meet Charity's as I flounder. She raises an eyebrow, discretely splaying four fingers. I turn to page four but it doesn't make it any clearer. I give up before I become obvious. These meetings are only ever about one thing: what we're doing to curb Lucy's need to be bad.

"I'm behind Charity's recommendation. I hope you give her the support needed to implement these changes. Lucy needs to be put firmly under lock and key."

Murmurs of approval lower my blood pressure. Even Electra seems satisfied.

Twenty minutes later the meeting finally unhooks itself from my day. People pack their documents up. I try to smile, conversing about obscure points of law and procedure with the stragglers. And then they're gone.

I sit down, sighing at the length of my day. Charity joins me on the sofa, placing a steaming cup of tea in my hands. I rub her arm, she's a lifesaver.

"Where were you during our meeting?"

I sip my tea, not able to answer a question I don't understand. My silence makes her clarify.

"Elle, you weren't paying any attention. You don't even know what my recommendations were, do you?"

I smile.

"I trust you and any proposals you would've made. I am completely confident in your ability to pause Lucy's crusade to annoy us for all eternity."

She chuckles as I lean back in the soft leather.

"But it still doesn't change the fact you were - luckily not noticeably or notably to others - absent."

I know I have to say what was on my mind instead of concentrating on bar graphs and yearly projections. She won't be happy, that's for sure.

"I have a meeting with Dizzy later today."

I concentrate on her face, and the change is instant. Her eyes narrow as she shakes her head.

"Is that wise?"

I shrug, not prepared to lie. It's self defeating to have a best friend you do that with.

"Probably not."

"And Discord is fine with this meeting?"

"She doesn't exactly know I'm taking it."

She stares at me for a second then removes the cup from my hands, putting it on the side table, knowing I'll use it as a distraction if her questions become too painful; the drawbacks of a friend you've grown up with.

"Why are you seeing her, and where are you having the meeting?"

Charity isn't in charge of the Bank for nothing. She can read between any number of lines, picking out relevant information as she goes.

"Her appraisal..."

She interrupts.

"Get someone else to do it."

I shake my head. It's as simple as this: I don't want to.

"I can control myself for half an hour."

She snorts a laugh. As well as reading between the lines, she's very observant.

"You shouldn't have to control yourself, Elle. It's not worth the risk."

Absence has made every part of me yearn for Dizzy, and no matter how much I understand the need for us to be apart, my heart is having none of it.

Charity reiterates her other question.

"Where?"

I steel myself for her reaction because any comments about this choice are well deserved.

"In my offices downstairs."

She cries out in desperation. I stare at the sofa, unwilling to watch her disappointment grow anymore. I wait for the barrage.

"Since when have you conducted appraisals in your private offices? In fact, since when have you conducted appraisals? There's no reason for you to be doing this. Unless..."

My words come out angrily.

"I want to speak to her. I'm an adult and I know what I'm doing."

The leather of the sofa shifts. She stands, gathering her files. I rise, shocked at the sudden end to our talk.

"That's it? You're not going to chastise me?"

Her head shakes as she puts her suit jacket back on. She opens her attaché case, slipping files in.

"Charity, I'm sorry for snapping."

Her case clicks shut and she heads towards the door. I follow, my voice raising before she manages to open it. I don't want everyone being privy to my business. That's happened enough lately.

"Please don't be angry with me. I can't help it."

I stand in the middle of my almost empty office in my definitely empty life feeling incredibly alone.

"I miss her so desperately."

Her hand stops on the door handle. She puts her case down and walks over, pulling me into a hug. I rest my head on her shoulder.

"I see her every day: passing in the halls, in the grounds, the training rooms. Her name's in the files I work on, she's mentioned in our meetings. She's everywhere and she's nowhere."

She massages my neck gently.

"I know."

Charity's my support when the world gets too tough. She's my whispering confidant, the person who's never selfish with her advice; it always comes from a pure place. But as much as I know I should listen to her regarding Dizzy, my heart is blocking my head.

Her quiet tones soothe me.

"You have to move on with your life, Elle. You can't interfere with Discord and Michelle, no matter what your feelings are."

A cold mist sinks down, making my skin prickle. I tense, pulling back.

"What do you mean?"

A flicker of surprise is her first reaction. Her eyes search mine for a minute before she speaks.

"I thought you knew." She sighs heavily. "I thought that was why you and..."

"That was once."

She nods, unimpressed.

"Once too many. Anyway, I heard the other day from someone in the training department. I mean, it could be a rumour. You know what this place is like, you only have to speak to someone twice and you're married."

"What? What did you hear?"

Her expression turns as serious as I'm sure mine looks. I steel myself, my heart beating wildly, willing her not to say...

"Discord and Michelle are seeing each other."

...what she has.

My brain repeats her words like a nauseating mantra.

"That's why I didn't understand your timing. I thought you were trying to stop it from happening." She pauses before speaking softly. "I thought you knew."

I should be happy for them, for the fact she's found someone else.

"It could be idle gossip, Elle."

Impossible feelings of jealousy rain down, and Charity grabbing at straws on my behalf doesn't make me feel better either. I put my best face on, the one that's lived with me since the break up, and hold tears back as Discord slips away again.

"I was shocked. I'll be okay."

I act for my audience of one, hoping for a standing ovation at the end of my performance. I continue, smiling a little, not wanting to overdo it.

"Perhaps this is for the best for everyone concerned."

Charity smiles contritely, cupping my cheek with her hand.

"You're good but I've known you too long. Your eyes are always your downfall, Elle."

My act gets neither the ovation nor the single red rose I wanted. Not wishing for an encore I leave my lies.

"I'm not okay with..." Her name sticks in my throat noticeably. "...Michelle, but I'll cope with it."

I think carefully about my next words. It may be the right thing to do but when has that ever made it easy?

"I'll pass Dizzy's appraisal onto someone else. I'll feign a busy schedule."

Charity tucks my hair behind my ear, keeping the errant in place.

"It's for the best, Elle."

However, that sentence doesn't makes it hurt any less.

## 22 CUPID'S INTRODUCTION

Elle didn't magic up any more reasons to see the lonesome cowgirl. Charity's advice was sinking into that head of hers.

Time went by as it always does. Lucy carried on being a bad kitty, Electra was clawing the furniture every time Elle's back was turned, and Earth, in general, was turning itself into a giant litter tray. So nothing new.

Back to the story. Now, the Heavens hadn't embraced Discord as well as it should. In fact it'd kicked her when she was down, so it wasn't surprising she no longer made the effort with anyone. She did her job, blasted her body in the gym then went home alone to eat and sleep. The only person she hung with was Michelle. Discord shouldn't have been living that way, it wasn't right. But like I've said before, right has a way of clawing its way out and screaming for attention.

Discord might have been misunderstood by almost everyone, but Michelle saw the lost little girl inside crying out for help.

## Chapter Twenty-Two: **Discord**
## **26th August, Year 2 - 19:00**
## **In The Beginning There Was Light**

I flick the channel over, hitting another chat show. I'm convinced no one planet can have so many disturbed people. I flick the channel again: infomercial. I change it again: how finding God ruined my life. That makes me turn the set off. TV should take you away from reality not throw you back into it. I open a magazine then shut it. Nothing here is helping take my mind off what it needs to forget. I pull some clothes on and head to the gym.

If there's one good thing about a bad split it's the amount of muscle you can develop. I've spent the majority of the last three months here cycling until my legs burnt, rowing until my shoulders couldn't move and turning myself into a slab of solid firmness. Of course, muscle doesn't make heartbreak easier to deal with, but it does make an exhausted sleep easier to achieve.

Out of the corner of my eye I see a familiar blonde approaching, reminding me of the sparring I've also been doing. Michelle's made my time working out less lonely. I sit on one of the benches around the outside of the room, watching her talking with a catlike brunette; all arched eyebrows and silky hair.

I've never been okay with people trying too hard to be my friend. There's always a reason behind everything. Now, that reason may not make much sense to anyone else but there always is one. Blondey here's no different. First off I thought Elle sent her to keep me out of trouble. But as the weeks went by I realized that wasn't the case. Elle doesn't even want to speak to me let alone send someone to help. Then I thought she wanted the low down on what went on, but she didn't ask any questions, never pried. Anyway, I don't think she's a gossip. The Amazons didn't send her. She proved that by saving me in the bar.

Michelle hugs the brunette, getting her hair ruffled in reply.

This leads me to my last conclusion. Blondey is very touchy-feely, so I thought she had a crush. But with me she doesn't over step the mark. There's been no pass or hint of one coming. A month of one on one fighting has given her enough opportunities.

I tape my knuckles up, wrapping the sticky fabric around tightly.

So I'm left with one conclusion: she's doing it to be my friend. On Earth I would have been suspicious. After what I've seen of here, I still am.

"Hey, ready to learn from a master?"

I glance up long legs, over a firm and muscled torso, pausing on ample breasts and up to Blondey's face - and wiggling eyebrows. I grunt my reply. If anything's going to be a distraction it'll be this woman. Ethically it may not be the best reason to get to know someone but when every moment of my day is filled beating myself up over Elle leaving then I'll take what I can to function, because I haven't been doing that of late. I've retreated into myself, something I thought I'd grown out of. I spent my childhood alone and I'm not going back there.

"Not feeling talkative?"

One reason she's still here is the fact, when I want, I can be silent around her. It scares everyone else, but she takes it in her stride.

She smiles, and for a second the blonde hair triggers a memory. I feel a terrible pang in my chest. It comes without warning and twists around inside, reminding me of what I've lost. I wrap the tape around my hands as tightly as I can.

I get up, grab my water bottle and go over to the body bag. I stare at it. There's a lot to be said about the joys of beating the Hell out of an inanimate object in the name of exercise, but after a while - I give the bag a small punch - it just gets boring. I let my arms fall to my sides. Like now.

A blonde head pokes around the bag, throwing a questioning look as to why I haven't landed any punches. She gets the joy of words out of me.

"Lucky I wasn't weighing up my next move."

I could've taken her head off.

"Lucky I'm quicker than you think."

Is her cocky answer.

I turn around, smiling to myself. She's a jackass.

I walk towards the exit.

"Should I wait here and play with myself?"

I turn around and stare at her. Her eyebrows furrow, but her mouth twists into a disarming smile.

"That came out wrong, sorry."

Yeah, she'll be a distraction. I turn and shout over my shoulder.

"I'm going to the bar. Only come if you can handle your drink."

I don't turn around. I have a feeling she'll be with me. I hear her jogging over. I was right.

We make our way to a corner booth. I'm ready to forget about Elle the adult way - with the aid of a bottle of Bourbon. I slide into the booth and lick my index and middle finger putting out three of the five candles on our table; I'm not in the mood for bright lights.

Blondey doesn't sit. She holds a hand up, telling me to wait. As I had no intention of moving I do just that.

I break a handful of toothpicks while I think about things I shouldn't. Miniature destruction is as valuable a tool as smashing the bar up. Two benefits: it lessens the amount of tidying up you have to do afterwards, and you don't get a beating that takes a week to mend. Anyway, I doubt this bar could take two instances of me acting like an ass.

A bottle of Bourbon lands in the middle of the table making the candles rock, the lights flicker. She slides in opposite and pushes a glass over. Her finger taps the bottle.

"I assumed."

The moment seems to demand I say at least one word.

"Thanks."

"Here's to welcoming you into the Heavens, Discord."

She pours the golden liquid out, a good triple in each glass, reminding me I still have company to act human in front of.

I can't help but get my word count up.

"It's been real welcoming so far."

I clink our glasses, emptying mine in one swift movement. I slam it down as my throat burns.

"Don't judge us too harshly. We're not all like the Amazons."

I stay silent. She downs her drink quickly, pouring us both another.

A quarter of a bottle later and I'm not feeling so bad. Elle hasn't miraculously appeared saying she was wrong to leave me, but after a lot of alcohol at least things don't seem so dark anymore. I've spent too long under a rain cloud.

"Hey, Blondey..."

She throws a hand up, making me stop. She's not drunk; I was right, she can hold her liquor. But she's not sober either.

"Okay, I've let it slide so it's partially my fault, but I hate it when you call me Blondey. My name's Michelle. Call me that or Mich, even 'Chelle, whatever, but not Blondey. Deal?"

Her sentence demands an answer. I shrug mine and even throw a word in for good measure.

"Sure."

I look into my glass as the silence stretches. My drunkenness starts to turn into something else as I remember where I used to be a little while ago. I squeeze my eyes shut. I don't like causing myself pain but getting a broken heart isn't something I'm used to. I'm not sure how to mend it.

A hand takes hold of mine for a second. My eyes flick open, not used to being touched.

"I'm sorry for what happened between you and Elle."

The name takes me by surprise. My brain kicks back in gear. What gear, I'm not sure.

"Yeah, well...."

A nagging thought slaps me back into consciousness.

"How did you know? Am I the latest gossip?"

Her hand covers mine again. She squeezes. She's warm and her fingers softer than I expected for a woman who trains as much as she does.

"There's no gossip. Psyche kind of hinted in the bar that time so I put two and two together."

I pull my hand away.

"Psyche and her big mouth, huh?"

"She's why you didn't end up in the brig. She's okay. Maybe a bit quirky, but those girls are in a world of their own, literally."

"I guess."

"I meant what I said. I'm sorry if you haven't had the best time here so far."

I look anywhere but at her. The drink isn't helping my usually solid reactions but I still have enough of an I.Q. not to snap.

"Can't be helped, Mich."

She's the first person who's said sorry for what happened. Not that it's her fault, but it always helps when a problem's recognized.

Her expression softens and she lifts her glass, saluting me.

"I'm not Blondey anymore. Now that deserves a toast. To better times?"

I stare at my glass for a moment then chink it with hers.

"Yeah, to better times."

The night goes quickly. Because of the drink, her, or a combination of both, I don't know. I stare down into my blurry glass. What I do know is I'm going to feel bad tomorrow morning and so is she. Those are constants that can be relied on, and for that I'm glad. I need some stability no matter what it is.

What happened next I'm not sure about. What I do know is, it's morning and I'm not in my own bed. The constant I thought my hangover would be, is here. I feel very, very ill. I sit up and then lie back down as my head protests.

A door opens, making me attempt to get vertical again. I manage it, for now. Mich carries a tray over and puts it on the empty side of the bed. I stare at the fruit juice and toast and fight the urge to tell her where she can put them.

She sounds unnaturally chirpy.

"Morning. You slept well. Have some toast and juice. You'll feel like death until you eat."

Shaking my head slightly I close my eyes, trying to put an end to the start of a spinning room and the wave of nausea greeting me.

"Thanks, but no."

The bed moves as she sits. The timing isn't welcome. I wonder what the odds are of me getting back to sleep feeling the way I do. I open my eyes realizing they're next to none.

She holds a piece of toast up. I don't argue; I only have energy for important battles now. I take it and manage a bite, forcing myself to swallow and not spit it out on her blanket. Satisfied she moves on to the glass of acid she expects me to drink. I draw my line.

"Mich. My brain is being thrown around my skull. Let me lie back down and die."

My hand is pried off the blanket and opened. I look down to see two white pills in my palm. They stare back waving flags and singing hymns. Praise medication. I make her feel better and knock them back with some fruity acid. I lie back, blocking the painful light with an arm.

My dazed brain finally realises it needs to clarify a few things. Simple deduction says we're at hers. I would like to know how we got here. Chunks of missing time are never good.

"This bed isn't mine. Did I do anything I should apologise for?"

Her laugh is quiet, probably on purpose due to my condition.

"It's my spare bed. You behaved like a drunk person should."

I pull my arm off from shielding my poor eyes, making the effort to look at her, the thought of the pills kicking in already making me feel better.

"But did I do anything I should say sorry for?"

She smiles, shaking her head.

"Nothing I want you to apologise for, no. I don't mind it a little bit rough, anyway."

I stare at her for a moment, forgetting about my nausea, throbbing skull and shipwrecked stomach. My brain begins to hurt from the effort of remembering.

"Rough? With what?"

She taps a finger gently on my arm.

"With me."

I stare at her and then down at me, suddenly aware under this blanket I'm naked. I blow a long breath out.

She slaps my arm, laughing.

"I'm kidding. We came back here and you went to bed. The end."

My sigh wasn't meant to be audible but when faced with a complete blank of a situation not every reaction can be controlled.

"Get some sleep."

I don't remember her leaving. I wake up alone, the room not as bright as before. She must have been back because a glass of water and two more pills are on the bedside table. I take them even though my head feels better - for now.

I drag my protesting body up, only then remembering I'm naked. A fluffy towel, fresh black tee and pair of jeans sit on a chair. I check the sizes; both mine. Then I realize these are mine. I recognise a nick in the tee's hem I made when I caught it.

My aching brain is uncooperative so that mystery is left, and I dress slowly, wishing I could've showered first to try and blast my brain back into motion.

The door opens and she pops her head around. She looks me up and down and answers the question I wasn't going to ask. Still, nice to know.

"I got them from your office. Hope you don't mind."

Compared to staying in clothes smelling of liquor, I'll forgive her. I shake my head, feeling better my pounding skull hasn't resurfaced.

Michelle reads my mind again.

"The shower is across the hall. Come down when you're finished. Dinner will be ready then."

I now understand the term, freshen up. After standing under the spray for ten minutes I feel a hundred times better. I rinse my mouth with the strongest mouthwash I've ever used. I bare my teeth in the mirror, checking it hasn't disintegrated them.

I audibly sigh when I put my fresh body in my fresh clothes. There's nothing worse than having a hangover hanging all over. Liquor is only fun for the small amount of time you're drinking it.

I walk down stairs I don't remember walking up. The lounge is empty.

I'm a curious girl, I like looking and touching things, I'm quite tactile. I pick up a flashy remote control wondering what it's for.

"That was quick."

I jump, unceremoniously dropping it noisily on the floor.

"Sorry."

She walks over, scooping it up, throwing it on a chair.

"Feeling better?"

I nod as I try to look comfortable standing in the middle of her room. Fact is I'm not. I feel sort of stupid for getting drunk and sleeping here.

"Gone back to being monosyllabic? I enjoyed getting two sentences at a time out of you last night."

Mich has extremely limited experience of what I'm really like. First I die, then I come to the Heavens as an Angel, then have a disastrous love affair with my boss, and now I have the edges of a hangover making me act and feel like a prehistoric monster. The real me hasn't had a chance up here - I'll add, yet, I'm trying to be hopeful.

I jam my hands in my back pockets, shrugging. She smiles and waves for me to follow her.

"Dinner is pasta and a salad. It's light and it'll make you feel better."

A fragile mind and body means I don't argue.

I sit down at a solid wooden table as she serves the food. My stomach rumbles in time to say the meal is welcome and won't be coming back up.

I have to ask. I'll die of curiosity if I don't.

"Are you a seasoned drinker..." A polite term for booze-hound. "...or is there a scientific reason you don't feel as bad as me?"

She grins, putting a little bit of everything on my plate.

"I drank a glass of water with every one of Bourbon, then took two vitamin C pills about three hours after...you know, we got back."

I admire people like her, having either an answer or movement for everything. She's not awkward like me or lost for words. Everything she does is smooth and seamless.

She taps her finger on the table.

"Is it dead yet?"

I glance up, no idea what she's talking about. She reaches over, carefully pulling the paper napkin I've been ripping up out of my fingers.

"Sorry."

I guess it's best if I eat and don't say or do anything else.

We don't eat in silence. She's a talker. She fills the space I'm leaving. It's nice to listen and not have to answer. I learn about her job. I knew she was in charge of training but now I get how complex it is. As she's telling me about some of the teaching they do, I wonder when my last proper meal was. I've been surviving on chips, dips and most other things either rhyming with that or having one syllable.

"What about you?"

I look up as I realise her question needs an answer. I stare into lively eyes and do my usual and shrug, then go back to staring at what's left of my food - which isn't much. As the silence continues I know I can't go on like this. As bad as I feel I have to start living again. I look back up at her happy face. I think Michelle will be good for me.

"Well...."

I start, not really knowing how to.

Her head rests in her palm, an elbow leaning on the table as she watches me. I play with a tomato on my plate.

"So far I've trashed a bar, pissed off most of the Amazons and alienated myself from nearly everyone else. I think I'm top ten on the most hated list up here."

Sometimes, though, silence is best.

"I don't hate you."

It's a good skill to have, dragging sentences back from dark depths.

"Thanks, but you don't know me that well."

You'd think I'd know when to shut up, especially when feeling sorry for myself is high on the agenda.

Her smile seems genuine.

"I think I know you a little more than you realise. I've been around for a long time. I've met a lot of people along the way. I'm more rounded than you think."

I look at her looking at me, and nod. So much up here isn't how I expected it to be.

I go back to concentrating on the tomato on my plate. Like me it's looking a little worse for wear. I decide to give it a break, hoping for some sort of cosmic payback, that maybe someone up high will give me a break? I then realise I am up high and no one's likely to be giving me any help any time soon. That's when it all hits home: the loneliness of being here, the fact that no matter what I do I'll always be the outsider or the woman who tried to lead Elle astray, that I've made a mess of things and I still have eternity to go. The realisation hits me like a slap in the face.

Mich proves she was right. She does know me better than I thought.

"You need to stop thinking. Stay here tonight. I can talk, you can listen."

Pity isn't one of my favourite emotions, not when it's being thrown in my direction. I shake my head.

"I'll be okay. I should go."

I stand up quickly, wishing I hadn't been so hasty as my headache restarts its subtle pounding. I'm not at my best when I don't have enough sleep, and I'm worse still when it's due to drinking.

"Thanks for the food and letting me stay."

Even though my tone sounds flat, I mean it. Last night was a nice break from my now usual brooding.

She leans back on her chair, rocking on two legs. Her smile stops me. Literally, as I'm about to take a step away from the table, I stop.

"It's nice to be able to cook for someone instead of defrosting a plastic tray in the microwave. You don't have to go. I get bored quickly on my own." She wiggles her fingers. "Idle hands."

Her genuineness is enviable.

I don't know how, but in the few seconds I stand there ready to bolt back to my place she changes my mind. It's the combination of small talk, hospitality and one more thing, her assumptions about me wanting to stay that keep me here. It's taken for granted that I like being on my own. It's true some of the time, but not all. I've found out since I've been here loneliness can be a killer.

I sit and watch her watching TV. She gives an intermittent comic commentary on the shows. In its own way it's fascinating, the way different people can see different things. It proves everyone has their own reality. Her chattiness even gets some intelligent responses from me, not morose or depressed ones like I've been giving over the past few months. She's managed a feat last night I didn't think possible. She's made me see a light at the end of the tunnel. Last night I thought I could find a good time in the bottom of a bottle of booze. Now I see how wrong that was.

I've been wondering about Michelle ever since I met her, about what category she fits into and I think that was the problem. She doesn't.

I sit back, get comfortable and watch the rest of the show.

## 23 CUPID'S INTRODUCTION

Dis stayed, chilled out and had, by the new girl's standards, a good time. Michelle kept well clear of laying the moves on that night. That spare bedroom got some solitary use. That's not to say Michelle wasn't still in lust. Sometimes it's hard to stop what you know will happen eventually. Or rather, what's already happened. Still, gotta give her points for trying to be good.

## Chapter Twenty-Three: Michelle
## 28th August, Year 2 - 21:00
## Deny Me Thrice

"**D**id she stay over?"
I can't help but smirk as I jump on my bed, grabbing a pillow and getting comfortable.
"How do you know about that?"
Gab wiggles an arched eyebrow and slides down next to me, trying to steal my space.
"I know everything, I'm Head of Intelligence."
I snort a laugh, pushing her legs away with my feet, protecting my side.
"Oh, okay. But really, how did you know?"
"John and Sam were in the bar. They saw you two leave."
"Gossip network."
Gab nods her head, smiling.
"Stop avoiding. Did she stay? I've been hanging for ever."
I dig a coin out of my pocket then flip it in the air. Heads I tell the truth, tails I don't. I watch it turning. I should be rooting for one or the other but they both have pros and cons. It lands softly in my palm and I stare at my fate. Heads. Who am I to argue? I drop the coin on my side table.
"Yes she stayed. She was drunk."
She stretches out like a cat. I wait, knowing she hasn't finished. Gabrielle needs time to consider things. It's a thoroughness that's saved me from enough scrapes in work and my private life.

"Where did she sleep?"

She raises an eyebrow, asking me a different question to the one she said aloud. I deliberate telling her a load of rubbish but she has an uncanny knack of knowing when I'm lying. Although, she should know me well enough to word her questions better, especially if she doesn't want to be here all night.

"In bed."

She does her usual and throws a pillow my way. Gab loves to show me displays of her mini temper. It's not grown up yet, it's still all small and girlie.

"You know what I mean, Michy. Your bed?"

I ignore her eyes boring into me.

During the time we've know each other our roles have become defined. She's the questioner and I'm the magician. She searches for the truth and I hide my rabbits in hats.

"No, the spare bed."

Her face falls when she thinks there's no absolute to find. I expected better, so I throw her a bone.

"The same one I slept in for part of the night."

Her eyes close in a long blink as she digests my titbit and thinks.

"Tell me everything. Don't leave a thing out."

I stay quiet, not sure I'm ready to deal with Gab's sensible line of questioning.

"Michy, don't be a tease."

I'm not sure I'm ready to deal with the constant berating of my silence either. Once I've started her she's like a spinning top, she'll go for a long time.

I roll over and prop myself up, looking down at her as she waits expectantly. I make a snap decision, one that sharing will be a positive thing. It'll help explain why I didn't let Discord in on some of the more pertinent facts - like sleeping together.

I play with her shirt collar as I think of how to word it, whether to dive right in or skim around the outside. I go for broke.

"Long and short, we were at the bar and got drunk. We went back to mine. We had sex. Then we had sex again. Then we went to sleep."

She holds onto my fingers, stopping them playing with her shirt. Her expressive eyebrow asks me what I'm leaving out. I clarify for her inquisitive mind.

"Oh, she doesn't remember about the 'us having sex' bit."

She gives my fingers a reactionary squeeze. Her mouth falls open and other eyebrow joins the first, up high.

"What do you mean she doesn't remember?"

I stare at her as if she's stupid.

"I mean, she doesn't remember. I woke up before her and had a shower and stuff."

She whistles out of tune.

"So much for our little talk on being her friend. Start from the beginning. What happened?"

I fall down on the bed, rolling onto my back. Gab, like the clumsy little cat she is, follows, mirroring the pose I had over her a moment ago. I throw my arms out to the sides, staring at my ceiling. If she's good for one thing it's hearing a story out to the end and giving an educated and thought-out verdict.

I get started on my tale of idiocy.

"We went for a drink - her idea not mine. To get to the point...."

Her hand slaps my shoulder.

"No, don't get to the point. Step by step, please. You're at the bar getting friendly, according to John and Sam."

"Okay, we talked in the bar. I mentioned Elle to gauge the reaction and she didn't fall apart, but she wasn't blasé either. Jury's still out."

"You always have to learn the hard way, Michy."

I kiss her cheek.

"It stays in my head better that way. So..."

"Wait, what did you talk about?"

"This is why my stories always take an entire night. We talked about work, life, stuff - although it was mainly me talking. You know what I'm like. It's a shame she's so quiet because when she does speak she's actually interesting. So, we were both pretty drunk and ended up at mine."

Gab butts in, clarifying for her decision on the morality of my tale.

"Your place by design or by convenience?"

"Why do you need so many details? Convenience. I started out with a master plan, but..." This is one hundred percent true. "...you and your subconscious implants. You were right. She's had a shitty time up here. I realised early on I wasn't going to put a move on her."

She rolls her eyes.

"And yet you didn't stick to it for very long."

"Listen!"

She smirks and motions for me to continue, sucking all the information up into her supercomputer brain.

"I introduced her to the spare bed. She was standing in the middle of the room and the drink was wearing off of me." I have a great sobering up rate. Of course, makes drinking to excess and staying drunk hard but it has a high point: limited hangover. "She looked so lost. I remembered your saying: even the toughest of us need to be hugged."

I get a little pat on the shoulder telling me well done.

"So I hugged her. I don't know what happened but it had a lot to do with the drink, being close and the fact I find her so damn attractive. Anyway, we started kissing."

She almost salivates at the thought of this new development. Gab's supercomputer tots it all up, spewing a question out.

"Did you kiss her?"

I redefine those parameters.

"Actually, no. I'm not into taking advantage. She kissed me first. I'm guilt free. I swear, I wasn't planning anything. Well, I was to begin with but all I could hear was your voice telling me off."

Her hand taps me, trying to get more information like I'm a Morse code machine. Tell - me - more - now, is what it says.

"My influence is finally paying off. What next? Was it good?"

I oblige, I'm not cruel. A warm feeling spreads through me as I close my eyes. If I'm going to have to spill the details I'm going to have fun remembering them.

"Good? It was..." I have to take a breath so my next sentence makes sense and isn't a jumble of vowels. "...better than good. She was very competent handling my body."

Gab grabs my collars, softly shaking me.

"Details."

I open my eyes, gently pushing her off. She has very little patience sometimes.

"I let her fuck me."

I wait for this one to hit. Her mouth forms an almost perfect circle as she blows a long breath out.

"You did what? You never let anyone do that. You'll have to marry her. She's obviously the one."

Fucking is a deeply personal act. To have someone inside me is intimacy at its highest level. Not everyone, and no one on a first screw, has got to do that. Even I don't understand why I let her. Temporary hormonal insanity perhaps? Whatever the reason, it felt damn good.

"Do you ever listen to a thing I say? I'm not looking for the one. Anyway, it'd hardly be a woman who didn't even remember we had sex."

She glances away now there's enough information for her chip to begin processing. I ready myself for a barrage of questioning. This is to quantify and confirm her final inference. It also gives me a fresh view on things I may not have thought about so I'm all for it. Gabrielle is fantastically predictable.

"Do you think she really forgot or did she not want to remember?"

I can see Dis' face after I said I was joking: complete relief.

"No, she doesn't know. Her face was horrified when she thought we'd had sex."

Gab pauses, shunting information from one side of her brain to the next. She starts her next run at info harvesting.

"How did that make you feel? Used? Cheap?"

I push my finger to her lips. She's beginning to sound like a therapist.

"Not until you mentioned it, no. I don't mull over things in my head, you know that. After I figured out she didn't remember I left her sleeping and answered my e-mails. Then I made dinner and we spent the night talking. She stayed again and took the spare bedroom. Alone."

She stares at me incredulously, picking one part of my statements out, laughing to punctuate the end of her sentence.

"You cooked?"

It isn't the norm, no, but then nothing during that night was. I went with the odd flow.

"Yup. Pasta with fresh pesto, and a salad."

"Wow. You made dinner? You never cook. You must really like this woman."

She grins. I slap her head.

"No. I made it because I really like fresh pesto."

Her stare is intense. Her next statement shows the downside of having a perceptive best friend.

"It's okay to like her, even a little bit, just as friends or whatever. It's also okay to have made her pesto. It's not a move that's legally binding, Michy. She can't make you pay alimony."

I hate it when she becomes the all knowing all seeing Gab. She's right, I have commitment issues. Not serious ones, playful ones. Anyway, a fling shouldn't interfere with those. One screw isn't like getting married.

She prods me in the side.

"You've skimmed over almost every juicy detail."

I try to remember what part I was at.

"So, we had urgent, raw, down and dirty sex. The gripping kind you end up fantasizing over when you get bored. She did everything right. That could be why I let her fuck me because she's my fantasy: silent, dark stranger, powerful attraction mixed with some alcohol and thrown in a bed and allowed to ravage the tall and athletic blonde."

Never underestimate the power of the Head of intelligence gathering. She commands the small details. She interrupts.

"Bruises, scratches?"

"None. Well, not on me." A fragment of memory unfolds itself in my head. "Oh, shit."

And it could seriously complicate things. I sit up, a little panicked.

"I scratched her back."

The moment demanded something to counteract the serious pleasure she was giving me. She sits up, puzzled.

"So?"

Intelligence gathering may be her forte but assimilating it takes a while.

"She doesn't remember why I would've had access to scratch it."

She taps my temple, realising what I do. Dis doesn't think we had sex and if that's the case what happens when she sees all of *my* scratches down *her* back?

"Michy, she's going to find those scratches and come callin'." She chuckles. "She really did...you know, do that, didn't she? And trying to keep it from me, too. Shame on you."

She may have advised me on the stupidity of getting it on with Dis, however, when faced with all the salacious details she's all for it.

"I haven't changed my rules about penetration. I was taken by surprise that I got her. I wasn't planning it. She literally fell in my lap - stop laughing. And you know what, quit hounding me and get me a plan."

Because I need a good one, too.

She considers my predicament, asking her first question.

"Is she only sleeping with you?"

I shrug.

"How am I supposed to know? Anyway, we're not sleeping together. We slept together."

She rolls her eyes but it's a serious point, we're not. We've been intimate but she's not my girlfriend. I haven't had one of those in way too many years.

"Okay, yes of course, mustn't use words associated with commitment. My point is, can anyone else be blamed for the scratches?"

I bite a nail as I think. I point a piece of obvious info out to her.

"You're Head of Intelligence. You find out."

She slowly nods, getting quicker as a plan forms in her head.

"I know who to ask."

She flips off of the bed and picks her bag up, rummaging around, getting the shiny high-tech phone/computer/microwave I got her, out.

"I'm calling a friend."

She puts her finger to her lips telling me to be quiet. I fall back on the bed as she talks. I close my eyes and think about last night. Discord Knight was a nice surprise. Of course, the lack of memory was another kind of surprise but I'm not looking on the downside. That type of behaviour is for people who insist on staying permanently depressed. I have all of eternity in front of me. I'm not living it on Prozac.

Gab flips her phone shut. I prop myself up on my elbows. She looks pleased with her call.

"She's single. No encounters apart from you know who. I'm reiterating, Elle will kill you when she finds out about this. But I'm not going to lecture. Let's move on to finding a plan now we've got no one to blame."

She stares at me so intensely I wonder if she's trying to transmit some wondrous answer to all our worries. She shrugs, at a loss. Obviously no surprise idea came to mind then.

Her face brightens.

"Tell her the truth."

Sometimes Gab has the stupidest ideas ever.

"Sure, what a great...."

I stop talking as I actually think about it. It seemed like a bad idea when I was caught in the headlights of the Discord Express with no way of getting off the tracks, but in the cold light of day, given ten seconds to think? There's no reason not to tell.

"Okay."

Gab double takes at my change of heart. She sits on the foot of the bed, patting my leg.

"We need to get you some consistency, Little Michy."

"No. I need some help in telling Dis what really happened."

A lot of help.

## 24 CUPID'S INTRODUCTION

Michelle might have been blasé about Discord but, trust me, Discord's charms had started to get to work. I'm not saying they were going to get married in a Vegas drive thru, more like there was a possibility that Discord's immediate future didn't have to go the same way as her immediate past. Michelle is a lot of fun to be around and if that fun could rub off on tall, dark and handsome then all the better.

Elle was also doing okay for herself. Well, she was managing. There was the odd bad day but overall her bling was brightening. Still, the Heavens don't stop running just because someone smashes your heart into a million pieces.

## Chapter Twenty-Four
## 29th August, Year 2 - 12:00
## Selection of the Fittest

"I gave you the files yesterday. Please don't tell me you've lost them, Sam."

Psyche watched curiously as Sam sifted through her in-tray, out-tray, desk drawers, even her bag. Sam scratched her head as her eyes darted over the blanket of papers covering her desk.

"It's not that they're lost." Sam looked up at the lithe brunette. "It's just, at this point I'm not exactly sure where they are."

Psyche turned away, sucking in a deep breath as she mentally counted to twenty. She turned back, stapling the most calm and serene look on her face she could manage considering her one night off this week looked to be ruined.

"I'll redo them. All of them. Every single one."

Sam's bottom lip began to tremble as she rechecked the drawers and trays, quickly becoming flustered as her search proved fruitless.

"I didn't mean to lose them." Sam sniffled, cuffing her eyes quickly. "I got Elle to authorise them, and they'd been stamped but..." A louder sniffle. "...now I can't remember where I put them."

Psyche blinked, a little taken aback.

"It's no problem." She went to pat Sam's hand but stopped, not wanting to tip her over the edge into a full blown tearful episode. "Just relax."

Psyche whipped around three-sixty, looking for help but reception was annoyingly empty.

Sam searched through the desk drawers trying to find some tissues, her words interspersed with loud sniffs.

"Relax? How can I relax? The heating is like a blast furnace: it melted the ball in my mouse yesterday and killed my cactus last week. The computer system shuts down whenever you use the letters L or B - guess whose initials they are. And someone took the blades out of the paper shredders so everything now comes out really well pressed. To top it all, I'm expected to organise Elle *and* everyone else. I can't do it all!"

Psyche closed her gaping mouth and rubbed the blonde's back, not really knowing what else to do. The women she normally dealt with were not criers.

The statuesque warrior pulled up a seat, keeping her voice low and even so as not to encourage anymore tears. In the time she'd known Sam she'd always found her a little ditzy but basically quite well organised. Lately, though, her reliability had dropped like a swatted fly.

"Sam, what's going on? I know it's not just..." She waved a hand around the mess on the desk. "...all of this."

Sam wiped her eyes, balling the tissue up and dropping it in the bin.

"I don't know. Stress, maybe? I've been an emotional wreck lately."

Psyche nodded but knew that wasn't it. Sam had dealt with more stress in the time she'd worked for Elle, so she delved a little deeper.

"Are you and John doing all right?"

Sam nodded and picked at her wrist rest.

"John's great. We're great. Maybe I'm ill? I spend my mornings being sick and my afternoons crying."

Psyche's eyes narrowed as something occurred to her. She glanced around reception, making sure they were alone, and then leaned in closer.

"When did you last have your period?"

Sam stared at Psyche and laughed. As the seconds dragged by the laughing stopped as her brain processed the answer to that question. Her face fell and expression changed from mirth to horror. Her reply sobbed out.

"I don't know!"

Elle's door opened, her head poking out as she looked to see what the commotion was. Her eyes darted between a shocked looking Psyche and even more shocked looking Sam.

"What's going on here?"

Elle frowned as she padded, bare foot, across reception. She glared at Psyche, arching an eyebrow.

"What have you done to her?"

Psyche stood, taking a step back.

"The Amazons are not to blame for *this* problem, Your Eminence. We don't have the necessary equipment."

Elle blinked, confused, and put her arm around Sam's shoulders. Her assistant clung tightly, sobbing into her silk dress. Psyche made a half moon shape over her stomach and pointed to Sam. Elle glanced between the two women. The warrior sighed and made a cradle out of her arms, rocking it back and forth. Elle's eyes went impossibly wide as she realised what the issue was.

"It's okay, Sam. Just relax and take some deep breaths," Elle said.

After a few minutes the sobs quietened and her assistant pulled back, cuffing her eyes. Sam stared at the wet imprint she'd made.

"Your dress. I'm so sorry. I mean, I'm so sorry, Your Eminence."

The sobbing would've restarted had Psyche not flicked the tip of Sam's nose making a half smile appear on her face.

Elle sat on the edge of the desk, hands crossed on her lap.

"How about this, today's been quiet so why don't you go home and relax in a nice warm bath?"

Sam stared at Psyche, buffing an eye with the heel of her hand, "But what about your paperwork?"

The warrior winked at Elle and then bent, catching the bloodshot eyes of the ditzy blonde.

"It's fine. I think...I *know* we have copies."

"You do?"

Psyche smiled, nodding.

"I'm sure we do. You go home and take a warm, not hot, bath."

Sam didn't need to be asked twice. She grabbed her bag, scooped up her coat and left with a little smile and wave to the two women.

Elle looked at Psyche.

"She needs to confirm she's pregnant. It'd explain her mood swings and the chaos my office is in. She may be ditzy but we've reached new levels this month."

Psyche nodded slowly as she spoke.

"I only saw John this morning. He'd be a nervous wreck if he thought they were going to have a baby."

Elle picked Samantha's glasses up off her desk, folding them as she pondered the situation.

"Gabrielle's close to Sam. I'll speak to her about organising a home test instead of going through the infirmary. I don't want idle gossip." She looked up at Psyche. "Potentially a mini Sam running around? What a scary thought."

"What's more scary are fifty percent of the genes coming from John."

Elle sighed as the rest of her working week reared its tightly crammed head.

"This can't be real. Not now. There's too much happening. Lucy's getting away with murder as it is."

Psyche nodded. It was true. Lucy was turning the Heavens into her personal playground. She thought hard for a moment before coming up with a plan.

"I'm sure Kreousa wouldn't mind loaning you one of her secretaries as a favour. I'll ask her to send one over for the rest of the day." Psyche glanced at Elle, with a mischievous twinkle in her eye. "One more thing, remember, she's a mortal so no hanky panky."

Elle suddenly flushed a deep crimson as she glared at the taller woman. Psyche simply bowed and winked.

"Your reputation precedes you, Your Eminence. I have to warn you or I'll have lines of Amazons signing up for the duty."

Elle grabbed a handful of paperclips, throwing them at the woman jogging away.

"Just get me someone who can type."

# 25 CUPID'S INTRODUCTION

John, the nerdy un-stud-like muffin, had potentially achieved something that didn't involve motherboards, just mothers. Don't get me wrong, I love him to bits, Sam and him make a great couple, but a baby taking the best parts of their D.N.A.? We're talking binary numbers for its I.Q.

So, anyway, while that was going on, Lucy was happy in the plush recesses of Hell. Her day involved: being naughty, flirting with Bee, naughty, flirting, naughty, flirting.... What can I say, great way to spend your time.

## Chapter Twenty-Five: Lucy
## 29th August, Year 2 - 13:00
## Keep Your Hands Inside The Carnage

"Come to dinner with me tonight, Bee?" I loll my head to the side, bored of what we're doing. My entire life is filled by Elle and her suffocating need for everything to be signed and filed, and to be honest, I'm in the mood for a break.

She slides another form over...

"Sign this, too."

...ignoring me as she sorts through even more.

I doodle on the edge of it in childlike script: Lucy loves Bee. I slide it over. She glances down and pushes it back, not missing a heartbeat. Her hands pull more forms out.

"Sign it properly, Lucy."

I sigh. The urge to be uncooperative is overwhelming but I control myself - just. I scribble my graffiti out, signing my name instead.

"Why are you so mean to me? Every other assistant I've had..."

She doesn't look up from her work.

"I bet you've had."

"Well, yes. Come on, make me happy, it's your job."

Bee closes the file and removes her glasses. She looks up, spearing me with an intense glare.

"You may have had every woman who's worked for you but that record stops with this one." She wags a finger. "I'm here to do a job, not to sleep with my boss. That dedication alone should be making you happy."

"But I always get what I want."

She snorts out a laugh, taking control of her face a moment too late. Her tone is amused.

"And you want me?"

I bite my bottom lip as I wonder if she's playing hard to get. I've never been refused before.

"Of course."

She motions with the sharp end of the pen. I push it away.

"Don't damage the merchandise before you've tried it."

"Lucy, I was hired to make sure we keep one step ahead of Elle. That's what you want and that's what you'll get."

"But, Bee..."

She jabs the pen in time with her words.

"Nothing. More. Nothing. Less."

She stares at me as her glasses go back on. She waits for a retort, for which none is coming, then goes back to her files.

This woman dumbfounds me and I'm not sure if that's good or bad. I watch her work in a silent efficiency that I could never match. Then I realise, I may be the naughtiness down here but the organizational brilliance is sitting in front of me, hair pulled back, wearing a tight black tailored suit and stylish dark framed glasses. Bee, the paperwork powerhouse of Hell.

## 26 CUPID'S INTRODUCTION

It was a normal evening, just a couple of days after Discord and Michelle's night of drink and sex - even if only one of them remembered. Mich had been trying to tell Dis the truth all day but with that kind of thing you need to pick your moment. It's not something you can drop into a passing shot in the hall, "Hey, Dis, forgot to say we fucked. Anyway, catch you later." Ton of bricks, smoking gun, heart-attack inducing.

So remember, the big secret still existed, only just. Goes to prove, when you throw shit at the fan eventually it's going to hit. The secret to a safe life is anticipating when and taking cover accordingly.

## Chapter Twenty-Six: Discord
## 29th August, Year 2 - 19:00
## And Then God Created... A Mess

I stand under the shower spray, washing my evening workout away. It's amazing how relaxing warm water can be. After ten minutes I have to force myself to get out. I dry off, pull my pants and a bra on then go to get my tee shirt. I catch my reflection in the full length mirror and everything stops. Razoring the glass with a hand removes the misty steam. Half a dozen scratch marks stare back me.

Someone comes in. My head flicks around and I glare. She backs out of the locker room, mouthing an apology.

I pull my tee on and sit on the bench, trying to remember what happened. After about three seconds my thinking stops. There's only one period of time I can't account for. My teeth grind. I head for Michelle's.

On my way I try to calm down, take some yoga breaths or do another form of anger management. My efforts don't amount to much. I manage to keep my temper calm enough not to pound on her door. I knock, cracking my knuckles as I wait. It opens. She smiles. That expression falls as she sees mine.

She pulls a face, her eyebrows lifting.

"You don't look happy. Come in."

I stand in the middle of her living room telling myself anger won't help. The temptation to start shouting is overwhelming.

She stops in front of me.

"I'm glad you came by. It's nice to see you again."

She smiles, looking genuinely pleased to see me. Sometimes Michelle can look more innocent than is necessary. But whatever, her words and expression have the desired effect. My muscles relax a little.

I concentrate on being level headed, and I almost manage it.

"Hoping I wouldn't notice the railroad tracks down my back?"

My badly toned, aggressive sentence makes me kick myself. I wait for the argument, but her reaction isn't what I expected. As I've come to realise she's not like the people I've known.

"That's a weight off my mind. I've been trying to tell you all day but I couldn't get time alone with you."

My body was ready for denial so any anger flops.

"Then we did...sleep together?"

She nods, matter-of-factly.

"Yup."

Fingertips massage the bridge of my nose.

"Why didn't you tell me?"

She raises an eyebrow.

"Why didn't you remember?"

Good counter. I should have, but then too many should haves often don't work out the way you expect.

"I was drunk."

"So was I."

My mouth opens but I don't know what to say. Legal Council for the defence directs wide green eyes my way. I feel like shouting for an objection, but the way my luck is going I'd get overruled.

She fills the silence, something she's good at.

"I did try to tell you. Your reaction wasn't great."

I concede the point, remembering when she said I wasn't gentle. I sit down heavily on her sofa, staring at my hands, not knowing what to do now I've been defused.

She sits next to me, nudging my shoulder with hers.

"I wasn't trying to be secretive. It didn't seem like something you wanted to have done. I gave you a break."

I glance over and know she's being honest. I also realise she's the first person who actually has cut me some fuckin' slack in all the time I've been up here. There is one thing to mention, though.

"The scratches were a giveaway."

Her eyes catch mine for a second and she starts chuckling.

"I'm not into marking territory. I'm not sure what happened."

No longer angry, just embarrassed, I'm at a complete dead-end.

"You've defused me. I don't know what to do."

She pats my leg and gets up.

"Well then, you can stay for dinner."

She talks while preparing a salad. I don't try to figure out how she made a bad situation a whole lot better. I don't think I could.

We eat. She talks about stuff that shouldn't be interesting but her enthusiasm makes me listen. As I'm helping with the dishes I have to ask. I know however hard I try it'll come out sounding terrible, so I just say it.

"I'm hazy on what happened. Between us, I mean."

I falter and come to a stop. I put the plate down, looking up at her.

"You want me to tell you what we did?"

I shrug, taking a deep breath, knowing how stupid I sound. My fingers pick at the towel I was using to dry up.

"Not in graphic detail, just the basics."

She laughs, takes my plate, dries it, and puts it away. Her hands fold her towel up into a little square.

"Lucky I'm not easily offended."

True, it's a nice change.

She glances at me out of the corner of her eye then straightens, holding one finger up.

"Firstly, we did this."

She takes a slow step forward so we're almost touching. The instinct to stand my ground stops me stepping back. She kisses me gently then pulls away, moving her mouth not her body.

She looks a lot more serious. Warm soft lips move to mine again, kissing me longer, fully. My eyes slide shut as I concentrate on this, on her hands gliding up my arms and resting on my shoulders, and my heart pounding. We stay like that for a long time.

From my initial reason for coming here to this? It's a difference and one I didn't expect, but sometimes you just have to deal with it.

She pulls away a little, and my body misses her heat instantly. My heart pounds. It's a feeling I've missed.

Heavy lidded eyes slip open as she steps back and holds up two fingers. Her voice is low and incredibly sexy.

"Secondly, Dis, you put two of these in me."

Not hoping to remember what we did, I think about inventing some new memories. I tug her shirt, pulling her closer. She wraps her arms around me as we kiss again. Deep, raw and way past gentle, slow becomes urgent.

It's then that ground zero happens: I think of Elle.

I didn't mean to, it just happened. I must have faltered, paused or something, because she pulls away. Warm hands rest on my hips, her thumb gently moving.

"What's wrong?"

Unable to convey my emotions at the best of times means I fall flat of how this is me not her. I shake my head and shrug, not knowing what I should give as an excuse; the truth is not going to happen.

I must look pathetic because she does the unexpected. Her face softens, her arms go up to my back and she pulls me in for a hug. I don't resist. I allow her to hold me because I'm sick of being strong all the time. I rest my head on her shoulder and close my eyes. Her pulse hammers against my chest and I bet mine is doing the same.

The thoughts that got me in this position are pushed out of my head. They're no use. Just a one way ticket to a painful place I want to get out of, not back into.

"I think we should just sit and talk."

She lets me go. I nod, determined to pull myself together.

Her tone becomes lighter as she rubs my arm.

"Or with your level of conversation I'll talk and you can listen. What do you say?"

Not much I can say to that selfless offer.

"Sure."

We sit down in her living room and I feel like a stupid teenager who got dumped and is about to have a talk with their folks about love and loss.

She leans back, crossing long legs, cocking her head. Mich does what she does best. She defuses.

"Now, I know it wasn't my technique because I'm very competent. I also know it's not a lack of attraction. You think I'm cute."

She says the last bit to me like a secret. Her fingers drum on a thigh as she continues.

"And it's not staunch morals due to the things we did the other night." She taps a finger on her lips. "You're not a virgin either, so it's not nerves."

She shifts, sitting side on, green eyes focused intently. I lean back on the sofa watching her watching me. The mood changes from joking to serious in a few seconds.

"Loves lost?"

Her simple question is unnerving. I look away, uncomfortable with where this is going. I do the decent thing and answer a direct question honestly.

"I guess."

I catch her slow nod, more to herself than anything else.

"I don't have any magic advice. None that'll make everything instantly better. Cliché, but time's a great healer. So are..." Her mouth twitches into a smile. "...athletic blondes. You should take one at least twice a day."

She flutters her eyelashes at me playfully. I can't help but laugh.

"Thanks. I'll keep you in mind."

"You have a nice laugh. You should practice it more often. Come on, let's forget about the heavy stuff. Your time up here shouldn't be a drag."

You're preaching to the choir.

She grabs my hand, pulling me up, and I let her. This woman has done me more good in the last three hours than the rest of the Heavens in all my time here.

We go back to her kitchen. She unlocks a wooden door I thought was a cupboard. We go through and I was clearly wrong. It's a narrow bare brick corridor lit by modern recessed spotlights. We can only just walk side by side.

Suddenly she spins around, walking backward in front of me.

"Ready for a surprise, Discord Knight?"

I shrug, not trying to think what she's up to now. Her hand goes up, so I stop. As I do she takes a step forward, quickly kissing me.

"That wasn't it. I had an urge. Close your eyes."

She makes an impatient face. You have to put your trust in something. I close my eyes. The heat of her body moves closer. I tease because she deserves it, but I'm not in charge of my tone and it comes out warningly low.

"Careful. You have my trust."

I kick myself as her body heat moves away. My eyes open. I reach out, holding her hand as she turns, her eyes fixed firmly elsewhere.

The last few months here have turned me into someone I barely recognise. I try to explain that without sounding retarded.

"I'm out of practise joking around. I didn't mean to sound...harsh. I'm sorry."

"No problem."

Her voice is quiet as though she doesn't quite believe me.

It's then I see we're not so different. Underneath that confident exterior is a sensitive woman, except I think she's even better at disguising it than I am.

I keep hold of her wrist, suddenly feeling very connected. It's a nice feeling.

I make the first move this time. I pull her gently and our bodies meet, fitting together too well. My lips move against hers, not fully connecting, just feeling her warm breath against them. Her body instantly relaxes; mine does the same.

I can't deny we have chemistry. I also can't deny my tendency to screw things up. Determined not to do that this time I concentrate on the person in front of me, nothing more.

Her free hand travels over my collarbone, settling on my shoulder. Her mouth forms a lazy smile under mine as words breathe out.

"You can't usurp my surprise like this. I had a plan and..."

I stop the rest of that sentence.

She's a good kisser. Unhurried, deliberate, sensual. It's a real pleasure.

Michelle is very passionate. I originally learnt that during our time sparring. She's dedicated, focused, and when she decides, very intense. It's not something you can see easily because she's the Queen of Disguise. I can feel that intensity now. Her tongue touches mine and I match her move for move.

My hands find their way under her shirt and drift over smooth warm skin. Suddenly I remember doing this before, when I was drunk. She pulls away thinking my pause is the same as earlier. It's no way the same.

"Are you okay?"

I hold a hand up and concentrate. I was rough with her, drunk and angry, too, I know that much. I sigh, not happy with some of my memories.

Open and honest green eyes stare at me, full of concern. She deserves more than to be constantly worrying about my state of mind tonight.

"Did I hurt you when we slept together?"

"Oh, flashback. Hurt? Nothing I wasn't happy with."

That answer doesn't help. In fact it makes me more concerned. It's not my usual thing to hurt the people I like enough to get intimate with.

"I was drunk. I'm not normally...you know."

I lean on the wall, annoyed at my ineptness to matching my feelings to words. She leans next to me, nudging shoulders.

"Don't worry about me. I can't be broken easily." She takes my hand and leads us along the corridor. "Come on, you."

We stop by a plain looking door that she opens. I feel the humidity first. It makes me blink as I walk in. The large cavernous room is well lit for what it is: an executive sized Jacuzzi.

Her smile has gone and she looks very serious again.

"There's only one way to do this."

She unbuttons her shirt, slipping the material off. She watches me intensely as her jeans go the same way. My eyes drift over her. No underwear.

"I'm not going to be shy around you. I think we've moved on from there."

I try not to stare but it's hard because she has an amazing body: firm breasts, flat muscled stomach, wide shoulders, lightly bronzed skin, zero tan lines and a natural blonde - even if there isn't much of that to judge her on.

Her bare feet pad on the floor as she walks over. I stand as still as I can. Part of me is nervous and I'm not sure why. Perhaps it's a little performance anxiety? Last time I wasn't in charge of what happened, the alcohol was. Now I've actively chosen this - if we even do anything. I mean, it's not a given.

Her padding feet stop short and she stares, deeply, almost into me. The charge in the room changes as that intense look disappears. She smiles, planting a quick kiss on my lips.

"Come and relax with me. Bubbles make all the bad stuff go away."

I watch her firm ass as she walks over to the tub. She lowers into it, flicking a switch. The air-pumps rumble to life, starting hundreds of jets, producing thousands of bubbles. Her head goes under momentarily then pops back up. She slowly slicks her blonde hair back. Arms slide over the rim as she leans her head back and closes her eyes.

Her voice is soft and gentle.

"This thing always melts my problems away. Come on, you, don't be shy."

She shifts, revelling in the water.

I make an important decision. Things have to start getting better. I've been doing that so far with her help, even the sparring has loosened me up. I have to stay on that track.

I kick my boots off, unbutton my shirt and jeans, and slip out of them. I leave my clothes in a little heap and walk towards the Jacuzzi, determined to start living again.

The water swallows my limbs, and warmth soaks through to my bones. I sit on a wide sunken step opposite her.

She grins.

"I thought it was only us blondes who tanned so evenly?"

I resist the urge to smile. She's something else.

"I thought you had your eyes shut?"

She cracks one eye open, then the other and smiles broadly.

"You thought wrong. I've seen it all before, anyway." Her head tilts. "Oh, you don't remember, that's right."

I duck my head under, covering my blush. I slick my hair back as I surface, and shrug, leaning back, mirroring her pose with my arms outstretched on the edge.

She stares at me, then the water, then back at me.

"You need more bubbles, more of a wave?"

The corners of my mouth lift. She's right, this is relaxing. I think it's more than just the rhythmic rippling waves. I think it's the company. She has a way about her. It's calming.

"Sure."

She moves over to my side, leaning across to the buttons. She presses one then stares at the effect on the water.

"How about smaller bubbles but more of them? Then it's like an all over massage."

She looks up, smiling, wrinkling her nose. It's then I notice how close we are. Her thigh brushes mine, getting more of a reaction than any amount of bubbles ever could.

Determined not to have a repeat of earlier I concentrate on keeping my voice light.

"I'm sorry if I was rough. You know, when we...."

Her eyes flick over my face and she loses her smile replacing it with that look of seriousness again. Her words breathe out.

"You didn't hurt me."

"You sure?"

She nods.

The water between us laps against my breasts. I tense from the pleasurable sensation, trying not to give too much away. But then her addition makes my reactions impossible to hide. A hand slides along my arm, stopping on my shoulder, a fingertip caressing my neck. Her body leans into mine and it's an immediate sigh of sensations.

Determined to have this run without a hitch I switch my mind off. We kiss. I focus on her mouth, her body, the feeling of her hands running though my hair. Nothing else seeps into my head.

She kneels on the step, straddling me, her firm thighs squeezing mine. I run my hands along them, feeling their strength and the muscles tensing. Mich is a strong, elegant fighter and it shows in the body she's got.

She leans closer, fingers entwining in my hair. The hot water laps some more. Our kisses turn deep and passionate. I lean back as she caresses me. Hands shimmer down the side of my breasts, over my skin, everywhere: my stomach, my hips, my inner thighs.... We drift somewhere else. Somewhere I haven't been before. Somewhere I've given up my control. For me that's a big step. I nearly did it for one other woman, the same woman I slam the door on in my mind, locking it and moving a safe distance away.

Lips slip down my neck and I'm brought back to the here and now as fingers easily slide into me. My eyes flick open and a concerned face stares back.

"Yes?"

I'd have to be insane to say no. I nod and my hips rise, seconding that answer. Sometimes your body knows best, knows just what it needs.

The rhythm set is leisurely. She moves and my head lolls on the side on the tub. I assume it's her thumb that starts to move in circles. I don't fight. I let go completely, going wherever she wants to take me because so far she's only taken me good places.

However many women have preceded me with Mich I'm grateful because she's very skilled: her fingers alternately curl and scissor inside me. My body arches slowly. My heart starts to pound. A warm mouth covers one of my nipples, sucking, tonguing, nibbling at intervals, sending waves of jagged electricity through me. I slip a hand into her wet hair, holding her where I need. The build up accelerates: the speed of her fingers as they move, her tongue and teeth on me, her other hand caressing, the warm water. I growl from deep inside. She bites down on my nipple, hard, forcing my eyes open in shock as her thumb pushes on my clit. A blindingly powerful orgasm forces through me, violently, making me buck up into her. She grabs the edge to keep balanced. My muscles tense and I grit my teeth at the suddenness as a low moan escapes. It's a feeling I've missed.

With fingertips on the back of her neck I guide her up, pulling her mouth onto mine. We kiss deeply. Her movements slow as those sudden pulses of electricity subside. I fall back against the edge of the tub. A warm hand combs stray strands of hair out of my face.

After a while her fingers slip out slowly. I sigh at the emptiness. Her body manages to mould into me effortlessly as her head rests on my shoulder. I blink, lazily, my energy sapped and the rest of me zapped. All of the stress from earlier has disappeared and for the first time in months I feel light, at ease. I lean over and kiss her forehead.

Steam curls around my nostrils, bubbles caress my skin, and I caress her. I turn the tables on this confident blonde.

## 27 CUPID'S INTRODUCTION

Dis put a crucial thing into motion: moving on. The rest of the night was filled with lots of that. She stayed again and a good time was had by all - even if they were doing this awkward dance around each other. Michelle was officially allergic to any commitment. Discord's personality didn't help. She was officially backward in coming forward. Still, she knew one thing. Life doesn't get any better if you spend your time feeling sorry for yourself. Sensible woman.

Back to the commitment-phobic Michelle. She had one major problem to overcome if she wanted to stay at arm's length with Discord: Gabrielle - and that woman knew her friend inside out. Avoiding was never going to be the topic de jour.

## Chapter Twenty-Seven: Michelle
## 2nd September, Year 2 - 22:00
## Hot Running Water

"**Y**ou're pensive."

Gab leftfields me with a well delivered stab in the dark. I side step it.

"I'm not pensive."

Her eyes narrow and I can almost see that super processor churning computations.

"You've caught it off of Discord."

I flick her behind with the tea towel.

"Shut up and wash."

I take the plate from her hands, drying it quickly, stacking it in the cupboard. I put my cloth down and lean on the kitchen counter. She glances over.

"Any news I should know about?"

"Loads. This new training selection programme with the Council..."

I proceed with a tale of my shitty week and the un-trainable Amazons. If she wants to feel my pain she can hear it, too.

"...so, I don't know what to do with them girls. They're allergic to learning."

"Get Psyche involved. They listen to her. Now." She splashes her hands up and down, shaking me out of my trance. "Any Discord news?"

"You were right. Elle and her were serious."

Gab pulls her hands out of the sink. They're covered in bubbles. She goes to put them around my neck - old trick. I pick my cloth back up and intercept, wiping them, keeping hold to stop her throttling me.

"I'm not going to say I told you." She shakes her head, tutting. "Instead I'll say, I was right like always. How'd you find out?"

I give her dry hands back.

"I asked. She nodded. She's not a talker. And before you say anything it's not a problem. If I want conversation I'll call you."

Gab is abnormally intuitive at times.

"All she did was nod?"

Lucky I'm feeling abnormally obtuse.

"No, I could sense it. Discord Knight has an aura of reticence about her." She laughs.

"An aura of reticence? That's one way to put it. But however you want to word it, I guess you'll have to back off now."

I focus on the dishcloth and get splashed with water. They say the sign of a good friend is their ability to finish your sentences for you. I finish hers with something I had no intention of saying but my blurty mouth decides to share.

"Or sleep with her again, which is probably better seeing as I've already done it."

Her hands go back to trying to throttle me.

"Michy!"

I bend and kiss her knuckles. This time I get a smile and hair ruffle. Gab is so easy to defuse.

"I didn't plan it."

"If you paid me every time you said that..."

"You'd have about enough to pay me back for the shirt you spilt wine down the other night."

A finger taps my chest.

"Okay, moving on. If you didn't plan it then how'd it happen? Start from the beginning. No skipping."

"What is this, live life vicariously through Michelle, month?"

"Yes. I'm working every day to clear our huge backlog of paperwork. I don't have a life. It's your job to help me live through yours."

One thing about Gab, when she finds a bone she never lets go.

"Quick version. She found the scratches and came around all guns blazing - a situation I am happy to say I defused. And..." I smile. "...she was wearing a tight top and looked so good I couldn't stop myself from kissing her. So I didn't. Ta da."

This was not exactly how it happened but I'm not in the mood for too many details.

"That's it? That's never it with you. What more? What about Elle?"

"I've told you about Elle."

"And you always forget stuff, normally the best stuff. As a reminder, I have no life and you have enough for both of us. Share."

"There's not much else to tell. Dis told me in that cryptic way that Psyche has. You know, they say stuff without saying it? So I had a sad and brooding, hot woman to cheer up."

"Wait, did you cook again?"

She raises her eyebrows. I shake my head. Technically it was a salad, I didn't cook anything. I'm telling the truth.

"Okay, what next?"

"I took her to the Jacuzzi and we had sex."

Gab gently slaps my forehead. It's her way of telling me I've been a bad girl. I get a lot of slaps.

"In it? Michy, I'm never going in that with you again!"

"You probably should've said that to me the day after I got it, because that Jacuzzi is not a virgin."

"What else? Where else? Should I not sit on your couch, or at the dinner table?"

"If you're going to be retentive about it then don't sit anywhere in my house. And never come in the bedroom, or kitchen - or bathroom. You know, even the stairs..."

A hand slaps over my mouth. I poke my tongue out, making her retract and wipe it on her leg.

"I'm kidding about the stairs. But you know your favourite chair?"

That same hand pinches my lips together. Gab is so cute when I say anything about that chair. It's her piece of territory and she guards it fiercely. She gradually relaxes her grip.

I tug her shirt, bored of kitchen duties now. However, in her world she now has her bone and a really whiny voice.

"My chair? With who?" She scrunches her nose up. "No, don't tell me, I don't want to...." Then there's this pause while she has an argument in her own head. She does that a lot. "No, tell me, because I need to know who not to speak to in the canteen."

"Make your mind up. Which is it? Remember, ignorance is bliss."

We walk into her living room. I'm exhausted. I've had a stressed out day. I need to relax.

My phone beeps and vibrates, and Gab does that eye roll thing she saves for when she's trying to make a point.

"Why can't they leave you alone for just a day?"

"I can't help my popularity."

"If that's what you want to call it."

I pull it out of my pocket, staring at the screen to see who my message is from: the cute brunette from the party the other week. Not urgent. I leave it on the table as I pass.

"Michy, who in my chair?"

I lie down on her sofa and stretch out. This space won't last long, I know that much.

"No one. Honestly. That's your little piece of sacred turf in my house."

Her arched eyebrows furrow as she thinks. She smiles then lies down, squashing me so we're face to face.

"See, you do love me."

"Only because you're such an idiot."

"I'm Head of Intelligence."

"And Sam is Elle's personal assistant. Go figure."

She laughs as her cold feet play with my toes. Her hands hold mine. At least these extremities are warm.

She stares at me, deeply, not saying a word. Of all the things I know about Gab this is the most solid: how she works up to an important question. The pause isn't due to nerves or being undecided about anything, it's her processing reams of information.

"Do you think it's wise to go after Discord if she's injured over Elle? Think about my question."

So I do. I remember back to the sofa when Dis confirmed it was loves lost, and how lonely she looked. Then my behaviour falls into place. It's not a nice feeling.

The revelation flies out of my mouth.

"I jumped her when she was vulnerable."

Gab's face screws up.

"I didn't like to mention it but I think you might have."

I pull my hands out from hers and sit. She props up on an elbow, frowning. Everything falls into place. I might've wanted her but not like that. I'm not an ass. Well, not completely.

"What's going on in that head of yours?"

How do you explain a mind full of confusion?

"I don't know. I think I'm having a pang of conscience because I took advantage. I didn't even think. Okay, you know what, I've had a really bad day and I don't need this. Let's watch a movie or something."

I go to stand but get pulled down. Gab sits next to me, a hand on my thigh, patting, rubbing, soothing, like she does the few times I get upset because my brain engages. She also uses her special low tone for when I do really stupid things.

"Let's not do your normal trick to avoid everything of importance. How did you leave it the next morning?"

I think back, a smile perking my mood slightly.

"We had breakfast..."

"You did cook!" She slaps my thigh, laughing. "I can't believe you're lying to me over this woman you've known, what, a week?"

"She's been here for about a year and a half."

"Oh, please. You haven't been paying attention to her for that long."

"Maybe not, but we've been hanging out for months, not weeks. And I didn't cook, we had some fruit."

Gab shakes her head. She's not angry. She's playing, trying to make me feel bad enough to give her all of the details easily. She likes to shift her modus operandi to catch me off guard.

I carry on.

"We talked about training and what she was doing that day. We walked to the office. I said bye and she said bye and we sort of..." I smile because it's a very visceral memory. "...kissed, in her office, with the door closed. She's such an amazing kisser. You know, intense and erotic. Anyway, then I went to work."

The rubbing hand stops and turns to a gentle squeeze.

"Then it doesn't sound like she's too hurt, right?"

"I guess. Okay, no more feeling bad then. Wow, that was short and sweet."

"Are you seeing her again?"

I shrug, not wanting to think about it. Then, not sure why I don't want to think about it, I think about it. We didn't make any plans.

"I don't know."

She pushes me in the side and I topple over. She climbs on, lying on my side, trapping my arms, one under me, one under her.

"I have to ask you one thing."

"Can't breathe. Make it quick."

She digs my shoulder with her chin making me crook my neck around to her smiling face.

"Count to ten first. Do you like her?"

So I indulge my friend because she has a way of getting to any issue even if I don't know it's bothering me. One. Two. Three. Four. Five. Do I like her? Six. Seven. Eight. Nine. Ten. Perhaps.

"I like everyone, Gab."

She smirks.

"Next time she's at yours do me a favour and don't make a pass at her. See what happens, okay?"

She smiles down at me then pushes off, tapping my nose to make her point.

"Remember, Michy, don't make a pass."

## 28 CUPID'S INTRODUCTION

Gabrielle can see through most of Michelle's defences, even if Michelle herself can't. Lucky really, because Discord and her needed a lot of prodding to get them onto the right path. One thing you should've learnt so far is that nothing important runs smoothly.

In contrast, Sam had got herself into a bit of trouble. In my personal line of work unplanned pregnancy is never an issue. Imagine hundreds of little Cupids running around. Exactly. I don't think this was really in Gab's remit either, but she's always up for this sort of stuff. Remember, she's the fixer, the sorter, the helper. Gab always makes a bad situation...better? Yeah, well, read on, my friends.

## Chapter Twenty-Eight
## 6th September, Year 2 - 20:00
## Welcome to the Mother-Zone

"**H**ave you read the instructions, Sam?"
Gabrielle cursed Michy for leaving her alone with this. Although, Michelle did leave her for the great company of Electra and the Nation's training requirements. Revenge was sweet.

"No."

Sam sounded nervous, but it was an understandable emotion for someone who could be pregnant. Gabrielle couldn't imagine being in her shoes - although with her love life it would be an immaculate conception.

She took the box and scrutinised the back. They were doing it properly, not half heartedly. There'd be no mistakes on her shift.

"Right. You have to pee on this thing..."

Sam interrupted.

"Which thing?"

Gabrielle waved the only thing she had in her hand. It was going to be a *long* night.

"This thing, Sam."

Sam nodded excessively. Gabrielle carried on before another silly question got asked. Sam was confusing enough, even more so with a valid reason.

"You pee on this then we wait for three minutes, and check to see if a little tick appears."

"And what if I get a tick?"

Sometimes Sam was classic proof the colour blonde could drain brain cells.

"Then you're pregnant."

Sam fell down on the sofa, cradling her face in her hands.

"I'm not ready for this. John's not ready for this."

Gabrielle wasn't sure the Heavens were ready for this. In fact, she could think that statement with certainty. Births normally stayed in the mortals' party zone. It was better suited to looking after them. They had crèche areas and playgrounds. It'd been so long since there was a baby running around, Gabrielle wasn't sure they'd know what to do. It'd get lost amongst the endless photocopiers, scanners and piles of files.

Gabrielle unpeeled Sam's hands from her face, and put the box into her well manicured fingers.

"Sam. Go pee. I'm desperate to know if you are or not. You're giving me an ulcer."

...and probably Michy, Psyche and Elle palpitations as they were waiting for the news.

Sam looked at the box then up at Gabrielle, then away, standing up slowly. Then back at Gabrielle, then at the box, then back at Gabrielle.

"Sam! Go pee."

"I'm not ready to be a mother."

As Sam walked out of the room Gabrielle added under her breath.

"Neither are we."

She timed the event with the stop watch on her cell phone - pretty much the only feature she could use. Michy bought it, ran through how it worked but all of that info fell out of her head long ago.

She paced for four minutes and twenty seconds before Sam walked back in. There was a desperate pause. Sam looked calm and held the paddle up, muttering something.

Gabrielle stared at her.

"What?"

Sam waved the paddle.

"Tick. The thing I had to pee on has a tick. And do you know how hard it was to do that - pee on it, I mean? Probably not, because it's not like you'd get in this situation, because you never date anyone."

"Thank you, Michelle."

Sam's eyebrows furrowed.

"No. I'm Sam."

Gabrielle stared at her and slapped a smile on. It wasn't her fault.

"I know. I was making a reference to...never mind."

Sam carried on, but her voice had an edge to it.

"I checked twice and at no point did it not have a tick. At no point. None. No. Point. Always the tick."

"Take a deep breath and..."

"I got a tick." Sam waved the paddle some more and suddenly Gabrielle was glad it'd had time to dry. "A small tick with a big meaning. The least they could do is make it a big tick for the importance, right?"

Sam's waving got manic. Her voice broke as she stared at it.

"I mean, it's not a tiny little thing. It's big, and the tick needs to show it's not something you take lightly. The tick needs to be bigger!" There was a pause, and she swallowed, adding, "I got a tick."

Then, as if in slow motion, Sam's face paled and body flopped. Gabrielle jumped forward just managing to grab hold of the limp blonde. She looked down. Sam was out cold. Cursing under her breath she carried that dead weight, which was not easy, to the bedroom. She glanced over to the picture of John on the bedside table.

"You had to be Mr Fertile, didn't you?"

Gabrielle gently placed her on the bed, the soft comforter squishing around limp limbs. Her legs went either side of Sam's stomach as she knelt over and started to undo buttons. She didn't want to damage the baby with a restrictive cardigan.

Sam's eyes flicked open, body jerked and a little squeal exited. Gabrielle almost lost her balance with the shock. It was at that point Mr Fertile decided to become Mr Bad Timing. Sam's bedroom door opened and he stood, slack jawed, staring at them.

His eyes did a darting glance.

"Gab, what are your hands doing?"

Gabrielle stared down, wondering why her hands had decided to use Sam's breasts to steady themselves. They unpeeled from the warm cleavage,

"Sorry."

"It's okay," Sam whispered.

John's tone was tight.

"I'm still here."

Aren't you just, Gabrielle thought.

"Oh, the hands. I was...helping."

"In case her breasts fell off?"

It's then Gabrielle saw the rest of this picture. Sam's arms were grasping her forearms and Sam's clothes were half undone. Gabrielle glanced back at his red face. Now was the time to offer an explanation.

"This is not what it looks like, John."

"You two? I thought you liked men and now you're trying to convert my girlfriend?"

"John!" Sam shouted.

Gabrielle untangled herself and got off of his girlfriend and his bed.

"I don't do girls and I'm not trying to convert anyone, thanks. There's nothing going on between Sam and me. It just...looks that way."

"You don't date for years and now you pick *my* Sam? I thought you were my friend?"

"I am your friend, and I do date, I just don't shout about it. Can we get back to the subject?"

John almost pouted.

"Which is?"

Gabrielle glanced down at Sam's wide eyes.

"For Elle's sake, Sam, tell him."

Sam looked at Gabrielle, then John, then as if she was going to cry. At no point did her mouth open to say anything.

"Tell me what?"

Hands on his hips and chest puffed out, Gabrielle realised this was his, 'I'm feeling threatened,' look. Any other time and it would have seemed laughable.

"Come on, Head of Intelligence, what were you trying to do to my girlfriend on our bed with your hands all over her?"

She took a deep breath. Her temperament was even, but this accusation? It was insulting and ridiculous.

"Nothing."

"Nothing? How dumb do you think I am?"

An answer to that question could push all of this down hill quickly.

"Sam, tell him!"

Finally, as if by magic, Sam offered some truth.

"I fainted. She was putting me to bed."

"That's what they call it these days, is it? Fainting?" He looked between the two of them, adding, "Why did you 'faint' then?"

"Because I'm pregnant!" Sam sobbed.

"Because you're pregnant?" He snorted then frowned, then, wide eyed, his jaw slackened and Gabrielle swore she heard it tumble to the floor. "Oh."

The thump as his legs crumpled and he dropped like a brick, reverberated. Gabrielle stared down at the little deflated peacock.

"Wow, you two are well suited."

## 29 CUPID'S INTRODUCTION

Where hard times are concerned you can do one of two things. You can fall to your knees begging the first God who walks by for some mercy. Good luck on *that* front. Alternatively, you can pick yourself up, dust yourself down, and sing something from, "Annie, the musical". Personally, it's a hard knock life and it's worth clinging to. Michelle helped Discord to do this. Remember, Mich is one of these people whose sun is always: shinning, about to shine or will be shinning in very near future. I'm not wishing a single raindrop on her parade, because it works for her, and it began to work for the lonesome cowgirl, too.

After the Jacuzzi of lust, things went well. It was good these two had come together, excuse the pun. Saying that, Discord wasn't stupid. She'd had a hard time since she arrived and wasn't giving anything up that easily again. Well, apart from the obvious. No, even friendship was going to be a tough one.

Anyway, onto the less mundane subject of Discord's new job. The Heavens had brought her up to speed with a couple of minor Grade B and C missions; the easier stuff. She passed without difficulty and graduated up to the next level. And with the new level came new stress. Vengeance is a harsh world, something Dis was finding out.

Her new mission had a distinct advantage. It made her take that important step in Michelle's direction. This part should read: Dis Gets A Break. Of course, there's one thing about getting a break, it always leaves something broken. That's a point to remember for the future.

## Chapter Twenty-Nine: Michelle
## 30th September, Year 2 -19:30
## The Tree Of Strife

I crush a drier load of washing to my chest with one hand and open the door with the other. Dis glances at my armful of clothes with a curious expression. I keep my surprise at seeing her to myself.

"I can't multitask. You knocked at the wrong time. Come in. Let me put these in to dry."

I dump my pile of semi wet clothes into the drier in my utility room, pushing the only button I ever use: number four. I don't know what it does but Gab uses it whenever she's here. If I trust anyone not to shrink my bras it's her.

I walk back to the living room. Dis is looking at a ceremonial knife on display. She glances over for permission. I shrug.

"Go ahead. I'm not anal. It's battle sharp. Don't slice a finger off."

She weighs it in her hand, turning it every angle, checking the workmanship, then puts it back in its stand, obviously happy.

"Nice."

That's good going, one word. It means she loves it. Words don't attach themselves well to Discord. Once I understood that she got a lot easier to deal with.

She turns, mumbling.

"I think I left my wallet here."

"Yup. Found it in the Jacuzzi room. I meant to drop it around weeks ago, but work was hectic and my brain is like a sieve."

I pull out crumpled receipts, gum wrappers, and yellow reminders from a drawer in my side table. Finally I find the wallet.

"I guess there was nothing important in it, seeing as I've had it so long?"

"Nothing I missed." She shakes her head and slips it out of my fingers, putting the slim leather into her jacket pocket. "Thanks."

She tries a terrible excuse for a smile. I'm no expert on Discord Knight but I will safely say she's not herself.

"What's up?"

As I walk closer I can smell shampoo which means she's been to the gym. It also means there's a problem. The gym for this woman equals a release of stress. That's the benefit of spending so much time together working out. I got to know the little secrets of why she does certain stuff.

She seems to struggle with her words, in the end settling for.

"Bad day."

"Anything in particular?"

She shrugs and exhales heavily, taking great interest in my floor.

"New mission. He hurts kids. It's difficult knowing this much about it. The details...."

Her words come to a stop.

Vengeance missions always feature the worst type of criminal. That's why we get involved, because society can't deal with or stop them. If there wasn't such a backlog, Earth would be a great place.

"Do you want to talk? Sometimes sharing can help."

She thinks about my offer. It's a first. Despite the time we've spent together she's still never consistently hit more than a paragraph at a time.

She shakes her head. I rub her solid forearm.

"We can rain check."

A bare nod accepts my offer.

Over the next hour I try to keep the subject matter light and airy. I'm known for my ability to talk and I use it. Dis isn't here to watch movies or to gossip, she's not the type. She's here because she's upset; like a wounded cat heading to somewhere familiar. Of course, being verbally retarded she doesn't say that but I know.

We end up in the kitchen, a wholly under utilised area but one that's experiencing a revival since she came on the scene. She likes my cooking. No, I'll amend that, she eats my cooking. I won't be too hopeful.

I've decided on a stir fry because my internal menu is limited. I chop some onions and garlic. My wounded cat still needs feeding.

My phone does its usual beeping telling me I have a message. I glance at the screen trying to place the name. All I come up with is a pretty blonde at a party the other night. As I'm about to type a quick answer I see Dis sitting dejectedly, playing with the fringes of the tablecloth. I stare at my phone then at her. I put it back down and get on with the cooking.

A little while later and I've finished most of the preparation. At least after this many years I no longer set off every smoke alarm.

For some reason, call it extra sensory perception if you want, I glance back around. Dis is staring at the floor. Suddenly her eyes slide up and meet mine. She looks devastated.

"Does it ever get easier, knowing everything?"

I consider lying but what's the point?

"No, not really. Why do you think I don't do it anymore?"

She nods slowly.

Vengeance is viciously brutal. There's no easy part. You're basically a justified murderer who gets to carry the gory details around for eternity. I completed over a hundred missions and the feeling after each one stayed the same. I felt dirty.

I try not to remember the reason I gave up, but my body isn't listening to my brain - often the case. A shiver runs down my spine so I do what I do best. I talk.

"You're more able to tune out but it's never easy. That's why we were shocked we got you, Dis. Modern day society isn't conducive to producing individuals for this kind of work."

Her voice is quiet and terribly sad.

"I don't know if I'll ever get used to doing this."

Who would?

I put the knife down, wipe my hands on a towel and walk over. My wounded cat stares up at me, not even trying to speak. She just leans her head into my stomach. I put my arms around her, stroking her hair for a while.

Finally I kneel and take her hands in mine.

"You don't get used to it, but you do learn to switch a part of yourself off."

Her words are quiet.

"Is that what you used to do?"

"Partly." I run my thumbs over her knuckles as I think back. "I'd focus on the crimes I was preventing not the bad things that'd happened. One thing that helped was finding some way to escape: the gym, reading, something. You're on the right track, you like the gym and we spar every week. But you have to talk about it. If you bottle it up you'll go mad."

I run my finger down the bridge of her nose then plant a kiss on the end.

"You have to stay here with me tonight. No arguments."

I don't get one. She just nods.


I finish making dinner and get her to help. Of course, anything needing the attention of a sharp bladed instrument is left for my hands. In the end we get a nice stir fry prepared, cooked and eaten.

I talk about my day. Throughout everything she remains distant, distracted. I mention something to do with Psyche and that gets the miracle of two words out of her.

"Psyche's attractive."

Well, *she* made an impression.

We don't touch on Vengeance again. I'm powerless with her pain. I can't work a miracle, that's something she has to struggle through. All I can do is provide support and listen, because despite centuries passing we don't quite seem to have understood: Vengeance isn't just about learning the right kicks, punches, holds or having the best gadgets. It's about being mentally strong enough to exist with what you know. It's not an easy course to teach.


We hit midnight, the witching hour. I pat Dis' hand.

"It's late. You need some rest. Come on, let's go up."

We stop by the guest bedroom and I tap the door. There haven't been any intimate overtones all night and Gab did tell me not to make a pass. I rub her arm and lean in to kiss her cheek. I don't know if she was turning to say something, but I catch the side of her mouth. It ignites parts of me that have only just died down. As I move away her hand holds onto mine, pulling me back.

"Sleep in here tonight?"

Is all she says. I search her eyes for a meaning I don't find.

I'm not one to shy away from the direct and straightforward.

"Are you asking me to sleep in here, or sleep with you?"

Suddenly Discord finds important words.

"Which one would make you say yes?"

And they're painfully honest. I open the guestroom door.

"Either. Let's go to bed."

The room where it all started.

I close the door and get a top and shorts out for both of us. I push the drawer back in and pause, an uncomfortable feeling creeping over my skin, the same one that always says hi when I think of my old days in Vengeance.

"I'm going to take a shower." I pat her pile of clothes. "Bed stuff."

I slip back into a familiar pattern. Vengeance equals lots of scalding water.

Ten minutes of steaming heat doesn't help. I lean my head against the cool tiles and pace my breathing, determined to snap out of it. My fist hits the tiles.

"Pull yourself together."

I dry off and put on my tee and shorts. I don't wipe the mirror. I don't want to look. Sometimes it's best not to.

When I go back in, Dis is sitting on the bed, looking very cute in my boxers and top. She has nice legs. One thing that can't be stopped is me noticing that kind of stuff. It's a safe constant in difficult times. I smile, pleased my brain hasn't entirely melted.

"Do you want to shower?"

She shakes her head.

"I had one after my workout."

She seems as lost now as she did when I was outside the gym looking in. I kneel and rest my hands on her knees, rubbing my thumbs over her skin.

"Your first jobs are always hard until you get accustomed. I'll help you anyway I can. Do you need to talk?"

She glances down at my hands and smashes the silence.

"It's not what I have to do that's the problem. It's...him. He's the problem."

With a deep shuddering breath she looks up, her eyes staring deeply into mine.

"Why'd you leave Vengeance?"

Her question takes me by surprise and I flounder for a moment.

"I...umm...."

My body reacts, pulling away, standing. She stands too, a hand out but not quite touching me, just floating in the space between us for a moment before almost skittering away.

"Sorry, I didn't mean to get too personal."

I make the effort to pat her shoulder before needing that all important distance as my flesh creeps.

I decide to get straight to my point and get out of the subject. The quicker you move the less chance it has to take hold.

"I left because..." I'm not going to lie to her. "...I could see the blood everywhere. Eating in the canteen, I'd see spots on my skin or the table. I'd see flashes of red in meetings. It took over every part of my existence. For weeks I could taste it in the back of my throat, and it didn't matter what I did, it wouldn't go away. I felt sick all the time."

My tongue runs over the tips of my teeth. I look directly at her.

"The last straw came after a really bad mission. The next day I accidentally cut myself and...I sort of flipped out." I remember back to that terrible day. "I couldn't breathe. I couldn't think straight. All of my training fell apart. I felt...claustrophobically trapped. They had to call Gab to calm me down. I took some time off and was transferred out."

Her face doesn't change. She stares into me, and for a rare moment I'm uncomfortable. But that's what happens when you're honest, when you actually speak something that isn't a line or joke. The truth isn't always so great to deal with.

"Did I shatter your illusions of some romantic end to my days?"

She doesn't look away. A simple shake of her head is her first answer.

Her second, wise words.

"You made it out in one piece."

She taps her head to show what she's really talking about. It's disarming.

"Some would disagree."

"But they don't know what we do."

I close my eyes for a second, relaxing with an exhale.

"No, they don't. Thanks."

I open my eyes in time to see a trademark shrug. My actions are automatic. I put my arms around her, pulling us into a hug. I think we both need one.

"I'm here to make sure you don't go the same way, okay?"

She nods as her body rests against mine. Her thighs are warm, but, and it's a unique feeling, it's not sexual. Gab will fall over when I tell her.

"Okay."

Resting forearms on her shoulders I smile into dark, dark eyes. I try to lighten the mood a little.

"One day I'll get you to say a whole paragraph."

Her lips curl into a lopsided grin. My hand runs through a thick mane of silky black hair.

"I'm not very verbal, am I?"

"No, Dis, you're not."

Her hands hold my waist. We stare at each other. She slowly moves her face closer, kissing my cheek.

"Thanks for telling me about what happened."

Her soft tone leaves me a little speechless. Our roles reverse as she gets to have the words because all I can manage is, "S'okay."

She lets my waist go and slowly we separate.

"Bathroom."

Is all she says.

The door clicks open then shut. I just stand in the middle of the room feeling numb and a little alone. It's not something I'm used to. Suddenly my mobile rings. It almost gives me a heart attack. The display flashes a name. Avoiding *this* woman would get me a slap upside my head.

"Yes, Gab?"

*"I wanted to show you I know how to use this thing. What are you doing?"*

I lower my voice.

"Dis is here."

*"Please don't tell me I interrupted something?"*

"Like I'd answer the phone in the middle of what you're referring to. No, we were talking."

*"She doesn't talk. What were you really doing?"*

I sit on the bed, taking a moment before answering.

"No, we were talking. Honest."

*"You sound down. Did she say something to you?"*

I let the silence stretch. Not on purpose but more because tonight has thrown me.

"It's not like that. She's stressed about her latest mission. We were talking about that, and, you know, when I did it."

Her exhaled breath makes the line crackle.

*"Are you alright? Where is she now?"*

"I'm fine. She's in the bathroom. I'm okay, though."

*"And that means you're not because you're repeating. Do you want me to come across?"*

"She's staying. I'm okay."

*"That's the third time you've told me."*

The door opens and I stare up at Dis who starts to back out of the room. I hold up my other hand and shake my head.

"No, it's just Gab."

*"Let me speak to her."*

"What? No way."

*"Michelle, either let me speak to her or I'm coming across right now. It's your choice."*

I pull the phone away from my ear and stare at it. She would come, too. I hand it over. Dis takes it like it'll bite.

"Hello? Oh, hey."

She stares at me and frowns. Well, not at me but obviously what Gab is saying. But then that frown falls and her eyes close. When they reopen her expression is - pretty expressive for Discord Knight.

She says one word.

"Sure."

She hands the phone back. I stare down at the blank screen. Gab's gone.

"What did she say?"

She puts a finger to her lips and shakes her head. She gets into bed and moves to the opposite side. Her hand points at the light then the empty side.

"But what did she say?"

She shakes her head and pulls the covers back, then simply points at the light and the bed again. I shrug and send us into darkness. I slide in and the covers are drawn over me. My eyes open fully, getting used to blackness.

Her voice makes my arms prickle because of the nearness.

"Lie on your side, facing the door."

"What...?"

"Don't argue."

I roll over and a warm arm glides over my waist. A hand holds onto mine. The rest of her body slides until all of her connects with all of me. Warm breath heats my neck, slipping across my skin. Lips kiss there once...

"Night."

...just like Gab used to do when I couldn't sleep. I instantly relax.

"Did she tell you to do this?"

"Yes."

"I'm okay."

"That's number four."

I squeeze her hand and close my eyes.

## 30 CUPID'S INTRODUCTION

Like I said, Gabrielle is a very clever woman. She's also a good judge of people - has to be working in Intelligence. She knew Discord and Michelle could be good for each other. Now, in what respect, lovers, friends, etc, was still to be determined. That was something, as a good friend, Gabrielle wasn't going to interfere with.

That night moved Dis and Michelle's friendship forward. Things weren't just about sex now. It'd subtly deepened their reliance on each other.

Dis was getting ready for her mission against Mr Child Killer. You can imagine, lots of paper, double checking facts, blah, blah. All takes time and it all takes its toll.

In the middle of it, the yearly office-bonding-thing came around again. You know, a time for all the departments to get together and relax. They usually grate on my nerves but not Elle's. She might be a God but she knows how to reward her staff.

The party happened in a fitting arena. Las Vegas. And boy was there going to be some rocking and rolling.

## Chapter Thirty: Discord
## 5th December, Year 2 - 03:00
## How Much Will You Gamble?

"I want to play the slot machines."

I pause snapping my toothpick. Everyone left in the bar, including me, stares at Elle. She shrugs and takes another sip of her blue cocktail. It's her third and considering she doesn't drink she's doing well. Still, it's not really my place to be worrying about her anymore.

A familiar catlike brunette opens and closes her cocktail umbrella. She catches my eye and winks as her voice fills the bar.

"You can't gamble. You're a God. It's a sin."

Elle chuckles, her cheeks a little flushed from the drink.

"Now, how can it be a sin if I've never tried it? If it displeases me I'll confirm its status, otherwise I'm going to take this place for all it's worth."

A wave of laughter sounds. She stands and slips back into her heels, increasing her height by a good four inches. I look away in case I'm staring, and graduate from my toothpick to peeling the label from my beer bottle.

A finger taps the wooden table next to my pile of shredded paper. I glare up at the owner of that hand. Psyche stares back. Her voice is low and considered.

"Someone has to go with her. She doesn't drink and I don't want her getting lost or making anyone a Saint."

I answer that insane suggestion with an obvious one of my own.

"You go."

She sighs as if I'm an idiot.

"I have my Queen and ten of the Royal Guard to watch and that's why I'm completely sober. Otherwise, believe me, I'd never be asking."

I glance over at Elle and try to keep my reasoning sound, and my temper in check at being spoken to as if I'm five.

"I'm here with Michelle."

Well, kind of, we travelled down together.

She takes a measured breath.

"I'm not asking you to rent a room together. Just look after her. Michelle won't even notice you're gone. I'll make sure of that. Be back in an hour."

I stare at her after that command.

"Are you ordering me?"

She straightens her shoulders and closes her eyes. They slowly reopen.

"No. I'm asking."

My brain reminds me Elle and I have ended our relationship, and at some point I'll have to be alone with her. I stare at my half finished beer. It's not as if I'll be driving this body under the influence. I glance across to a poker machine in the corner. Mich and that catlike brunette are hitting all of the buttons in no particular order, laughing and joking.

As if sensing my hung decision, Psyche adds.

"I'm asking because you're the most visually discouraging to hangers-on, and more importantly, I've watched you and that beer. You're sober and no one else in this room is."

I take a deep breath and whisper.

"If this is some kind of trick to get Elle in trouble with the Council...."

She puts her hand over mine, bending down, looking directly at me. Her tone softens.

"I'm on your side. I also want Elle back in one piece. You better hurry before she gets away from you."

She already got away from me.

Elle grabs her purse and heads out of the bar. I leave it for a count of ten then get up and follow.

She's surprisingly quick in heels. I guess she's had years of practise. I jog to catch up. A quick glance from her turns into a double take. She stops before we enter the casino floor. I lean against the thick brass railing. The noise from the machines makes everything seem surreal.

She raises a questioning eyebrow. I shrug.

"I'm here to protect you."

She smiles softly.

"From myself or the public?"

I look away, across the casino floor, over the heads of the twenty or so people who are up at this hour.

"Both." I remember my manners, having got out of practice from not being in her company for so long. "Your Eminence."

Her hand touches mine. I turn and those eyes hit me, too.

"You don't need to call me that, Dizzy. It's okay."

No, it's not.

I keep my hands by my sides and change the topic back to where it should be.

"You want to play the slots?"

"That's the plan."

A waitress in a tight fitting uniform stops.

"Cocktails, ladies?"

I open my mouth to order a diet coke for Elle but she beats me to it.

"Can you make real cocktails?"

The woman smiles.

"We can make anything you want and very well, ma'am."

"Excellent. I'll have a Bikini Martini." She turns to me thoughtfully. "And a Pussycat for my friend. Thank you."

The waitress jots our order down on her pad.

"Where will you be, ma'am?"

Elle turns around, pointing to the quarter slot nearest. The waitress nods, leaving us alone.

"I normally drink beer."

She sits down at the machine, patting the seat next to her. I sit, glad the chairs are wide enough to give us some distance.

"I remember but you'll like a Pussycat. It's a tough drink with an underlying sweetness."

I nod. I don't have to finish it.

Elle stares at the buttons and takes a hundred out of her purse. She sounds excited, which is one sign of the alcohol, I guess.

"What do I do?"

I make sure I only touch the note as I take it from her outstretched hand. Folding it up I drop it back in her purse.

"We'll start small and work up to that later."

I fish around in my pocket and pull out a twenty. I grab a plastic bucket and feed the note into the slot. Elle's face lights up as I hit the payout button. Quarters ding in the metal tray as my twenty converts into change.

"Thought you'd like to put the coins in instead of playing the note."

She looks ecstatic and pulls handfuls of coins out, dropping them into the bucket. She tucks a stray strand of hair behind her ear, and then those blue eyes turn on me. She rubs my arm and my jaw tightens.

"This is fun already. We should sit here and change notes all night. At least we won't lose anything."

The waitress arrives. I tip her a ten to make sure she keeps coming back.

My drink doesn't look lethal so I take a sip. I shouldn't have doubted her. It's good

"I thought you'd like it - Pussycat."

She chuckles teasingly. I stare into the dark contents of my glass. I keep things safe, muttering, "It's nice."

Silence. Even the machines have taken a pause. Then her hand lies on top of mine. I can't help but look into eyes that give me shivers.

"I was hoping we wouldn't be uncomfortable or stilted around each other."

Yeah, so was I. I don't tell her that because there's no point, but more importantly I'm here as a guardian nothing more.

I offer something nice and safe.

"This is a good chance to work on it."

She squeezes my hand. It slips away and taps the machine.

"So, how do we win?"

"By not playing."

I spend the next few minutes explaining the slots to her. I don't think she cares about winning. She always liked glittery things so I guess she's playing more for the noise and colours. She's also still handling her alcohol a lot better than I thought. Apart from being a little flushed and more playful you'd never notice. It's a real gift.

After a deep breath, she makes her announcement.

"I am ready to start."

Her eyebrows furrow as I feed four coins in and press to play them all.

"If you play four at once you get a chance at hitting the jackpot that is..." I stare up at the amounts on a screen on the top of the machine. "...eight thousand dollars. If you play any less you get a tenth of that."

"Four it is, then."

Her hand taps the play button and the machine hums to life. The lights flash, the speakers vibrate and Elle wins - nothing.

She takes another sip of her cocktail, tapping the bucket of coins I'm holding.

"More. Put more in."

I insert another four. This time she takes a deep breath and crosses her fingers. She looks at me from the corner of her eyes.

"I have lucky hands, remember."

Yeah, I remember.

She hits the play button. I wonder if all newcomers are so hopeful on their first trips to Vegas with.... The slot machine starts beeping and throwing coins out. I lean over, staring at the lines. All sevens. Jackpot.

She jumps up...

"We won! We won!"

...then ducks down, pulling handfuls of coins out, dropping them into the bucket. My ears fill with intense noise, her elation, and metallic chinking. I slump in my seat, thankful we're not drawing attention to ourselves.

"Quick. Go get another bucket!"

I walk to the end of the line of slots and motion to an attendant. Our machine will only pay out so much before the cashier needs to settle the rest; not even a Las Vegas slot machine holds eight thousand dollars worth of quarters. As I turn back I'm greeted by a huge crowd surrounding her. I got my distraction. It's not just Elle and me. Now it's Elle, me, and the rest of the casino floor.

A man pats her on the back as I push my way through. I stand in his personal space. I have a good five inches over him. I growl my words out.

"Less laying on hands."

He turns and recoils swiftly. I always recognise that look because I used to get it enough when I was alive. It's shock. Benefits of being a female over six foot.

Elle leans closer. I jam my hands in my back pockets.

"He was only congratulating me."

Yeah, bet he was.

"I'm here to make sure you stay safe."

"Thank you." She smiles. "Now if you don't mind, I'm going to go and put more coins into my bucket."

I stand back, being what I'm best at, a deterrent. No one gets too close. The attendant who prints a voucher for the rest of her win keeps his distance, and it only takes a few sentences to stop the Armani suited pit-boss from calling their publicity people. Eventually another machine hits a jackpot and our fickle onlookers move away to their fresh meat.

I grab three heavy buckets of coins and Elle takes one. We head off to find an open booth. I spot an automated payout machine in the corner.

"We can swap this for notes and cash the voucher in over there."

The noise of the machines fills our silence as we walk over to our quiet corner. I dump my buckets down on the top of the payout machine.

"Damn!"

Suddenly hers falls out of her hands. Her eyes squeeze shut the instant it hits the floor, spilling quarters everywhere. She reopens them one at a time, chuckling.

"Perhaps that last cocktail wasn't such a good idea?"

I stare down into a puddle of coins glad most of the winnings are in voucher form.

"No problem. There are only two hundred quarters to pick up."

My knees sink into the plush carpet and I start to corral them into a pile. Even in heels and that skirt she makes her descent seem elegant. Her lips curl into a slight smile as she picks the coins up one by one, dropping them back into the bucket with a cheery ding. I make sure my fingers aren't in the pile when hers are.

Suddenly I realise I'm the only one shifting coins. I glance up and she's paused, watching me intently. My fingers loosen their grip as we stare at each other.

"I'm sorry, Dizzy."

I don't look away.

"It was an accident."

Her head tilts as she smiles sadly.

"I don't mean about this."

Her hand lifts slowly across our gap. Fingertips graze my lower lip. My pulse speeds up at her touch, as if my skin remembers what it should be doing - or more like, shouldn't. Every part of me screams to pull away, but I don't. Inhibitions I've struggled to control, explode messily. My body sways towards hers. Painful inches keep me on the side of sane, and her on the side of someone I should be over. Then her warm breath covers my lips, and my eyes slide shut. My hand rests on her arm, keeping her near. A second later and that teasing gap closes. Her lips touch mine. We kiss urgently, my body heating up in an instant. Hands slide into my hair and pull me closer, and it's exactly how it used to be. My need for her flares into frightening proportions.

Then she's gone. It all stops, the suddenness brutal. I keep my eyes closed for that one moment, some part of me hoping my nightmare won't happen, but hiding didn't help me before and it doesn't help now.

I open them. Her shocked face says hello back.

"I didn't mean to...."

I feel like asking why she did then.

Her hand touches my arm and I recoil, physically moving away. I push the coins back in the bucket.

"Dizzy..."

"Don't." My tone is fierce but I can't help it. "For once, just don't."

I glance up and her face is stone. I wish I could switch that on so quickly.

I finish cashing her coins and voucher in, and check the notes. Eight thousand dollars is a lot of good luck, none of it mine.

We walk back in silence. I don't look at her. I don't try and act like that kiss hasn't affected me. It has. It hurts. It hurts even more when we're outside the bar and I see Mich laughing with that brunette. After everything she's done for me I do this? I feel like a grade-A asshole. Then I wonder why I'm thinking that? Mich and I aren't involved...really. Confusion is not something I'm good at and to add to mine...

"Dizzy?"

I turn, suddenly, ripped out of my thoughts. Elle comes to an abrupt stop.

"*What?*"

She pulls me to the side, behind a partition, away from prying eyes. I rip my arm out of her grip. I'm not angry with her but me. I spend all this time getting over her to slide all the way back? What kind of idiot am I?

"I didn't plan that."

"I know."

I don't know what else to say.

Her blue eyes spear me even though I try to get away.

"I still care a lot about you."

Sense makes me clamp down. My fist hits the wooden panelled wall, hard, noisily. She jumps, startled.

For once my words come in order and making some kind of sense.

"You can't say this kind of thing to me anymore. I'm moving on and you're not ruining that, Elle."

She whispers, almost angrily.

"It wasn't just me. You kissed me back."

My mouth opens then shuts. I did.

"And I'm already regretting it."

As soon as the words are out I know I shouldn't have said them. She takes the impact. Arms cross defensively over her chest now she has nothing left to defend.

I want to say I didn't mean it, that I'm sorry if I hurt her, but I don't. I can't take it back. Nothing can go back.

I turn and start to walk away.

"Dizzy, wait."

I guess my legs still listen to her because I stop. Her heads tilts as she continues.

"I don't want us to hate each other. Please."

This time I tell the truth. The whole truth.

"I could never hate you." The painful truth. "But I'll never love you again."

The shock on her face is instant.

I get control of my legs and walk back into the bar, feeling more angry and hurt than I have in a long time. Only Psyche notices my arrival. She starts talking to Mich, meaning I slip back in unnoticed.

I hear Elle's announcement.

"Las Vegas is eight thousand dollars lighter."

A loud round of applause sounds as I order a double Scotch. Psyche walks by, pausing long enough to whisper.

"One piece. Well done."

Well done me.

"My pleasure," in an alternative reality where ripping your insides out is actually pleasant.

Then, as if sensing I'm having a really shitty day, Mich arrives. I flounder as a wave of guilt swallows me.

I stare into my drink for a moment before she nudges my shoulder.

"You don't look like you're having much fun."

I'm not.

"I'm okay. Relaxing, you know."

I down my drink in one. A warm arm slips around my shoulders and she stares at me in the mirror behind the bar. Her lips form a slow smile. I close my eyes, savouring this feeling of safety.

She whispers.

"Want to come and watch me lose a few hundred bucks? I'll even let you press my buttons."

I meet those happy green eyes in our reflection. She wiggles her eyebrows. I catch Elle looking over and that decides it for me.

"Sure."

I get up and go with her, leaving Elle far away, where she should've stayed.

I concentrate on the slot machine. That same catlike brunette winks at me. Mich prods her in the side.

"Best friend, Gabrielle. She heads intelligence. Oxymoron."

Gabrielle. A face to the name and voice. She rolls her eyes and holds her hand out. We shake. She's got a firm grip. It's a good sign.

"You've probably already figured out that Michy talks too much."

Despite myself, I let a half smile out.

"She's not quiet."

Gabrielle snorts a laugh before wiggling her empty glass and pointing to the bar.

"Well, I wouldn't know about that."

I stare at her back as heat creeps on my cheeks. Mich holds her forehead.

"She's had too many cocktails. I'll kill her for that. Sorry."

I remember what I was doing ten minutes ago. I glance across. Elle's talking to Sam, but for a second she catches my eye. Pools of ice blue try to hold on. I shift, turning away.

"No harm."

Her hand slaps the side of a slot machine.

"How about we lose some cash? I mean, it's only paper, right?"

The next half an hour is a pleasurable blur. I don't know what I expected, maybe to feel awful and have a bad time? I don't, and I'm having a good time considering what's gone on. The miracle that's raised my mood has been Gabrielle and Mich. I've listened to them bicker, more than play the slots. It's been unique.

Mich pats my arm, snapping me out of my trance.

"Ladies room. Back soon."

I flick a stray peanut off of our table.

"You look more relaxed than the beginning of the night, Discord."

Gabrielle sits down opposite.

"I am."

This is one of my problems. I'm worse than awful at small talk. My teenage years were spent with horses or nature not people or nurture. But, and I can see why they get on, Gabrielle has the same skill as Mich. They both fill gaps effortlessly.

Her hands play with a coaster, tapping it on the table.

"Vegas is great for relaxing in. You can sit and do nothing, but still watch so much going on. Lights, cameras and action, huh?"

I make a special effort to say something meaningful. She is Mich's best friend. I don't want to look like an ass.

"The city of sin never sleeps. Lucky for the casinos, I guess."

She smiles.

"I didn't get a chance to say thanks for helping the other night. Talking about why she left Vengeance always throws her."

She's being totally genuine. I return the compliment.

"She's helped me enough. It's about time I gave something back."

Her next sentence takes me by surprise.

"I think I'm going to like you, Discord."

What do you say to that?

"Thanks."

"Pleasure. What floor did they put you on?"

I blink, left fielded. I dig my swipe card out of my pocket and stare at the accompanying tag.

"Umm...fourteen."

"That's us, too. I'm heading up when she comes back. I'll leave you two at the mercy of the machines. It was good to finally meet you."

I nod.

"Same here."

"One more thing. Tomorrow...I mean, if you guys hang out at all tomorrow, make sure she drinks plenty of water? She's been on wine most of the night and that's not good. I have a seminar to give on Monday so my attention span is fully booked."

I force my mouth to say more than one word.

"I'll be in charge of hangover recovery."

Gabrielle's entire face changes into a stunning smile. That's when Mich bangs into the table.

"Ouch. If I get a bruise."

She rubs her leg where the table connected. Gabrielle stands and takes her arm.

"Michy, I'm heading up. It's you two versus the casino."

Mich frowns.

"Vegas is boring now. All these machines do is eat my cash." She turns to me, raising her eyebrows. "You want to come up? I have a huge room, it's not crowded."

I catch a glimpse of Elle in one of the mirrors. She stares at me before turning away suddenly, taking Sam's arm.

"I'm on the fourteenth, too. Sure."

We make it up without incident. I sit down as Mich takes delivery of room service in preparation for tomorrow: two litres of water, some Advil, and a bucket of fruit. I flick through infomercial after infomercial, settling on a B-Movie with too many ads.

Mich floats about the room. It didn't take me long to realise that she's a little drunk. Not that you can tell right off, just her normal chattiness isn't so coherent - it's just as funny, though.

Gabrielle pokes her head through the adjoining door.

"I know, I'm a wimp, but I'm off to bed."

Mich's head whips around and she throws her hands up.

"We only just got here."

Gabrielle rests her head on the side of the open door.

"I have a mammoth headache coming and that seminar to write tomorrow. Discord will keep you company."

Mich turns to me and shrugs an apology. Gabrielle adds as a reminder.

"Make her drink her water or she'll be a beast tomorrow. I'm gone."

The door closes at the same time Mich shouts.

"Lightweight."

She walks to the table and pours out a glass of water.

"Wine doesn't agree with me. I don't know why I drank so much."

She sits on the corner of this huge bed and downs the water. I stay where I am and stare at the remote in my hand: cheap plastic, typical, too many buttons.... Suddenly a tanned hand slips it from mine. The bed bounces as she moves and sits next to me. She starts to flick through the channels.

"There's nothing...Resident Evil, great film. You wanna watch with me?"

She nudges my shoulder with hers. She's very warm.

"Sure."

The film's good just like she said. It's kept my mind off of what it shouldn't be on and for that I'm thankful.

Suddenly the phone rings. She leans over to pick up, giving me goose bumps when her hand rests lightly on my thigh. I force thoughts of sex out of my mind, but it's not easy, she's a good looking woman.

"No, we're still up. No, watching a film. Okay, thank you. I'll speak to you tomorrow."

The phone goes down. She says one word, "Gab," and jerks her eyebrows. The phone rings again.

"I'm Miss Popular."

She picks up, leaning over again, resting her body on my thighs.

"Gab, can't you.... Oh, hello." She shifts off of me. "Um...I can't. I know, but - I'm busy."

I tap her arm and point to the door. I don't want to interrupt anything. She squeezes my arm and shakes her head.

"Listen, we can talk tomorrow when we get back.... Hello? Hello?"

The phone goes back down and she chuckles deeply.

"Guess I'm a little less popular now."

"If you have something you need to do, I can go?"

She smiles, leans back on the headboard and flicks through the channels, stopping on CNN.

"There's nothing I need to do."

For the next ten minutes we listen to details of civil unrest, political insurrection, football scores, and the weather around a place I used to pay attention to. She flicks over to a cartoon, then mutes the TV and stares at the remote.

"I was thinking. What are you doing for New Year? Just, Gab and me are having a party and I thought you might like to come."

At least she's consistent in her weird train of thought.

"I'm not great at parties."

My people skills are nonexistent, parties are torture.

"You'll be with me. I mean, I'll look after you. It's more a gathering than a full on party. You don't have to. I won't be offended if you say no."

She pats my leg but leaves her hand there. I get a waft of her perfume.

She smells nice.

"Yes? No?"

Mich has never failed to be good company, and more importantly I'd like to spend it with her. I need to see the next year in on a more positive note.

"Sure, but I'm not great with conversation, so...."

Her hand squeezes my thigh, a thumb rubbing the seam of my jeans.

"I'll cover for you."

I cover for me as I try not to notice her hand and what it's doing.

"Who's going?"

"Gab, me and now you. John and Sam. I think Gab's asked her secretary pool - who are all crazy, I hope they come. Also, my assistant Jen and her boyfriend. So, small but perfectly formed."

"I guess I can cope with that."

"Excellent."

She gets up, wrinkling her nose.

"That wine's kicking in. I need Advil and some sleep."

I swing my legs off of the bed, grabbing my jacket because there's nothing worse than an unwelcome visitor.

"I should get going."

"Oh." She frowns and scratches her forehead, and for the first time looks confused and uncomfortable. "Okay, I'll see you tomorrow...today - later on, whatever."

Her arms cross. Gabrielle was right, she isn't good with wine.

"Remember to drink your water."

I tap the bottle as I pass. The phone rings and she holds the receiver to her chest as I open the door.

"Give me a knock when you're heading down for breakfast if you want some company?"

"Sure."

I close the door and try and remember which way my room is. These halls are like rabbit warrens. I stare at the signs and fish my swipe card out. Before I take three steps another door opens and Gabrielle's head pops out. She jiggles an ice bucket.

"Do you want to escort me to the ice machine?"

My smile isn't forced. Neither is my answer.

"Sure. I'd hate for you to get hijacked on the way back."

She chuckles.

"Vegas is full of ice thieves. It is a desert, after all."

I lean on the machine while she holds the button, shaking the bucket to level the cubes. An olive skinned woman passes, carrying a huge plastic cup of coins. Looks like Elle wasn't the only one who took Vegas for some change.

"Hey, Gab." Her eyes slide down me and she winks. "Dashing."

My cheeks burn. Gabrielle pats my arm, shaking her head with a smile.

"Hello, Jen. This is Discord."

Jen's eyebrows raise and she cradles the plastic container, holding her hand out. I shake it. Another firm grip.

"Sorry, I thought you were with Gab." She nudges Gabrielle with an elbow. "But then you'd need to date someone to get someone, wouldn't you, Gabrielle."

Jen moves quickly, ducking an incoming ice cube as she runs down the hall.

"I'll tell Michelle you need some training for that arm!"

She dives into her room leaving us alone by the machine. Gabrielle clarifies, explaining their playfulness.

"Jen is Michy's assistant."

"I wondered."

I catch an escaping cube, putting it back in her bucket.

"I know I said it downstairs, but I thought I'd say it again. I appreciate you being there for Michy. I can try to understand but I never truly will. You put my mind at rest."

I make a distinct effort to speak more than two words.

"It's not like it was a hardship."

She smiles, levelling off the ice with the palm of her hand then wiping the moisture off on her pants.

"She's easy to get along with, isn't she?"

My mouth twitches into a smile all on its own.

"Yes, she is."

I carry her ice bucket.

She motions towards Mich's door as we walk back to her room. Gabrielle switches direction effortlessly.

"Are you two not hanging out?"

"The wine made her tired."

"She's had a hard week, too, which is probably why she drank all the wine. My week is why I had that third cocktail. It's not doing good things to my head. I'm not going to get much work done tomorrow."

She opens her door and takes the bucket back, smiling, mirroring Mich's offer.

"Come and knock for us if you want company at breakfast. And thanks for protecting me from those ice thieves."

I give her a deep bow.

"Pleasure, ma'am."

Gabrielle curtseys.

"Charmed, I'm sure." She pats my arm. "Night, Discord."

"Night."

Her door shuts.

They're well suited. Both are great at putting me at ease and that's not a simple thing to do.

Suddenly, Gabrielle's neighbour opens her door. A surprised blonde stares at me like I have two heads. Mich then looks along the hall, then back at me.

"You lost?"

"I met Gabrielle. Helped with ice gathering. Mission accomplished."

She leans on the door frame, her legs crossed at the ankles.

"She's had too many cocktails. She needs it for her head."

"I thought you were going to sleep?"

A soft smile lights up her face.

"I was, but I heard what I thought was the sound of Discord Knight speaking. I had to come and investigate."

I can't help but laugh.

"She's easy to talk to."

Just like you.

"One of the reasons I love her to bits."

We stare at each other for a moment.

"Listen, I'm not going to sleep right away. Even if I do, I have a huge bed." She hooks a thumb over her shoulder. "You wanna play sleepovers?"

It's not a difficult choice, but I pause to make it seem like I'm at least thinking about it.

"Sure."

She smiles and moves out of the way.

The room comes equipped with two miniatures of everything including toothbrushes, and weirdly, shoeshine kits. I have a quick shower and put on a loaned tee and shorts; a woman's clothes I can borrow are a rare thing. When I exit only the TV and a small lamp, light the room. Mich is lying on her stomach, on top of the covers, to one side of the bed. She's flicking through the channels, shaking her head as she moves on each time.

"So many channels and so little to watch. How does that work?"

She rolls over, sitting up, smiling. Her voice is soft.

"Feel better?"

I throw my towel on a chair and she mutes the TV.

"A lot."

Her smile relaxes away and she pats the empty side of the bed. I lie down and look along my naked thighs then up at a TV silently reporting a hurricane somewhere. I wiggle my toes as houses and trees blow from one side of the screen to the other.

"Is that us? Did we do that?"

I point my toes at the screen and glance over as she settles closer.

"Might be a big Vengeance case we need a lot of cover for. Could be Lucy being bad, or you know what, it could be the Earth doing its own thing. Let's face it, we can't even control what we do have."

She shrugs. I turn back to houses being picked up like they're made of Balsa and torrential water swirling around, sucking towns from their foundations. I press a button and the pictures implode down into a small white dot. The screen goes black.

Mich rolls over, propping her head up on a hand. She smiles and it reaches all the way up to those green eyes. She's everything you'd expect of an Angel: blonde, perfect features, beautiful. And she's nothing you'd expect of an Angel: tempting, sexual, and, as her hand reaches over to mine and removes the remote, aggressive. She throws it somewhere and slides closer until our bodies are almost touching.

I rest my hand on her hip. She's very warm. Her fingertips touch my face and slide off, down my neck, coming to a stop on my shoulder. I'm pushed onto my back. She watches her own hand move down my chest, glancing up as she pauses on my breast. She gently moves it over the material of my top. I try not to show how good it feels but it's a challenge. Then she takes that softly moving hand away and slides it down to push the hem up. My eyes close. There's a pause. I wait. No hand touches me. My eyes open. She's frowning and I feel why. A finger slowly traces around a light jagged scar near my ribs. It makes me tense.

"I never saw this before. Guess I was occupied."

I push up on my elbows and stare down. Not that I have to. I know what it is. It is impossible to forget.

I stare down into raising eyebrows.

"Interesting story behind it?"

I sigh.

"It was how I ended up dead."

Green eyes disappear in a long blink. Her finger pauses.

"I guess that's pretty interesting. What happened?"

She folds her arms and leans them on my stomach. Her chin rests on her knuckles as she stares at my scar.

"Car crash."

My stomach muscles tense in time with her breathing. Also, despite the subject matter, she's still touching me, and some part of me obviously likes that. It's a confusing mix of emotions and feelings.

"Do you not want to talk about it?"

I wonder if I want to get into all of this, because I can't easily get back out. Then I remember what it must have taken for her to tell me about crashing out of Vengeance. That took courage.

"No, it's okay."

Except my mouth clamps shut, refusing to give up all of its secrets.

"I shouldn't push you, car accidents are bad."

I press a finger against her lips, willing to give a little.

"I didn't die from the car crash. I drowned."

Her eyebrows sink. My mouth takes on a life of its own.

"I was coming back from a funeral. It was dark, raining. I was upset and the road slippery. I must've spaced out. My car flipped into a river. It was too much of a shock. My hands couldn't get my safety belt off or the door open."

She kisses my finger before softly speaking meaningful words.

"A funeral for a funeral."

You have no idea.

I take a moment to settle, and then do what I've done since I've been here. I bury the real truth where it has to live: deep down in dark recesses where it can be controlled.

"Yeah, well...."

"So, how did you get the scar?"

My stomach muscles jerk, feeling a small amount of the same shock they did on that night. I try not to shift too obviously.

"I crashed through a safety barrier to get into the river. I took part of it with me. Sliced clean through the windscreen and into my ribs. Still, it made it quick. What with that and the cold there was nothing I could do."

She kisses my stomach, just below my scar. It echoes through me.

"I'm sorry."

Is all she says. It's all she has to.

Her finger traces along it then off, following the bend of a rib.

Some say the past can drag you down, and they're right, the truth pulled me into a river to drown in the dark, alone.

"We all have to die sometime, Mich."

I tug on her shirt, pulling her up, trying to stop all of the memories that haunt me even now. I kiss her as hands slide under my top, circling my nipples. My body pushes into hers, wanting more, much more. She kisses my neck and whispers.

"Not anymore, we don't."

I finish what she started.

# 31 CUPID'S INTRODUCTION

That little fiasco in Vegas hit Elle hard. Charity picked the pieces up. I know what you're thinking, she bought it on herself. Maybe she did, but feelings can't be turned off like a faucet.

Despite everything going on in the Heavens, Lucy was still being Lucy. Her stats had spent the last month suffering. The souls her people were allowed to bring in were diminishing. Before that hiccup in Vegas, Elle had gone into super overdrive on detecting Lucy's soul stealing schemes. Miss Efficient, Charity Nature, ensured every soul audit was correct down to the last anally retentive decimal point. Lucy was getting more and more frustrated. No matter what her marketing people did the gap wasn't closing.

Understand, Lucy's agents were everywhere, following mortals and Gods alike. Nowhere or no one was safe. She had blanket coverage and used every means available to win. Remember, a bored Devil is a dangerous one.

Just like the Amazons, Lucy caught the two doomed ex-lovers being complacent. And, boy, were they going to pay for it.

## Chapter Thirty-One: Lucy
## 7th December, Year 2 - 12:30
## The Camera Never Lies

"**W**hat is it, Bee? I'm busy."

I lift my head up from my desk, resisting the urge to rub my eyes and smudge my mascara.

"You were asleep."

I explain even though I don't have to.

"I was dreaming up nasty things to do to those *Angles* in the Heavens. You interrupted a fruitful and time saving exercise."

A hand goes up in surrender. One thing about Bee, she knows her place. It's a pleasant change from my usual power hungry assistants. I was lucky to get her.

"We've had reports from our agents about Discord and Elle."

She waves an envelope then pauses, deciding she'd rather move from her usual stoicism to shifting about. Bee has yet to learn a very important lesson. I've been alive since time began. I've heard all the bad news there is to hear. Nothing's a shock anymore.

I lean my chin in my palm, watching and waiting. I'm tired. I've had a hard day. I want to soak in the hot tub not drag info out of my assistant. I click my fingers repeatedly, yawning. She finally opens the envelope.

"You might want to take a look at these pictures."

She slides the contents across my desk and leaves quickly. I've seen death and destruction - actually I've been the cause of most of it. I've been witness to plagues and massacres. I have personally examined most of the inside of the human form when it's been on the outside. I flip the pictures over quickly, already bored with this. I want to be doing bad things to good people, not sitting in my office.... My eyes widen as my jaw clenches so hard my teeth creek. A flash of heat spreads through me threatening to ignite my explosive temper. I slam my fist down, rising quickly.

*"Bee!"*

Her head pokes around my door.

"I knew you'd be angry."

I swivel the picture around.

"What is this?"

She drops the tone of her voice making it as smooth as velvet. However, that won't appease me after this.

"It's a picture of Elle and Discord."

I grab one of them, waving it at her. I've been irritable all week. My stats are two points lower than last quarter. Elle's not going to win. Not after this picture, anyway.

She senses I'm on the edge of my temper precipice.

"Try to remain calm. It was taken a couple of days ago in Vegas."

I'm incredulous.

"I can't steal a kitten's soul and she's gambling in the city of sin?"

I walk around my desk, rubbing the back of my neck, trying to find the underlying cause of this.

"I thought they were over, Bee?"

She shrugs, her fingers playing with her pen, clicking the lid on and off. I make her uncomfortable when I'm like this. I should. I own this body and I have no idea what I'll do.

"Intelligence said they were."

I stare at the picture again. The crisp image of Elle and Discord kissing imprints into my consciousness. I don't like surprises unless I'm giving them.

I wave it in front of her, my voice rising.

"This doesn't look like they're over, does it?"

A bare shake of her head is all I get. I verge into a rant, because the more I think about it the more annoyed I am.

"This looks to me like they are a disgraceful item. This looks to me as though my people aren't doing their jobs properly. This looks to me..." I stop and move my face to within inches of hers. "...as though you're not doing your job properly. I thought the Amazons had dealt with this relationship?"

Her eyes narrow the slightest amount at the accusation. Bee will take a lot but she's not cowardly. She stands up to me when I'm wrong - which isn't often, but it's enough for me to respect her heaving bosom.

She defends her honour. Her hands settle on her hips.

"They did deal with them and I am doing my job properly. I've checked our surveillance, and if this is to be trusted as evidence of a rekindled relationship then it's only just happened."

I turn away so she can't see me smiling. Bee's great.

I sit on the edge of my desk and think out loud.

"There's only one way to find out what's going on, and that's to ask our Wondrous Highness herself." I stand. "I'm going to see Elle."

I pick the envelope up off my desk, sliding the close-up in.

"Do I get a good luck kiss?"

She stares at me, her face blank.

"No."

"Never hurts to ask."

I click my fingers and transport myself in to Elle's reception. My eyes take a few seconds to get accustomed to the low lighting she has up here. It's much brighter downstairs. I pop a glucose tablet, crunching quickly to top my energy levels up; wouldn't do to pass out in a devily little heap on Elle's floor.

Sam stands, pointing, shocked at my arrival.

"You don't have an appointment!"

I stare at that finger and without warning hiss. She retracts her arm in a fraction of a second.

"I don't need a *fuckin'* appointment, Sam. And point that at me again and I'll eat it."

She squeaks as I walk towards Elle's door. Normally I'd be more intelligent with my threats but my mood is waning, I'm hungry, and this picture is the last straw. I push her Holy Highness's door open. Sam comes running up, trying to stop me. As if. I turn around and bark. She screams and comes to an abrupt screeching stop.

Elle forms a frowning blockade.

"Don't scare her, Lucy, you could damage the baby." She winks at the blonde paperweight she has posing as a P.A. "It's okay, Sam, I'll deal with her."

"Damage the baby? I think her genes may cause more problems than a raised voice."

Elle glares at me, ushering her back to her desk with a soothing wave. Whatever.

"Your Gracious and Illustrious Wonderfulness, forgive my intrusion."

In a figure hugging herringbone dress she looks edible. She shakes her head, turns and walks back in. I follow.

"I do have an appointment system, Lucy."

She sits behind her desk, looking tired and not her usual glowing self.

"I know, your Elite Perfectness, but think how boring your day would be without a surprise from your favourite Angel."

I sweep her paperwork into a pile and perch on the edge of her desk. My fingers flick idly through some files. She sighs and slides them away. Doesn't trust me. Sensible. I wouldn't.

"What do you want? Your window of opportunity is five minutes."

She leans back, the black leather creaking flirtatiously as her fingers tap on the wooden arm. I put my manila envelope on the desk and slide it over. She watches it curiously, and then glances up.

"What is this, Lucy?"

I smile, safe in the knowledge she'll imminently lose her temper. Elle's very controlled so her explosions are like Hailey's comet - they come around infrequently but are well worth watching. I keep my fingers crossed.

"It's a terrible, terrible thing, Ellie. Seems someone has found out your little secret."

She looks perplexed. Her fingers take hold of the envelope, opening it. I savour the next part. She slips the picture out and her face pales. She looks up suddenly. Her fingers freeze, held just above it as if afraid to touch.

I suck a deep breath of her vulnerability into my lungs. I know her better than she knows herself; a hunter should always know their prey. Her mind is running through excuses, reasons, a way to get out of what she's seen and done. She's weighing up the pros and cons of convincing me not to show this to anyone else. She's also wondering what she can offer and at the same times reconcile with her conscience. Elle does not like making deals with me.

"This is a forgery, Lucy. Nice try."

She throws the picture back and it floats in the air. I stare deeply into her eyes and hold my hand out. Like a feather, my evidence gently lands in my palm. I hold it up, cocking my head, looking at it from all angles.

"Liar, liar, pants on fire, Your Most Illustrious Untruthfulness."

I pace back and forth. She hates me doing it which is more than enough reason. I'm predictably annoying at times, especially when I've lost a week's worth of sleep due to her reign over my stats. The way things are at present, the Earth is heading for six months of happiness, and my staff for six months of emptiness and boredom. Clearly unacceptable.

I stare at the image, running a finger over my lower lip.

"If the lighting was better it could be erotic. If her hands were lower, mildly pornographic. As it is? It's just very, very troubling. A God and a mortal? The Amazons aren't going to like this one bit, Ellie."

Her jaw tenses. I turn the picture towards her, holding it against my chest, keeping it in her field of view.

"What do you want?"

"Aha, we come to the part I enjoy the most. Having you over a barrel. I've already had you over my desk and I enjoyed the practise, so..."

*"What do you want?"*

I sit in the black leather chair in front of her desk. I tap the picture on the arm repeatedly. Her eyes follow it.

"I want you to tell Discord about us. You know, Ellie, the us that's going to be painful for her."

"I don't know what you mean."

I roll my eyes, sighing.

"Let me remind you. After you and Dispawed split up you fell into my loving arms.... Actually, you fell across my desk and we..."

"*Enough.*"

She gets to her feet, her face flushed, enraged. She never looks more alluring than when immersed in drowning anger. She glows.

There's silence for a moment as her eyes dart, as she tries to think this through. Her voice is low.

"And what if I don't tell her?"

She's annoyed to the point of no return. Good. About time something got her riled.

"Then my conscience will have no choice but to show this to the Amazons. They won't be happy, Ellie. I can see a replay of my days here."

I lean back in the seat, closing my eyes as I recall the old times when I sat at her right hand.

"Do you remember it, the charge in the air when we argued, the months of uncertainty over the future of the Heavens? They were interesting days, admit it. Not like these, full of intense boredom, fighting over percentages, figures, numbers, pretend battles with no winners or losers."

"You're insane."

I open my eyes feeling her daggers sticking in to every part of me.

"Elle, please, I like to think of myself as quirky."

"You can't expect me to do this to her, Lucy?"

The corners of my mouth lift in a smile.

"Oh, I do. You wouldn't be lying. You'd be stopping the lies. It's either that or the Amazons will revolt." I stand, smoothing my skirt. "As always, you're the supreme ruler, so it's your choice."

She walks around her desk, her movements lacking her normal grace; she's stiff and tense, shaken and stirred. She stops inches away.

"Why are you doing this?"

I gently caress her cheek with my fingertips. Her skin is baby soft, her eyes the brightest blue you could never imagine. Her beauty is devastating. I'm sure she knows the real reason but I don't offer that.

"Because being bad is what I do best. It's what you expect, and I always try to live up to expectations."

Without breaking our eye contact I reach for her hand and put the picture in it. I lean close and softly kiss her lips, savouring that second of contact, then move my mouth to her ear.

"As you're the boss I'll give you an hour."

Three steps backward and I take one last look before I go. Agonisingly devastated are the two words to describe her.

I leave her alone to think about that oh so difficult problem of how to tell Discord.

## 32 CUPID'S INTRODUCTION

Luce showed her true colours, but I need to repeat, she's not evil, she's just been carrying that torch for Elle so long it's burned more than her fingers.

Elle needed some help with this so she called on Charity. Now, Charity may have been a Don Juan in her own life - she always had a new girl on her arm - but she didn't let that colour her advice. She's good like that. Charity thinks with her head not other parts of her anatomy.

Elle had been upbeat but as she crawled out of the depths of her despair it just meant there was further down to fall.

Rollercoaster time, people. Do up those seatbelts and get ready to hit the bottom of the loop.

# Chapter Thirty-Two: Elle
# 7th December, Year 2 - 13:00
# Dwindling Congregations

**M**y responsibilities as a God are never easy, especially as I carry more than most people could imagine. I turn the glorious Technicolor image over, speed dialling Charity's number as my composure begins to dissolve. I push the receiver to my ear and close my eyes, waiting impatiently. Her answer machine sounds. I slam the phone down, speed dialling her mobile instead. It rings three times before she answers.

*"Charity Nature."*

I don't know what to say.

"It's Elle."

Her voice lowers. She's clearly not alone in her office.

*"Is something wrong?"*

My throat tightens, threatening to betray me.

"Yes."

*"I see. I'll be there as soon as I can."*

"Thank you."

*"You spent all last week listening to me drone on about work, the least I can do is down tools."*

The next thirty minutes feel like hours. I pace, I wait, I try to think of a way out of this mess. I'm not stupid, Lucy's right, this will make Electra's day. It'll give her the excuse she seeks. How ironic. One kiss and my castle threaten to crumble again.

Charity arrives. She sits us down on my sofa, leading me through my story coherently. When I'm finished she doesn't repeat the one explosion she had when I told her about Lucy all those months ago. She keeps her comments as minimal as before.

"There are some things I wish you'd never gotten into. Lucy is one."

If things weren't bad enough, her reaction to that picture makes me lose any hope of us being able to get out of this. Her face is shocked, her eyes wide.

"Is this genuine?"

I want to say no but today untruths have proved they will always come back to haunt me. I nod.

"How did they get it? Don't you have a security net set up to follow Lucy's agents?"

"Normally, but you know John has his hands full with Sam, and I changed the location the night before. Clearly we weren't set up in time."

She grimaces and stares at it, thinking.

"The night before what? When did this happen?"

I look at my hands in my lap. Everything is going badly at present.

"Las Vegas."

"I knew I should've come to that! Oh, Elle, this isn't good. You know that, don't you?"

"Yes."

Her face is a covered in a thick veil of concentration. Suddenly she glances up.

"Are you and Discord seeing each other again?"

I catch a little surprise in her voice.

"No. It was.... It just happened. Nothing else did and nothing else will."

This is not how I imagined eternity going but the fault is mine, I should've known better.

Her fingers tap on her thigh as she bites her lip.

"What would Discord do if she found out about you and Lucy?"

I fall back on the sofa, cursing the impossible situation I'm in again.

"She already hates me so that can't get worse. But it'd hurt her terribly."

She asks a similar question.

"And what would Electra do if she found out about you and Discord?"

"It'd be the end of things as we know it. She'd break the Heavens apart."

Charity takes my hand, rubbing it gently. Her words mirror my thoughts.

"Then I think you have your answer, Elle."

I look at my best friend. Of all of my confidants she's the one I trust implicitly. It's not that the others are untrustworthy just I respect Charity's judgement without reservation. She's my rock.

"All I seem to do is ruin her life. She doesn't deserve this."

She kisses my knuckles.

"Sometimes two people who shouldn't be together get locked into a cycle of self destruction, wrecking everything around them. You and Discord? Bad things happen. The quicker you separate, the quicker you'll find happiness and peace inside yourself and with the Amazons. Why can't you see that? It's just not meant to be."

She squeezes my hand as I offer a colourless statement.

"Everything I did, I did with a pure heart."

I never meant to hurt anyone.

"You're in a terrible position, Elle. Sometimes I wonder how you deal with the pressure, because from your throne so high up, the only way off is down."

She's right, it's impossible to match so many expectations. I rub my temples and look around the room, trying to understand what's going on, not just here, but in my entire life.

Charity continues.

"As for Discord deserving to be hurt. No she doesn't, but she's stronger than you think. Michelle will look after her."

Her words elicit an impossible to rationalise jealousy.

"Yes. She has solid support."

"One more point. If Michelle sees that picture you're guaranteeing Discord's fate. You can stop this misery before it hits the fan."

I hold Dizzy's happiness in my hand, the same happiness guaranteeing my unhappiness. The irony isn't lost.

We talk. Rather, Charity talks and I listen. I try to justify what I'm about to do. Charity says it's the only option, as does my brain. However, my heart? That's another matter. It's whispering that what I'm doing isn't right. It's also telling me I should've had more sense than to sleep with Lucy.

Barely a month after Discord left my life I hit my lowest point. I'd come out of a crippling meeting with the Amazons when Lucy arrived. I'm not going to be pious and blame her because she may have started it but I certainly blew on the flames. She caught the wrong moment at the right time. I was feeling powerless, utterly crushed, all I could see was a solitary eternity stretching out in front of me. Charity was away for a week with work, my support network crumbled and Lucy caught me. It was easy to fall back into the old days with her, even if it was just for one night.

What a series of terrible decisions from a person whose job it is to know better.

I turn to Charity.

"Well then, I should go and deliver the bad news. Never delay hurting Dizzy, that's what I always say."

"It's the only thing you can do."

She squeezes my hand.

"I know, and that makes it even harder."

## 33 CUPID'S INTRODUCTION

What you think will happen often doesn't. Dis, with Michelle's help, wasn't the rabbit in headlights that'd walked in almost two years ago. She was slowly finding herself again. Still, she was in for a whole heap of problems with Elle's coming confession. See, in my experience you shouldn't try to go back with an ex. Look forward and put those proverbial blinkers on, there's always a fresh set of breasts around the corner. However, not everyone can do that.

No matter how hard Discord tried, her heart was still fragile. It wasn't that she was still in love with Elle - I don't think Elle's M.O. with the split meant they ever had another chance - but Discord was still dealing with a lot of hurt and anger. And we all know how she deals with things like that. Badly.

## Chapter Thirty-Three: Discord
## 7th December, Year 2 - 13:15
## In The Bed You Made

Today's been a dog of a day. I haven't managed to get to the gym, I missed breakfast with Mich, and my work is already backing up. I push my office door open with my foot, an armful of files threatening to scatter. I feel like a circus performer attempting my greatest trick. If I pass the balancing act maybe I'll graduate to plate spinning. I've already jumped through hoops.

A figure standing in the middle of my office makes me jump. The threat becomes reality and files rain down all around. My brain catches up a millisecond later, identifying my mystery guest as Elle.

"Hey," I say a little breathlessly.

I stare at the mess my neat paperwork is now in. I bend down, picking it up quickly, looking forward to spending another hour sorting again.

"I didn't mean to startle you."

I nod, dumping it in a heap.

Elle smiles. Her hair is tied back. She's wearing a figure hugging dress.

She looks stunning.

I should be angry with her after Vegas, but I'm not. It was as much me as her. In fact, I'm worse because I've been sleeping with Mich. I should know better.

She uncharacteristically bites a nail; she prides herself on that fact they're as well manicured as the rest of her.

Curiosity gets the better of me.

"Is there a problem?"

When I came here I remember watching her. She was everything I wanted to be: confident, assured, calm and collected. Today she doesn't seem any of those. She seems distracted, worried; nervous, even.

She stops biting her nail and smiles quickly, uncomfortably.

"Elle, is there a problem?"

Her arms cross over her chest. The rest of her body subtly shifts away from me. I notice details like those. The ability to read people is essential in combat, but also in general applications, like now.

"Sit down. I have something to tell you."

I don't sit.

She tucks a strand of hair behind her ear; smooth, silky hair. I walk over and lift a hand, almost touching her arm. Then I realise that's not something I should do. My arm falls.

One deep breath later she puts some distance between us by stepping away. Despite being surrounded by people almost all of her waking hours she prefers a lot of personal space. It's a weird thing I learnt from our time together.

She walks over to my office plant. I used to forget to water it all the time. I got told off whenever she visited. Her fingers touch a purple flower and she turns, perplexed.

"It's bloomed, Dizzy."

That name used to be followed by a sharp pain, but not anymore. Now that ache has dulled to almost nothing. It's weird how changes sneak up on you without warning.

I nod.

"I've learnt to look after the things I love." She smiles sadly as I mumble the rest. "You taught me that."

She turns back to the plant, her fingers sliding from the flower.

"I'm glad. It's beautiful."

It is. She gave it to me as an office warming present. She picked the position out, too, said it was, "The most conducive to it actually staying alive."

I cut to the chase.

"Why are you here?"

She laughs a little weirdly then turns, searching my eyes for something I don't think she finds.

"I've been reconciling a few of my more questionable actions, coming to terms with the good things and bad things I've done. They say the truth sets you free."

The truth never sets you free.

I lean back on my desk, crossing my arms, her cryptic statement worrying me, her behaviour not far behind it.

"I'm here to tell you something. It's hard because I know you'll hate me but I don't have a choice."

Every now and again she glances my way, but her eyes always slide back to safety.

"I don't understand."

I don't, not one bit. That's my problem, I never could hate her.

"When we parted I was adrift."

As soon as I realise where this is going my heart speaks up, not waiting for my head because it's tired of always getting a raw deal.

"Elle, it's in the past."

I don't want to hear the rest of her story. Mine hurt enough. I don't think I could deal with hearing it from her point of view as well.

"You have to let me finish. Please, Dizzy?"

After a moment I nod, realising I don't have much choice.

"When we parted I was adrift, I was lost. Everything came crashing down for me in those months. Work didn't help, either. The Amazons sensed my grip was loosening and they came in like sharks. I felt like everyone was against me. The one person I wanted to hold me and say everything would be all right wasn't allowed within twenty feet."

"It was a time of..." She pauses and glances over, a painful expression on her face. "...very questionable decisions on my part. I don't expect you to understand why because even I don't, but...." Her eyes squeeze shut for a moment. "I'm not very good at this, sorry."

"Just tell me. It's easier that way."

She stares at her fingers as they touch the flower, then she stops, turning to face me. She straightens up and takes a breath.

"After we stopped seeing each other I had a brief fling with Lucy - and it was brief. Please, hear me out."

My throat constricts painfully. I stop listening to what she says and push myself up from my desk.

"Lucy?"

She winces, managing a bare nod to confirm my insane question. I don't stop there.

"You couldn't see me because of the risk to the Heavens, but you could sleep with her?"

"Dizzy, let me explain..."

I slam my hand down on my desk, making her flinch, making *me* flinch at my anger. I'm sick of being hurt.

"No! You don't get to explain. Not with that."

I try to pretend it's okay, that we weren't together so it doesn't matter, that I don't feel betrayed, but I can't. Feelings aren't easily controlled. Not mine, anyway.

I stare at my desk; the weird wood grains, the patterns, anything I can to stop from thinking about what she just said. The hand I slammed down crushes into a fist. I try not to remember how devastated I was when we split up. I try not to think of how *she* consoled herself.

178

I turn and face her, keeping as calm as I can.

"You left me because of the risk to your position, and you slept with Lucy?"

All of the anger that should've come out a long time ago hits a raging boil.

"It doesn't make much sense, I know..."

"The Amazons didn't approve of me, but they were okay with her?"

The volume between us creeps up.

"I understand your..."

Higher.

"No. No, you don't. If you did you wouldn't be here telling me this."

Higher.

"I don't have a choice!"

Highest.

"Of course you have a choice, you're a God! You have every choice you could want! I don't have a choice." I jab a finger in my chest. "Me! This is what not having a choice looks like."

Her voice is almost a shout.

"If I had a choice do you think I'd be here now, telling you this? If I had a choice do you think I would've given you up?"

I grit my teeth. My hands splay across my desk as I lean down, trying to catch my breath.

"I don't know."

I shirk her hand on my arm, moving away, not wanting to be touched.

My phone rings, and I jump. I stare at it ringing, ringing, ringing. I grip the receiver tightly as I look at Elle. Her eyes slide away.

A familiar voice sounds happy. Mich has amazing timing.

*"Want to come for a late lunch with me seeing as you blew me out earlier? I'll even let you steal my fries."*

I turn away from Elle and push the earpiece closer.

"I'm..."

About to lie to you? Except this isn't Vegas, I've learnt my lesson.

"...in a meeting with Elle."

*"Oh."* There's a long pause. *"Okay, well...no problem. Just thought I'd ask. I'll speak to you later."*

My fingers crush the handset.

"Wait." I take a deep breath. "Give me twenty minutes to wrap this up?"

Another pause and I can imagine what she's thinking, because we both know I don't have any reasons to be in a meeting with Elle. I wait for her anger or at least a spiked sentence but I get neither. Her voice sounds lighter. She's smiling, I can tell.

*"I'll grab a table in the canteen. See you soon. Bye."*

I have to respect the way she always pulls things back from the edge.

I carefully put the receiver back, staring at it, taking a moment. Then I turn to Elle. Her arms are crossed, her blue eyes hold mine. There's only one thing I want to know.

"Why tell me now?"

She stares at some far off point behind me, shaking her head slightly.

"I told you because I was reconciling things and...."

She comes to a stop.

My anger froths up. Anger at this, at her sleeping with Lucy, but also anger at me for what happened in Vegas. And then it dawns on me, her revelation.

"Is this about me and Mich?"

She shifts, but her reply is devoid of any malice.

"No. I always hoped you'd find someone who would be right for you. Michelle is..." She pauses. "...nice."

"You don't sound too convinced."

Her lips part and she looks taken aback - because it's true or because it's not, I don't know. She snorts a laugh.

"This has nothing to do with you and Michelle. This is about you and me..."

"There is no you and me."

Her expression hardens as the volume begins to creep up again. Hands slide up the sides of her face, pulling her hair back.

"I know that."

"Then why tell me now? Why come in here when you know I'm happy with someone else?"

Her hands fly out, sparks of blue electricity leaping from her fingertips, reminding me why she's a God and why I should watch my mouth.

*"Lucy's blackmailing me."*

I try and keep up. My face must be a picture. I know hers is. Classic body language as her fingers settle on her mouth, covering now it's too late. They fall away as she takes a moment before speaking.

"This isn't about you or Michelle or even me, really. This is about our kiss which Lucy has a picture of. This is about me keeping the Council happy again."

She starts to pace. My mouth goes dry.

"A picture? How did she get a picture?"

"John's been caught up with Sam.... I don't know how. She has it, I've seen it and our deal was I tell you about the assignation or she informs the Council, and by default, I would assume, Michelle."

Her words stop, but she keeps moving.

"And you trust her?"

"Her fun is having control and asserting it. If she wanted to destroy me she wouldn't have given me a choice, she would've delivered it directly to Electra. I couldn't call her bluff on this."

For a moment I just want to talk to Mich, let her make everything better in that effortless way she has.

Elle finally sits down on my sofa, cradling her head in her hands. She looks up, eyes tearful. My body refuses to go near her.

"I'm sorry. This isn't how I wanted things to be between us. Please believe me."

"You're always sorry, Elle."

"Dizzy..."

Pain spills out between us.

"I've always hated that name. It's Discord." And to make my point. "Your Eminence."

She straightens.

We stay in very painful silence for what seems like forever. I do what I've become an expert at. I push the pain somewhere I can't find it.

She gets to her feet.

"Try to understand. I have a position and all of the Heavens to think about. My decisions are dictated to. That's the ironic thing about being where I am, I have no power."

"Poor you."

She glares, nostrils flaring, her eyes, slithers of ice.

"Should I let her show Michelle, because I still can?" Those slithers disappear for a moment before reappearing. "I didn't mean that, I'm sorry."

I think sensible thoughts, making an effort to remain as calm as I can. It's not easy. It's like trying to put out a forest fire with a cup of gasoline; it's not going to work.

"What'll happen to the picture now?"

"I'll see Lucy later and get it back off of her."

I run my tongue over the backs of my teeth, feeling sick at the thought of Mich seeing it.

"Where does this leave us, Discord?"

Exhaling deeply, I know I have to take a walk, move, do something to work this anger off.

"I have a lunch date in fifteen minutes."

For a moment there's an impassable drop between us, a void I don't think can ever be turned into anything other than what it is: a dead man's land. Then she turns, and without looking back, leaves. There's no door slam, just a small click to signify what's happened.

My hands relax their tight fists. I stare at my bloodied nails and cut palms. Lucy. Fuckin' bitch. My temples throb, my temper forms a white hot rage. I can't fight all of the battles all of the time but I can fight one.

I have someone to see before lunch.

# 34 CUPID'S INTRODUCTION

There was a lot of love between Elle and Discord but also a lot of unresolved hurt and anger. It had to leak out somewhere. Personally, if I'm not meant to be kissing a chick because of - and I delete as necessary: boyfriend, girlfriend, manic Mother/Father who may or may not be a God and able to crush my bones, then I tend to keep my smooching and feeling up in private, not go into the middle of a freakin' casino and tongue them! Someone obvious failed to teach Elle the basic, 'Eight easy steps to get hot and horny with someone you shouldn't.'

Now, Discord going to see Lucy was a problem. Why? It's a simple story of jealousy. A few millennia ago Elle and Lucy were a serious item. It was going to go official. Lucy was set to sit at Elle's right hand; she was going to share the leadership - or so she planned. But there was an argument over...you know, I can't even remember what it was about. Something and nothing, probably, you know what Lucy's like now. Things deteriorated rapidly and she escalated everything. Luce was immovable in the old days; things went her way or no way. She was well liked and her friends backed her, then Elle's friends backed her - you can see where I'm going with this. After a stand off it all hit the fan and the Heavens were torn apart under a cloud of viciousness. A month later, after the debris settled, Luce licked her wounds in her new home.

So, you see, she's never going to like anyone dating her ex, especially since Discord got to have Elle on even terms and more than once. Luce could've been anyone when Elle got sweaty with her again. Elle was living to my rules. She was taking her port in the storm and dropping anchor, then, the next day when there was some calm, moving her ship on.

Oh, one more thing. Discord's temper was getting worse with the stress of the last few months. Big problem if you mix that with Lucy.

# Chapter Thirty-Four: Lucy
## 7th December, Year 2 - 13:30
## Holy Backstabbing!

**M**y door flies open as I hear frantic tones outside. Bee pushes by Discord, standing in between us in my office.

"I tried to stop her, Lucy."

I put my nail file down. It seems no one else takes grooming as seriously as I do.

The leather of my chair sighs as I lean back, eying my intruder. Discord doesn't look happy, which is hardly a departure from the norm. She's never been exceptionally chirpy.

I smile at Bee.

"Leave us alone. If she isn't out in five minutes tell Elle to come and collect her body."

Bee goes, knowing I can take care of myself.

Discord's eyes narrow but, impeccably, she keeps her anger in check. As I've always said, if at first you don't succeed, bait them 'til they break. It's not a bind. Of all the mortals I hate, which is almost all of them, she's number one. I don't like people pawing my territory.

"To what do I owe your visit, Discord? Have you come to give me your soul? Don't bother. I don't want it. You cause more trouble in the Heavens than you ever could working for me."

Her eyes wander as she ignores me. I follow her gaze, trying to see what she's looking for. She walks over to my glass memento case. Even I have to collect something. I have the spent bullet casings from some of my most inspirational moments: JFK, Ghandi, Lennon, Arch Duke Ferdinand, Rasputin, Lincoln. They're some of my most treasured items.

Her fingers follow the casing's oak frame. She turns, smiling broadly, smugly.

"Nice collection. Something you value. Good."

I'll have to have her fingerprints polished off of it.

"What do you want, Dispawed?"

Her elbow smashes into the glass. I stand instantly, vexed to the utmost. She watches me as her hands pull the frame off the wall. It crashes to the floor, spilling my small murderous collection everywhere. If this woman wants to see the worst part of me then she's going about it the right way.

"The only reason you're not dead is because of my personal courtesy towards your boss. Remember that."

She snorts a laugh. A chilling urge to make her pay for ruining my collection descends.

I walk around my desk as she picks up my favourite casing: Arch Duke Ferdinand. She holds the crushed metal up to the light as if examining it. Then it dawns on me what this little visit is. It's hardly rocket science. Elle's betrayed me, the naughty little minx. That God always forgets one thing: she can't out fox me.

My fists clench. I hiss.

"You're playing with the mother of all fires, little girl."

She holds the casing in her fingertips then turns, bends, and pushes it deeply into the earth surrounding a plant. My teeth grind as she wipes the dirt on her pants.

She takes a step towards me illustrating our height difference. I don't think she's realized one small point yet. I raise an eyebrow. Size doesn't matter. It's what you do with it that does. My arms force their way into her chest, pushing her backward. She flies through the air, hitting my far wall. The plaster cracks as she bounces off. Even the air in the room reverberates.

I stare down at the heap of Angel in front of me, quite thrilled I haven't lost my viciousness. I use it less and less often so I worry it won't be as sharp and painful as it used to be - shouldn't have bothered.

I bend down as she tries to stand. I grab her shirt, picking her up. I throw her against the other wall. Plaster shatters, raining down.

I've come to terms with the destruction of my office. Those two seconds of decisiveness were an annoying waste of my time. Now I'm enjoying the fun times of pulverising this woman.

She flips up, clicking her neck. It's not intimidating, just annoying she's still able to move.

She wipes the side of her mouth with a finger, staring at the dark red tip before wiping it on her torn shirt.

"You're such a stud, Lucy."

"Someone in this room has to be."

She dives, taking me off guard, and we crash into my filing cabinets. Her hands go around my neck, mine settle on her hips. I prove my metal. I lock my arms out, pushing her away, making her take several steadying steps backward.

My office door flies open. Bee, my tardy self-proclaimed protector. I shout, not annoyed at her specifically, more her intrusion and this Angel's cheek.

*"Can't a girl get some privacy?"*

I point at the door. Bee looks between us then nods. It closes with a dull click. In less than thirty seconds I'll have enough staff outside to kill half of the Heavens. Not that I need them, but it's the thought that counts.

I turn my attention back to Discord the Dusty.

"This can go one of two ways. I can kill you slowly, or...you know, I retract, it can only really go the one way."

As the Devil I have eons of battle experience. I know the benefits of a direct attack - she makes a grab for me and I let her pull me close - moreover, I know the benefits of letting your enemy come to you.

I concentrate on a requisite from being old school. My scalpel sharp claws pierce the skin of my fingertips, extending their full three inches. Elle may have evolved most of her new Angels into clawless, fangless entities, but not me. I've kept mine. I don't like to run with the crowd.

I *slide* them into her stomach, pushing harder as I catch several ribs. I hold her close as she struggles, showing the power I have is as physical as it is anything else. Her rich growl makes my heart pound.

I finally let her retreat because I want to see her face, gauge her reactions, make sure I'm doing everything just right; I always try to please.

Her pupils dilate. Her mouth falls open.

I gently twist my hand, listening to the sound of flesh cutting - it's a subtle noise, you can miss it if you're not careful. I caress the nape of her neck, crushing her body back into mine.

I fight to keep my balance in four-inch heels, and whisper.

"You're beautiful when you're dying."

I run my lips over the skin of her neck, barely touching her, tasting the saltiness of the moisture that's prickled up. I twist my claws again, closing my eyes, savouring this. My mouth moves back to her ear. I want these moments to be as memorable for her as they are for me.

"Did I ever tell you I had Elle in this office? Seems I've had both of you now. I took her on that desk. She was a vision, glistening wet and ready for me. She begged me to go harder, faster, more fingers. She screamed when she came. She screamed out my name."

I jam my claws up to my fingertips suddenly, because it wasn't my name. For a moment the memory hurts as much as it did that night, but, as I did then, I do now: I concentrate on other things. Like the person whose name she did call.

Discord's eyes close, trying to block me out. She should know there's no escaping. Not once I have my claws in, anyway.

I gently kiss her cheek.

"I love being inside a woman. It's so intimate."

I push her away, claws reluctantly leaving her body, pulling my arm as she stumbles back. My hand reaches out to experience that delicious feeling again. My claws sink back and I watch the vision in front of me. Her arms hang limply as she stares, blankly, eyes blinking quickly.

I know the rules. Angels can heal simple wounds. It's a benefit of being one of the ranks. One thing we can't heal ourselves are injuries sustained from each other. And that would be little ol' me.

She stands, still, staring. Neither of us moves. The potentially deadly silence in my office is captivating.

"You know, I always exhaust the women I'm with. It's a real problem being so virile."

Her chest rises and falls as her breathing gets shallower and shallower. The material of her shirt spreads blood rapidly, turning it from white to red in seconds.

"Remember this moment, Discord. Was it good for you, too?"

Her answer is whispered.

"Fuck you."

My lips curl into a smile.

"Maybe one day."

She takes a jarring step backward, a hand feeling for my wall, controlling her slide down. And all the time she never looks away. It's a challenging connection.

I smile, then open my mouth and scream one name out, not prepared to be her murderer - just yet.

*"Elle!"*

Another thing we all possess as Angels is we all have the ability - a bright light blinds me for a second as Elle flashes into my office - to hear each other's cries for help. Elle stares at my bloodied hand, then iced eyes meet mine. Her eyebrows furrow, her face falls, and she slowly turns around.

"My gift to you, Your Eminence."

Discord's head turns to Elle as she tries to speak. Unfortunately she seems to be at a total loss for words. I suppose I'm quite an experience.

I seize this opportunity and lift a blood covered finger to my lips. I flick my tongue out and lick the tip as Elle's shocked face turns back.

"You know, I always wondered what you saw in her, Ellie." I groan appreciatively as I smack my lips. "But now I understand. She really is quite delicious."

I sit in my chair, kicking my heels off as I relax into the soft leather.

"Now, do me the courtesy of getting that mess out of my office before it stains my vintage oak flooring."

She kneels, a hand resting on Discord's shoulder. The other almost touches the pretty hole I made. Elle's expression is a beautiful mixture of pain and utter panic.

"What have you done to her, Lucy?"

I pull a face, the one that always used to annoy her. Her eyes blaze. Still does by the looks of things.

I chuckle, more to annoy than because this is amusing. Elle offers nothing. I was expecting more.

"If you'd kept your side of the bargain this wouldn't have happened. You owe me a favour for not killing her. I'll collect at a time most inconvenient to you."

She seethes. Blue sparks of electricity fall from her fingertips.

"I lost my mind the night I slept with you."

I roll my eyes.

"It certainly wasn't your virginity. Now if you don't mind, I need a cigarette after all that exertion. Speak to you soon." I smile, reclining in my seat. "Oh, despite double crossing me, this was better than helping Electra's bitches. Call us quits on that front."

She puts her arm around the fallen Angel, her voice growlingly low.

"Remember, Lucy, I'm a God. One day you'll go too far."

"I went too far before and I took half of the Heavens with me when I came to a stop. Want me to do it again?"

Her eyes narrow into sharp slits but she stays silent. A second later a flash fills my office. They're gone.

I pull a wet wipe from my desk drawer, cleaning Discord off my hands. I've gone too far? What a stupid statement. I can never go too far.

## 35 CUPID'S INTRODUCTION

Elle could've, should've, but never really would've, followed the correct procedures with her injured love. Every rule went out of the window along with sense, brains and her keep off deal with the Amazons. She played doctors and nurses with her wounded ex. Of course, Elle being Elle she missed the opportunity to do some checking of vital organs like: lips, breasts, inner thighs - the important stuff. Still, I guess what happened was for the best. Elle finally saw what she'd been trying to hide from for so long. It was a wake up call with an alarm clock the size of an elephant.

## Chapter Thirty-Five: Elle
## 7th December, Year 2 - 14:30
## Smell The Coffee

I pace beside my bed, every now and again glancing over at Dizzy, thankful she's resting now.

I clench and unclench my freezing hands, tying to encourage the blood to come back to my dead arms. Mending her injuries has left me drained. That's the downside to being a God and having everything done for you. You eventually get so out of practice you're almost redundant as anything other than a figurehead.

Her bloodied top is dragged of off my floor and dropped into the bin. Charity's words flood my mind.

*"Sometimes two people who shouldn't be together get locked into a cycle of self-destruction, wrecking everything around them...".*

Understanding their meaning seems a lot clearer now. Even if seeing Dizzy's injured made me realise how much I still care, it was a harsh jolt back to reality. Her chest rises and falls rhythmically. I rest my hand on her shoulder. Her skin is warm. A reality with room for only me. I get up and leave.

Today has been exhausting, both physically and mentally. In fact my whole week has been hectic. If I haven't been in meetings it's been visits to various departments, or networking, or chairing board meetings. Bureaucracy is the inhibitor of my days.

In the kitchen I pour out a glass of fruit juice, adding a large spoonful of sugar to help my energy levels. In my reception the phone beeps as I press speed dial one. Her voice instantly lowers my level of tension.

*"Charity Nature."*

I sit, cradling the receiver between my ear and shoulder.

"It's me."

I sip my drink and close my eyes. Talking to Charity always makes me feel better. To know you have someone at the most stressful times can be the difference between surviving and falling at the first hurdle.

She sounds happy to speak to me.

*"Hello, me. What are you doing?"*

I tell her the short version of what happened. She listens to my story of Lucy against Dizzy. She listens as I tell her how I bought her here. She listens to my recount of her healing.

Her first question is easy.

*"Have you had something sugary? You'll pass out otherwise."*

"Fruit juice with a large spoonful to help the medicine go down."

Her second is not so easy.

*"Why didn't you take Discord to the infirmary?"*

"I panicked. She was covered in blood and Lucy was being a bitch."

*"She's always a bitch."*

I can't argue with that.

We talk. Charity says the right things and doesn't judge me. I don't think I could take a lecture now.

*"Do you want me to come over? I finish in half an hour."*

I take another sip of my juice as I try to dilute the adrenalin. I ponder the offer but she can't keep rescuing me.

"No. You have a nice evening relaxing with...who are you seeing today?"

She laughs at my cheekiness, however it's my prerogative as best friend.

*"No one. I'm single. I'm trying to detox."*

"How, by flushing women out of your system? I don't think it works like that."

*"I need to be in top form for the All Souls Ball at New Years. Are you still coming? Mother was looking forward to hearing your news, but if you don't want to I'll make something up."*

I curse my memory because I'd forgotten. For a moment I wonder if I want to be there, but perhaps being around others, especially May, will be good for me? I make a snap decision.

"Of course I'm coming. What time are you picking me up?"

I mentally review my wardrobe.

*"Seven. FYI, I'm wearing a white suit and Mother's in blue."*

We say our goodbyes. I write a reminder to get my white dress cleaned. May will love the fact Charity and I are both in white. I slap the note on the hallway mirror and walk back up the stairs to my room, happy I gave poor Davis the day off. I think he would have died at the shock of this afternoon.

I check on the patient. I sit next to my sleeping giant, sinking into the thick quilt, but keeping a safe distance. Her eyes slide open, eyelashes fluttering as she focuses. She turns to me, grimacing at the movement. Lucy is a pro at damaging things. Any more and I wouldn't have been able to heal it. Even this God has her limits.

Dizzy doesn't say anything but simply stares, her eyes deeply hypnotic. I fight the urge to move closer.

"My hero?"

I refer to a conversation we used to have. I once called her my white knight, and it's true, for a long time she was my protector - or it felt that way anyway, and that's all that mattered. But when betrayal twisted our perfect union not even she could protect me from myself.

Her voice is hoarse.

"I don't feel like one."

"Heroes never do."

Her eyes never leave mine as I continue.

"I'd never have forgiven myself if...."

I remember about Michelle. I leave that unsaid and switch to safer ground.

"How are you feeling?"

She whispers, her voice low.

"I've felt better."

We stare at each other. Las Vegas and the argument in her office have erected a wall of steel between us. The affair with Lucy has surrounded that wall in barbed wire.

"Considering Lucy almost eviscerated you I'd say you're doing well."

My fingertips barely connect with hers, an innocent gesture but I feel the same electricity I always have when we touch. The basic senses are the most powerful, touch especially. It can be reassuring, comforting, or at the extreme, highly charged and sexual. Or it can mean much more to one person than the other. She moves her hand away and mumbles, pulling her trademark shrug short with a grimace.

"I guess."

"It wasn't the most sensible thing to take on Lucy. Notice not even I do that."

"I went to shout at her. I lost my temper."

It's believable. Lucy has a talent for escalating situations.

"I'm sorry about this, Diz...Discord. Please believe me."

Her jaw muscles tense, those dark eyes holding their perpetual sadness close. Then she explodes the silence with choice words.

"I wish I could hate you."

I'm as honest as I can be.

"I'm glad you can't."

And so is she.

"I can't stay. Electra will find out."

Yes, it's always about others.

"I'll call the infirmary ambulance. They're very loyal to Charity and I."

My telephone begins to ring, startling me and breaking our almost moment. I take the easy way out and grab the handset, going into the hallway to take it.

"Hello, you."

I thought it was Charity. It's not.

*"Your Eminence, it's Michelle. I'm sorry to be calling you at home but I heard there was a problem with Lucy and Discord.... She was meant to be meeting me for lunch, and no one knows where she is. I need to know she's okay."*

The gossip has already started.

"Tell everyone she's in the infirmary."

*"But I've just checked and she's not there. Your Eminence."*

She sounds uncomfortable calling me. I suppose in some way I'm the other woman to her. I think in some way I'm still the other woman to me, too.

The urge to say she's fine and leave it there is strong, however my compassion has always been my greatest and worst trait.

"No, she's not. She's here. I think she'd like to see you before the ambulance comes."

There's a pause. If I were in her position I'd be wondering why Dizzy was here and not already in the infirmary, but Michelle has no recourse against my decisions. Finally, a benefit of being a God!

Her words stutter out.

*"Right.... Thank you."*

I should feel proud for being magnanimous, however I don't. Emotions never work to defined rules.

She says a polite goodbye and I know she'll be here shortly. I know because I would.


I wait in my reception, thinking about everything I threw away, and about my life as it was with Dizzy and my life as it is now, alone. What a depressing series of events.

Within five minutes there's a knock at the door. Michelle is looking harried, in a shambles, and extremely uncomfortable. She pushes her hair back, her eyes dart around. I know who she's looking for. I stand aside and let her in.

I offer my excuses for Dizzy's benefit, not hers.

"Lucy caused a lot of damage. I've done the hard work. The infirmary will do the rest."

"I appreciate it, Your Eminence."

I bet you do.

I stare at her, her expression unwaveringly solid. I was expecting this awkward moment. I'm sure there are a million questions she won't ask. I'm positive there are a million answers I won't be offering.

She takes a deep breath, the only thing giving her away. I know her thoughts lie with the woman in my bed, and it's now I cease my uphill struggle. I give up whatever it is I'm trying unsuccessfully to do. We ascend the stairs in silence. I focus on every step instead of what I'm doing. At the door to my room I stop, my fingers resting on the handle as I look at the woman who has filled my shoes rather well. I push the door open.

"Go in."

She walks to my patient's side and her eyes dart over to me once, but that once stops me. I stand back, watching like a seedy voyeur.

Her voice is soft and caring.

"Have you been playing with sharp objects again?"

Dizzy opens her eyes and blinks at the new face. Michelle sits and whispers something, stroking her hair as I did ten minutes ago. I'm too far away to hear but I can imagine. Discord's hand reaches up. Her fingers touch Michelle's lips for a brief moment. The action slices my insides into tiny pieces, shuffling them like a deck of cards. It's almost too much to bear, so I leave them. I retreat to my reception and call the Director of the infirmary - one of Charity's ex-girlfriends. The private ambulance will arrive in less than five minutes.

I speed dial my best friend, mumbling her name repeatedly, almost as if she'll hear and pick up quicker.

*"Charity Nature. Hello, me."*

I smile into the receiver. She's finally put my new number into her phone.

"Hello, you."

I sink down into the soft brown leather of my favourite chair, its deep cushions hugging me.

"Dizzy's going to the infirmary. But...."

*"But?"*

"Michelle's here."

*"Oh."* Is all Charity says in reply at first, but after a pause, adds. *"How does that make you feel?"*

I laugh.

"You sound like my therapist."

*"I'm cheaper and I know all your problems already. You should switch to me and I'll blame everything on your absentee relationship with your mother."*

We switch to talking about her last fling and how truly awful it was. The subject is refreshing. By the time we say goodbye we're both feeling much better. It doesn't stop my thoughts of what's happening in the next room, nevertheless it's a distraction, and that's what it's all about: doing whatever is necessary to function.

I pick a magazine up, my distraction at this moment, and wait for the ambulance.

# 36 CUPID'S INTRODUCTION

Dis went to the hospital in a serious amount of secrecy. Elle made sure no gossip got back to Electra and the Council hounds. For once things worked out okay.

Dis was kept in for a couple of days to make sure everything still worked. Michelle did her usual of rerouting approaching rain clouds. She kept Discord company and was a very good nurse. Then the patient was allowed home. But nothing is ever easy, is it? Especially with those strong silent types.

## Chapter Thirty-Six: Michelle
### 10th December, Year 2 - 15:30
### Revelations

Two metallic keys stare back at me from my palm. My eyes follow the wood grain until they reach the keyhole on Dis' door. They slide back to those keys.

"She's hurt, you're not moving in."

My...her key slides in easily. The door noiselessly pivots. I stare down her long hall, at the small high table, at the big mirror at the other end and me staring back. Some things should be worried about. This shouldn't. Not when the patient's only just come out of hospital.

I put my bag down and pick her post up, going through it, kicking the door shut. Junk, so I leave it on the small table, but the files she wanted I do pull from my bag.

"Hey, Dis, it's Michelle. Don't jump me, I'm not Lucy trying to break in and finish the job."

A crash, a curse, and a bang make me run into the lounge. Dis looks up from staring at a broken vase. She grimaces and unsteadily lowers herself into a chair.

"Finished running with scissors so playing bull in a china shop?"

She stares at me, nostrils flared, silent.

"Hurts?"

She nods, just taking short breaths.

"Don't move. I'll clear it up."

"I can..."

I give her shoulder a squeeze.

"Just break more things. You need to learn when to stop. And now's that time."

A minute later, a lot of frowning from her, and the breakage is cleared. Her voice is interspersed with pauses.

"I thought we were meant to heal quickly?"

"We are, but playing, 'cut me a new stomach,' with Lucy negates that. She's an Angel, you're an Angel, it's always going to be vicious. Lucky she didn't clip your wings. Your powers would've gone like..." I click my fingers. "...that. You would've been d-e-d after those claws."

She came close enough this time. I spoke to the doctors. I know what they said. It's an uncomfortable thought. Uncomfortable because of my reaction: panic. And then confusion because of the panic, and then thinking because of the panic, and confusion because of the thinking about the panic.... Whole can of worms.

She grimaces and repeats a well known phrase slowly.

"Wings are for Vengeance missions only."

My lips curl into a smile.

"And I remember you telling me you binned those laminated cards from training."

I sit, laying a hand on her soft pants, her hot thigh warming my palm. Dark eyes meet mine.

"I lied."

I tap her nose gently.

"And why was that?"

A hint of a smile, then a scowl at the pain.

"You annoyed me."

"Glad I made an impression."

She stares at me for a second then her eyes slide away.

"You did."

She can be so cute. I give her thigh a gentle squeeze.

"Come on, soldier, on your feet. Let's get you to bed. The doctor said you weren't meant to be up."

She sighs heavily, shaking her head.

"He said I have to be careful. I've been lying down all day. I need a break. Did you get those files?"

I hand her the envelope from Gab. As she goes to take it, I pull it away.

"Listen, I know this is your case and I'm not trying to be all motherly but you're meant to be taking it easy."

"It'll keep my mind active."

I can't argue with that. I hand her the file.

"You hungry?"

Two dark eyes stare at me and she nods.

"Listen, you sit here and do your active mind stuff and I'll get lunch ready. How about pasta?"

"Sure."

I get up to go but a hand takes hold of my arm. I'm amazed at how very cute she looks.

"I wanted to say thanks for helping and...sorry for shouting yesterday at the hospital. I get frustrated being like this."

She stares up at me. I sit back down, taking her hand, rubbing my thumb over her soft skin.

"It was more a ratty shout than shouting. You're forgiven. And it's no problem, helping. I'd worry about you if I wasn't here...."

My mouth comes to a screeching stop as something sounding like a blatantly caring statement exits. I almost stutter the rest.

"I mean...with breakages and, you know, you've already killed your vase."

She glances over at the empty space on the shelf, in her own world.

"It doesn't matter. It was a present from...." Her eyebrows furrow. "I won't miss it."

Elle's everywhere. I don't know why it's even a minimal shock.

"A present from Elle?"

Dis, welcome to my blurty mouth.

"Yeah."

I try to tread carefully but blurty mouth doesn't really work that way.

"Maybe she can get you a new one?"

Narrowed eyes slide to mine.

"Is there something you want to ask?"

"Let's talk about it another time."

"Let's not."

On the spot I flounder for a moment before her fingers gently squeeze mine, encouraging rather than stopping.

"It's just.... I was surprised Elle didn't take you straight to the infirmary."

She nods and her eyebrows lift, waiting for more. Blurting is a fine art, meaning everything you want to say slides right out into the open.

"And that she took such an interest that you ended up in her bed."

Dark eyes disappear in a slow blink. Her tone is low as her hand leaves mine.

"I didn't have a say where I ended up, Mich."

I try to lighten the moment because a full on argument is not a destination I want to go with her.

"Lucy's not someone you should mess with. If you wanted to spar you should've called me."

Her hand holds her stomach with a grimace as she shifts.

"I lost my temper. I only went to talk."

"Sorry. I didn't mean to push it."

For a moment she looks even more uncomfortable than normal as her words tumble out.

"I don't have feelings for her if that's the problem."

"Lucy? Glad to hear it."

She almost smiles.

"You know who I mean."

Yes I do. Elle casts a big shadow.

"I don't mean to get personal. I'm here to try and brighten your day up."

"I know. You're doing a good job."

"That's because I'm an expert." I pat her hand, standing. "Let's have some lunch. You hold tight here."

The layout of her kitchen shows she doesn't use it much. Some of the knives look like they've never been out of the block. I have to wonder what she eats. I open her fridge: a colourful mix of fruit, vegetables, cold meats, yoghurts, and two lone beers at the top. Shame on me for thinking her diet is bad.

I don't try and figure out what's going on with Elle, not that it sounds like anything is. No, I'll save that for Gab, that's her territory. She's the thinker, I'm the doer.

Fifteen minutes later and lunch is almost ready. I wipe my hands on a cloth and walk to the edge of the lounge. Dis is staring at the file, elbow on knee, head resting in palm. Her expression makes me stop, because I know the kind of thing that's on those pages. Personally I never wanted each victim's details: names, family background, funeral pictures. But everyone's different. Dis will find what's right for her.

"Maybe you should read that another day, when you're feeling better?"

She keeps staring at the page. She lifts a picture. Maybe it's one of the victims, maybe the target himself? I lean on the doorframe, giving her some space. These missions are hard. Doesn't matter if you've completed one or a thousand, you can't change the impact they have.

"Gabrielle gave you this?"

"Not exactly. It was from a stack of files they hadn't had a chance to go through yet. She knows I have it. Problem?"

She looks at the picture, then flicks through the pages quickly.

"He did all of this to these girls?"

I go to walk over but she raises a hand, shaking her head. Understandable, the need to be alone.

"It was sealed a few months ago so it won't include his latest victims, but it's as comprehensive as it gets."

"Have you read any of it?"

"Nope. Should I have?"

"No. Guess not."

Her hand tears at a page, removing it slowly. She folds it carefully and slips in into her pocket, along with the picture.

"That's the only copy we have, Dis."

She stares over, eyes empty, face blank.

"Good. Let's eat."

We don't eat. I eat. She plays with her food.

"Is it that bad?"

She blinks, looking up at me.

"No, it's great."

Her eyebrows furrow and she stares back down at the plate.

I try for a smile but her mood is worrying. I take the fork from her hand, laying it down.

"Do you want to talk about that file?"

She runs a hand through her hair, staring vacantly at the table.

"No."

"It's understandable to find it upsetting. If it wasn't we wouldn't be called in."

"Just leave it, please."

"While you brood your way through...."

Dark eyes turn on me.

"Leave it, Michelle."

I sit back in my seat, wondering what's going on. After a minute of silence she interrupts my thoughts.

"Everything in that file's been confirmed, right? It's definite? He's guilty?"

I nod.

"The only things left to do are to run our final set of checks, then you do a visit to get comfortable with the target, Gab sets the date, Elle okays it and we have a judgement."

She nods, then her face twists for a second and she clutches her side. And this explains her ratty mood. Pain. I get up and put an arm around her shoulders.

"You're going to lie down. No arguments."

She looks up at me with watering eyes. A slight nod of her head is my answer.

It doesn't take me long. She doesn't put up a fight. In less than five minutes she's lying down, breathing a lot easier. I sit on the edge of the bed.

"This reminds me of when you wanted to fight every Amazon in the bar."

Her head turns, her eyes so sad. It's an emotion I'm not used to around her. She's always so tough and strong, and this...? It makes me feel like I'm not doing enough to help.

"It was a bad day."

"For everyone. Those Amazons, my stomach, your entire body and Psyche, because I heard she had to lie through her teeth to cover that up."

I smooth out her frown with a fingertip.

"I didn't realise."

"Psyche likes filling in paperwork. She gets to do it every month with those girls of hers."

She nods, looking even more tired. Her hand slides closer to mine but she doesn't touch me.

"About earlier."

"You're not at your best. I'll forgive you."

"But..."

I press a finger to her soft lips.

"It's time for sleeping."

Her eyes blink slower then flutter closed. I slide my finger along her lower lip, and then kiss it. I get up and leave her breathing deeply.

I clean up the lunch stuff and check the lounge to make sure the entire vase is gone. That closed file stares at me from the couch. I pick it up, flicking through, and there's nothing special apart from the jump from victim number three to victim number five. Ragged edges of paper are where victim number four used to be. I guess we all need our motivation, who am I to judge where Discord gets hers?

Suddenly my mobile rings. Gab. Not even a hello, straight into things, that's my best friend.

"How's the patient, got any more patience?"

She must have this place bugged.

"No. She's ratty as Hell."

"Same as you when you're not well. Unbearably snappy to the point I feel the need to smother you."

"I love you, too."

Her laugh makes the line buzz.

*"Did you sign that file out or just take it like usual?"*

"No, I signed your fifteen forms then signed the other ten and the other twenty, then I sold my soul to..."

"Okay, thank you, Michy. Now answer the door."

"What?"

A knock sounds at the door. My head twists in that direction.

"Have you bugged this place?"

Silence. I walk to the door and open it. Gab stares back, still talking into her mobile. I get her voice in surround sound.

"No, I haven't bugged it." She lowers the phone and holds a sealed plastic dish out. "Instead I bought chicken soup."

I sigh and click the phone off, putting it on the hall table. Gab doesn't move, just holds the dish out.

"Do you need an invite over the threshold?"

"No, stupid, my car's waiting. Some of us can't leave our jobs to come and play doctors and nurses."

I take the dish and she plants a noisy kiss on my cheek. My statement whines out.

"But you only ever make this soup for me."

"Jealous?"

"No." I look through the glass lid. It even has noodles. "Yes. This is Michy's-ill-food!"

She grins, pointing over to her car.

"I have to go. Don't overheat it, you'll scald the noodles."

I know I'm pouting but I don't care.

"She helps you get ice and suddenly she's your new best friend?"

She whirls around, walking backward.
"She charmed me. I'm gone."
The car door opens then closes. She drives away.
I hold my smile back. She charmed me, too.

## 37 CUPID'S INTRODUCTION

Time moved on. Charity's ex at the infirmary had let Elle know that Discord was all right. That settled her mind so she could focus on work, or rather, throw herself into everything she could.

Along came the All Souls Ball at New Years - nothing like a distraction to keep your mind off of the painful stuff. I was meant to be going but I got grounded again. Something about messing up half of Hollywood's elite.... Ah, I don't know what my Ma is on about. So, me and my Love Girls had a party, got a bit fried and shot some arrows off. Not sure what the problem is. Big deal, a few movies got delayed, not like anyone died. Serious overreaction if you ask me.

Anyway, glad I missed it. Fate doesn't like Elle's choices you can imagine the way she gets on with mine whenever we cross paths. Of course, Charity can do no wrong. I've never figured that one out, especially since she's been through more women than Elle and me put together. I guess, love it or the it, it's a parental right of selective disapproval.

Anyway, here's the Ball.

## Chapter Thirty-Seven: Elle
## 31st December, Year 2 - 19:10
## Road To Recovery

*"E*lle, I'm getting dehydrated out here."
"I'm almost ready."

I cradle my mobile between my cheek and shoulder. My feet slip into white Manolos and I grab my clutch bag. I can almost see Charity tapping her fingers, so I make my excuses.

"I'm in white. I have to be careful not to touch anything. Right, I'm coming."

I make it down stairs without incident. I jog, in four-inch heels, to the open door of her Limo. I slide in, closing the door to keep the cold night air out considering my scant dress.

"Wow."

Is all Charity says when she sees my outfit. I look up, mirroring her exclamation.

"Wow to you, too. Are you planning on those staying put tonight?"

She's in a fitted white Armani suit. The jacket is cut extremely low, showing her lack of anything underneath.

She laughs and tugs at the edges of her jacket.

"Taped. I'm not stupid. I'm taking no chances if Mother's in attendance."

Which reminds me.

"Where is May?"

She makes a face telling me I won't like her answer. Her hand pats my knee. No, I definitely won't.

"She's coming. With Fate. I didn't know until half an hour ago. Last minute thing, sorry."

I seethe.

"The last thing I need is my overbearing, moralistic mother telling me how badly I'm doing at everything. I was hoping to relax tonight."

Something I desperately need.

Her warm hand slips over mine.

"We'll lose them after the initial speeches and go and be naughty on our own. How does that sound?"

"Perfect."

We arrive and make our way to our table. Even from here I can see my mother laughing with May. I grit my teeth. After tonight I can justify not seeing her for another few months.

May rises, smiling. She kisses Charity but wraps her arms around me, hugging tightly. She lets go and glances at my dress with a smile.

"You look beautiful, Elle."

"So do you. Is Poseidon here?"

She's wearing an amazing figure hugging dress in deep blue. It's Poseidon's favourite colour.

"If he is my dance card is already full."

My mother gets up.

"Elle," is the sum of her greeting.

No, sorry, and an air kiss, too. She glances at my dress. Her eyebrows slide upwards. She doesn't smile. Instead she moves across and puts an arm around Charity, pulling her in.

"Those are two assets I'd like to think you'll be keeping to yourself tonight, Charity."

"I'll be trying, unless I get a very attractive offer."

My mother laughs and sits back down without another word. Charity stares at me sadly. I shrug. It's hardly anything new.

The speeches seem to drag. May does the unthinkable and asks about my love life. Even with Charity between us I can feel my mother bristle.

Her fingers tap on the table as she turns her brutal attention over to me.

"Yes, Elle. A husband on the horizon? Or even a date?"

May and Charity exchange looks. May glances at me as I fight to stay calm in this public arena.

"No, mother. I'm single."

Even mentioning Dizzy in the abstract makes my stomach sink. I pull my emergency cigarettes out of my bag, the ones I made Charity stop and buy when I knew she'd be here.

"I thought you'd given up?"

No getting one by you, is there? I light one.

"I did, but some situations dictate I slide back into old habits."

Charity's hand pats my leg under the table. I inhale, blowing my smoke away, putting my own over the top of hers. She dives in and saves me.

"It's not like it'll kill her. More Champagne, Fate?"

My mother smiles, putting her hand over her glass.

"No, thank you, Charity."

A pause as she stares at her. I cross my fingers she doesn't ask about her buoyant love life.

"It's been so long since I last saw you. I'm glad to see the red hair has gone. It suits you eau natural."

I can't help but laugh as I remember that hair colour. It shows how long it is since we've all been together like this.

"I've changed a lot since those days, Fate."

"Yes, you have."

Is all my mother says before we're interrupted by more speeches.

The next hour is a distracting mix of good and bad. My mother makes several tacky comments about my, "choices," as she puts it. Eventually she heads off with May to mingle, leaving us safely on our own.

Charity turns, smiling sheepishly.

"She looks well. I thought you were soon to be from an officially broken home?"

I snort a laugh. So did I.

"As far as I know they're still separated. I spoke to dad the other day, and she sent him the papers to sign, so...."

I shrug, not really wanting to touch the still raw subject of the imminent divorce of my parents or who the catalyst was: Charity's, almost estranged sister, Hope.

We both stand. I smooth my dress off as she whispers.

"Let's not get into that or we'll both be ranting. You about your mother, and me about my sister. Let's go and dance the dance of two single, yet devastatingly attractive, women."

"Single, yes."

And likely to stay that way for a frightening amount of time. Obviously I'm not as good at covering my emotions as some people.

Her fingers brush my arm.

"Sorry, I didn't think. We can sit and judge people on their fashion mishaps if you'd prefer?"

I look at my friend who's doing her very best to help me through this. I force a determined smile.

"No, it's about time I started coming to terms with the fact it's over."
I adjust her jacket, smiling at her choice of clothes.
"Come on Ms Nature. Let's dance."

# 38 CUPID'S INTRODUCTION

Charity and Elle had a good night, especially since they managed to avoid Fate for the rest of it. You can see why Elle is such a great diplomat, because she's had enough practice with her mom. Harsh woman.

Both Elle and Charity got some vital downtime to recharge their batteries. They work damn hard to keep the Heavens running smoothly. It's good for them to get a break every now and then.

Now, on the other side of town there was a private party going on for the girls in white: Michelle and Gabrielle's New Year's bash. It's a great time to be out with the old and in with the new. And boy was there going to be some new news tonight.

## Chapter Thirty-Eight: Gabrielle
## 31st December, Year 2 - 21:00
## You Can Open Your Eyes Now

"I thought this was a quiet party?"

Michy frowns as she slides one of my plants across the hallway to where it originally was before she moved it five minutes ago.

"It is."

I stare at her outfit. Sprayed on shirt, low-cut jeans and heeled boots.

The doorbell interrupts and she walks off.

"That'll be Dis."

I run and catch up, grabbing her arm, dragging her to a stop.

"Discord's coming?"

She nods and smiles, raising an eyebrow.

"Problem?"

"No, it's great, but...you never said anything. When did you ask her?"

"In Vegas."

"And she's up to partying with us?"

"I won't be dirty dancing with her, but she's well enough for the other stuff. Oh, she said thanks for the soup."

"When?"

"After I gave it to her."

"That was three weeks ago. Thank you for relaying the message, Michelle."

"It's okay, Gabrielle. I was busy being the Nurse - minus the uniform, of course."

I press a finger to her lips as she wiggles her eyebrows suggestively.

"I don't want to know."

She smiles and pulls it away.

"It's not like that."

I do up two of the buttons on her shirt, shaking my head. Only one person should be seeing those, and she's not here yet.

"It's always like that with you, Michy."

Her face falls.

"Not this..."

The bell rings again, interrupting.... I'm not sure what. My brain doesn't have enough info. Yet.

Michy has recovered and is back to smiling. She stares down at my fingers still on her buttons.

"Gab. Let me open the door."

My fingers let go.

The door opens to Sam and John. She sighs and her shoulders drop. Sam and John glance between us as she doesn't move.

"Michy?" In the end I elbow her out of the way. "Come in, guys, great to see you."

John whispers.

"Is she security tonight?"

I watch her undoing one of her shirt buttons. I pull her hand off.

"You'd think so."

He shrugs and they go through to the other room, to a chorus of greetings from my secretary pool. I turn and slap Michelle on the shoulder.

"Forgot to plug your legs in?"

She rubs where I slapped, making her classic pouty face, which is adorable and at times can still swing an argument with us.

"Ow. No."

"You've been spiky all day. Have I done something?"

Michy is dependably chirpy, and I know she's been looking forward to New Years for months. She loves parties, but recently....

She tuts and shakes her head.

"No, it's nothing you've done."

"The Vengeance stuff?"

She sighs, not looking at me, taking a long time to answer - a sign her brain is plugged in.

"Partly, I guess."

She frequently needs prodding. She doesn't offer information freely when something bothers her. It's not an obstacle I'm unaware of after this long being best friends.

"I hate it when you think about those days. But what's the partly referring to?"

"I've been..." She lowers her voice, looking very uncomfortable. "...thinking about things to do with..."

She shifts about so I finish her sentence with a stab in the dark. "Discord?"

She leans back on the wall, resting her head on it. Her eyes squeeze shut. "Maybe. No.... I don't know. Yes, I guess."

"That's a lot of answers. It's fine she's coming. I don't mind and no one else will if that's part of the problem. I like her."

"It's not that."

"Care to volunteer what it is?"

She bites her lip and frowns; she's building up to it. We will get there in the end.

"Something's bugging her. She's been moody since Lucy tried to skewer her."

I can't help it.

"We won't notice the difference then."

I get a sharp poke in the side as she fixes me with a stare.

"She's not moody, she's quiet, there's a difference."

"Joke."

"Forgiven."

"What's the problem then?"

"I don't know. It's just..."

The doorbell rings and she growls, shaking her head. She inhales deeply, her mood changer. She smoothes her shirt, looks in the mirror and smiles. That smile stays fixed as she opens the door to - Jen.

Jen laughs, highlighting their shared sense of humour.

"Theme party? Working girls? I wish you'd told me."

I snort a laugh. Michy turns around with a glare. I bite the inside of my cheek.

She pokes Jen in the side as she walks by.

"Where's your man, J-girl?"

Jen hands me a bottle of very expensive wine. Her hand rests on my shoulder and she kisses my cheek then turns, answering.

"He might come later on. We had a row. I'll call him in a while." She smiles then throws her hands up. "So, who do I need to f...?"

"Drinks are in there."

I point to the other room. Only then do I notice her outfit: tight dark red dress, seemed stockings, heels. I stare down at mine. Black pants, black top. At least I have heels on my boots.

"Why do I get the feeling I'm underdressed for this?"

Michy smiles, looking into the mirror as she runs a hand through her hair.

"Because you are?"

"I guess I'll go and change into something less...motherly later. So, anyway, we were talking about Discord, and you were about to tell me something serious."

She runs a finger under her eyes, checking for eyeliner smudges.

"Was I?"

She glances at me. I lean on the wall, next to the mirror, tilting my head to get her attention.

"Yes, you were."

"You know how I hate to be serious. I think you've got your wires crossed."

"But..."

The doorbell sounds and she winks.

"Saved by the bell."

The door swings open. Discord manages a pretty good smile. A slight quirk of an eyebrow confirms Michy's outfit went down well.

"Hey, Mich."

Her eyes slide down the rest of my best friend. She leans in and kisses Michy on the cheek. Too cute.

I poke my static guard in the ribs.

"Are you a doorman? Move out of the way and let our guest in."

She turns and stares at me blankly, then suddenly side steps. That's when I see Discord's outfit. Striking. Pants that make her legs look a mile long and a shirt that proves she might have muscles but she's also got two other things.

Michy looks at me, narrowing her eyes.

"I'm not a doorman." She turns to our guest. "Sorry. I'm in a daze. Come in."

Discord hands me two bottles.

"Hey, Gabrielle. Champagne. New Year and all."

I take the two heavy bottles and rest them on my hallway table.

"Thanks, we'll open them on the stroke of midnight. Actually, Michy, can you get the champagne glasses from the cellar? I forgot to bring them up."

Her eyes widen and she points to her heels. I frown. Her nose wrinkles. She finally rolls her eyes.

"Why are they in the cellar?"

"Because you've systematically broken every single expensive glass I have to such an extent, I now keep the good stuff away from your paws."

"Okay, mom. You coming, Dis? We can look through Gab's prized collection of things she doesn't really want me to touch but is asking me to fetch."

I talk to her back as they walk away.

"Be careful down there." She ignores me. "Michelle? Don't break anything!"

Ten minutes later the almost couple bring the glasses back upstairs. I can't help it.

"What were you doing down there, making the glass yourselves?"

Discord jams her hands into her back pockets. Michy winks at me.

"We couldn't find them amongst your hordes of boxes."

I bet.

I take the opportunity to be less mumsy and slide myself into a more appropriate tight dark blue dress. As Michy said, *"If you'd loosen up there'd be a long line of men waiting to..."* I managed to get that mouth in time for once.

The next two hours go well. I hostess, but food does not make itself. Hosting is a hard job especially as I thought I'd have help tonight. But everyone's having a good time and that's all that's important at this time of year.

I finally run into Michy as she's getting some drinks. I lean back on the counter and lift an eyebrow. She doesn't look at me, but grins.

"Yes, Gabrielle?"

I tease.

"You've left me to manage this whole thing on my own."

Her shoulders drop and she deposits her glasses back down.

"I didn't think. What do I need to do?"

"Tell me what you were doing in the basement for ten minutes."

She tuts and shakes her head.

"A lady never tells."

"You're not a lady. What did you do?"

She shrugs, her face becoming serious for a moment.

"We talked."

"About?"

"You're such a detail whore. She's not saying much, but her latest mission is getting to her big time."

I think for a moment, and then it occurs to me.

"Well, we have a rota's problem with the kill prequel. There's no one to be the second. Do you want to go, strictly backup, to make sure she's alright? It'll save me rescheduling it."

I watch her carefully. One thing I don't want is to set her off on the downward spiral Vengeance brings. But she's worked as backup before. It's a completely safe position. There are rarely ever problems with the information gathering side.

She nods, and I voice my main fear.

"Preferably calling us if there's a problem. No going heroic."

She smiles, flicking my ear. I frown, poking her ribs.

"Are you worrying about big strong Michelle? I promise, mom, no playing out after dark with the big kids."

John comes up and leans in-between us, staring at the food.

"Sorry, ladies, but your guests are wasting away."

Michy prods his stomach.

"We'd have to leave you in the wilderness for a year before your body worked that off."

He pats his slightly round belly.

"I worked hard to get this extra layer of protection."

She snorts.

"I can imagine. All that chewing must've been exhausting. Go and hand these around."

Michy exchanges his drink for a platter of nibbles. He lifts the plate up to his mouth, picking a mini pastry off with his teeth. He chews then opens his mouth and shows us both. I push him away as he speaks with his mouthful.

"Last time I saw a platter like this my head was on it."

Michy rolls her eyes.

"How could you if your head was on it?"

"Der. When I was on Earth doing my Baptist thing? Is it just me that remembers those days?" He sighs. "Pay attention, Michelle."

"You want me to call your mom over here?"

Michy looks over to where Sam is and opens her mouth as if to shout. John sighs and starts walking away.

"Alright, I'm going to distribute food stuffs."

If I'd realised it was that easy I would've got his help earlier.

I catch sight of Jen and Discord in a corner. Jen obviously tells an interesting story because she manages to drag a slight smile out of Michy's girl, a feat I wouldn't have thought possible a few months ago. I tug an arm of Michy's shirt, directing her attention to the corner. Her eyebrows furrow.

I tease because it's my chosen theme for the night.

"Jealous?"

Her arms cross as she glares over.

"No. She can do what she wants. We're not married."

My eyebrows lift at her stern tone, because this isn't my ball of fun Michy. This is some scary monster that's taken over her body.

"Follow me, please."

She doesn't move but keeps staring at them. I tug her shirt.

"Michelle, honey, come on."

Her head jerks, she blinks.

"Sorry. Sure."

I close the bedroom door behind us and lean back on it.

"What's going on?"

She shifts about, obviously annoyed. I try and remember ever seeing her this bothered by any thing let alone any one.

"Nothing's going on. Can't a girl get a bit of P.M.S. without everyone questioning her?"

"I'm not everyone. I'm your best friend. You can talk to me."

There's an almost painful pause before her words softly exit.

"I know I can."

She sighs but offers nothing more.

My sentence is hardly a stab in the dark. I've been watching them together for a while now.

"Honey, it's all right to have even the smallest of feelings for Discord. Have some fun and relax. It's New Years."

She runs a hand through her hair and nods.

"I'm sorry. I'm screwing things up, aren't I? I think I need to get drunk or something."

And now I know there's a problem. Michy doesn't need to get drunk. She's lively enough with out excessive alcohol.

"If you want, get smashed, but...."

Something's nagging me: the jealousy, the time they've been spending together, Michy's preoccupation.

"Do you have *serious* feelings for Discord?"

She stares at me, hands going to her hips. That answers my question before she can deny it.

"Don't be crazy."

I repeat myself, my tone showing this is not the norm. I'm incredulous. I'm not going to disguise it.

"Michelle, do you have serious feelings for Discord?"

There's a pause, a long one, and she doesn't look at me.

"I think.... Maybe. I don't know - yes. Yes, probably."

Her face falls as the last word is out. Mine fell well before that.

"I don't know what to say."

She throws her hands up.

"Hey, welcome to my world. One minute everything's fine, I'm having a good time and then,..." She starts to pace, but falters, her hands going to her head. "...I don't know, a whole heap of stupid feelings sneak up on me. It's crazy, and you know what, not me. Maybe I'm having a moment or something?"

She doesn't worry often, but when she does....

"How serious?"

She stares at me, not defiantly just a little shocked as her arms drop to her sides.

"Michy, how serious?"

I walk over and take her hand, squeezing it. What comes out of my mouth is not what either of us expected.

"Are you in lo...?"

This time her finger presses down on my lips, stopping my last word. It slides off slowly.

"Don't ask me that."

She looks at her hand in mine. Her face is shell-shocked. We stand in silence as my brain attempts to process this new development. I try to find something useful to say, something pertinent.

"Why are you worried about lo...liking her?"

"Because...."

Her eyebrows furrow at my question. She looks at me, puzzled then sighs.

"It's not me, that's the point. I'm a good time girl. I like my freedom. I like to be able to do what I want with who I want."

She tuts and exhaled her stress in a big puff. I take my intro and run with it. Michelle's great if you can pinpoint her worries, and answer them.

"It's not a problem. Your feelings, I mean. Think about it. She's totally single. She's stable. She's good looking. She's not possessive at all. She's not demanding, in fact she's beyond laid back. You share the same interests. She's clever, she knows about the Vengeance stuff. If you could like anyone you picked a good one."

Her head cocks as she digests my words.

It makes sense. Discord resembles every trait Michy likes. In fact, I should've seen this coming.

"And liking someone isn't a jail term. It can be...you can have fun. You're having fun now, right?"

She nods, but then sighs.

"Only because she doesn't know. You know what I'm like. I'll blurt, I always do. I have zero control over my mouth. I'm surprised I haven't done it already. I wanted to in the basement, so I kissed her instead."

"You said you talked."

She smiles, seeming a lot calmer now everything's in the open.

"We did, but we kissed, too." Her smile falls. "Gab, this is so complicated. What should I do?"

I rub her arm.

"You're going to go back outside and have some fun. It's New Year's Eve and you have a very sexy woman waiting for you to come out and spend time with her. Just be yourself and don't worry too much. Relax and see the year in with a blast."

"Sounds like something I'd say."

"Good, then you'll probably do it. Go on, scoot."

She smiles, throwing her arms around me, picking me up in a bear hug.

"You I have no problem loving."

Her Freudian slip is lost on her, but not me. She kisses my cheek and sets me down. I ruffle her hair before she leaves.

I close the door, keeping the party at bay for a few important minutes. I take my drink and sit on my bed, trying to digest what I've found out: Michy's in love with Discord. I spend decades setting her up with women and she goes and finds one of her own to get serious about. I get up and give my lipstick another coat, staring at myself in the mirror. Michy's, potentially, got a serious girlfriend? My mouth breaks into a huge beaming smile.

"Finally."

Now, one thing is her propensity to whiplash away from intimacy when she panics. I make a mental note to keep her on an even keel whatever it takes. I down my drink and make my way out into the party zone.

The dawning of a brand New Year approaches. Having had so many you'd think it'd lessen the excitement. Rarely. It just makes it easier to plan your next twenty parties.

The countdown happens and Jen grabs my arm.

"You can't be on your own on the strike of midnight, Gabrielle."

I stare into hazel eyes wondering what she's talking about. Five, four, three, two, one. Her eyes close. Soft warm lips gently meet mine as she kisses me for much longer than necessary. She pulls away with a very naughty smile.

"Good kisser. The boys don't know what they're missing out on with you."

My brain lets out some words oddly making sense.

"Where's your boyfriend?"

"Dumped. New Year, new start, watch out."

Chuckling, she disappears into another room. I catch my reflection in the mirror. I hold the backs of my hands against my cheeks, trying to get rid of my blush. That's when I see where a certain duo got to: on the decking out back, gently lit by the burning torches. I couldn't have planned a more subtly romantic moment if I'd tried. Thankfully, things like that often go over the top of Michy's head. More ignorance, less freaking is fine with me.

She's in full swing, looking a thousand times calmer than earlier, telling some stupid story I bet. She nudges Discord's shoulder and they subtly get closer and closer. I can't help but smile, because I've wanted to see her settled for too long.

"Gaby, you voyeur."

I jump, splashing myself with my drink.

"Sam!"

She hands me a napkin and I pat my dress down.

"Is this how you get your intelligence? Who's she out there with?"

She looks out onto the decking, and then straightens up, eyes wide.

"That's Discord. Elle will...." She covers her eyes with a hand. "I'm not watching. Walking away now. Walking."

She bangs into a small table, almost knocking some drinks over. I gently grab her, pulling her hand off of her eyes. I hold onto her arms, rubbing her belly.

"Watch the baby, honey."

She clamps her mouth down in a comical manner, which makes me wonder, why would she be doing that?

"Are Elle and Dis still involved?"

She snorts and rolls her eyes, obviously forgetting about that clamped mouth.

"I hear Elle and Charity talking all the time and.... I mean, I don't know anything at all. Nothing."

I keep a hold of her, determined to confirm all the rumours, especially after Michy's admission. There'll be no loose ends on my watch.

"You don't have to say anything, so you won't be telling me. But I need you to nod for yes and shake for no. It's very important. Very. Okay?"

Innocent blue eyes sparkle as she nods.

"Are Elle and Discord definitely over?"

She pauses and glances out onto the decking, and nods. I almost sigh in thanks.

"Were Elle and Discord serious?"

Her eyes go wide and she nods very quickly.

"Is Elle still.... Does she still have feelings for Discord?"

Her head nods slowly. Another question enters my head. A dangerous one.

"Did they ever get back together again?"

She stares at me and shakes her head, but then stops, wrinkles her nose and shrugs. Her mouth pops open.

"I don't know. I don't think so."

It's as good as it's going to get. I'm happy. I pull her in for a quick hug, whispering.

"Thank you. You go and make John change the music to something you like."

I pull back and she smiles up at me.

"You'll regret saying that."

She almost runs off. And I turn, just in time. My lips curl at the scene that greets me: Michy wrapping her arms around Discord as they kiss. The perfect way to see in the New Year.

## 39 CUPID'S INTRODUCTION

Gabrielle didn't bring up Michelle's revelation, but she did work hard to keep her as calm as she could. Good job too because as you know, love does not run smoothly in our universe. And Hell? That was the same as ever, full of an eternally naughty Lucy. Gotta love that woman's consistency.

## Chapter Thirty-Nine: Lucy
## 7th January, Year 3 - 13:00
## Crucial Memory

"**W**here are they?"

I perch on the end of Bee's desk, taking a sip of my latte. She glances up.

"Where are what?"

I sigh.

"The deluge of files that are my daily greeting. I'm trying to be a helpful boss for a change. I'm not avoiding this morning, I'll sign them all."

Bee stares at me yet touch types at a vicious speed. I lean down and stop her hands.

"Don't tease me with the speed of those fingers. I won't be able to contain myself soon. Give me a distraction. I'll sign anything you want."

"There's nothing to sign."

I take her hand and put it on my arm.

"Pinch me. Go on."

She does, quite hard. I'm proud of that strength of character. Her eyebrow slides up as she looks at the little red mark on my arm.

"You're not dreaming, Lucy."

I lounge across the desk, very close to her. I can smell her sensible lipstick.

"I didn't think I was. I had a dream about you last night. You were in leather, holding a whip and you pinched me before pushing..."

"But you can always help with the backlog of bank paperwork I have to complete."

It's amazing the sheer number of times my passes can be thwarted. Still, I always find a thoroughly unproductive game amusing.

I crinkle my nose up at her suggestion.

"Do I have to?"

I lean over, putting my chest disgustingly near to her face as I get a pen from the other side of her desk. She sits back in her seat, flicking through some files.

"You don't have to do anything you don't want to."

I roll my eyes at the fact I'm not winning this battle of wits. Then my brain assimilates what she said sixty seconds ago.

"Why don't I have any papers to sign? I always have papers. Every day of the last Century I've had papers. Why none today?"

Her expression is defiant. One day I will break her. I'm certainly enjoying the build up.

"Elle hasn't sent us any."

I prop my head in my palm and shift closer. Bee doesn't pull away but narrows her eyes for a moment, a silent warning. I ignore her and lower my voice to a bare whisper.

"Do you think jamming their air conditioning system to the high heat setting was the straw that broke Her Mighty Glowing Brightness' back?"

I move our lips near so they're almost touching. Sexual harassment? Of course. It's character building. I carry on.

"I also arranged for their cold water supply to be heated up, and cancelled the bottled water deliveries for a week. It's like a desert up there. Do you like it hot, Bee?"

She simply shakes her head.

"You never stop, do you, Lucy."

"I do have amazing stamina, it's true."

She pushes her seat back.

"If you were a man and I felt threatened, then your behaviour would be a problem. You know that, don't you?"

I get up, understanding my game won't work this time.

"But I'm not a man and you don't feel threatened, do you?"

With a deadpan expression she puts her glasses on.

"No."

"Bee, you're such a delight. Let's go home early and spend the afternoon in my Jacuzzi."

She doesn't look up from the files she's putting into order.

"I have work to do. You feel free. I can hold the fort."

"When are you going to stop playing hard to get?"

"Never." She glances up at me. "Have you ever thought how productive we could be if you spent your time working instead of flirting?"

"Yes, but I have a reputation to uphold."

Her next sentence ends our moment of sharing.

"Okay, but Stats Man is waiting in your office."

I double take, a little annoyed.

"Why is he in my office instead of out here?"

"Because it makes him more uncomfortable. He's been there for an hour and the heating is on full."

It makes sense.

"Want to come in and watch, Bee? I have a lot of unresolved tension to get out of my system since you're not..."

"Of course I want to watch. I still have the syndicate to smash."

"Your timing interrupting me is impeccable."

Her lips twitch into the barest of smiles.

"I know."

I push my office door open quickly, making it bang against the wall. A yelp fills the air. Stats Man kneels, picking up his files.

I take prime Alpha-female positioning and sit on the edge of my desk, looking down on him. Bee walks across his papers. He retracts his hands quickly; her heels are lethal. She sits in a chair, ready to observe and win her bet.

"So, how am I doing in this quarter's race?"

He grabs a file, smiling nervously, flicking through pages as I wait.

"No pressure, Stats Boy, but I'll need an answer some time today."

I pick a pen up, tapping it noisily on my desk. Bee sighs loudly.

"I'm trying to find your figures."

Bee tuts again, pokerfaced. He glances over, apologetically. Her face doesn't change; his hands start to shake.

I walk into the middle of his papers.

"Why are you always trying to find?"

He stops, looking up at me. I can't help myself - not that I'm trying that hard.

"I like Angels on their knees. It fills me with a feeling of accomplishment. What did you say your name was?"

He blinks. A bead of sweat drips down the side of his face.

"David."

"Are you married?"

He seems perplexed. So am I. I never know if I have a point.

"Um...yes. She's very..."

"I'm sure she is, Daniel."

"David."

"Whatever. Found those figures yet?"

"Oh, yes. Here. You were..."

"Changed my mind. Woman's prerogative. If I manage to take an extra seven percent of souls over the next week, will I match the totals for last quarter, Daniel?"

"It's David. I need some time to work that out. Seven percent?"

"Eleven. Over the last six periods."

He stares up at me, more sweat beading off of his head.

"I thought you said seven?"

I bend down, glaring. Now is the time to prove that my ancient form is as impressive as this one. I elongate my front teeth, turning them into fangs. I hiss like a cat.

"Don't tell me what I think, Danny. Totals. Now."

He recoils and swallows. His voice sounds like a prepubescent boy's.

"Eleven percent over the last six periods is...."

His hands shake on the buttons of his calculator. He grimaces and clears the totals once, twice, then a third time.

Bee can't help herself.

"An eleven percent rise would leave you ahead by three percent, Lucy."

I throw my arms out, sighing loudly.

"Aha! An answer. It's all I wanted, Danny. An answer. Nothing out of the ordinary."

"It's D..."

"Whatever."

I bend down, licking a fang for show, then carry on.

"Your incompetence annoys me."

I push him in the chest and like a good little puppy he falls back without resistance. He is the archetypal victim; limited eye contact, no argument and very little fight in him. I kick through his papers, sending a cloud into the air.

"I hate the way you can't do your job. Bee, send a complaint into Elle. Copy in the Council and Nature. I want a recount on the last year's figures."

"No, no, that won't be necessary."

"Uh oh," is all Bee says.

I join in our little game.

"Are you trying to cover up your incompetence, Danny?"

He wipes his moist brow. One of his eyes blinks quicker than the other.

"No, that's not what I meant. But you don't have to call Her Eminence."

Even Bee can see the start of the crack.

"You're asking me to commit fraud? To lie to Elle, the Council and that little bitch Nature? I can't believe you want me to do that on your behalf."

"Th - that's not what I said."

"But that's what you meant. Oh, Danny, Danny, Danny, it didn't have to end like this, you know. I'll tell your wife you were a good man. Well, not really, you were a liar, but..."

He shoots up from the floor. His eyes brim over with tears as he sniffs, noisily.

"I don't need this from you! I'm a good p - p..."

Bee saves me from slapping that word out of his mouth.

"Pineapple?"

He stares at her impassive face.

"What?"

"Pilchard? Puppy? Pom-pom? Prick? I know you're one of those."

He actually seems taken aback by this addition to the conversation. It makes two of us. I have to wonder where she hid such a dirty mouth. He blinks rapidly.

"Prick?"

As Hell's net closes, his mental cracking elongates. I jump in with both feet.

"Don't speak to her like that, Donald."

"But I d - didn't say anything."

"You called her a prick, which is actually anatomically incorrect, but anyway, I won't have her insulted like that. She's been nothing if not friendly."

"B - but.... I was repeating her words to me."

I turn to Bee.

"Was he?"

She hides her face in her hands, sobbing.

"No. I don't deserve to be spoken to like this, Lucy. I'm here to take notes not to be cursed at."

She sniffs loudly. I walk over, taking full advantage of the situation. I put an arm around her, pulling her into my cleavage.

"It's okay, Bee. I know."

Something jabs me in the ribs. I muffle my surprise, pulling back. She stares, waving her pen like a sword. I shrug, smoothing her brow, whispering.

"Do you want to win or not?"

She narrows her eyes for a moment then finally nods. I turn back to Elle's little spy.

"This is going into my letter of complaint, Derek."

"It's D - David. And I'm going to have to leave now. I...I don't feel very well."

I pat him on the back, pushing him towards the door.

"You're not very anything."

Opening it I shove him, stumbling, into my reception.

"You take care now. Be back tomorrow at three - a.m. I'm an early riser and we have a long day ahead."

He stares at me, cuffing his eyes with a sleeve.

"I don't think I'll b - be in tomorrow, Lucy."

"Shame."

I smile and slam my door. Bee says it all.

"I wish I'd got more people in the syndicate, now."

## 40 CUPID'S INTRODUCTION

Lucy sent an encyclopaedia of complaints up about Daniel...I mean David. I guess she was turning the tables and burying Elle in paperwork, too. David was medically signed off for three months pending a psychic evaluation.

Bee was quietly ecstatic. Whenever I.T. came up she gloated in that minimalist way she has - by putting lots of holiday brochures on her desk.

Anyway, let's swing over to other things. Sam's normally ditzy self got even worse with those pregnancy hormones. John was doing his best, but he was stressed to the max. Lucy was still disrupting things where she could. Add them all together and the Heavens were swimming in problems. So, normal day really.

## Chapter Forty: Elle
## 9th January, Year 3 - 14:00
## Cumulative Hell

"**I** think that brings things to a close. We're adjourned." My head almost collapses onto the oval meeting table as I finally end today. Exhausted doesn't beginning to describe how I feel. I slip my feet back into heels, not caring these new shoes pinch. Manolo pain is always less than any other kind.

Gabrielle rubs an eye as she picks her papers up.

"It's been a long day, Your Eminence."

"Imagine my week with three more of these in it and Lucy trying to send every member of the statistics team insane."

Her hand makes the shape of a gun and she puts it to her temple, pulling the trigger. At exactly the same time Sam takes the opportunity to drop a tray full of crockery. I hold my heart as everyone in the room jumps. Gabrielle stares at her fingers then at Sam, sighing.

"I was about to say, I didn't think they were loaded."

She goes over to help, rubbing Sam's arm, announcing to our paused onlookers.

"Okay, people, nothing to see here."

The rest of the room files out as I stare down at what were my best antique china cups in pieces. The sound of quiet sobbing refocuses my attention on my poor little assistant.

"Don't cry over split Ming." I glance between the two of them. "Split Ming? Spilt milk? The cups are Ming." They stare at me. "Right then, moving on."

Gabrielle gives Sam a hug as I realise there is a difference between Gods and Angels, mainly in frames of reference. It's times like these I wish Charity could be on permanent speakerphone. She always gets my abysmal jokes.

I pour some fruit juice and watch; it's nice to be almost on the outside, looking in. Sam sniffs and pulls a tissue out of her pocket, blowing her nose loudly.

Gabrielle rubs her tummy.

"You have to calm down for the baby's sake."

"Oh, I'm being very good. I've even cut out dairy, and I'm onto everything that's brown: bread, pasta, sugar."

"Good girl, we don't want you with swollen ankles."

"John says we should get married so the baby has proper parents."

I wonder when someone swapped my assistant for one who has a little sense. I take this opportunity to speak up.

"You can't be an unmarried mother."

Gabrielle looks as if I'm trying to pass a law to kill all newborns. Even Sam stares at me oddly. I clarify.

"A stable family environment means you have less chance of raising a socially dysfunctional child, that's all."

It's only then I think about my parents, my mother especially. I suddenly realise it doesn't really matter if your parents are married or not, they can still send you askew.

Sam glances at Gabrielle then back.

"But I don't want to lose my individuality and be swallowed up as just John's wife. I'm also not happy with the whole shotgun wedding theme."

Her words stop me with their intelligence. Gabrielle quirks an eyebrow. I manage a few slightly shocked blinks.

Gabrielle's words to Sam bring about a complete change, though, as she goes from sad to madly glad in less than a blink of an eye.

"Or you could think of the presents you'd get with a wedding and a baby shower."

She squeals in delight, throwing her arms around Gabrielle, teaching me an important lesson: never judge an Angel by her dim cover.

They leave, chatting, completely forgetting about me. It's a pleasant feeling.

My cell phone rings. It's Charity.

*"Elle, is Samantha on maternity leave yet?"*

"No. Perhaps that's something to enforce early? She just spent the last five minutes destroying my best china."

Charity laughs as I sit down. She proves that we were obviously separated at birth - which would explain why I like her mother more than mine.

*"Don't cry over split Ming."*

"That's what I said and no one got it!"

*"You should keep me on speaker phone. I could be rent-a-laugh."*

"It'd be the only way I'd get someone to laugh at my tired jokes. Now, why did you need to know if Sam's on leave? Has she done something peculiar again?"

*"Sort of. What do you want me to do with the eight files of papers on Intelligence's latest Vengeance missions delivered to me by mistake?"*

I sigh, kicking my shoes off, curling my legs under me. Ever since Lucy let those mice loose I'm wary of putting my feet on the floor. I pick my heels up, putting them on the table.

"Do they look urgent?"

*"They don't have anything stamped across them. The closing date is a while yet. There's time. I'll bring them all up when I feel like lifting heavy paperwork. It's under the name of Clipper if you need them urgently."*

We go on to talk about relaxing matters. We briefly touch on Discord but I'm not feeling brave so I divert. Charity doesn't miss my tactic but does let it slide. We gossip for ten minutes before her next meeting looms.

I close my cell phone after our goodbyes and glance at the clock. My next meeting isn't for another hour. I close my eyes, willing my brain to come up with a solution for my organisationally challenged pregnant assistant. Between Sam and Lucy my life is going to get a lot worse before it gets better.

Sometimes the Heavens are Hellish.

## 41 CUPID'S INTRODUCTION

Sam was doing her best, but...well, Sam's Sam, her best still isn't great. Anyway, it was only paperwork, right? Nothing in the Heavens is just paperwork.

Michelle and Dis had been busy. All the departments were understaffed and overworked. It was a stressful time. Relationship-wise they were still being careful. It'd been almost six months since they first slept together. I've never dated a woman for that long, let alone hung in there for something more. They did the usual: met up for lunch, worked out in the gym, enjoyed each other's company - even if it was more than simply enjoying for Michelle.

In the mean time, I crossed paths with Elle in the mall. She was in the class above me in school. I had a crush on her for, like, a couple of generations. Anyway, we're both easygoing, we had a good time. Elle did the shoe shop. I did the woman serving at the cookie counter. Elle picked some new heels. I picked chocolate chips out of my bra. Elle got her nails painted. I also got my fingers coated. We bonded. Retail therapy is a valuable form of recovery.

Discord, on the other hand, finally got to focus all of her irreconcilable anger. Her painful mission was hitting full speed. It was time for our Vengeance girl to go and do the recognisance for her next mission: Mr Child Killer. It was going to turn everything upside down.

# Chapter Forty-One: **Discord**
## 14th January, Year 3 - 07:00
## Lock And Load

Today has hardly started. It's seven and already it's not going great. I've been here since five, staring at an ivy covered condominium in a quiet street. My eyeballs are getting dry from my lack of blinking.

I shift around on my car seat. It's hot and my air-con. has decided to act up. The inside of my car is getting muggy, there's no breeze, and I need to

221

pee. I wind my window down. It doesn't make it cooler but it makes me feel less claustrophobic. I've never liked small spaces and at over six foot, most spaces are verging on tiny.

I pull a picture out of my back pocket, running my thumb over the face of victim number four. My motivation. Nice of them to give her a number. Real personal.

"He'll get what's coming."

I put the picture back into my pocket and concentrate on what I need to do, not how bad I'm feeling inside. Brooding on stuff won't help me now, but staying focused will. I've waited too long for this. I'm not losing it now.

The door I'm watching opens. I grab my digital camera, zooming in on the figure coming out. And I finally get to see him in the flesh, the man who's caused so much pain to everyone he's touched, and a few others by default. Jacob Clipper shields his eyes from the bright sunshine. He puts on a baseball cap then sunglasses. As he walks he tugs on the bottom of his off-white tee, trying to make it cover his stomach. I stare at him in the viewer on the camera. I once watched this programme about ancient tribes. Some of the elders believed cameras stole your soul. I click some pictures for the records; this way we can set a date for the kill once intelligence have confirmed everything for the twentieth time. Cameras don't steal souls. I stare at him. I do. I'm the executioner after the judge and jury decide a soul's final destination, and it's always the one place, Hell. For once I'm glad Lucy exists. I've heard about her tar pits. I know what his eternity involves.

He walks down the road towards his car. I checked it out earlier: old Chevy parked a hundred yards away with the insides covered in rubbish. This man is a slob.

I get out and follow. I stay on the opposite side of the road and keep to the shadows. Someone walks by. She winks.

"Nice ass."

I shake my head at my backup. Michelle keeps walking, staying in the shadows like me.

Leaning on a tree I watch him drive off. I make sure his car turns at the end of the street. Never cut corners when doing a job because the repercussions outweigh saving time.

Now it starts. I walk back to his house. I don't think about what he is, what he's done, or who he did it to. I do wonder what his neighbours think of him, this monster. I just hope they don't let him baby-sit.

I stop for a moment, just taking five seconds to clear my head. I remember what Michy said about not being able to change the past, but instead making the future a better place. They were clever words, but then she's a clever woman. I'm glad I've allowed myself to get to know her. I'm also glad she's hung in there. I'm not easy, not by any definition of the word.

I take a deep breath and get back to it.

I walk along his winding path. Large flowery bushes hide the door. That's stupid on his part and fortunate on mine. I side step a whirring sprinkler system. Latex gloves snap over the skin of my hands. The secret to a successful job is not to leave an audit trail: no sightings from curious neighbours, no meeting the victim, always pay parking meters, don't speed, never park in front of hydrants. When you no longer exist on Earth it's best if no one gets to question that fact.

My lock pick gun slides into the cylinder. Twelve seconds and the door clicks open. I shut my eyes and count to ten. Only an idiot goes from bright sunshine to darkness. Never get blinded by the light.

I leave the lights off and as many of my feelings as I can outside. My boots take me over the threshold and into darkness. My eyes open and I'm able to see even though the curtains are drawn. I stand in Jacob Clipper's house, my skin creeping from my toes right up to my scalp. It's a slithering slide through every part of me.

I begin my fact-finding mission, as hard as it is considering I'd rather be removing his head from his body. Nobody's going to say I don't do things by the rules.

I try to get a sense of him. The house is nothing special. No hallway, straight into an L shaped lounge. He doesn't have a cleaner, that's clear from the dirty plates all over the place. I walk into a back room, obviously where he sleeps. It looks trashed. Dirty clothes everywhere, even dirtier sheets on the bed, and a packed ashtray makes the place stink. Suddenly I wonder if he raped anyone in here. I back out of there. No one said it'd be easy.

My fingers flick my camera on, and I look through the digital viewer, taking some pictures for our files. The grainy image of his bedroom looks back. It's weird how you can capture a little bit of evil onto a computer chip, ready to upload it later like it doesn't mean a thing.

I take some more and move on.

I tread on a magazine and pick it up. A woman is spread-eagled, wearing only a cowboy hat. Porn, adult, perfectly legal. I place it back where I found it. My finger runs over a stack of dustless books. I lift one up: Satanism. I lift another: Revelations, Chapters twenty-three onwards. I lift another: Necromancy. Glad to see he's been doing his research and will be happy to see Lucy. Then something makes me stop. I've only been on a few other missions but I have a sixth sense, and there's something in here that's triggering it off. I turn, looking around. It's a pit but nothing else is out of the ordinary. Then I realize what's wrong. The smell. It's not of him but something a lot different. I try to place it, closing my eyes to concentrate. My feet walk me over to a pale wooden door. That smell gets stronger. My fingers rest on the handle. My heart hammers in my throat. My cell phone vibrates on my belt and I jump out of my skin.

My fists clench, I take a deep breath, trying to steady my nerves. Caller ID: Mich? I don't speak, just listen.

*"Dis, get out of there!"*

I break protocol and talk, because I don't know what she's going on about.

"I'm almost through."

*"He's coming back."*

Words no operative wants to hear.

My heart pounds. I stare at the door then around for somewhere to hide. I push the phone to my ear, searching for another way out, but I don't know if he prefers the back or front door. His windows are locked shut. I don't have a safe exit. For a moment I remember the picture in my pocket and the fact she didn't escape. My fists clench as I wonder if escaping is what I really want to do.

My mouth works automatically.

"How do you know?"

*"I'm watching him walking up the path. He went to the store not to work."*

In my downward spiral I land back on Earth. And panic.

Keys jangle outside as I frantically look for anywhere that can hide a six foot two woman.

I push the cell to my ear, whispering.

"I'm screwed."

I grab the handle on the pale wooden door and pull it open, diving in. The smell almost makes me retch. Along with the darkness it's intense and smothering. I curse my luck at ending up in the slob's rubbish room.

As my door clicks closed another clicks open. I turn the volume down on my phone, pushing it to my ear as hard as I can, trying to keep her voice in.

*"Dis? Discord? What's happening?"*

I say one thing to her.

"Shhh."

My eyes don't get used to the small dark room. It's like an intensely smothering coffin. I keep my eyes front as I listen with a free ear, trying not to let my claustrophobia freak me out.

Footsteps. Answer machine clicked on and checked. No messages.

I slide my knife out of the scabbard on my belt. This was a fact-finding mission. The kill was later, not yet. I bring the thin blade up to what I know is his neck height. I'll slit his throat wearing a smile if forced, but I'd prefer not to. Giving the Amazons even more ammo isn't all that appealing.

I stand, still, my eyes focused on that thin broken sliver of light under the door, the one telling me he's standing right there. I hope Mich doesn't take this moment to start shouting on my cell.

A knock at the door becomes a beautiful distraction. Heavy awkward footsteps reverberate on the floor, and his shadow moves away. I bring my knife down and breathe carefully through my mouth - minimises sound and stops this damn smell from making me nauseous.

A familiar female voice makes me whisper into my cell.

"What?"

Then I realize it's not from there the sound is coming. It's from the front door he just answered. The unravelling of my most important mission hits its peak. I almost have an aneurysm as I hear Mich asking him survey details.

I wonder what I'm going to put in the report. The Amazons will have a field day when this hits the fan. That's when I think about the stupidity of standing in my target's house while thinking about the consequences of being found. I should be hauling ass!

I turn the door handle slowly. It's oiled and makes no sound. Make or break. I stop pressing my cell to my ear and walk out. I see his back, his tee is grubby and creased. For a moment I stand there, staring at the man who doesn't belong on the Earth. My tongue slides along the back of my teeth, over and over. But then a certain blonde grabs my attention. Mich ticks things off on a clipboard as she asks what cable channels he likes. She doesn't look at me or stutter her sentences even though I'm less then fifteen feet away. I didn't think it was possible but I have more respect for her now, and clearly a lot to learn. I also have a lot to make up for.

Like walking through a minefield my boots plant down carefully. Then something makes me pause. My head cocks. Carefully I pick up a pen from the floor; my memento. I slip it into a pocket and turn to close that pale wooden door. He's opened the curtains. Light from the house floods into my coffin shaped room illuminating my surprise companion. Instantly I realise what that smell was: death. She's hanging by her arms from a meat hook on the ceiling, right at the back of the room. Head to the side, eyes taped shut, she's purple and her skin swollen. Her legs are cut with thick pieces of dark red skin hanging off. All she's wearing is white...*once* white underwear, most of it discoloured with dried blood. My mouth waters. I'm about to be sick. My ears start ringing as I stare.

Michelle coughs, waking me back up. I close the door so softly as she rustles her papers. I walk on eggshells to the back door, opening it carefully, taking a deep gulp of fresh air, running to the front of the house, through the light film of water from the sprinklers, forgetting not to draw attention to myself with the neighbours, and jog down the road to my car. I get in and start it. I do not think about what I just saw.

I dial Mich's cell.

"I'm out."

I click it off. A painfully long minute later she jumps in the passenger seat and throws her clipboard in the back. I drive us slowly around a corner. We continue for five minutes in silence until we hit a deserted area of town.

She finally speaks.

"To say that was no fun is an understatement."

Something digs into me and I pull the pen out of my pocket. I glance down at my memento then slam the brakes on, pitching us forward. Her palms slap the dashboard. She leans across, steadying the wheel, stopping us from ploughing into a wall of bushes as we skid to a stop. I push my door open. My stomach heaves violently and I start throwing up.

A warm hand massages the back of my neck.

"It's okay. Just relax."

She carries on rubbing my muscles as I unromantically throw my entire stomach contents up. I finally will myself to stop. I close the car door and rest my head on my hands on the steering wheel. Mich gives me a bottle of ice cold water. Only now do I let go of my memento. I put it on the dash.

I wash out my mouth, spitting it out of the window, and drive away from my shamefully weak moment, feeling stupid, like an amateur, and embarrassed I had an audience, especially her.

I don't know where I'm going and I don't care. Eventually we come to a stop. I stare out of the windshield at nothing, just a haze of colours with no focus.

Michelle can't be silent for too long, her mind protests.

"It's stress. Try and relax. Missions affect people in different ways. Don't feel bad. I threw up once."

I don't believe her, but I have to clarify why I did.

"There was a dead girl in the room I was in."

I open the door again, afraid I'll start retching. My body sucks in air as I resist the urge to bring that water up. This time she rubs my shoulders. I pour the rest of the bottle over my neck and face.

I sit back in the driver's seat, definitely not in charge. This isn't my first mission. I've killed twice before. Violently and messily. It goes with the territory. No one wants to go to die. But this? This was different.

She forces me back to reality.

"They haven't found the body of victim number six."

They found the body of victim number four. I have her picture in my pocket.

I nod, not trusting my voice or my open mouth. Mich fills the silence again, something I'm beginning to rely on.

"She was definitely dead?"

I stare incredulously at her.

"She was rotting with flesh hanging off of her limbs."

She pulls a disgusted face.

"Understandable reaction then."

I make sure my tone is even.

"Why has it taken this long to catch him? Why didn't we take him out after the first or second, or even the third? We could've spared a lot of heartache."

I pop a chewing gum in my mouth, trying to get rid of the smell in my nostrils and the memories in my head.

She shrugs and sighs softly.

"Same reason I'm your second today. Backlog."

And that's it, the explanation for everything all boils down to: we're too busy. What a joke! I push the car door open quickly and get out, slamming it as hard as I can. The car shudders, just like me.

When my temper goes it's best if I get some sort of physical exercise. It restricts unreasonable thoughts and forces me not to think about what's driving me insane. I walk away, needing my feet to be moving.

Mich catches up, keeping in step.

"Where are you going?"

I shrug, because if I start talking I'll lose my temper completely, and as much as I need someone to shout at, it's not going to be her. She doesn't deserve that.

She takes hold of my arm, dragging me to a stop. I stare down at her fingers.

"Sorry." She lets go like I burnt her. "I know you're upset. I am too, but you have to channel your anger and make it work in your favour or it'll eat away at you."

She looks at me for a second, shrugging, silently asking if I agree. I can't even pull enough words together to answer. Instead I look around at where we are, in the middle of a beautiful nowhere. Make it work in my favour? I hear the birds singing. Feel the sun blazing down on my face. The wind gently whips around me, cooling my hothead. No matter what happens the world still turns, life carries on regardless, so I can either keep myself together and get the job done, or lose it and live up to everyone's low expectations.

I let a long breath out, relaxing my whole body, and sit on a fallen tree trunk in a pathetic little heap.

Mich kneels down and does what's becoming a regular thing. She puts her arms around me without wanting anything in return. I relax my head down on her shoulder as she strokes my hair. Nowhere in my life have I given someone as much control or trust as her. Not even Elle and I thought I gave her my all.

As always, she has some words to share. Her arms loosen but a hand stays on my knee.

"How's your stomach doing?"

My earlier episode rears its head. I hope my embarrassment isn't obvious because I feel like an idiot.

"It's all right."

It's not, it's hurting and I feel light-headed, but my stupid pride got in first and answered. A fried breakfast would be a blessing right now.

"I need some food. You sure you don't want to have something from the diner with me? I saw one a mile back."

I stare at her, wondering about this ability to give me just what I need when I need it. It'd be unnerving if I thought too much. So I don't.

"Sure."

My one word gets a soft smile from her. She runs her hand lazily down my leg as she gets up. I watch it move over my pants, making my skin prickle. She starts talking about something in that cheerful way she has. I stare up into glittering eyes, wondering how she's become this amazing grounding presence.

She misinterprets my expression.

"What's that look for? What did I do?"

I stand.

"Nothing. Breakfast?"

She nods, still concerned, but Michelle's good, she never pushes any point. I appreciate that, especially now.

She drives to the diner. I watch the winding roads, bare skeleton trees, and, in the mirror, our dust trail. I keep occupied so my attention isn't taken by that clawing room in Clipper's house, or more importantly, what he left hanging up like a discarded coat.

The lot is full of cars and trucks as Michelle smoothly slides us into a space. Bright sunlight streams in from behind making her blonde hair glow and bright eyes, sparkle. She pats my thigh and smiles.

"Come on, you."
I take my travel toothbrush in and clean up in the bathroom.

We sit in a booth at the back. I enjoy doing normal things like this. It's nice to forget what I am now, and pretend my life is as it was.
I play with the toothpicks. My hands don't like to be idle. Mich props an elbow on the table, her head rests in her palm. She stares at my growing pile of broken wood. I push it into a neat little heap.
"Your favourite habit?"
I try for a smile, not really achieving it, but still doing my best.
"Better than biting my nails."
Her smile reaches all the way up to beautiful green eyes. She tucks a strand of blonde hair behind her ear as she gently prods a stray piece of wood back into my pile with a fingertip.
"You're such a puzzle, Dis."
The statement comes out of the blue. I'm not sure how to comment.
"Thanks?"
She chuckles, her finger still playing with my toothpicks. Her unblinking eyes seem to bore straight into me. I try to hold her gaze for as long as I can but I can't read it. I stare down at the plastic tablecloth, unnerved by her intensity. She coughs and looks around for our server. The intensity lifts.
Her fingers tap a little rhythm out on the tablecloth.
"I'm starving. Where's the food?"
On cue we're served two huge plates of heart attack inducing breakfast. For once we eat in silence. For once I find it off-putting. I don't associate being with her this way. She's always talkative. It's one of the things I really like about her.
Our server smiles.
"Coffee?"
Mich nods and gets a refill as she passes.
I watch her sipping her coffee and watching the room, and wonder when she managed to slip by all of my defences without even an alarm sounding.
Her green eyes catch mine. Her eyebrows furrow.
"You look like something important is going on in that head of yours. One day you'll have to share some of those thoughts with me."
"One day you'll get more than a few sentences, I promise."
She smiles, wrinkling her nose.
"I look forward to it."
I nod, staring down at the horrible tablecloth again.

We finish our food in silence. Every now and then I catch her eye but she looks away. Another quarter of an hour passes and she hasn't talked about Gabrielle or work or clothes, or...what she had for dinner last night. She's just sat and looked into her coffee cup or around for a refill or at the other diners. Finally I can't stand it.
"You're not speaking!"
My words come out as a plea. She looks like I've done something incredulous. Then she steals *my* answer and shrugs. I almost smile. She

stares into her obviously interesting coffee cup again, playing with a sachet of sugar which she doesn't even take. She looks up. Her fingers drop the sachet.

"I like you a lot, Dis."

I fumble for something to say.

"I like you, too."

Her eyes dart around and she shifts in her seat.

"I think I'm in love with you. There, I said it."

I don't take a breath for the next ten seconds. In that time she looks as shocked as I probably do. Then, with a slight shake of her head, she sits back in her seat and sips her coffee before continuing.

"Look, it's no big deal. I just thought you should know. You need a refill?"

I glance down at my empty cup then back up at her.

"I.... No. No coffee, thanks."

She stares at me for a moment, and I know my expression can't be good. She sighs, takes a twenty out, and leaves it on the table.

"Lead balloon, huh. I'm going to the washroom. Back in a minute."

I stare at our table wondering what just happened. I'm scared, I know that much. After my disaster with Elle I don't think I could go through that again. But then, this woman isn't Elle and that doesn't feel like it's a problem. Just the timing with Clipper.... I sit and wait, drowning in my own fears and confusion.

A hand presses firmly on my back.

"Come on then. Let's go."

We walk to the car. She chats about the inside of the washroom, telling me how the soap smelt nice, obviously finding those words she lost earlier. I tug on her sleeve. She stops, turns, and smiles. I seem to have found some of my own, too.

"We're just leaving that sentence?"

Her eyebrows raise.

"About the soap? Well, no, not if you don't want to."

I look away trying to get a grip on my thoughts. I'm not eloquent or particularly verbal about my feelings, however at times it is necessary. I pinch the bridge of my nose, taking a moment.

"Not the soap, your feelings."

"Okay." Her arms cross over her chest. "We've spent a lot of time together, and I know it's a shock, because it is to me too. I blurt sometimes and...." She shifts from one foot to the other. "Listen, it doesn't need to be an issue."

I fumble for words that will be adequate.

"I like you, a lot, Mich. You've been a good friend, but things are complicated for me with this case and...."

I search but still don't find anything more. I trail off into silence.

She holds a hand up, her face not entirely joking as she tries to lighten the mood.

"This is sounding like a Dear John. Don't say anything more. Come on. Let's go. I won't die of the rejection."

She walks to the car leaving me staring at her back. I sigh, annoyed at myself for not getting my point across, the point that I like her a lot and that she's good for me, but that this couldn't have come at a worst time. I can only have one focus at the moment.

I get into the car and turn on the ignition, letting the engine idle as my brain races. Like a flash of lightening the last few hours spike: the mission, the body, him, Mich, confusion, fear, loneliness. It's overwhelming. I push my foot down on the accelerator, flooring it, making a Hell of a lot of noise but not going anywhere. Her hands splay across the seat as she braces. I bang my hand down on the steering wheel, turning to face her. My words twist what I want to say into an aggressive shout.

"What do you want from me?"

She looks shocked. This is why I say very little. I always push things down hill. She stares out of the windshield. Her mouth opens but she sighs instead of answering. Her fingers play with the gear change lever, and with a deep breath she turns and meets my eyes with sad green ones.

"I don't want to screw up being friends with you, Dis. I enjoy the sound of my own voice too much. I need to learn when to shut up." She looks away. "Like now. I won't mention it again."

She looks out of the window.

I grip the wheel, digging nails into hard plastic, then put the car into gear, backing us out of the space.

We drive in silence for a few miles before I'm overwhelmed by the sheer amount of stuff in my mind. I pull us over to the side of the dirt track, slamming the brakes on, determined to at least attempt an explanation.

She holds a hand up to her head, pushing her hair back.

"Will you stop doing that?"

I stare at my hands on the wheel, trying to put my words in the right order, but they're whizzing around so quickly. I struggle, really struggle.

"What you said was a shock. I didn't know you felt like that."

Her hand gently slips onto my thigh, making my muscles tense. Her smile is forced.

"It kind of snuck up on me, too. It's okay. I'll deal with it. I'll put it back where it came from."

I'm scared. I want to go back to my apartment where I can sit and think, where I can sort out what all these feelings mean. Of course, I don't say any of that.

"I value our friendship."

Is all I can get out before I came to an obvious stop.

"You value our friendship? Oh, I know where this is going. You don't have to be polite. Can we just get back? We have a debriefing in twenty minutes and the portal is fifteen away."

She looks out of the window, her arms crossed tightly over her chest.

I put the car in gear and drive.

# 42 CUPID'S INTRODUCTION

If you've only learnt one thing so far it should be that love does not run smoothly. Michelle had guts. For a commitment phobic to say what she did was admirable - even if it was more blurting than a discerning revelation. But Discord's battlements were guarded against all comers. Or maybe her heart wasn't guarding itself as well as she thought? It'd let Mich in this far, and that blonde wasn't going anywhere. But neither was Clipper, and his influence ran deeper than anyone realised.

## Chapter Forty-Two: Michelle
## 14th January, Year 3 - 09:50
## What Would I Give?

I pace up and down in Gab's waiting room. Every now and again I sneak a look at Dis. She's sitting, leaning elbows on knees, staring at her hands. She hasn't moved in ten minutes. I wonder if she's thinking about what to say to Gab or my mistimed revelation? I can't decide so I don't think about it.

Better people than me have gone insane, pondering lesser points than this.

I pick up some healthcare leaflets, trying to stay occupied. I make one into a paper plane. Gab's door opens, stopping my launch sequence. She stares at us, me in particular then at my plane. I put it down. She shakes her head at my misappropriation of the healthcare literature.

"Discord, Michelle. Come in."

Her voice is stern. I hope I'm not going to get a detention from my best friend.

Without saying a word Dis stands, rolling her shoulders. I can't help but watch. Suddenly she glances straight at me. I look away quickly.

We follow the Head of Intelligence, not Gab my best friend; she knows how to compartmentalise. She seats us in front of her desk, picking our statements up, glancing over them. The leather of her large ornate chair creaks as she moves. Her hand taps a Mont Blanc pen on her desk; I got her

231

that a few years ago.

Her eyes flick between us. Gab's been reading our statements and cross-referencing everything with her files since we got back. She opens a black folder labelled, Clipper, J. She scans the pages. Her voice is a monotone, as if she'd done this twenty times this week. She probably has, there's a horrendous backlog of work, because this month's been manic.

"I read your statements. I'm sorry your information wasn't as comprehensive as possible. Of course, you'll both get a written apology because of the corpse, and a commendation for how you handled the incident."

Dis sits up straight and I cringe at the use of the word corpse. Her eyes bore into an oblivious Gab. My finger taps on the arm of my chair, trying to get her attention. I will her to look up before she carries on. She doesn't. The repetition in her tone continues, and it makes my stomach sink.

"Take a week off with our compliments. I'll authorise the condominiums in Europe to be made available. Get some sun. Relax. I'll look into the matter and..."

Dis shoots up, glaring at an interrupted Gab who only now glances at her. Dis' hands are on hips, forearms tensed. Her voice is low and angry.

"Who was the corpse?"

Gab looks shocked as she flicks through the notes. I cross my fingers as I pray she says her name and not...

"Victim number six."

...a number. I fall back in my seat, covering my face with hands. I split my fingers and watch. Dis balls her copy of our statement up and throws it at the Head of Intelligence, just missing her. She storms out and slams the door.

Gab stares at me, no idea what's gone on.

"That isn't the Discord I've come to know and approve of. What was that about?"

"This job's got to her. Did you have to say a number?"

She pulls a pitiful face and flicks through the pages, as if proving her point.

"It's how they're listed on my sheets. As numbers, not names." She holds a picture up. "See? It even says six on it."

This is the crux of the matter. It might seem emotionless but it's functional. She deals with the most heinous crimes. If you think of them as people, the sheer volume becomes impossible.

She puts her pen down on the table then double takes something in her in-tray. Her nose almost touches it as she moves closer.

"Why is it always me? It was me earlier today with the box of evidence we managed to lose between Elle's floor and this one - how is that even possible? And now here we are again. The wheel has come full circle."

She slides out a large brown envelope. The name on it makes me sigh: Jacob Clipper. It's ripped open quickly. She falls back in her seat and holds a yellow sticky up as she flicks through the contents of the package.

"Charity saying it was sent by Sam to her offices by mistake. And these would be the papers telling me where the corpse was. Clipper's place.

Should I go after her?"

I walk around her desk and give her a tight hug.

"No, you stay here and make sure that there are no more bits of paper in our backlog."

I'm careful to say our. It's not her fault. If it's not missing paperwork it's corrupted servers or phone lines not working. We're all trying to swim in this sudden deluge of problems. Lucy has a lot to answer for. Actually, John, too. Sam was bad enough without that hormone rollercoaster adding to things.

"Will you be able to calm her down?"

I nod, letting her go.

"I know where she'll be. I'll give her a head start so she can kick out some sit ups or something."

I get gently poked in my ribs.

"How are you doing after the diner incident? I thought you were calling from halfway up a mountain."

"The washrooms make everything echo, sorry."

She takes my hand and kisses my knuckles.

"Oh, Michy, what am I going to do with you? You're not very good at choosing the right time to make revelations are you?"

That's the understatement of the century. I don't have enough practise, and the practise I do have, today included, is awful.

"You know what my mouth is like. It walks to the beat of its own drum."

"I know, mouth opened, words fell out. We're going to have to get that problem sorted one of these days."

I nod, we are.

Gab continues.

"How did you leave things with her?"

I sigh, a deep sigh that relaxes my shoulders, showing me how tense I really am over this whole thing. I lean on her desk.

"She gave me the, 'I value our friendship,' speech."

Her eyebrows slide upwards.

"Ironic seeing as that's your favourite way of dumping girls."

I frown and probably pout as well. I'm not too proud to say this wasn't one of my better moments.

"Thanks, Gab."

She squeezes her eyes shut for a moment.

"I'm sorry, honey. I think we both need some time to adjust."

"Or maybe not as I'm only friend material. Look at that, for once I don't get what I want. Kind of funny - you know, in a way that isn't funny one bit."

"Maybe with time she'll grow to..."

And that's just it.

"I don't want her to have to grow to do anything with me, Gab."

"Sorry."

She taps a fingernail on her desk, thinking, processing, deciding. Her next suggestion is more painful than appealing.

"Maybe you have to be content with being close friends?"

She squeezes my hand tightly. She's been thinking about this a lot, I know. Her serious face and lack of the usual barrage of questions means she's come to her analysis.

"You're not going to like what I say next." She pauses, confirming I won't. "I think you need to back off and let her come to you when she's sorted everything out in her head."

I take a moment to think about it. One question comes to mind.

"And what if she doesn't come to me?"

She smiles sadly.

"Then you only get to have her as a friend."

My voice goes into the childish tone I save for really horrible things.

"That doesn't sound like fun."

She chuckles.

"No, Michelle, love is not fun sometimes."

I mumble, and I know I must be pouting again because her laugh grows.

"See, and you're always, 'Why don't you go after Miss Right, not Miss Right now'. This is why. Because it's no fun."

"But think of the fun if she wants to be more than friends."

It's a valid point.

"All right, you pulled that one back from the edge." I squeeze her hand. "Maybe I should go and see if this is going to be fun or no fun, then?"

"The gym I'd presume?"

I nod.

"Go on, scoot."

I put my arms around my best friend ever, hugging her tightly.

"How are you still single?"

She ruffles my hair, pushing some in my face. I pull her hands away, smiling at her stupid ways.

"We'll answer that question after you've sorted out your little problem. Go on, go."

I head to the gym because Dis is a creature of habit. I peer through the glass of the door. She's in her kit doing pull-ups, her feet crossed at the ankle. Her thick shoulder muscles tense with the effort. A couple of Amazons are watching. One smiles to the other, nudging her with an elbow. I push the door open noisily and walk over, glaring at them. They get back to their workout.

I lean on one of the stanchions keeping the bar up and watch. Her body holds such amazing grace when she moves. She pauses, muscles holding mid pull-up as dark eyes stare at me. I don't say anything. I just run a finger down the bridge of her nose, catching a bead of sweat before it falls. I kiss her forehead and those pained eyes lose some of their famed darkness as she visibly relaxes.

Her legs drop and she stands, running a hand through tendrils of damp hair, shaking it out.

Best to dive right in.

"Come back to mine and I'll fix some dinner while we talk about today?"

The pause is probably reticence to do with my revelation. I expect a shrug but get the miracle of speech instead.

Her words are gentle.

"That sounds nice."

I don't make a comment.

We go to mine and I chat about stuff in general. I do it to keep her mind off of today and mine off of her. Difficult feelings shouldn't be dwelled on and corpses should be forgotten as quickly as possible. Of course, nothing works out like that, but it's a cute thought.

She comes back down from her shower with lightly towel dried hair, and for a moment I catch myself staring. I turn and put away the first thing my hands come upon: some old magazines. And when that doesn't work, it's time for small talk and dinner.

She's bending, watching something on the counter. I lean across trying to see what's so interesting. I can't help but laugh.

"You've found my sea monkeys."

Her nose almost touches the plastic of their small aquarium.

"They don't look like the picture on the packet. Still, I always wanted them. I just got real horses as a kid."

It's curious, because she's never really volunteered personal information before, especially about her old life, and I never wanted to pry.

"I always wanted real horses. I just got these."

She rests her head down on folded arms, on the counter. Then, of all the strange things, Discord Knight fills the gap in conversation.

"Real horses are a lot of work: feeding, grooming, riding. Good fun, but you need to be dedicated and have plenty of time."

I'm lost in the intimacy of the moment. My words are automatic, perhaps a little stupid, but still true.

"I always wanted to be a cowgirl on a ranch. I watched from a distance but never managed it. We were always too busy up here."

Her mouth twitches into a smile. This new side makes me want to catch her off guard all the time.

"My folks had a small ranch. I guess I got what you always wanted."

More than you'll ever appreciate. Of course, that stays in my head. Our boundaries have been drawn, and I'm firmly on the side of friendship.

She tilts her head the other way as she continues.

"Maybe that's why I grew up tall, because of all the lifting and lugging things about?"

"Maybe. Where was your folk's ranch?"

She smiles, still watching my pets. It's a priceless moment.

"Gallatin County, Montana."

"I'm not good with places anymore."

"It has lots of space and greenery. Not too many neighbours where we were, just my Aunt and cousin Faith a few miles away." A pause and that smile drops slightly. She shifts a little, uncomfortably. "So...probably why I'm not good with people. Limited practice."

"You're okay with me."

She holds my gaze for a moment before glancing away.

"Yeah, I guess."

"Were you close to your Aunt and cousin?"

A long pause then a bare nod.

"But death came between us."

There's not much else I can say to that, except...

"I'm sorry, Dis."

"So am I."

"I'm sure Elle could authorise you seeing your family when they join us. We don't get many of you guys in this section so there are no ground rules, but I think it'd be all right."

Another shrug.

"I need to clear this mission before I can think about that."

"It gets easier."

She barely nods.

"I hope so."

She returns to watching my sea monkeys swimming, her head moving, following them. Then she straightens up, her eyes darting around, hands jamming into the back pockets of her jeans. I try not to smile as I chop the peppers. She's looking very cute.

"Do you need me to help?"

She taps the tip of her boot gently onto my floor. At over six foot she can't be adorable but it's a tempting word to use.

"Guests don't get to help, they get to watch."

A naughty piece of pepper tries to escape but is caught by a quick hand. She drops it back on the chopping board. I nudge her away and she smiles. I finish the salad, keeping busy, trying not to think of how I'm going to get over my feelings for her if she keeps behaving like this.

We eat. I talk, as usual, keeping her mind off of stuff. I don't get a reoccurrence of before. There are no more insights into Discord Knight. In fact she doesn't even look like she's here.

We finish and I clear the plates up. No time is good, so I dive right in and ask about Clipper's house.

"Today was a difficult job. Are you still seeing her face?"

Her nostrils flare as she breathes deeply, nodding. I open the fridge looking for some beers.

"I won't lie. Something like that remains with you for a long time."

I grab two from the back, twisting the lids off. I hand her one but she doesn't take it. Her dark eyes are sad again. I keep holding the bottle out.

"Kids are always worse. They stay in your nightmares. There's no way around it, Dis. You have to work through it, workout through it, talk through it, something."

Her eyes search mine for a moment then she takes hold of the bottle, slipping it from my hand. I take a sip, enjoying the chill as liquid fills my mouth.

We go into the lounge and sit down.

Now, when I have something to say with a meaning, I get to it quickly;

always achieve catharsis minus the boredom.

"My last mission was a child killer about..." I try to remember. "...ten years ago. He kept the heads of his victims in boxes. I found them. All of them. One was fresh."

I take another sip, trying to mask a taste not really present in my mouth.

"Victim number eleven. His box was smaller than the others and still warm. He looked young, about six. He had such beautiful eyes."

I take a moment as it crawls over my skin, making me feel dirty.

"I don't even remember finishing the mission. Apparently I slit the target's throat - not very well - and then sat down with that box on my lap. The bottom of it was warm and wet. It soaked right through my pants. I was there for a few hours until Gab came and got me."

It's still traumatic. I still want to wash it off me. I still know that never works.

I take a swig of beer before carrying on.

"Things can go one of two ways. You can let it drag you down and make you useless, like it did me, or you can harness your anger and carry on trying to do good. With or without us bad deeds will always happen, but our work does get to even the scales up a little."

She picks at her beer bottle label. Dis, as I've found out, is a serial paper shredder.

Her voice is quiet.

"The scales are evening up for these girls too late."

I shrug, she's right, but it's not something we can change.

"There are billions of people on Earth and a handful of us. We try our best. Who's to say how many bad deeds we stop with the work we do?"

She leans back on the sofa, staring at the bottle in her hands. Silent Discord beating herself up in her own head. Except she shows me a little piece of her thoughts, a frightening glimpse.

"Her eyes were taped shut. You only do that if they can see. You can only see if you're alive. The body at Clipper's isn't the problem. It's the time before she became just a body that is."

Her next sentence is a flat emotionless whisper.

"I read another file on her today. It said her name was Katie. She was only thirteen."

I try to stop this before it begins.

"You can't identify with them. Your work can never be personal, that's how it starts."

However, I'm too late and also too stupid, because this is her first serious mission. She retreats into herself, closing that little window I got to look through.

She growls her response.

"It's already personal."

I rub my forehead, annoyed at my mouth.

"I didn't mean that the way it sounded."

Her beer slams down.

"Save it."

She gets up, grabbing her jacket, royally pissed. I stand between her and the door. There's no way I can let her go like this. She tries to side step me so I match her movements. She goes the other way. So do I. Her nostrils flare.

One thing I've learnt is she responds well to anything tactile. It was surprising to realise because she doesn't look the type. I take a slow step forward, looking her straight in the eye. I lay a hand on her chest, above her hammering heart.

"You can't save Katie but you can stop him. Learn to concentrate on the things you can do instead of the things you can't."

Her tense muscles deflate and shoulders drop as she nods. I don't move my hand as she leans towards me. I close the gap and slide that hand up to her neck, leaning my forehead against hers, fingers stroking her warm skin.

"It's okay for you to be upset around me. I know what it feels like."

She nods imperceptibly and a hand casually rests on my hip. Her thumb slowly moves back and forth. The other settles on my side, and I can feel her warmth through my thin top.

The gap closes, my eyes slide shut. The heat of our bodies is quite something, and there's one thing about heat - you have to have chemistry. Her lips move closer, her breath warming my mouth.

I realise our position and what we're going to do. If anything, it'll be a pressure release for both of us. I want her, she wants this, we both come away happy - ish.

That thumb moves under my top, sliding over my skin, making me shiver. Then she kisses me. I don't move. I just stand here being kissed by this incredibly attractive woman.

I've kissed a lot of women. I've been alive for bucket loads of years. Few could turn me on by doing it. I'm not saying it was them. I think it was a simple compatibility issue. For me I'm compatible with the woman I'm touching now. Her hand slides under my top, up my stomach, making a shudder run through me. I break our kiss, trying not to pant my sentence.

"Come to bed?"

Her pause is long, and I know it has to do with what I said earlier. Then her expression softens as she nods. I take her hand and lead us upstairs.

I switch on the lamp in my room, turning the darkness into a beautiful warm glow. I cup her cheek, kissing her lightly, starting this slowly. I look into eyes that aren't as sad as they were earlier. But then something catches me by surprise: her eyes are midnight blue, just so dark they seem almost pitch black. Blurty mouth can't help it.

"Your eyes are blue."

She smiles.

"Only in the right light."

Just shows, you can look for a long time but never see what's right in front of you. It also makes me wonder what else I've missed.

We stand close, and she lets me pull her top off. I run my hands up her sides and remove her bra. She has great breasts, firm and high. Fingertips dance over the sides of them and her eyes darken. I slide a hand down her solid stomach, flicking the top button of her pants open. She suddenly tugs my arm and our bodies meet, her mouth on mine in an instant.

My clothes are swiftly and expertly removed by hands I expected to be rougher. The cold metal button of her jeans pushes into my stomach. It makes me gasp at the same time her hands slide up my sides and cup my breasts. We fall into bed, never breaking our kiss.

She slides a firm thigh between mine, setting a rhythm of slow movements that make me moan. The roughness of the denim rubs my skin. She kisses my neck, then my collarbone. Her tongue slowly glides. I run my hands over her back, feeling her muscles tensing, feeling her power.

I'm a quick build up girl. I don't need a lot of playing with. I'm also multi orgasmic so I can have fun all night long, literally. Suddenly she pulls that thigh away and I almost scream in frustration.

"You can't leave me like..."

Before I can finish, a warm hand makes all my internal muscles clench, almost giving me an orgasm. Her finger moves. Her eyes close as she feels how wet I am. Me, I'm not surprised. There's something about her that turns me on at a primal level.

Her other hand caresses my breast at the same time she slides two fingers into me. My muscles clench around her. I moan, loudly. I'm not the silent type.

Gradually more of her body weight is on me. It's an unusual, but nice, feeling. Her proportion of muscle tone helps because she's incredibly solid. Most of the women I've slept with have been shorter, smaller. It's always been a given I'd have to be careful or on my back. Discord's the first one who's matched me for size and strength. It's a real curve ball.

We move together, rhythmically. Our kisses are hungry, her tongue's in my mouth, and my whole body seems to be feeling some part of her: fingers in me, fingers on me, thighs against mine, breasts pushed together, and a film of sweat covering both of us. Everything culminates as my muscles tense. Her thumb pushes me over the edge. Forceful circles bring me to a powerful, and vocal, orgasm, as every one of my muscles clutches, tenses and shudders. My fingers dig into her shoulders, squeezing, gripping, pulling her closer as I ride it out.

I break our kiss as we slow to a stop. She slips out gently. I wrap my legs around her hips, pulling her in. She grinds her body.

I said I was multi orgasmic and I didn't lie. I can have one after the other. It's made a lot of women jealous. It's made a lot of me very fulfilled. Discord picked that up quickly because she's not a lazy lover.

Her forehead rests against mine and we lay still for a few minutes. Her breath pants. I run my hands along her shoulders, feeling the moisture.

Her mouth moves to my ear. Soft warm lips leave feather light kisses as she breathes words.

"Turn over."

I think about the obvious thing she would want to do with me in that position. It's not my favourite. I'm not a silent lover, no use if you want to enjoy yourself. I move her face up with a hand, looking into her eyes, making sure my voice is soft so I don't offend.

"I'm not really into anal."

"Me neither. I want to take you from behind, but not in that way."

I don't even have to think about that offer. I've never said anything but this is one of my favourite positions. She lifts, allowing me to turn. The moisture on me makes the sheet stick.

Hard nipples graze my back as she slides down. Warm wet kisses plant a slow trail of fire along my shoulder blades, then my spine. It sensitises every inch of my body, even parts she's yet to get to.

A knee moves my legs apart as fingers find me again. A single one enters. I try to control the intense feeling this angle brings. I can't.

I lock my hands behind my head and my muscles tense as she quickens the pace. A warm hand slides my leg up the bed, allowing for deeper penetration.

My hands grip each other tightly, the force making my biceps shake. I bury my face into the soft sheets as so many sensations overwhelm me. She leisurely licks her way up my back, then warm lips dance over my neck, and all the time her hand doesn't stop what it's doing. She adds another finger as her tongue traces my ear, making me shiver and shake at the same time. I grit my teeth as it becomes too much. Expert fingers switch from long hard strokes to short shallow ones. My hips buck as the bed muffles my cry. My orgasm is strong. In the next thirty seconds intense contractions explode all over my body.

Hands gently unlock my arms. Warm lips kiss my neck. Hands stroke my skin. I take a deep breath and relax, sinking into the soft sheets.

My eyes open and dart about. The room is dark, I'm on my back and her arm is over my stomach. As I get my senses back a rush of excruciating embarrassment descends. I squeeze my eyes shut, my palm slaps my forehead. I fell asleep.

I grit my teeth at being such a selfish idiot. She must be kicking herself. I mean, all work and no play can lead to a frustrated sleep. Not that I'd know, I got all the fun. I watch her sleeping. She doesn't look frustrated just incredibly peaceful. If everyone could see her like this there'd be no misunderstandings. It's a stark contrast to how she looks when awake, and it's not helping me get over my feelings.

On her stomach, an arm still casually resting over me, she stirs. I turn on my side. Her eyelids lazily slide open and she blinks, clearing her throat, moving the hand resting on me, off. Her tone is confused.

"It's still dark."

"It's about..." I glance over at the digital clock. "...three a.m."

I run my hand down the strong muscles of her back. She sighs and shifts. Her fingertips touch the skin of my thigh. I scoot closer, wanting to get my apology over in the forgiving darkness.

"Sorry for passing out like that."

Her mouth forms a lazy, sleepy smile.

"Understandable. I wore you out."

I chuckle. I like this sleepy Discord.

"I didn't get to wear you out."

I move my thumb over her skin, following the ridges and dips of muscle.

"I'll rain check."

I plant a kiss on her shoulder, tasting salt from our...my earlier workout. Her breathing gets deeper and I settle next to her, leaving my hand where it is.

I wonder where this leaves us. Friends who fuck?  Gab is going to love having to sort this one out.

# 43 CUPID'S INTRODUCTION

The next week went better. Michelle's personality helped because if there's sun hidden above the clouds she'll find it.

They met up for lunch, the gym, etc. Michelle made herself available for moral support and guidance, consoling herself with a friendship she thought was better than nothing. In reality Dis was being careful. She didn't trust her own judgement where love was concerned. Also, she was caught up in this horrible job. Work's timing really sucked.

But now over to Hell. Lucy never thinks. She just does. If you're talking about putting chocolate spread on a naked woman's inner thighs then that's cool, more power to you. But this? I'm drawing the line. Lucy was low.

## Chapter Forty-Three: Lucy
## 21st January, Year 3 - 14:00
## Pay The Boatman

**B**ee hands me a videotape. I stare at it, wondering what I should be doing exactly.

"Yes?"

She seems pleased with herself. In fact, if she had feathers she'd be fluffing and puffing herself up.

"That..." She points at the tape. "...is a video of a series of therapy sessions and funerals. We got it by mistake from Sam. Her brain is obviously full of babies."

I throw it back. Her hands fumble to catch. She holds it tightly to her chest as if it's a prize piece of china.

"If I want to watch unhinged people whining and sobbing, I'll turn on Jerry Springer."

I recline my seat. My stats are down this quarter and nothing I do is shifting the balance. I'm in a foul mood.

"Okay, think of it more as a montage of death and mayhem caused by - and you're going to hate this part, Lucy - a Satanist."

I groan and wave for her to continue.

242

"The session is to do with Clipper."

I flick a pencil and it spins off my desk.

"Don't care, Bee. I'm bored. Let's go and..."

She raises her voice.

"Lucy, will you please listen to me?"

I raise an eyebrow.

"I like it when you're dominating."

"This is important. This tape was meant for the Vengeance department. It features Clipper's sixth victim, the corpse Discord found. Lucy, concentrate, please."

I drum two fingers on my lips. His name is familiar. Then I remember: Clipper, the last batch of paperwork we intercepted and rerouted.

"We've already disrupted that case. Anyway, we'll have his soul next quarter. Elle's made that judgement. Been there, done it, bored now."

She sighs.

"This time the count is close. From my figures one or two souls could swing it."

I raise an eyebrow as she continues.

"I know a way that Clipper can get into this quarter's figures. What do you say to that?"

"I say, yes, please, thank you, Bee."

She continues. I try not to watch her breasts move as she talks. It's a challenge.

"Sam's hormones mean we got this tape by mistake. I watched it, it's horrible but...." She looks down at the tape then up at me. "Lucy, you need to see it."

"I don't have the will. Condense it down into three lines."

"No."

"Don't get too used to saying that word around me. I'm not keen on it."

She rolls her eyes, shakes her head, and then slips the tape in my machine, holding a finger up to silence me before I even open my mouth. My television comes to life. I sigh. The sound is low, the picture of disgusting quality. Don't the authorities know it's the digital age?

Bee taps a finger to the screen as a picture flashes up, then pushes the pause button. The grainy image flickers back and forth. My eyes go wide as I move closer to the screen.

"Is that...?"

I can't finish because my mouth has dropped open. Bee shakes her head.

"Not exactly, but there's a real family resemblance, isn't there?"

I manage to snap my mouth shut as words start to reform.

"Yes, there is. What's going on? Who is she?"

"She was Clipper's forth victim. He abducted, raped, and murdered her over two years ago, then left her body on her own front porch. Her neighbour found her." There's a dramatic pause. "Her cousin."

She quirks an eyebrow and nods her head. My eyes widen as I salivate.

"Don't tell me. Her cousin Discord." My smile beams as I take a moment to gloat. "That's tragically beautiful."

My gloating may have been short but it was not unfulfilling. However, there is business to conclude.

"Why did they give her the case? That's cruel and unusual. You'd expect it of me not Elle."

Bee shrugs, flicking through a thick file.

"We've been in a paperwork war with Elle for the last five years. They probably lost the file. Anyway, why would they check the details properly? It's normally us doing the work and we don't have mortal relatives. I did get a copy of some of the files, though."

She hands me a thick manila folder. I frown at the weight and hand it back.

"This you can condense into three lines."

"Of course." Her eyes narrow. "Was that one of them?"

"No, you still have three."

She flicks her index finger up.

"One, Clipper kills her cousin." Another joins it. "Two, Discord finds the body." And finally one more. "Three, the night of the funeral, Discord dies in a crash." She shrugs. "Tragic."

"That made it four. Are you sure Elle knows nothing about this?"

"Discord would never have been given the case if anyone knew."

I sigh, trying to think through this. My avenue is obvious, and that's what worries me.

"It all seems too good to be true. Is this a trap?"

Bee bites her lip, her nose wrinkling as she answers.

"I knew last week but didn't tell you until everything had been checked. This is real, Lucy. If we can push the kill forward we can win and control the next quarter."

I look up at the paused picture as it flickers. The young woman looks back, the spitting image of Discord Knight except for one thing, the beaming smile.

I shake my head, getting back on track.

"Give me that tape, Bee."

I walk around my desk and she offers it to me like it's made of diamonds. I stare at this beautiful piece of naughtiness covered in a distinctly dirty aura.

"We no longer have to be content with hiding paperwork or burying them in their own bureaucracy. This..." I wave the tape. "...is serious ammunition." I hand it back. "Make a copy and send it to Discord's office, special one hour delivery so I can time her reaction. Get Clipper followed from now. I want to be kept informed of every move that little Satanic slug makes."

She nods. Something comes to mind.

"Wait, is Clipper in a cult?"

"No. Lone operator."

"Damn, less to kill. Okay, off you go."

She leaves, with a hint of a smile brightening up her wonderfully stoic self.

My actions could be perceived as evil but I work with the tools I'm given. Mortals aren't mine, they're Elle's. It's only fair she should get the benefits.

# 44 CUPID'S INTRODUCTION

The Devil can be a bitch at times. Well, almost all the time, really. Lucy also has an amazing sense of timing. She can choose just the right moment to do something über bad, like now.

Dis was at breaking point with the stress of this case. It's one thing dealing with drug dealers or dictators, but the killer of one of your own family? That's another. Fate's automated lines were holding - just as stubborn as she was - and Michelle was hanging in there, trying to feel happy with the friendship thing. I have to say one thing, I'm glad those two met or all of this could've gone down hill in a massively bad way. That's not to say what happened next was good. It wasn't anywhere near.

## Chapter Forty-Four: Michelle
## 21st January, Year 3, 19:00
## The Devil Comes In Many Forms

I stare at Discord's office door and knock again, but there's still no answer. I glance at my watch: seven. The hallway clock: seven. I knock again. Patience is not one of my virtues. Opening the door I poke my head in.

"Dis it's seven. Did you forget about..." Her office is empty. "...dinner?"

A low hum of voices comes from the plasma screen on her wall. As I'm about to leave I hear a name mentioned: Knight. I turn back to the screen, to grainy black and white images I recognise the general look of as evidence for a judgment. A Police logo sits in the top right corner and pictures of victims stare back at me one by one; and I thought they'd have moved on with technology since the last time I did it. Clearly not.

The tape plays, sickeningly, captivatingly. For victim number one there's a crying family at her grave side. For victim number two there's a white outline on a bloodied carpet. For victim number three there are stills taken at school. But it's the next one that makes my eyes go wide. Barely out of her teens with inky hair, dark eyes and a smile, her details run along the bottom of the screen. It's like a punch to the guts. Faith Knight, only sixteen, raped and murdered. It flashes off as quickly as it flashed on. Then her funeral shows for a fraction of a second. It confirms the unbelievable. My jaw drops, my skin prickles. Pens, folders, everything crashes to the floor as I hunt for the remote on her desk. I rewind then pause the tape and walk towards the screen, dazed, feeling more than a little sick. One figure by the side of the grave gets my attention. In the periphery is a lone woman dressed in black, arms crossed tightly, looking more lost and alone than ever.

"Dis?"

My fingers touch the grainy image of her as my chest constricts so suddenly I have to take a moment to catch my breath. I press play. The tape shows the rest of the victims, except there's one just listed as missing but presumed his last. Number six makes me want to bring my lunch up. It's a picture of a girl and her family at a party. I know that girl. The words on a banner hanging from the ceiling bring it all home: happy birthday, Katie.

Katie. Number six.

It slots together like a perverse jigsaw puzzle. If this is Katie's killer, then...it's also Faith's killer.

I press stop and the screen goes black. A cold sweat settles. I close my eyes as I realise what we've made Dis deal with.

Leaning against her desk the rest of a puzzle I didn't even realise I was attempting to finish falls together. My eyes flick back open. I'm in Dis' empty office with this playing? A tape shaped delivery box catches my eye and I grab it, recognising the handwriting. Bee. Lucy, you bitch!

The door bangs back on the wall as I yank it open and run to where she must have gone. But the gym is empty. The locker room, too. I call her cell. Off. I wait for the automaton woman to let me leave a message.

"Dis. Michelle. I saw the tape. Please call me, I'm worried about you."

I make my way to the one person who'll know what to do. Gab.

I fly into her office without knocking; benefits of being best friends. I skid to a stop as Charity, Elle, and Gab stare at me. I groan inwardly. It's the weekly management meeting.

Gab sighs, tossing her pen on the desk. I rush my sentence out to justify my presence.

"You all need to watch this."

Elle tone is polite but firm.

"Michelle, perhaps we can do that another time?"

I forget about all of my training and good manners, protocol and etiquette, because none of that matters now.

"No, I don't think so, Elle."

I push the tape into the player and rewind it halfway. I press play. Perfect timing. We see the end of victim number three. I glance over at Gab whose eyes are wide in an intense glare.

"Trust me and watch it."

I try to do just that, but the girl's face makes me look away. I can see too much of Dis in her features. The funeral comes on and I press pause. I lift my finger up and tap the screen.

"Does she look familiar to anyone? Want to know something else? The man who killed her is Dis' latest mission."

Elle sits back in her seat, her face ashen. Gabrielle closes her eyes. Charity takes hold of Elle's hand.

I speak more to Gab than anyone else.

"I can't find her. I think she's moved the kill forward."

Gab mutters one word, "Damn," as she thinks. I came here first because she's always good in a crisis, it's her forte.

Charity pipes up, still holding Elle's hand.

"There are rules and regulations to a kill. She's breaking..."

Blurty mouth sharpens its projectiles.

"I'm more concerned with her mental state than getting some stupid piece of paper rubber stamped!"

I glare at Elle's new girlfriend as she sits in her pristinely pressed Armani suit. I doubt she's ever got the bottoms of her designer boots dirty let alone had to kill someone.

Elle points a finger at me.

"Michelle."

Her voice is calm but that action tells me I'm walking on thin ice. She's good at protecting the wrong person.

Charity shakes her head, talking to Elle.

"That's not what I meant."

Elle pats her hand.

"I know it's not." Then she turns to Gab. "Why didn't we know about this?"

And it all hits the fan.

Gab just blinks for a moment before her mouth kicks back into life. The change in her demeanour is instant. Head of Intelligence stares directly at Elle.

"The mortals never cross from their area to here. Faith would've had no way of knowing about Discord to even have brought it up. And the forms Discord filled out on entry gave us no indication. The tags you asked to highlight arrivals from Discord's family didn't activate until both Faith and her were here, so we've only been watching for the other members."

Elle's palm hits the table as she stands.

"But why didn't we check double-check?"

Gab's jaw tenses as she sits still.

"We had no reason to, Your Eminence."

"What about the last name in the files? Why didn't our systems cross reference it and realise we had two Knights from the same recent gene stock?"

"We don't cross reference last names. This is our first mortal in a long time."

I press stop, sending those images back where they came from: a black hole.

"Do you all want to know how she got the tape?"

Everyone stares at me. I throw the courier box over to Elle and she reads the label.

"That's it. I'm going to kill her!"

My gaze doesn't falter because I'm madder at her than Lucy. Elle's in charge, she's probably still in love with Dis and she's failed her over and over.

"Why? She's just doing what she does. That's Lucy. But you? Why didn't you...?"

Gab says one word, "No." She leans over, grabbing my arm. Elle glares at me.

"Why didn't I what, Michelle? Why didn't I what?"

The tape box slams on the desk. The hand squeezes my arm tighter, making my words stall. But, as I look into Elle's eyes I know I don't have to say a thing to make her feel guilty. She's doing it all by herself.

I take a deep breath.

"Nothing. Your Eminence." Gab's hand slowly lets go, rubbing where she gripped once. "I know Discord's moved the kill forward. I want permission to give her backup."

Elle narrows her eyes at my tone but I don't have time to mess about because Dis is somewhere on her own.

Elle looks at Charity with an expression I can't read. Miss Armani quirks an eyebrow.

"We don't know if Lucy's sent a copy to anyone else. Electra could be watching through a microscope. You need to stay out of this, Elle."

Elle's words growl.

"Because Electra is the one in charge, after all."

Hauntingly blue eyes slide my way. That's when I get the permission I need. This God speaks to me, her tone dropping the temperature within a second.

"Michelle, go to Discord. You have my full approval. I'm authorising the kill for now. She's in your capable hands. Be careful." She grabs her bag as Charity watches. "I can't be seen to be involved in this."

The door opens and slams as she leaves. And that was Elle's total help. No wonder they split up.

Charity stands, turning to me before she leaves. Her sentence isn't exactly verging on obscure.

"Don't judge her until you've walked in her shoes."

"It's not about judging her, it's about the facts. Why didn't she know about something like that?"

"Did you know?" Charity moves very close. "Well? Exactly."

I take a step back, feeling Gab's eyes boring into me. I tell Charity everything that's important to me now.

"All I care about is that Discord's all right."

She sighs, closing her eyes for a moment, rubbing her forehead. When they reopen the change is noticeable.

"And all I care about is that Elle's all right. I'm glad we both have pure motives."

We stand in silence for a moment before she raises an eyebrow.

"Don't you have a girl to get?"

I nod.

She turns on her heels, closing the door behind her.

Gab shakes her head. A finger flicks her pen sideways, sending it spinning across the table. I take it that's her new stress reliever.

"I thought Elle was going to exude sparks. You got her so angry, Michy."

"Really? I didn't notice through the heaps of concern that shone out."

Gab gives me her, 'you're being silly,' look. I get it a lot.

"What did you expect, a nervous breakdown? She's a God."

"Whatever."

"Look, let's concentrate on finding Discord."

"Fine by me."

She reaches over and takes my hand, rubbing her thumb over my palm.

"Take a breath. We'll find her and make this better. She has us now, okay?"

I sigh, rolling my shoulders to get rid of some of my tension.

"I'm stressed. Lucy is such a...." I leave that unsaid. "Why can't we send her somewhere?"

"We did. She made Hell and came back."

I roll my eyes.

"You know what I mean. Anyway, we're wasting time."

"Yes we are. But first, if I'd known about any of this...."

I pull her close, hugging tightly.

"I know. At least we get a chance to make it better."

She kisses my cheek and ruffles my hair. I slap her stupid hands away, smiling despite my mood. Gab always knows what to do.

"Yes, we do."

She sits at the computer and clicks open the resources files, accessing Discord's folder. One hand moves the mouse, the other writes down notes on a pad. I read over her shoulder.

"Died in Montana..." One especially, catches my attention. "...after coming back from a funeral?"

Her eyebrows furrow as she nods.

"Bad luck."

I tap the screen with my finger on the last line of that paragraph.

"Faith's funeral."

She sits back in her seat for a moment, shaking her head.

"What a huge mess."

Then, with a steadying nod of her head, she concentrates and skim reads the rest.

"Michy, bring me the Clipper map."

I hunt around in a folder, dragging it out quickly, spilling other papers on the floor. I smooth it on the table and kick the mess on the floor into a little pile.

"Michelle." A sign that what she's about to say is of utmost importance. "His attacks all took place around a central point, right?"

She leans over, stress relieving pen in hand, and draws a large circle around where the girls were snatched. She marks the centre as she continues.

"And that central point is where he works. Mount Pleasant Cemetery."

I look between her, the map, and our notes as she continues.

"It looks like your girl has gone home in more ways than one."

She circles a sentence on her writing pad. I stare at those small but very important words.

"Mount Pleasant Cemetery, where Faith's funeral was. Clipper buried her, too? Oh, shit. Why didn't we know any of this?"

I regret my snapping tone as soon as I say it.

"Because I'm working five people's jobs. So are you, so is Elle. We don't know everything."

"I'm sorry." I rub her shoulder. "I didn't mean that the way it sounded."

A small detail flickers in my brain. I process it with super speed.

"Gab, I gave her the file."

Her head falls back on the headrest and she stares up at me.

"What file?"

A wave of painful nausea hits me.

"The file. The one with the details in. The one I took from your office. I hand delivered it myself. You remember, you came around with the soup, I said she was acting weird. I started all of this."

I bang my hand against a filing cabinet as I remember the page she removed. Victim four, Faith. I thought she was looking for motivation when she already had it.

My words fly out.

"I'm going to kill Lucy for this!"

Gab gets up and takes my hands, squeezing them gently. I blow a long breath out, trying to regain control.

"Let Elle deal with her."

"They deserve each other."

"Don't get sidetracked, you have a girl to get."

She reaches up and pulls me into a tight hug. I hold her for a moment as I steady so many emotions inside. I blow out a deep breath, letting go, slapping her hair ruffling hands away.

I nod, knowing what I have to do.

"I already have her. I just need to go and save her now."

Gab was right, Dis has us now. And I'm going to prove how important that is.

## 45 CUPID'S INTRODUCTION

Dis was wired, strung out, not thinking straight. She was playing God baseball with a frankfurter as a bat. She was screwed, basically, and that's never a good thing. Still, it put that final piece of the puzzle into place: why Dis had been so freaked out about this whole mission.

Imagine it was you. No one knows she's your cousin, and if they find out you'll never be allowed to continue and have your revenge, but the more you deal with it the more it slithers into your head and messes you up. Tough stuff. Lucy pushing her over the edge wasn't exactly great, either, but, as I've mentioned before, right has a way of forcing itself out.

Now, like we did before, we're going to go back in time, just a few hours, nothing major.

While Michelle wasn't even aware she'd gone, Discord was somewhere far from her office.

## Chapter Forty-five: **Discord**
## 21st January, Year 3 - 15:30
## Hell's Gates

**M**y boots sink in the well maintained grass. The sun beats down on my back. It's a beautiful day.

I loosen my grip on the bunch of flowers, not wanting to crush them, and concentrate on the map, trying to figure out where I'm going. I don't want to get more lost than I already am.

After five minutes of wandering, I finally find some direction. I see one of the things I'm looking for. I stand over plot number seventy-three, and it's then I notice plot seventy-four. My hand slides down the cold granite as I kneel. Plain functional headstone, no philosophical inscription, just a name, date of birth and date of death. The ground has settled well, grass covers the plot. I'm glad I've fitted in somewhere.

I take a single rose out of the bunch and drop it onto my grave. It's the only flower here. I always thought the Heavens brought families together after death. I never thought they'd keep us apart. I take a deep steadying breath, laying the rest of the bunch down on the grave next to mine, the one I came for.

"Hey, Faith, look what I got you. I know you liked red, so...."

I struggle with the tears that always come when I think about what happened. But you don't get mad, you get even. Or as Mich said, best to channel the anger and make it work in your favour. I click my shoulders out, determined to make that monster pay for what he did, because now is my time not his.

I go back to staring at the map, trying to point myself in the right direction. That's when I see it, in the distance, the gravediggers' hut where Jacob Clipper works. Everything focuses very quickly.

I glance up at the midday sun, shielding my eyes from the intense glare, then back at the hut. It's still too early. He's just started his late shift. I look down on plot seventy-four. It's not as if I'm being rude, it is mine. I shift my flower over, sitting on the grass, leaning back against my headstone.

For a while I try to think about some of the good times I had when Faith was with me. Until it all went so bad. Until he took her. Until he hurt her. Until he brought her back. My nails dig into my palms. Until I found her.

Like it always does when I think about it, the images change, morphing into bloody pictures in my mind - why I always locked it away. And now the pictures have company: Katie, but also, him, Clipper, the man who took six - I bring my knees up, hugging them - seven people's souls.

Now the tide has turned. I stare at her headstone, knowing she's safe.

"Family sticks together, right? We get our chance to make everything even. I won't let you down."

I pat the ground and wait for sundown.

The day goes by quickly. I don't move. I don't think anymore. I just sit and wait for darkness to fall. The gravestone shields me from most of the sun's heat. Finally, even the birds go to bed. The bright light of day gives way to a low orangey haze of evening. Over a thousand gravestones cast identical shadows on the ground. It's a sight to behold.

The wind has picked up. It whips around, blowing my hair back as I rise from my grave. I know I'm in trouble for doing this my way but sometimes you have to look further than what you're allowed to do, and do what your conscience tells you, you should. You have to be true to yourself or else what else do you have? Time to go and see Jacob.

As I get near to the hut I wait under a weeping willow. The wind whips dust and leaves. The temperature drops. Dark clouds fill the sky. Something big is on the horizon. I put a hand over my heart and close my eyes, speaking words I know off by heart, the same ones we say before our missions.

"The Heavens open and send forth this messenger of light. In righteousness, I bring Vengeance for my eyes carry the flame of truth." Thunder shudders through the air. "I am the Word of the Gods."

A low glow surrounds me, building from my feet upwards, swallowing everything in a blue blaze. I squeeze my eyes shut as my muscles and bones shake at the force. I feel my clothes finish morphing into my uniform; the only one we can wear when we cast judgment. My dark robes ripple in the breeze, and the heavy hood shields my face. I blend in with my darkness.

Then the pain starts.

Heat, intense, burning the backs of my eyes. A hum fills my ears, then my skull, and my knees almost buckle. A wild roar tears from my throat; it's hard to get used to the sound of your own flesh tearing. Bones readjust, warm drops of blood trickle down my back. Creaking, cracking, thunder swallows my cry. And my wings finally unfold. They flap once, settling, drying in the gale. Intense light floods around me as I transform into what I am. An Angel of Vengeance. A bringer of death.

The trunk of my weeping willow is rough against my forehead. I wait, taking a moment, catching my breath. Fingertips trace the bark as I count to twenty then straighten. I turn towards his hut.

"Judgement has been cast, Jacob Clipper."

# 46 CUPID'S INTRODUCTION

What do you want me to do, tell you everything was going to get better and be okay? Hey, I might be your narrator here but I'm not going to lie to you. Things were not going to get better, and they were no where near okay, not for anyone concerned.

We're back to the present, with the blonde bombshell, Michelle.

The ripple's had started and it was a case of sink or swim in the backwash.

## Chapter Forty-Six: Michelle
## 21st January, Year 3 - 19:20
## Leave Me Lying Here

The dull haze of brightness fades as the portal closes behind me. I stare at the short thick metal railings of the cemetery. With a run up, I plant a hand on top and vault them in one fluid motion.

I've never been on time for anything, but for once I pray I'm not too late here. A flash of blue in the cemetery; the prelim to a kill. My shoes crunch in the shallow gravel and I run as quickly as I can, covering almost a mile in record time. Then I stop, my boots sinking in the sodden earth. I wonder where I'm going since I don't know where I am. I turn around, staring at row after row of identical graves.

"Shit."

I kick a broken branch as hard as I can, frustrated I came so unprepared. A gun shot rings out, then another and another. I squint in that direction. In the half light I can just make out a small shed in the distance.

Dark clouds begin to fill the sky. A fine mist softly pelts me. Thunder sounds in the distance, almost like the gunshots. We try to plan a storm during judgments, it covers our tracks. I sort of regret being nasty to Charity if her mom's done this.

Then I see her as I get nearer. She makes for an imposing sight: heavy black robes that refuse to flow in the storm surrounding us, and unmistakably frightening wings. Sometimes I wish Lucy had the right to kill these people and leave us out of it. I slow my run to a walk.

Clipper glows in white overalls. With a shovel in one hand and a revolver in the other, he looks reassuringly panicked. I would be too if a six foot plus, winged, hooded creature confronted me in the middle of a thunderstorm. At least fear is on our side.

Dis whips around, her face hidden by the heavy hood. She holds her palm out. I stop, mid footstep. I take a step backward.

"I'm not here to interfere. Just to make sure you're okay."

The hooded figure nods. Is that what they used to see when I did it? No wonder a large percentage begged. I would, too.

She starts to recite our words, the ones I used to say so long ago. My stomach sinks as I listen.

"I bring Justice and Vengeance for your crimes."

She pauses, changing direction, veering off of how we cast Judgments. Her voice is a worrying monotone.

"The name Jacob is from Genesis. Angels spoke to him while he slept."

He drops the shovel, cocking the revolver, aiming it right at her. Of course it never works. Fighting back, I mean. We're Angels. We have a God on our side. You can't fight that - although, like Jacob, you can give it a go. The Divine right to fight, I guess.

The wind is heavy. Her wings shudder. His voice cracks.

"Don't take another step or you're dead!"

She shrugs, carrying on. Her words are conversational as if she's talking about the weather or a good book.

"When Jacob awoke he looked into the face of God. Except I'm here to tell you she knows what you've done and she doesn't want you."

A clap of thunder makes me jump at the same moment she lunges at him. My body jerks, wanting to help, but my brain steps in and overrules my legs as I go back in time to when I worked Vengeance. I try to clear the feeling of thousands of ants crawling all over me.

She grabs his shirt, pushing him backward. Another clap of thunder and he skids across the ground, hitting a tree stump with a thud. His slumped body doesn't move and neither do I. I doubt he's dead, just out cold. Dis wouldn't be sloppy with someone of such importance.

I finally make my stupid legs walk. Her hands take hold of the heavy hood, pushing it back. It's only as I get close I notice she's hurt. Sure she can heal it, but it's not an instantaneous process and it looks like it could do with a few stitches. My skin prickles. My hand goes out. It doesn't get far before it stops, useless, held out near the blood on her top. My fingers curl back into a fist. My arm drops.

"You're hurt."

She stares back blankly, and I know that expression. I used to see it in the mirror enough times. It's when you focus your mind into what you have to do.

"His shovel was sharp. It's not serious."

I snort but keep a lid on the panic filling my shoes.

"I'll decide that. I'm here as your backup. Let me do my job."

I blink the cold wind away and tie my hair back, trying to keep everything in place.

Her words show she's not a lost case - yet. It's a fine line.

"I know I'm in trouble. Let me do this and I'll come back with you."

I'm not willing to risk her for this man. I'm not willing to risk her for anything.

"You're not in trouble. Elle personally authorised the kill for today. Listen, we'll get a cleaner in to finish this off."

Her growling tone makes me snap back to reality, sinking in the gravity of this out of control situation.

"To prove I can't even do this right?"

I glance at the blood seeping into her robes, making the darkness darker still. I get a flash of red as I did when Gab had to pull me out of the black hole I'd sunk into. My breath stutters before I get control.

"We won't get a cleaner then, but you're hurt and he's out cold."

Her head cocks, her eyes soften, she looks lost. Except her words show me she knows exactly where she is.

"You know, don't you? That's why you're here."

I sigh, not willing to lie.

"I saw the tape. Why didn't you tell me?"

Her eyes, a void, holding my gaze.

"So you could say sorry or tell me everything would be fine? It wouldn't have made anything better."

I take a step, slowly inching my way closer.

"Maybe not, but.... I'm your friend, remember? I said I'd help you any way I could. I meant it. That's why I'm here, to make sure you're okay."

A tear cuts a track down her cheek. It shines out as I soften my tone.

"And you're not okay, are you?"

I take another small step forward so I'm almost touching her. Her dark eyes are watery as she shakes her head. I wipe the start of a new tear away with my thumb and tuck a strand of hair behind her ear.

"I'm here to make everything better, Dis."

The lightening flashes, thunder roars and the rain pounds. Except there's one thing we forgot. A loud report makes my ears ring. I jump. Warm rain splashes my face and my eyes squeeze shut. I lick my lips and my eyes flick open. It wasn't rain. Rain isn't sticky and it doesn't taste like this.

Dis stares at me for a moment, her head cocking. She looks around and one of her wings is broken at the tip: dripping, open, raw. Her eyelashes flutter heavily. My mind goes blank, every piece of training I've had becomes useless. She falls to one knee then the other. And in her place is Jacob Clipper. Arm extended, gun smoking, smiling.

## 47 CUPID'S INTRODUCTION

Mich proved herself again. She was falling deeper and deeper in love with Discord, and at Michelle's deepest she offered up the greatest of sacrifices. The only thing we Gods listen to. Michelle offered us her life. And who are we to say no?

## Chapter Forty-Seven: **Discord**
### 21st January, Year 3 - 18:30
### It's Been A Bad Day

I crumple down to the ground. My ears ring. My body feels numb. The world changes trajectory. My horizon skews.

The grass is cold and wet against my cheek. My muscles relax, like a deep sigh that helps after a bad day. A feeling of peace begins to warm my skin. But then all that screeches to a halt; his voice tears through the yards of darkness, hooking into me, dragging me back.

"You'll be next if you don't shut up and follow me. Or do you want me to finish her off? Without those wings she's an easy target."

I rejoin the night sinking, the wind screaming, the rain pouring, and my wound howling. Mich's voice curls around, tugging at me, her calm tone gone.

"Who are you?"

"Someone who's done his research."

I grit my teeth, thinking of Faith, Katie, the others, and now me and Mich. My focus returns. Orbs of rain weigh down blades of grass, millimetres from my eyelashes. I lie in a hazy shade of darkness; not night, not day, not anything. My fingers jerk, knocking those orbs off and depositing me back in the here and now with a sword of pain delivered silently through my spine. My body burns.

The rain doesn't help dampen that pain but there is a way to work through it if you're determined enough. I finally lift my head and blink the haze back, focusing on him manhandling her.

His voice slithers into my head.

"Pick the shovel up, Blondey."

"I'm dying my hair when this is over."

I glance at my wing, the holder of my powers as an Angel. Bone hangs at weird angles, shattered and splintered, the white now a splattered watery red.

The wind whips up a storm, the thunder shouts for me to get up, my fingers jerk in the cold wet mud. That's the thing with life, it has a way of finding its way back to where it belongs; even if technically I don't own any, it doesn't seem to realise that.

Paralysed I watch. Mich bends down and picks the shovel up, thrusting it at him.

"One shovel."

He smiles, leering and vile. If ever I needed motivation....

"Good. Now we're going somewhere private."

"Fuck you."

"No, that's what I plan to do to you. Or do you need me to empty your friend's skull first?"

That hands me the motivation.

His laugh is frenzied, his movements staccato; Jacob is falling off the edge. Not fast enough.

I take two deep breaths, telling myself on the third I'm getting up. As with my time in the gym I grit my teeth and work through the pain.

Water soaks through the back of my robes. The cold rain revives me. It slides over my face, into my eyes, flooding my ears. I sit and breathe a fine mist out. My head cocks as he pushes her. No pain, no gain, nothing in this world is free. An eye for an eye, a soul for a soul, it's all about those clichés.

I stand unsteadily as my legs work on a slight time delay. I take a step forward, but this finale decides to ignore its happy ending. I must make a sound, something, because Jacob swings around abruptly.

I stare down the barrel of a gun.

He swings it back to Mich, covering both of us. He moves so close I could snap his neck - if he didn't have that gun.

"I've been waiting for you." He doesn't blink. "A man like me knows where he'll end up. I've already guaranteed my alignment with Satan. He needs a loyal servant like me to stand by his side."

He waves the gun at my broken wing before carrying on.

"And if my research is correct, I've just clipped your wings. You can die like the rest of them now. Praise the internet and the information it brings to us all." He smiles "What's your name?"

I blink, trying to sort through all of this information, especially that he knows too much. Then I realise it doesn't matter. Clipped wings, no power, I'm still going to kill him. I'll also still enjoy it.

"Discord."

"What are you, an Arch Angel, a Seraph?"

I stare over his shoulder, at a tombstone in the shape of a cross. How many more of his victims are buried here? How many more of their graves is he gloating over? My hands ball.

"I'm just me."

"Well, me, you're amongst equals now. How does it feel?"

"It feels warm and fluffy."

He snarls and dives forward, taking me by surprise. I'm only quick enough to feel something hard hit me in the face, forcing me back. I bang into the thick metal railings around his hut, catching my wing. They clang. I cry out. For whom the bell tolls.

A torrent of pain floods my mind. It's a smothering of sensations and none of them good. Something cold hits my wrist.

"This'll keep you still, Discord."

My vision slowly reforms into a very clear picture: a dead man and a beautiful Angel.

Rain slides down my skin, dripping off of my nose. I realise I'm not moving, not helping. I take two quick steps. A clink and I'm dragged back sharply. My eyes follow the source of my interrupted movements. A large silver handcuff is attached to my wrist and the other end to a thick iron railing. I lift my arm and the cuff grates against the railings.

His voice is a shattering call, like a siren. My head follows the sound.

"How does it feel now, still warm and fluffy?"

My mouth drops as I glance back at my mini prison. I tug my wrist and it clinks. Realisation punches me hard in the guts.

Mich catches my eye, looking anything but calm and collected. Her hand wipes at her face, at the haze of my blood. She stares at her fingertips. Measured breaths puff out of her mouth. Her arm falls to her side.

I start to panic. The cuffs glint as lightening strikes. He joins the party, grinning with yellowed teeth.

"You like them, Discord?"

Mich grunts as he jams the gun into her ribs. He moves behind her, a free hand trailing over her thigh. He stretches up and rests his chin on her shoulder, staring at me, eyes unblinking. His hand snakes around her waist. Her eyes close. She bares her teeth. So do I.

I shoulder barge the railings once, forgetting about my new addition of a broken wing. The inferno of pain almost makes my knees give way. I hold on as tight as I can to stay upright.

My voice growls, tickling my throat.

"Don't touch her."

His voice is an arrogant smile that I want to stop from sounding.

"I'm going to do more than that."

I pull my arm so hard my eyes tear up.

"She's nice. She smells good enough to eat. You done that to her, huh?"

Not even Michelle's words make me calm down.

"Stop it. He's feeding off of you."

"When I get these things off...."

His tone is high, mocking.

"When I get these things off." It changes to a snarl. "What? You don't have any powers, little girl. So what are you gonna do to me? Huh?"

The revolver clicks, and I pause because one good shot and all of this is over for both of us. I stop struggling and stare into the face of a smiling monster.

Mich closes her eyes, taking several deep breaths. When they slide open something's changed. She holds her arm out, a finger pointing at me. Her tone's different. It's slow and low.

"Stay. Still."

He growls a shout.

"Say another word and I'll shoot you in front of her, Blondey."

She turns back to him.

"My name's not Blondey."

In one fluid motion, in a fraction of a fraction of a second she side steps, cocks her arm, twists, and punches him in the face. Her body follows through, all of the weight transferring into his skull. I feel the impact travel through the ground to where I am. It makes my teeth itch. He hits the floor and lands on his back. The gun tumbles to his feet.

A flash of lightening congratulates her. She massages her knuckles, her face pulling into a sneer, something I've never seen.

"That's what I do to people who touch me like that."

I'm thankful for a multitude of things: she's not dead, neither am I, we didn't have to call for help, and Jacob's out of action. We can still clean this mess up.

I look around at my wound. Not too good. Neither is the feeling of vagueness sneaking into my mind. No use being a tough girl now. I turn to Mich just in time to see her grabbing Clipper. She holds him up, his legs hanging limply. Her other hand slaps him right out of unconsciousness and into a deep groan. Her face contorts as I get to watch from the outside instead of feel from the inside. That low glow of blue light blazes up from her feet. I watch in awe as she's cocooned in brilliance. A familiar sound of bone shifting, skin tearing. She screams and my skin prickles.

Her wings buzz into existence and unfold, wet and heavy. They flap, settling. A fierce gust of wind skids across the smooth white surface. But we don't stop there. Lightening forks the ground, electricity illuminating her. Sinews tense in her neck as her head twists slowly. Two arched fangs elongate like a Vampire movie. She hisses like a wild cat.

I stand, watching, water dripping into my open mouth.

Her fist slams into his face. I barely recognise her voice; the fangs, I guess.

"I used to kill mortals like you every day."

She hits him again, his body moving like a rag doll.

"One after the other." She grabs one of his fingers and jerks. "Like a conveyor belt."

I feel it snap. He screams. The thunder lays over us, keeping us safe in the cold night.

"You think you know Hell, Jacob? You don't even know the Heavens."

She grabs another finger, but this time there's a different reaction. His knee jerks up, catching her awkwardly in the ribs, making her double over and drop to the floor. He scrabbles around for the gun, splashing through dark puddles. He picks it up clumsily; I pull my cuffs, almost removing my arm from its socket.

My mouth opens to warn her as she tries to stand, but I'm too late. He pistol whips her in the face. There's no finesse, just a brute's force. She drops, instantly, silently.

He kneels, putting the muzzle to her right wing and squeezes the trigger twice. A haze of red fills the air. She jerks awake and he slams the gun into her face again. Mich falls back.

I kick at the bars, once, twice, three times. Tears mix with the rain, mud, blood on my cheeks as my frustration hits manic boiling point. I make my decision: we've failed. My mouth opens to call Elle. It's then I experience a miracle, my first one in all of my time on Earth and the Heavens. The thunder stops, the wind drops, the rain slows to a soft pelt. A bright ball of fire signals her entrance. The heat makes me recoil. It's not who I expect.

A figure walks through the flames, her eyes reflecting their colour. Blonde hair blowing in a gale that isn't present, arms out to her sides as if revelling in the heat, she stands in the middle of the roaring fire, breathing it in. And then, with a finger to her lips and one word, "Shhh," the flames die.

Lucy arrives and everything stops.

She looks up at the sky and tuts.

"May and her pretty little diversions. My hair's ruined now." She glares at me, pointing a finger. "You're lucky I have spies everywhere, a deep need for this man's soul, and an inability to snap his neck like a twig. Why Elle insists on you girls performing the kill, or not, is beyond me."

She whirls around to face Jacob as he reloads quickly. He fires a round forcing her back a step. She quirks an eyebrow, looking down at the smoking hole in her stomach that now begins to close.

"What do you think you're doing? I'm not some ten a penny Angel whose insides you can spray everywhere."

She takes a step towards him. He fires again. She jerks backward, this time snarling.

*"This dress is irreplaceable. You on the other hand? I can make you from snips and snails and puppy dog tails."*

His voice wavers.

"Another step and I'll kill you!"

Lightening forks the ground, inches from her. All the vegetation nearby wilts, and a heavy mist floats around her feet. Lucy doesn't move. Jacob steps back, startled.

Her voice is almost a scream as she doubles from the delivery.

"You can't kill me, you little worm!"

Our lost direction wanders further off the beaten track.

"Then I won't." He blinks and moves the gun to Mich who's struggling to stand. "Your friend?"

Lucy's eyebrows knit together.

"We're not exactly close."

"Then you won't miss her."

I concentrate on his finger pulling the trigger. Frame by frame it happens. I kick at the railings. Mich's eyes meet mine, no longer Angelical, but more a deadly killing machine. I reach my free hand out to her. A bang, a flash, I pause. She takes the force in the chest, lifting her in the air, along with a spray of blood. My real life eight millimetres plays out too slowly for me to do anything. Her wings flicker, hazing into nothing as they disappear. She hits the floor, forcing dirty water up. Each splash fixes itself in my head.

I watch, incapable of speech, incapable of being anything other than what I am. Useless. Mouth open I stare. My arm falls. Lightening flashes and thunder roars louder than at any other time tonight. The rain sinks down onto us. Her eyes stay open as her face gets wetter and wetter. She doesn't blink. Her fangs slowly slide back.

I look to Lucy.

"Do something!"

Her jaw clenches and she stares at Mich then back at me. After a moment she turns away.

I slide my cuff down the railing, kneeling, stretching. I try to reach out, to touch her, to help. My fingers sink in the dirty earth, inches short of her hand.

"Do something!"

Cold mud squirms under my nails. I kick at the bars, stretching, stretching, stretching, with everything I have, trying to get a centimetre, a millimetre, just a fraction more. The cuff slices into my skin, almost peeling my wrist. I get nothing. I punch the ground. I slowly bring my arm back and sit up in a mix of my own blood and cold rain, watching her lie still. My mouth opens slowly and words stumble out, swallowed by a clap of thunder.

"Mich?"

I look up at Jacob. If ever I wanted to kill someone. He waves the gun between Lucy and me.

"Stay still or I'll kill the other one."

Lucy snorts.

"You'd be doing me a favour."

She walks over and stares down at Mich. No smile, no jokes.

"Oh, Jacob, if you weren't already marked you'd be in big trouble with Elle for what you did to this one."

"Shut up!"

Lucy blinks and slowly cocks her head, staring at him.

"Come on, put two and two together. You're surrounded by girls with wings, your big shiny gun is useless against me, and I arrived in a ball of flames. Hello?" She taps her head with a finger. "Anyone home?"

His arm falls, the gun bounces against the side of his thigh.

"But...."

"What? It's because I'm gorgeous. I know. It's such a cross to bear."

"You're a woman?"

Her eyes roll.

"It's the breasts, isn't it?" Her hands cup her chest as she stares down. "They're such a giveaway."

Jacob blinks, not hearing the sarcasm in her tone. His eyes suddenly go wide.

"Of course, to lead men astray. But I'm already your servant, Lucifer."

Lucy stares at him, shaking her head.

"You are not well."

He gets down on his knees.

"Look what I've done for you. Haven't I proved my worth as your right hand?"

"Anyone wanting to be my right hand normally has to pay for dinner and buy me something pretty."

His eyebrows furrow.

"But...I've been waiting for this day for so long. Everything I did, I did it for you."

She sighs, shaking her head.

"You have no idea how much I dislike Satanists. My marketing department has it hard enough without you people undoing their work."

"I don't understand. I'm giving you two of God's Angels. Doesn't this prove my commitment to you?"

Lucy snarls, glancing back at Mich.

"I happened to like looking at that one, and now you've gone and spoilt it. As for commitment? What do you want, to marry me? Take a ticket and get in line, there's a long queue. Anyway, Jacob, we're forgetting one important thing." She moves closer. "I don't like rapists." She grabs him, pulling him close so their noses almost touch. "You were given the gift of free will and you decided to do that with it?" Her lips peel back into a snarl. "You could've done anything. You could've tried to make yourself better, could've worked to invent something meaningful, could've helped better your race of retarded monkeys, and you didn't." She throws him onto the ground. "Who are you to take lives?" She seethes. "Monkeys aren't Gods!"

Her hand raises and flames tunnel out: golden, orange, red, beautiful, a vision; blinding, bright, hot, even where I am. He falls back, crying out as they smother him.

I go back to watching blonde hair floating in a muddy puddle.

"Mich?"

A hand takes hold of my arm and yanks it. The railings bend, the cuffs snaps, my own bones move in a way they're not meant to. I hear my own scream as I fall forward, barely staying on my knees. Fingers grab a handful of hair, lifting my head, and I stare into intense eyes. A calm expression contrasts her extreme heat, making me blink.

"What are you, a Keystone Cop? Let me explain this obviously incredibly complex situation to you. I want his soul for my figures. Kill him."

I try to speak but nothing is working. She shakes me hard, jumpstarting my mind, body and spirit.

"Come on, Discord, there are only a few hours left of today and the end of this quarters figures. I'm not asking you to sign your soul over, just his. I want Clipper."

I look over at him, a writhing mess on the ground, his hair smoking, his flesh burnt and black.

"Then help Michelle."

"He raped and murdered Faith. What more motivation do you want?"

"Help her!"

She glances across at Mich then back.

"Kill him!"

Her eyes narrow a fraction and she throws me back. I land heavily, painfully. I stare up at racing black clouds in an inky sky. A flash of lightening then Lucy appears. She glares down, inches away, stealing my view.

I speak up, finally.

"I'm calling Elle."

My mouth opens as my collars are grabbed. I'm pulled up sharply.

"If she cared, Discord, she'd be here already."

I shout as loud as my throat allows.

"Then you won't care if I call her."

Her growl is loud, her words louder.

"You don't dictate to me."

I bare my teeth as pain explodes through my body. It expels in a scream of words.

*"This time I do!"*

I get shaken once, hard, jarring everything. She pulls me so close our lips touch as she speaks.

"I really do not like you, Discord." Her breath is warm. "Fine, I'll help her." Another short sharp shake. "Kill him before I change my mind and tear you to pieces."

I'm deposited on the ground, my legs barely holding me steady. Lucy tilts her head and takes a step back, watching. I feel like an animal in a zoo.

I move, and each step feels like molten metal is being dripped over my body. Each step and I'm ripped apart by pain. I stand over Jacob. My nose twitches from the smell: burnt flesh, still burning flesh, and dirt. Everything smells of dirt.

I concentrate on calming everything in my head, concentrate on that bit of safe ground, that oasis, because in the middle of it is her, Michelle. It took me long enough to realise and I'm not losing her now. I get down on my knees and roll Jacob onto his stomach. In this night of the dead what more does one make? I'm just completing my mission, that's all.

I put my hand down onto the back of his head and push him into the soft earth. I glance around at Lucy.

"Keep your side of the deal."

She pulls a limp, wingless blonde up by her shirt, and runs a finger along her bloodied bottom lip. With a wink she kisses her then splays open her hand. Mich drops back like a rag doll.

Lucy sways as she straightens. Her lips curl into a smile.

"Me and your girlfriends. We seem to have a theme here, don't we?"

I take my hand off of Clipper's head as I wait. Lucy smiles.

"Don't you trust me? I'm hurt."

Michelle's hand twitches, her body convulses once, and she rolls over, coughing.

"Ta da." Lucy curtsies. "Remember who helped you today."

I grit my teeth and push Jacob's head into the ground as hard as I can. His body flaps like a grounded fish. His hands claw at mine, nails tearing into my skin. I close my eyes, trying not to think about all of this, trying not to feel.

Clinically dead to a soulless in just over two years. It's kind of funny.

But then something stops me. I realise what I have in the palm of my hand: the man who killed Faith. I stop pushing and flip him over. Crispy skin peels from his face, his hair a matted, melted mess. He gasps, trying to drag air into his body, biding time, delaying the inevitable.

I sit down on the dirty Earth, crossing my legs.

"You wanted to know who I was."

His eyes are wide, his face is black.

"I'll do whatever you want."

"I'm Faith's cousin. You probably don't remember..."

"Please..."

"...her. She looked like me, just, smaller, younger. You hurt..."

"...I'll stop."

"...her, you raped her, and then you killed her. Then you brought her back and left her for me to find."

"I'm sorry!"

I get up, slowly, my wet pants sticking to my legs.

"You're sorry?"

He cowers as he realises the extent of this. There's no escape, nothing's going to save him. I grab his shirt, pulling him up, closer.

"I saw what you did, so I don't care how sorry you are."

I throw him backward and he bounces in the soft wet dirt. My boots sink as I stand over him. Mich taught me, when you know what you want to do, do it quickly, don't transmit your intentions. I drop down and kneel on his chest, keeping him pinned. He screams as I take hold of one arm and hook my foot around the other.

"You put these fingers on her."

I sit on his hips to keep the rest of him still. Complete lockdown.

"Did she scream when you hurt her?"

My voice breaks as a tornado of memories crawls through every inch of my mind, claiming me, taking me back to that place. To that night. To when I walked up the steps of the porch. To when the wood creaked and the fireflies buzzed. To when everything went wrong.

"Did she scream when you raped her?"

I grab his wrist. His hand is blue from Mich's earlier attention.

I blink the rain away as I remember finding Faith propped up against a wall on the porch. At wondering if she was sleeping or drunk and passed out. At asking her. At not getting a reply. At never getting a reply from her again.

I peel his fingers out from a balled fist and slam them into the ground.

At kneeling down. At looking closely. At seeing her clothes were dirty. At realising they were all on wrong: buttons done up oddly, shoelaces loose. At seeing the scratches on her thighs, at touching them, at feeling how cold she was. At not understanding.

"Did she scream when you killed her?"

The cold wind pounds my back as I blink more than the rain away. As I slide my knife out of the scabbard on my belt. As I see a red stained belt, off, on the porch next to her. The belt I gave her for her birthday. As I still didn't understand.

"Please! Don't!"

I hear her voice saying the same thing to him as he hurt her. As she begged for him to stop. As she probably prayed to someone who couldn't hear her. As she didn't understand.

"You don't deserve to have these anymore. Not if you can't control them."

I understand now.

I push the blade down in-between the bones of a knuckle and bang my weight on it. Resistance to no resistance in under a second. He screams. Lightening strikes, thunder roars, my body goes cold as the rain pile drives into me. But what stays with me is the look in Faith's eyes as I lifted one of her eyelids, thinking she was kidding. It was cold, glazed, empty, as she stared at nothing.

All of my weigh sits on his writhing torso. Lucy's voice snakes around me as my muscles shake.

"Minimal playtime, Discord. Then I want his soul."

My mouth answers for me.

"We'll both get what we want."

He screams again and my ears ring at the pitch and tone as I remove another finger. I put it next to the first, in a sick little line. Drops of rain sit heavily on the tips of my eyelashes.

His voice rolls around inside my skull, but it doesn't remove the image I have as I shook her, trying to get her to wake up. Tears slip over my lips, into my mouth. My eyes squeeze shut as I remember: the shock after I called the police, then sitting down with her, guarding, keeping her safe when it didn't matter anymore. Stroking her hair until they arrived and poked, prodded, photographed her, then put her in a black bag like she was trash. Not knowing what to do when everyone left, when the authorities had taken what they came for.

Hours, days, weeks, they all merged. Time went weird. Nothing was the same, not even breathing. It went from automatic to a burden, something I had to force, had to remember to do. Not sleeping, not eating, just sitting on my porch and hearing crying from inside the house. Everyone was crying, crying, crying, all of the time. Everyone except me.

Day after day, night after night, darkness, light, shade and shadows all came and went and nothing got better, nothing helped, nothing changed.

Then the day when they gave her back to us in a sealed casket because of what they'd had to do: cut her open, cut us open, it was all the same. They told us not to look, and we didn't, because it wouldn't have been right, and after all, what was right meant a lot now everything was so wrong. But I didn't have to look because I could still see her in my head when I blinked. The ugliness was branded in a deep dark place that I couldn't heal, and no matter what I did it burned and burned and burned until it was all that kept me going, until the burning felt right, until I couldn't imagine a time without it. So I took comfort in my pain as I sat on the porch and listened to the crying that wouldn't stop.

Later, hours, days, who knows, I watched them put her into the cold ground, in a box, on her own. I waited, stayed with her until the sky cried tears, until the thunder howled, and the lightning lit up nothing. And then I waited some more, until my legs shook from the cold and I couldn't see because the storm was all around me. Only then did I leave her, where no one would look after her, where no one cared.

The darkness came as I sat in my car, as I stared out into the graveyard, as the thunder roared through me, soaking up the sound of the engine as it started. I don't remember leaving but suddenly there were no more graves just endless roads ahead of me; endless roads with no possibilities. I wondered when it had all become a dead end, when all of my dreams and needs, and loves and hates had disappeared. Then I remembered when the wood of the porch creaked and the fireflies buzzed. That was when.

And then it happened. The burning stopped as I followed the winding road, as the rain pounded my windshield. No more burning, no more comfort in the familiar, because now I felt something else: lost, empty, dead inside, but at the same time there was sadness everywhere. Hurting, deep, like an echo I couldn't hear, couldn't find, couldn't get away from. Drowning in something I didn't know how to stop.

Then, as I turned a corner, I saw how I could stop it, I realised what to do. Like a revelation, my headlights lit up a blindingly white placard: Lake Pleasant. So I listened to my divine sign. I turned my wipers off, took my hands from the wheel and closed my eyes.

The impact, the force, the metal crashing through the car and tearing into me, pinning me to the seat. Water everywhere, colder than I could ever remember feeling. The shock made me gasp, made my eyes widen as I sank down deep in my very own coffin, all on my own. But then a change, because my body wasn't in agreement, it didn't want to go, didn't want to leave like that.

Struggling with the seat belt, with the metal impaled in my side, my fingers frozen, not working properly, slipping off of everything I tried to hold on to. Ice cold water filling up the space, soaking through my clothes, making my muscles seize. Fighting, fighting, fighting. The jolt as the car hit the bottom, as I strained to breathe in the last of the air, as I stretched my neck up, gasping, sucking in each mouthful like it was my last.

And then it was my last. I held my breath.

It was dark, but I could see clearly as my own blood turned the water red, as my hair floated up like a dark curtain all around me. My eyelids were heavy from the cold and I felt tired. I opened my mouth and the last air bubble rose to the roof.

So I stopped struggling.

No more fighting and no more pain as the water took all of that away. It was just the cold, the dark and me. My mouth opened. The water came in. It was suddenly peaceful. It was suddenly calm and quiet.

I closed my eyes and it all went dark.

"Dis?"

Something touches my shoulder and my eyes slowly open to the here and now. To row after row of graves, to a light haze of cold rain falling onto everything, to the thunder bellowing softly in the distance. I stare up into the worried face of a bloodied blonde Angel. She kneels, taking the knife out of my hands; shaking, cold, wet hands. Warmer ones hold onto mine as green eyes tell me it's all going to be okay now. My demons slowly fade back into the shadows, just like they did before. She kisses the tip of my nose and stands, moving away, giving me space.

The bitter winds don't let up. They buffet everything living and dead as she leans on a tree, sliding down, cheeks puffed in an exhale.

I've fought so hard to keep control, to stay in charge. My shoulders sag now I don't have to be. I stare back down at him, seeing everything a little more clearly now the end is in sight, now the fight is almost over.

I always wondered what would happen when my demons were set free. Now I know and I'm glad I kept them in until the time was right, until it was safe, until I could let them tear up the person who deserved their fury. I stare at his fingers on the red soaked ground. A row of digits that have hurt so many people, ruined so many lives, stare back at me.

I get up from his bloodied, still body.

"I want his soul, Discord."

I turn and put a finger to my lips, "Quiet," smelling his blood on my hand.

I look at Lucy. Her blonde hair wet, dress filled with scorch marks and small holes. Her eyes flick between Clipper and me, then the pile of fingers. But there are no more jokes, no more smart comments. Now she gives me a gift: silence.

It's then I'm drawn over to someone else. I never thought anything would interfere with the moment I got to avenge everything. I was wrong. I go to Mich's side. My pant legs soak as I kneel next to the person who came through for me every single time. I help her shift and get more comfortable against the tree. I tuck a piece of wet hair behind her ear.

She groans.

"My..." Pressing down gently on her mouth I try and stop her speaking but she pulls my hand away, squeezing it before letting go. "...phone. Inside pocket. I need to call Gab."

I dig around in her wet jacket then help her with the call; the cavalry are coming now the battle's almost over.

Her green eyes are bloodshot and barely open. She lifts a hand to my face, cupping my cheek.

"Are you all right?"

"I should be asking you that."

Her lips curl into the slightest smile.

"I wouldn't say no to an hour in the Jacuzzi. Wanna join me?"

Despite everything I smile.

"Sure."

Her eyes shift slowly away, over my shoulder.

"Gab can tie up that loose end if you want?"

I slowly turn and stare at Jacob Clipper, remembering what I said I'd do. I glance at Lucy as I answer.

"No. I made a deal."

I stand, looking at the crux of the problem, and not just mine but so many people's. My boots walk me back, but this time I do one important thing and turn my brain off because those demons have had their playtime. Now it's back to business. I lean down and pull his eyelids open letting the icy rain in. He blinks slowly, a low moan curling out of his dirty lips. It floats around me, trying to get in and trigger off another memory bomb. I glance over at Mich and she winks. I'm in control now. Also, more importantly, I have someone who can and will pull me back when it all gets too much.

His body twitches, dragging my attention away from her. He jerks as I kick him in the ribs breaking one or maybe more. I don't know and I don't care. Rain fills my eyes, reminding me to blink. I put my boot over his face because I don't want this man on my hands anymore. I punch all of my weight into it and he howls like the animal he is. My sole slips and I reposition because now isn't the time to miss. I raise my boot and slam it down on his head. Something gives way, cracks, caves. Finally all life here ceases. And now it's just me, the darkness and the smell of burning, blood and dirt.

He's been stopped as has everything: no more thunder, lightening, rain. No more pounding my body and mind into submission to make up for the way I failed Faith. No more risk to anyone anywhere. I stare at my wet and sticky hands and sit on the cold earth, in a place the dead can rest again. Warm tears fall down my cheeks. It's all over. I stare into the darkness.

Suddenly a voice cuts through the calm, slicing it into shreds. Lucy's laugh is loud.

"Welcome to life as an Angel, Discord."

## 48 CUPID'S INTRODUCTION

This is an important lesson. Time moves on and we do, too. Scream and shout for that fact to change but no one's listening. You have to leave the past in the past and move yourself into the present, and hopefully a better future. That's the way of your world, my world and an infinities worth of alternative realities.

It was time for some old doors to close and some new ones to open, and not just in life and death, but in love, too.

# Chapter Forty-Eight: Discord
## 22nd January, Year 3 - 07:00
## Pro-Choices

I push the button on the hot drinks machine. Nothing happens. I push it again, ducking my head down to where the cup's meant to drop. Zero noise, zero movement, zero coffee. I slam my fist against it, taking my frustration out at having to wait in an infirmary for so long. I bring my fist back again, looking to teach this machine a lesson. A warm hand takes hold of my wrist. I spin around and ice blue eyes smile into mine. I relax my arm, ashamed at being out of control. Elle's fingers slip away.

I mumble, pointing to the machine.

"It won't give me my coffee."

I cringe at my childlike words. Thankfully Elle smiles, knowing me better than I know myself.

"Let's see what we can do about that."

She tucks a strand of hair behind her ear then takes a coin out of her purse. She throws me a sideways glance, arching an eyebrow, and inserts the coin, pressing number three, my usual. The machine hums to life. Ten seconds later she hands me a steaming cup of coffee.

"I suppose I just have magic hands."

She pauses, holding onto the same cup I am. Her smile is warm and it lights up every part of her. She's as beautiful as that first moment I saw her, except now there's a slight difference. There's emptiness in the space between us, a hole sucking everything in. Finally her grip loosens and the cup is mine. She leans against the machine.

"I'm glad you and Michelle are safe."

I wait, because there's a but coming. I've known her long enough to recognise that tone.

"But there'll be repercussions because of what happened, of Lucy intervening."

She sighs, shaking her head, eyebrows furrowed as we hit a topic I wish we didn't have to.

"Why didn't you tell me about Faith, about everything that happened?"

I stare down at my boots and shrug. If I had an answer to that I wouldn't have got into this whole mess.

"I can't force you to tell me the reason, I suppose."

I keep staring at my boots as she sighs.

"But despite everything that happened between us why didn't you at least call me to help you with Clipper?"

That's when a little piece of truth breaks free, a revelation for both of us. It hurts to say and I know it'll hurt to receive. I look up into the bluest eyes I'll ever see.

"I wasn't sure you'd help. You've always been busy with other things."

And I guess this was always the crux of my problem, thinking everyone else was too busy, too caught up in other, more important things.

She blinks and straightens, shocked.

"Is that what you think, that I would've been too busy?"

I nod, not willing to lie anymore.

"You've always left me on my own before. I'm not blaming you, just explaining why."

"I.... I would've helped you, no matter what."

I shrug because it doesn't really matter now.

She looks deflated. Despite it all I don't want to hurt her. Her life is full of people like that, people she should be able to trust but can't. So I take a little bit of it back, just a little bit as I make my excuses.

"I know. I'm sorry. Look, I've had zero sleep and I'm worried about Mich."

Her words are slightly mistimed.

"She'll be fine. The doctors are good. They mended you quickly."

I nod, not knowing what else to say. Elle does.

"I'll do what I can with the Council."

My mouth and brain join forces and produce a sentence that's spikier than I wanted.

"Don't risk anything for me."

Her expression flicks direction and she glares at this sitting target. I hold my hand up.

"I mean, I don't want you getting in trouble, Elle. I'm tired, my words..."

Delicate fingers lay themselves on my forearm, stopping my sentence. Blue eyes soften their assault.

"Always come out wrong. I know."

A cough from one of our doctors drowns our moment. Her hand slides off, creating a trail like a line of fire ants. The doctor rolls his grenade into our camp.

"Michelle's awake if you want to see her."

He disappears as quickly as he arrived, the explosion leaving its crater. Elle smiles sadly.

"It's time you went, Discord."

I nod. I don't know what to say. Goodbye would be sensible but life is rarely that. She fills the silence instead, voicing a point I already know.

"Michelle's a good woman."

I stay quiet. Elle doesn't. Her voice cracks.

"Every night I wish things could've been different between us."

There's so much I want to say, but this isn't the place to try to understand why all our bridges were burnt, how something so good turned so bad.

My voice is a whisper.

"I'm sorry."

I am. Whatever's happened I don't like seeing her upset. Also, I know a little part of me still loves her and always will. I know because I can feel a pain deep inside.

"Never apologise for wanting to be happy, Dizzy."

"Maybe one day we can be friends?"

She doesn't smile or change her expression.

"I look forward to that day, I really do." She barely nods. "I need you to understand one thing, just so you know. I never wanted to let you go, not once."

She sighs and turns to go but I hold onto her arm gently. I shouldn't say it, but there's been a lot of that done lately.

"I never wanted to be let go of."

Her eyes hit me with an intensity I remember from our early days together.

"There's one thing I value about being here. I have eternity to get back what I've lost."

She moves closer and stretches up. Her warm lips glide across my cheek as fingers squeeze my shoulder. Then she's gone. Without looking back she disappears around the corner leaving me in the blast radius of those sentences.

I stand still for what seems like an age, just concentrating on my own breathing. I look at the space she occupied, then at Mich's door. So much has happened, so much has changed. I'm different now. I've found someone who'll stand by my side. Elle was right, Mich is a good woman. I look towards her room finally understanding the futility of Elle versus the possibilities of Michelle. I put my coffee down on a table, aware of what it signifies. My fingers peel away from the scorching hot cup. I go to Michelle.

The swinging door almost hits me as Gabrielle comes out of Mich's room. I nod and move aside.

"Hey, Gabrielle."

She pulls the door shut, blocking my way, crossing her arms. She looks away for a long moment, then back, frowning.

"I don't want you hurting Michy if you're still involved with Elle. I'm her best friend, Discord. She deserves better."

I pinch the bridge of my nose, trying to understand what this woman is saying. I feel like I've missed a whole conversation.

"I don't understand what you're talking about."

She taps a finger to the circle of almost black glass in Michelle's door. Both hands settle on her hips.

"I saw you and Elle. Michy can't stand so she didn't have the pleasure."

A knot of frustration forms while I stare at the darkened glass. My eyes close as I lean against the wall.

"It wasn't what it seemed."

Her voice is a low whisper.

"It seemed overly close to me."

I snort a laugh. It was anything but, really. It sure wasn't the closeness she's thinking of, anyway.

"Well, it wasn't. I'm not involved with Elle. At all."

She pins me under an intense stare. I don't look away because I've made my choice. Suddenly her face relaxes and she nods.

"Good. I'm just watching out for Michy. She's bruised and battered enough."

It must be nice to have a friend who always looks out for you, someone who just wants you to be safe and happy. Mich is a lucky woman.

Gabrielle glances back at that door.

"She's not looking or feeling her best so get ready for the visual shock."

"I'm sorry about all of this."

Her voice is a low whisper.

"Good, then you'll feel guilty enough to do whatever you have to, to make her feel better." There's a pause. She moves closer. "While we're on the subject of sorry, I need.... I want to apologise for giving you Faith's case. I should've spotted it."

I don't know what to say to such a frank admission.

"She's safe now. I guess it all worked out in the end."

"In the mortals' area she can have everything she ever wanted, Discord. It really can erase all of the bad things."

"I hope so."

She moves forward, putting her arms around me, pulling me into a warm soft hug. Her voice whispers as my defences slide.

"I'm sorry about what happened to her as well. Losing people you love is hard enough, but like that? It shouldn't happen."

The change in me is strange as my arms go around her. It's something I would never have done a few days ago. I stay silent, knowing my voice will betray me. When she finally lets go she takes my hands, gripping tightly.

"If you ever need to talk I'm a great listener. So is Michy. The past is better out that in. Okay?"

I nod.

"Thanks."

Her hand touches my arm before she walks away. Then she stops and returns.

"I like you, Discord."

She stares deeply, her eyes flicking over me. Obviously satisfied with what she sees, she smiles, turns, and walks away.

I take a deep breath, trying to compose myself, switching to a mode that can be useful to the injured patient. I push the door open. Mich is lying on top of the bed covers. Her eyes flick to meet mine in an instant. Gabrielle was right, she looks terrible. One eye is black, her lip cut, cheek bruised. I keep my surprise to myself.

Her voice is croaky, her tone flat.

"Hi."

I stand next to the bed, jamming my hands in my back pockets. I try to find my words except she beats me to it.

"What a screwed up mission."

No denying it. I nod.

"I never meant for you to get involved."

Her bloodshot eyes meet mine.

"I'd never leave you on your own after I saw that tape."

She pauses and shifts, grimacing at the sudden movement. I move to help but she shakes her head, showing me again how strong and self-sufficient she is.

"Why didn't you come and find me, Dis?"

The time for lies has gone. There's no use hiding demons, they find you even in the dark.

"Because I'd kept it secret so long, I thought...maybe you'd be angry I hadn't told you about it before. Or that you wouldn't want to get involved. I know how busy you are."

She waits for a long time but I don't offer anymore. It's as much of a confession as I can give at this moment. Even I don't fully understand everything that went on.

"Have I ever been too busy for you before?"

I don't have to think.

"No."

"I told you I wasn't letting you deal with this stuff alone. I always keep my promises."

Yes you do.

"I know."

"Do you want to talk about it now?"

I take a breath and shake my head.

"Maybe another time. For now we both need a rest from him."

"Sure. But if you ever need to talk, I'm right here and I'm a great listener. Remember that."

"Gabrielle said the same thing."

"She's had enough practice listening to me talk over the years." She tries for a smile but sighs instead, her hand touch her lip. "At least breathing isn't painful - yet. Maybe it will be tomorrow."

I look down at the woman who effortlessly removed all of my defences and stood by me no matter what. For the first time I see what I have within my reach. I have what I envied outside. Someone who's looking out for me, a person who wants me to be safe and happy, even if what she gets in return doesn't make her as happy as it could - the diner comes to mind.

"You're a good friend, Mich."

Her head nods slowly before she speaks.

"It's better than a bad friend, I guess."

I sit down in the chair next to her. I try to become the Discord I was, not the Discord I've made myself into up here. I promised Gabrielle I'd make her feel better no matter what, and I won't let anyone down, not after everything that's happened.

"You're not looking so hot, though, Mich. I mean, have you seen the nurses up here?"

She blinks and her mouth drops open. I quirk an eyebrow. She laughs, pulling the sound short, a hand covering her ribs.

"Don't. My side."

But so out of practice I trip myself up.

"You'll never get one of them if they see you like this."

Her expression falls and I want to kick myself.

"Yeah, well...."

There's a time and place for everything but this isn't it. Not for a serious talk anyway. However, Mich steps in. Her directness takes me by surprise, proving that for her this is the time and place.

"Listen, I'm just going to dive right in. It's best that way, clear the air and all. After what happened between us I need you to feel like we're on solid ground." A slight pause. "About what I said in the diner. It's okay, you know. For us just to be friends, I mean."

She thinks over her words. Whatever I failed to say needs to be amended now. My mouth opens, and for once she fills a gap I wish she hadn't.

"It's better this way. I mean, why ruin a great friendship, right? Lovers are.... I can get any amount of those, but good solid friends? They're precious."

She doesn't smile or try to lighten her statement with a joke. She pats my hand and my skin tingles. I sit back in my seat and offer up the only three words I can now.

"Yes they are."

We remain silent for a long time. Finally I speak because I told Gabrielle I'd do whatever I had to.

"How long are you in for?"

"A day or so. I'm a good healer but I'm still allergic to bullets. What about you, are you good as new?"

I nod.

"Bullet went right through. I'm just a little more holey than when I started all this."

She smiles then frowns, touching her split lip.

"Where have all these jokes come from? Not that I don't like them."

I shrug. I try not to feel sad. I try to look on the bright side of being friends. I take a deep breath and my mouth answers automatically.

"I'm getting back to my old self, I guess."

It's not always what a person says that's the best judge. Her eyes blink for a brief moment. She recovers beautifully.

"Then all this was worth it. I like the Discord I've met so far, very much. I bet I like the old one even more."

Her green eyes sparkle. I stumble into my meaningless sentence.

"You'd think there'd be an easier way."

She glides into her important one.

"Nothing worth anything is ever easy, Dis."

She smiles down. A sincere genuine smile on the face of a beautiful Angel.

"No it's not."

I make as much conversation as a person like me can. Mich takes care of the rest. She fills my gaps and covers my pauses. We make a good team. We make good friends. A big part of me wishes we could make something else.

A knock on the door interrupts. A head pokes around and I recognise the olive-skinned woman: Jen her assistant.

Mich tries for a smile.

"Hey, J-girl. I hope you're bearing gifts containing calories and not work."

Jen looks between the two of us, her eyebrows lifting in a hello.

"No work. Training is taken care of. Psyche and Gaby are working together to cover you. I was here to keep you company, but you kind of got someone already. I'll come back later - with my chocolate - from Belgium."

Mich holds a hand out then grimaces.

"Don't make me beg."

"But it'd be the only chance I'd get."

Jen winks at me and comes in. She sits on the edge of the bed and deposits a huge box of chocolates down. Mich tries, unsuccessfully, to get to it. Her fingers tap the bed.

"Don't tease. I can't stretch."

"I'm not teasing. If you can't move you're not well enough to eat them, right Discord?"

Mich eyes me like a puppy wanting a treat. I can't help but smile.

"It's true. Imagine the hard centres with your jaw."

Mich recoils and folds her arms slowly.

"Okay, fine, but don't leave them where I can see them."

Jen slides the box into the bedside cabinet. She leans closer to Mich, looking her over.

"You look like that time you got beaten up by that Amazon in the arena competition."

Mich blushes, eyes wide.

"Don't you have lots of things to be doing, Jennifer?"

Jen grins at me, perking up instantly.

"She was the one you beat, Discord." She turns and faces glaring green eyes. "And yes, I do have things to be doing. And yes, I am going. Thank you and goodbye."

With a kiss on the cheek for Mich and a wave for me she whirls out like a cyclone.

"You got beaten up by...?"

"No. It was a very close match."

The door opens again. Gabrielle this time. Mich waves her fingers without lifting her arm as she carries on.

"The referee was dating one of Psyche's friends. I mean, it was never going to go in my favour."

Gabrielle laughs.

"What, that time you got your ass kicked in..." Mich growls. "Okay, I'm going. I forgot my favourite pen from my favourite best friend."

She grabs it from the side table and opens the door to leave. She side steps and Psyche smiles at her and comes in as Mich raises her voice.

"I didn't get my ass kicked. It was a points decision."

Psyche looks at Gabrielle.

"Are we talking about that time when..." Gabrielle nods and Psyche's eyes widen. "I should wait outside before the shouting starts."

"I'm not going to shout!"

Mich says shouting.

I lean back, watching, because all of these people have come together for one thing. To make sure Mich is okay. It makes me see the Heavens in a new light.

Psyche nods at me then goes to leave, holding the door open for Gabrielle.

"Glad to see you both made it back alive. And I hope to see you back in the arena soon, Michelle. We could do with an easy victory."

The door closes and Mich shows her determination as one of her pillows hits it.

"It was a points decision and she got a couple of lucky hits. My face bruises easily, see?"

She points to her lips then cheek. I nod with a chuckle.

"I hope it mends as easily."

"Not so pretty to look at, huh?"

My fingers pick at the edge of the blanket. She slowly runs a hand through her tousled blonde hair. Despite her bruises and cuts she's still beautiful, there's no doubt about it.

"I wouldn't say that."

Her fingers move to mine then up to my knuckles, gently running across them. I look up into a serious face of someone who's just my friend. My cheeks burn so I move my hand away because a person shouldn't be thinking about a friend the way I am.

I've heard mumbling come out of my mouth but I never imagined it would from hers.

"Sorry. I.... So...."

A flash outside makes the glass window in the door light up. The door opens, deflating the tension instantly. Unfortunately the visitor heightens it again. Lucy stares at me then Mich.

"I wanted to thank you in person. I won, Elle lost, and boy are you two going to be in a lot of trouble. Anyway, enough gloating, I have the next quarter to plan."

The door slams. I offer up the only thing that comes to mind when I think of Lucy.

"I hate that woman."

Mich laughs quietly.

"I think the feeling's mutual."

We talk about something and nothing. As time moves on her questions and answers become less frequent, her voice slower, lower, as she begins to drift off. Her blonde head lulls against the pillow as she yawns. I stand, making as little noise as possible. Her eyes slide open.

"I wasn't sleeping. Don't go," she says, sleepily.

Her hand reaches for mine. Tanned fingers hold me with surprising strength. I look down at our hands then up into half-closed eyes.

"I'm going to get some coffee. I'll be right back."

Her childlike voice makes me smile.

"Promise? I don't like hospitals."

I lay her hand back down on the bed.

"I'll be here when you wake up."

Her voice is quiet. She's barely awake.

"Even if it's late?"

"No matter what time it is."

She smiles sleepily, snuggles down into the covers, and begins to breathe deeply.

I remember back to the time in the bar when she helped. Who'd have thought all of this would've come of it? Not me, that's for sure.

I watch her for a long time before leaving to get my coffee. I walk over to the same machine as before. I put my coin in. I press number three. A steaming cup of coffee appears in less than ten seconds. I finally get what I ask for.

I push the door open and lean on the doorframe, sipping my coffee, watching her breathing deeply. Would I ever find someone who meant as much as Elle did? That's a question that's kept me awake for too many nights. Mich shifts, her fingers jerking slightly. Her lips smile the smallest amount. Mine do the same. I'm happy with the answer sleeping in front of me. Even if what I want isn't what I'll get, a friendship is exactly what she said, precious.

I sit, get comfortable, and wait for her to wake up.

## THE END

www.ingramcontent.com/pod-product-compliance
Lightning Source LLC
Chambersburg PA
CBHW070855180626
46817CB00003B/778